# Moonfall

ALSO BY ED CROCKER

*Lightfall: Book One of The Everlands*

# Moonfall

Book Two of

THE EVERLANDS

ED CROCKER

ST. MARTIN'S PRESS
NEW YORK

This is a work of fiction. All of the names, characters, organizations, places, and events portrayed in this work are either products of the author's imagination or used fictitiously.

First published in the United States by St. Martin's Press, an imprint of St. Martin's Publishing Group

*EU Representative:* Macmillan Publishers Ireland Ltd, 1st Floor, The Liffey Trust Centre, 117–126 Sheriff Street Upper, Dublin 1, D01 YC43



www.stmartins.com

Map artwork by L. N. Bayen

The Library of Congress Cataloging-in-Publication Data is available upon request.

ISBN 978-1-250-28775-5 (hardcover)
ISBN 978-1-250-28776-2 (ebook)



First Edition: 2026

10 9 8 7 6 5 4 3 2 1

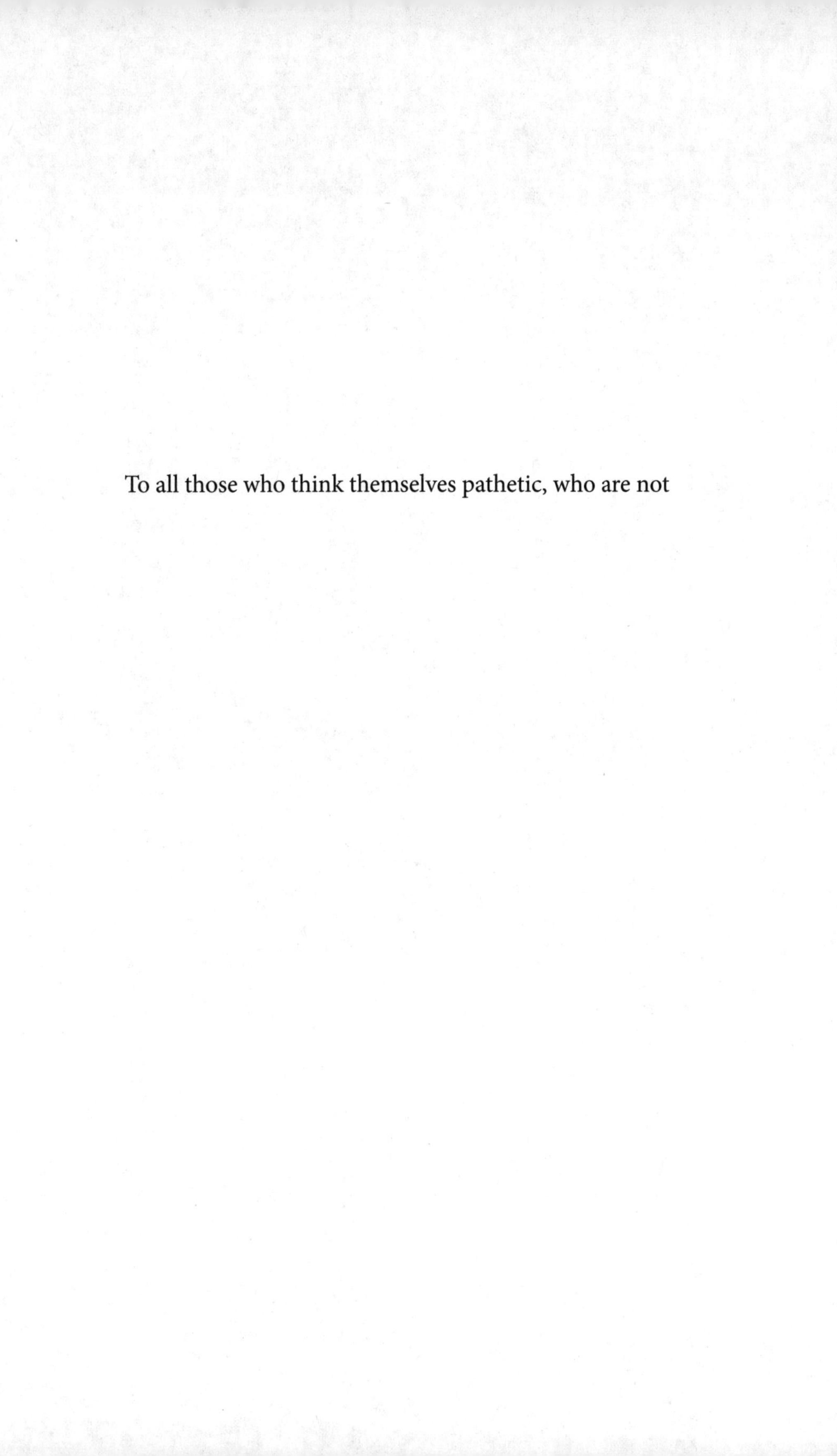

To all those who think themselves pathetic, who are not

The Everlands
G: abandoned due to Grays
N
E
S
W
Shadowfall
G
First Light
The Borderlands
The Wolflands
Lightfall
G
Cult of Humanis
Dawn Death
G
Luce
Last Light
The Ashlands

# Moonfall

# *Previously, in the Everlands*

First, Grayfall happened. Mysterious killers with gray cloaks and deadly weapons, forcing the Centerlands cities of the Everlands to vacate. A hundred years later, the last vampire city of First Light is ruthlessly administrated by the Lords. The Worn peasant class get the worst of the blood, while the nobles hoard the best kind, wolfblood, for a future battle date with the Grays.

Enter Samantha Ingle, palace maid, her mother, father, and sister all killed due to the Lords. When the youngest son of First Light's ruler, Azzuri, is murdered, Sam finds a vital clue to his murder and seeks out the Leeches, the fabled spy ring of First Light composed of servants who blackmail the Lords. She discovers that society belle noblewoman Daphnée Hocquard is their leader, with Alanna, a survivor of the fabled lost city of Last Light, beside her. Soon they are joined by Sage Bailey and Jacob, magickless Quantas sorcerers from the Cult of Humanis, who believe in the myths of mortals. They suspect the involvement of mortal relics. The notorious werewolf assassin Raven Ansbach, currently helping the vampires catch wolf escapees who are bled for their wolfblood, also joins our heroes. The situation is further complicated by the presence of Neuras Sinassion, the infamous mind-reading sorcerer who tried to take over the continent two centuries previous with his Neuras army, the Shades' in the Twin War.

Eventually—and after First Lord Azzuri's psychotic son Rufous has killed Sam's best friend Beth by repeatedly dropping her out of the sky, and after Lady Hocquard has been fatally shot—they discover the conspiracy at the heart of Grayfall that Azzuri's son was killed to protect: The Grays are, in fact, Neuras Sinassion's old army, the Shades, not killed at the end of the Twin War but repurposed by Spymaster Saxe and his secret cadre of Lords into obedient assassins. Their weapons? A discovered gun cache of the mortals.

With this information, Sam confronts Azzuri and his council, only to discover that Saxe has already told them of the conspiracy within their ranks and they are mostly happy with it. Our heroes are imprisoned. However, First Lord Azzuri frees them, then tries to take his own life as well as kill Saxe as revenge for his son. Azzuri is saved by his loyal servant Redgrave, secretly a rebel spy.

Meanwhile, our heroes take on Rufous and his First Guard and defeat them; in doing so, Sage reveals (via the use of a bullet-toting metal suit) that the Cult of Humanis hoards actual weapons of the mortals, who definitely existed, and Sam defeats Rufous Azzuri in one-on-one combat, though spares his life. Jacob, Sage, and Raven flee for the Wolflands to tell the wolfkind the truth of the conspiracy. Sam elects to stay behind and help her city, done with big plans. Yet plans find her, as a month later Alanna appears to her and reveals that Lady Hocquard is still alive, saved somehow by Alanna. They take Sam into a room at an inn to meet the leaders of the revolution, Molly Threetimes and Hands Parker, only to see Redgrave, closely followed by the now ex–First Lord Azzuri, join the party.

Key Dates: [AL = After Light]

–400 AL: The Great Intelligence [date is best guess]
0 AL: Founding of the first Everlands city, First Light
50 AL: Founding of Luce
200 AL: Founding of Lightfall
250 AL: Founding of Last Light
420 AL: The Twin War begins
440 AL: The Twin War ends
450 AL: Last Light falls
500 AL: Grayfall
600 AL: Present day

# Prologue

## The Rules of the Hunt

If you want to understand the difference between vampire, wolf, and sorcerer society, you could do worse than study their attitude to rules. Vampires have the most, often pointless, frivolous, petty societal things, but they work the hardest to break them all, especially those in power. Wolves have a moderate amount but they stick rigidly to them, for they are all connected with who they really are. To break a rule for a wolf is to sever their link to the land. Sorcerers have the least; they steal and murder at levels that would shock even a vampire Lord, but the rules they do follow they have no choice to obey, because the magick within them can be unforgiving that way.

Cardinale Ciani, *Reflections on Eternitie Volume II*

### Raven Ansbach

There are three rules to a wolfhunt. The first is that the hunted should always know they are so. This one is normally fairly easy, because it is not as if they are just running away for the fun of it. Occasionally there are times when the hunt will begin with the prey already in transit. If it is one wolf hunting another—the true hunt, the only one worth its name—then this is easily solved by scent; at some point the hunted will be told by its nose that another wolf is on their tail, and the hunting wolf will scent this in the slight change of their emotion, and this will be enough to satisfy the rule. If it is not a wolf? Make yourself known. Howl or something. Use your initiative.

The second rule is that the hunted must have a head start. If there is no head start it is a murderous chase, and nothing fit for wolves. What if there is no fun? What if it is a simple desire to kill? Then you are not a wolf and this advice is not for the likes of you. There is always fun—not for frivolity, no, but for the sake of being alive. Being alive, in the forests, running, hunting, feeling the wind, feeling the thrill, with the scents whistling through your nostrils like a breeze sent straight to your brain, with a different message every time, one made of pure emotions wrapped in common scents magnified to their essence. That is when a wolf is most alive, and if you never feel that alive then I pity your walking corpse.

So give them a head start. Hours, ideally. Let them get the lie of the land, and see how much good it does them.

The third rule of a wolfhunt is that if they escape you, if the hunt fails, then they are duty bound to one day hunt you back. So make sure you catch them more often than you don't, or you'll be looking over your shoulder in the light of the moon your whole life, and our lives tend to the fucking long.

I do not look over my shoulder much.

## Jacob

**Three Weeks in the Future**

I'm not enjoying being hunted by a wolf. It's not meant to be an enjoyable experience, I realize, but even so it's worth emphasizing just how shading annoying this is.

It wasn't meant to come to this. I was meant to be the hero for once. Not Sage. Me. The mage who drinks too much who solved a murder and stopped a war. But now I'm going to be disemboweled and probably eaten in the middle of a snowy forest, deep in the Wolflands, hundreds of miles from home, and I'm suddenly discovering that the price for trying to be the hero is one that I seriously can't afford.

The trees rush past me as I push myself to the edge of my speed, the edge of my abilities. Which, for a sorcerer, is not that fast. Maybe if I was an Atmos I could summon some currents to fly on. Those smug shits get around pretty speedily. But every other sorcerer, especially a magickless kind like me, can run for, what, twenty miles an hourglass for . . . a while? We don't get tired too easily but we can't keep on forever. A full wolf can run at the peak of their fitness at forty-five miles an hourglass . . . for a full hourglass. I didn't use to know that. But I had a lot of time to spend reading about these bloody wolves in the past two months in the Wolflands, even before Raven put on me the frankly unfair responsibility to solve a murder as if it were *me* who used to be an inquirer in the sorcerer capital, not Sage.

So even though I know I can't outrun the wolf on my tail, I know I can't rest, unless I want my rest to go in a little more permanent direction than I'd like.

I come to the crest of a hill. Beyond, the valley stretches out before me, a flat expanse of white. Mages are not built for running in the snow. I'm used to the desert and I'm cold and I'm tired and I'm running in snow boots with various furs wrapped over my robes and despite these, I'm starting to lose sensation in my extremities. Things are not looking good.

At the end of the valley, hidden by a copse of eastern pines but there all the same, is the territory of Pack Gevaudan. More knowledge from my recent studies. That's where the wolves closest in allegiance to the Ansbachs are. The ones most likely to help me.

More to the point, they're the only other wolfpack for a hundred miles, so most likely or not they'll have to do. But then the person on my tail knows that, too, and they won't let me get there. I have a funny feeling that they could have caught me by now, and that they might be playing with me.

I look down at the canopy of trees below the crest, a hundred feet down. I could jump, I suppose. I can't practice magick, but whatever made me strong like all the sorcerers put the Light in me, and I'd break a couple of bones and have one of the worst days of my life but I'd heal eventually. But what good would that do? It would only delay the inevitable. But if I don't jump, if I don't at least try, then a lot of people are going to die. Beginning with me, primarily.

Jump it is, then.

"Let me save you the bother."

I smile at the voice, and acceptance comes immediately with the smile. I turn and face the murderer, who at some point between catching up to me and watching me contemplate the jump has shifted to person form, naked and smug amid the snow, teeth and claws still long and sharp, eyeing me with a predatory gaze.

For a moment, I allow myself to imagine Raven darting out of the trees to save me. I imagine the last conversation we had, the look in her eyes. I would have liked to continue that. But it's too late for that. That's not an option anymore.

"It isn't fair," I try. "I don't deserve this. This isn't how it should have ended."

But even as I speak the words, they sound ridiculous to me. I allowed myself to think I was someone else, that the drunkard Sage found all those years ago in an inn, bitter at his destiny, at being a Quantas, the worst of the five kinds, the magickless fucks, could be someone better. The person Sage always wanted me to be, who Raven had helped me become. But I realize now that the more you dream, the more you can't see the ground shifting below you.

Out here in the Wolflands, there's no hiding from the reality of life. No one is thinking about what you deserve. Certainly not the forest, anyway. I take comfort from the fact that, despite being a mage in a land of wolves, I'm thinking like a wolf in my final moments.

Maybe, then, people can change. But my transformation has come to an abrupt end.

"I wish," I say, facing my death, as it looms before me and opens its jaws, jaws ever so wide, "that there had been pockets in these furs for a drink."

Then those jaws close, and that's the end of me.

PART I

# A Peaceful Revolution

## 1

# Rebels with Cause

> The powerful will always be accountable for their actions. If it doesn't come from above or sideways, it will come from below, and that is the most terrifying kind, because you think you are king of the world right up until the moment the small people in your periphery bite back.
>
> Redstorm Bellpull, *The Dynamicks of Lightfall*

## Samantha Ingle

**The Present**

The last time I was in a prayhall, I was surrounded by Grays and had to bleed a wolf assassin half dry to escape.

This isn't that prayhall. I'm not in First Gods, with its huge spired towers and great vaulted arches. I'm in Fifth Gods, which is one of the smallest of the major prayhalls in the city, situated on the east end of Westfall, near the border with Centerfall.

And my task isn't that hard. But I'm still nervous. This is my first spot of rebel business, and I don't want to disappoint.

*Rebel business.*

Am I really a rebel? And if not, what am I?

I'm not Sam the cleaning maid. She died when I found the only clue to the murder of the youngest son of First Lord Azzuri.

I'm not Sam the secret spy. She had her time, helping to uncover the conspiracy that stretched right up to the Lords, discovering a bond with two sorcerers, a wolf, a countess and . . . whatever Alanna is.

I'm not Sam the brutal wolfblood fighter, who drank half of Raven Ansbach, challenged the Lords with the evidence of their crimes, escaped from their jail, helped to massacre their finest fighters, and then won against Rufous Azzuri in single combat. She still lingers in my skull, the memory of those wild scenes making me wake up in cold, tingling sweats, the breath taken right out of me.

And I'm not Sam the shadow, the girl who wants to slip back into Worn life and live like normal people and never achieve anything of note again. That brief period lasted right up until Daphnée appeared to me in an alley, alive and well, and invited me back into the great game of it all.

But if I'm to be Sam the rebel, then I'm done with death. Done with causing it, blood slick on my hands. Done with being responsible for it. This time, I'm doing it my way.

I just need to work out what my way is.

Maybe my task here will help. In a few moments, Lord Skye is going to walk into the prayhall, and straight into me and Alanna.

Lord Skye is the head of one of the smaller councils, the Beastblood Council, a smaller offshoot of the Blood Council that regulates various less than exciting activities such as the upkeep of the animals in the Blood Farms in Northwestfall, where a wide assortment of creatures winged, furred, and scaled are kept to be drained for their precious red stuff. Molly Threetimes, the leader of the rebels, would like some information from him on how the Blood Farms work. I'm not sure why, but I suspect I'll find out soon if this turns out as planned.

Skye has been on the outer rings of the Leeches' web for a while. When Lady Hocquard—or Daphnée, as I'm still learning to call her now she's given up her mansion and title and is slumming it like the rest of us—and Alanna formed the Leeches the best part of ninety years ago, he was one of the first Lords they heard rumors about. That he would break the laws on using wolfblood recreationally (rules that the Lords generally respect as it's pretty obvious when you're on the stuff) and purloin himself a vial of it. Then he would do things high on it that would make you burn the entire ruling class in the morning sun if you had the will and the way. Anyone who spoke out found themselves punished, too. Magicked stag would suddenly appear in their rooms and they would be sunburst for the thieving of it.

According to Alanna, he's "the most deserving bastard to be given a touch o' the Leech charm."

Problem is, they never had anything on him. Nothing to blackmail him with. He wasn't stupid enough to leave any evidence of his wolfblood thieving. He was the one who got away.

Until now.

A maid who works for the Blood Guard is one of ours, and she was there when Lord Skye approached the Guard's wolfblood stores. Other than the vault in the First Lord's palace, and various small batches that have made their way from that vault into the wider city over the years, that's the only place Lords can get their hands on wolfblood. The wolfblood in the Guard's stores is meant for the winged guard, for when they need to fly the short space past the city walls to scout for Grays or emergencies when they need to fly across the city. It makes sense that Lord Skye would try to get it from there rather than the palace; it's easier but it's blooddamn riskier as well, because the Guard always ask for a written chit for any requesting Lords. Which would have been fine for Lord Skye because it's not like anyone's going to check those unless they have a reason to.

Except that day Skye wrote the chit but made a mangling of his signature at the end, and being the vain prickard he is (show me a Lord who isn't, I'll wait) he screwed it up, and thrust it in his pocket and wrote another. But it fell out of his pocket as he walked away, and who should be there? Our Leechmaid, who knew all about Skye's scheming, of course, and, sensing the opportunity of a century, picked it up before anyone could notice it.

On such small pieces of luck is a Leech network made.

Now I wait in the apse of the prayhall for Lord Skye to swagger in, presumably quite angrily, as he would've seen the very rude and provocative note I sent him asking him to meet a stranger here.

I look around Fifth Gods. It's empty this soon after nightfall, just as we planned. I'm standing next to the altar, next to the sinstone, with its razor-sharp edge where those who believe in the Blood Gods bleed away their sins. I've never bled, though I've bled in other ways, more than I should have for a Worn my age.

I feel excitement course through me: the same sensation as when I found out Lady Hocquard was the Queen Leech, the same as when she asked me to explain the history of Neuras Sinassion at her house for the others' benefit, when I realized that all my learning was being noticed, that *I* was being noticed, that my ambitions were finally spooling out in front of me.

I thought I'd given my dreams up, the guilt of death hanging over me (for a moment I think of one dead name in particular, but then I hear the beat of wings, Rufous's wings, and I push it back down in my mind).

But I'm back in the thick of it more than ever now, deep in the thickets of this city once again.

I peer through the shadows to the back, the pews, behind which Alanna is crouched, like a mountain cat ready to pounce. She has the easy role here. Mine is the tough one. It's my first big catch.

Alanna says I'm ready.

I'm not so sure.

Suddenly there's loud footsteps and the prayhall doors are banged open and in comes Lord Skye, stomping his feet and trying to make his stride longer in that way that men have when they have business, and angry business at that.

"Right," he says, bluster packed tight in his voice to hide his fear. "Where are you? I have little time for these games. Come out of the shadows, you scarecock."

I'm kneeling before the altar now. I don't want him to see me straightaway. A thousand thoughts lance through my mind. Of what he can do, and what he will do. My muddy blouse and skirt scrape the floor as I kneel. My straw-blond wig scratches my scalp. I smell the patches of dirt on my neck and face; I had foxblood to steel me for this so I smell them better than most dirty Worns ever do.

I will come to him as the lowest of the Worns, to give him his truth. It's how Daphnée does it herself, and I kneel in her legacy, hoping I don't dirty myself the wrong way.

I hear him stop as he sees me. "Leave this place, girl," he shouts. "I have business here. Go on, be on your way."

I don't move. I feel his outrage burning off him.

"I said move, girl. You'll be sorry if I have to repeat myself again."

I turn then, and I smile slowly.

"Right, Wornbitch, you've had fair warning. I may as well have some fun with you while I'm waiting," he says, striding forward.

"Oh, Lord Skye, it's me who'll be havin' the fun," I reply, my first words in this performance coming out quieter than I would have liked but still full of the evils, as Alanna likes to say.

He stops mid-stride. His face takes on the expression of someone who's been slapped mid-sentence and then slipped on his own piss.

"How do you know . . ." he begins, quiet now.

"I know who you are, m'lord, and I know all the little things you been up to." I stand now. My Southwestfall Worn twang holds. I could've used my own voice. It's not like he'll remember me in the unlikely event we cross paths again. Lords don't think like that about us. We're not a thousand different variations of accent to them. We're all the same.

But, as Alanna is fond of reminding me, details save lives, specifically ours, and so I practiced for the last two days the strong eliding of consonants that marks the Southwestfall sound. Why Southwestfall? Because we don't want him coming back to Westfall looking for me if things go wrong. Who would believe we'd meet where we live now?

"You just killed yourself, Worn girl," says Lord Skye, and he sounds so angry he can barely spit the words out. "You should tell me what this is all about right now and I might make it easy on you, girl. Or you'll die slow and in various pieces, that I promise."

"Oh, it'll be you who'll die slow when they find out, m'lord," I reply. "Find out you've been smuggling a little wolfblood on t' side. What's the penalty for takin' wolfblood that don't belong to you? I'm fairly sure it's death, m'lord. I bet they'll make an example of you. Can't let the Worns go around thinkin' that some Lords are secretly drinkin' the good stuff, instead of savin' it for t' wars to come, right?"

Lord Skye has lost his voice, it seems. I carry on.

"I mean, everyone knows the Lords have a thimbleful of it now and then. But you're meant to be sneaky about it, not sell it on t' black market, you fat little moron."

Lord Skye finds the remains of his voice jammed down his sweaty little throat and uses them to carve out some words.

"How?" he says. Then, "Who?"

"It don't matter who. And it don't matter how, though I doubt you'd even understand. All that matters is that I know your secret, and others do, too, so there's no use in killin' me now. If you do as I say, no one'll ever know. You 'ave my word on that. You don't know me from Misbabel, so you'll just 'ave to trust my word is good. But if you don't, First Lord Azzuri will have proof of your little game—and you'd better believe we have the proof, a note-taking of your last smuggled batch from t' Blood Bank clerk you've been paying off—and it'll be sunburst for you, Lord or no Lord. I hear Rufous is runnin' things a little more crueler these days. There 'asn't been a Lord sunburst for decades, but I bet he'll make an exception for you." At this, I raise my arm, point at him, and wink.

Lord Skye seems to be in a state of confusion now. I can almost read his damp little thoughts. I imagine him looking at my brown-stained rags clinging to my chest and thinking, like always, *I want it. When can I have it?* But he can't have it. Not this time.

"But . . . you're just a Worn . . ."

I smile, and in my mind's eye I see Daphnée wink approvingly. "Yet see the damage I do."

Lord Skye hangs his head. "What do you want me to do?" He's as deflated as a bloodsucked calf.

"Keep your hands off your maid, for a start," I reply, and my eyes narrow and my cheery tone goes all quiet and cold. "If you don't, we'll know. Then it'll be you who are fucked, m'lord, not her. Oh, and we want the answers to these questions." I pull out a small bit of parchment from my petticoats and hand it to him. "Just a few facts about the Blood Farms. Nothin' too strenuous, I'm sure. One of ours will be around your way to collect the answers before lightfall. So be quick about it, now."

"Why do you—" he begins, but then he gasps, because Alanna has slipped in behind him and shoved her dagger up against the small of his back.

"That's enough. I reckon it's time to be thinkin' of leavin' now," she says. He goes to mouth some words, but Alanna kicks the back of his knee ferociously hard and he kneels to the floor in pain. Then she turns the dagger so she's holding it by the blade, calm as you like, and hits him on the back of the neck hard with the pommel, causing him to bow his head in front of me as if preparing to bleed away his sins to the sinstone.

"Actually," finishes Alanna, the green emerald set into the hilt of the dagger winking in the dim light as she pockets it back into her undergarments, "we'll leave first."

And then she knocks his skull hard with the flat of her hand and he falls at my feet into unconsciousness, small droplets of blood spotting my boots.

We reach our lodgings deeper into Westfall by five bells. At this time of year there's plenty of the night left, and much to be done. The new abode of the Leeches is, like most of the buildings in this part of First Light, tall, rickety, and grown up rather than sideways.

Unlike Worntown, the home of the Worns spread across Southwestfall and Southeastfall, the buildings here are sturdier, of solid timber from the Borderlands rather than mud and wood reeds and straw and whatever can be cobbled together. Some in the center are even stone—these are the homes of the wealthier Midways, the merchants and suchlike, although most of the rich ones are in the true Midway home, Eastfall. Westfall is the place where Worns and Midways meet, a place where class divides are broken down through a love of the one thing the Lords can't take away from us: the arts.

As I climb the stairs to the very top of our lodgings, the seventh floor, my ears pick up the trills of a harpist practicing in the next house to ours. If I listen more carefully—and my foxblood hasn't quite worn off yet, so I can do this with fair ease—I hear the muted shouts of an acting company a street away, practicing in a courtyard. A few houses down, a musicscene singer hits a high note, the chord hanging in the air before dying a small death. I'm taken back to the fine singing of my mother in the early evening air, and I linger for a second in the memories of a time I had a family. I even fancy I hear the warming up of the crowd in the Sunway, the stagetale house in Westfall where Worns are packed in tighter than cows at a bleeding. It's less grand than the Sunsphere in Centerfall where Lords sit in their boxes and watch the great Midway performers of the day, but a lot more fun, and if you've seen enough stagetales I don't need to tell you that.

Finally I reach the top, and I let Alanna overtake me. She slips a key from under her petticoat—I briefly wonder whether she keeps it next to her blade, much good will those thoughts do me—and then bends down to slide across a panel at shoe height in an otherwise blank wall where a room should be. The key turns in the lock beyond the panel, and with a grunt she pulls at the wall itself until it hinges open from the bottom. It's a strange way to do it, but you wouldn't look down there for a secret lock, would you? It helps to get into Alanna's head when designing secret rooms, even if the designing of them is something of a headache.

Once we're in, I sit down at the small gelmwood desk that, other than a bronze safebox in the corner, is the only furnishing in the room, and I open a drawer to reveal a small leather-bound volume that smells slightly of damp. I dip the quill on the desk in some ink, and I turn to a page with Lord Skye's name on it and place an *X* next to him. It's a Leech ritual, and it feels all the sweeter for the lengthy chase of the man.

Then I turn to Alanna and I say what I've been girding myself to since Lord Skye was unceremoniously introduced to an unexpected sleep with her dagger.

"That was quite an ending you gave to him." I smile, to show I mean it friendly, which is something I still do a lot to Alanna, who's easy to become familiar with in the same way a twenty-foot snaptail in the swamp is easy to wrestle.

"Say what you mean, Sammy," she says, her voice singsong but her meaning clear.

"It's nothing, it's just I thought we were going to let him walk out, all humiliated. You . . . gave him quite a knock."

Alanna steps a little closer to me and studies my eyes for a second. Her normally narrow eyes are wide and open, and if you didn't know her well you'd say there wasn't much thought in them, but I know her well, or at least well enough to know what she can do. Daphnée has left me with a weapon, I'm just not sure who it's aimed at.

"I did give him quite the hit, and he won't be of the forgets for a while about it. So when he's had a few blood shots with a little Wolfsbane whiskey mixed in down at the Rushes, and he starts to be of the mind to find out who those little upstarts were who took him down from his high perch and made a meal out of him, just as he be doin' to his servants, well then, he'll rub his neck and touch his knee and remember better of it."

I nod. "That makes sense."

"But if you don't want me to be attemptin' such a thing in the future, then ask me and I'll do it."

I study Alanna for a few moments. I look into those eyes, those strange peepers that can hold anger or wisdom, I haven't really found out which yet. What I do know, I realize, is that I'm not as scared of her anymore. So I try a little honesty.

"No. I'm sorry, Alanna. I don't really care, it's just . . . I thought I was done with . . . I don't know, violence, I suppose. A month ago I killed several vampires, and bested Rufous Azzuri in combat. And it felt amazing, with the wolfblood in me. But then I crashed, and I realized that all I did was cause chaos around me. I'd got what I wanted—I was playing a role in the city. A big role. But then I saw all the death around me and I wanted very much to go back to . . . not being someone."

Alanna regards me with a beat of silence. "And then me and Daffers brought you back out of it and straight into the life again." There's a glimmer of a smile on her face that I hope is sympathy.

"This must sound ridiculous to you, Alanna, I know," I say. "I can't imagine you ever had such a quiet life, or one free of violence."

She laughs then, one of her signature cackles that always makes me jump a little no matter how many times I've heard it. "Oh, you would be surprised, Sammy. I fair think your petticoats would shrink to hear the truth from my lips. I was once more quiet, as you put it, than you have ever thought to be."

I wait for more. More on Last Light. That fabled city on the southern continent of the Ashlands, founded by four vampire families. The city full of wonders that lasted two centuries, all of it silent to the rest of us, until its destruction a century and a half ago. The city with a thousand rumors about it and no confirmed truths. I've seen Alanna jump off First Gods unharmed, not even any wolfblood in her. I've seen her fight like a dance of death. And with all my books inside me and still more to read, I find myself wanting the knowledge of her just as much as anything still left in the library.

But instead she just sidles nearer to me and whispers, "And I miss it, too, by the by, Sammy. Sometimes, even I miss it, too."

There's a silence then, and I don't know how to fill it. Luckily Alanna saves me.

"Oh . . . Before I forgets . . . a strange little Leech tale has come to us from one of the girls. 'Bout a mage."

My head turns to her from the record book a little too quickly, and she grins. "Not *that* mage, Sammy. But our girl, Thea, thinks there's a sorcerer livin' secretly on the edge of Westfall, where it meets the Fang Tips."

I frown. "One of the bloodmages, you mean? Or the Neuras?" Other than the Kinet sorcerers who improve the blood—who are all restricted to the Blood Farms—and the handful of Neuras sorcerers employed by the nobles to group together and transmit simple messages with their mind across the continent to the wolves and mages when needed, there shouldn't be any other sorcerers in the city now that Sage and Jacob have left.

"She don't know. She heard a rumor of a mage comin' and goin', getting up in the daytime so as to be all about the secrets, and then she thinks she saw him herself when she went to investigate. A canny one is our Thea, so I trusts her."

My thoughts turn to dark and shadows. "Sinassion?" The most feared sorcerer of all claimed he wasn't the real enemy the last time we heard from him, trapped on the roof of First Gods; he told us that his old army had been turned into the Grays by the Lords. But I'm still loath to take the word of a mass murderer, a mage whose Shade army killed thousands, in the Twin War.

Alanna nods. "Could be. If he's still in the city. Which is why I'll be extra of the carefuls when I creep into his business. And bring both my daggers just in case."

"I'm coming, too," I say.

The hint of a smile haunts Alanna's mouth. "Thought you were done with violence?"

I shrug, badly affecting nonchalance. "Well, we'd better make it a friendly visit then, hadn't we?"

## 2

# You Can't Go Back

> People have forgotten how scary it was when you heard a new sorcerer was in town. Nowadays a sorcerer in a vampire city is most likely to be one of these newfangled bloodmages, or just a Cloak or basic-level Atmos looking for work. People have forgotten when an Atmos assassin could level a town with bolt magic, or even the days when a Kinet could crash a rock face onto a village. A vampire's fear of the mage went with the War. I wonder if it will ever return.
>
> George Dunn, in a letter dated five years before Grayfall

### Sam

The house that apparently contains a rogue sorcerer secretly living in First Light is a modest two-story abode made of mortared white-gray stone, like a smaller version of the Westfall buildings north of where I'm staying where all the richer traders live. But unusually for a building that's stone, not timber, it's all on its own, far removed from the Westfall main, hugging the very western border of First Light where the brutal peaks of the Fang Tips begin.

"What's this doing here?" I ask Alanna, not unreasonably, as we hide behind a copse of trees a couple of hundred yards away, the hustle and bustle of Westfall proper a good quart-mile behind us.

"Maybe it was a watch-post once of a time," she replies, shrugging.

I look up at the Fang Tips searing into the night sky just beyond the house. It's hard to imagine any invading army getting over those, which is why a simple wall made First Light so impenetrable for centuries; no one's getting in by the mountain west or the northern sea. And east you have the problem of wolves, although Grays wouldn't have an issue with that . . . but they've never tried, just like they've never tried to breach the wall. Which, of course, makes sense now I know they were never an invading army. Just a smoke screen created by a cadre of Lords to pump out fear.

"I suppose once upon a time it was easy to get wolfblood and fly over the mountains," I muse.

"Time and a place for your library things, Sammy," Alanna says, not unkindly. Maybe she's warming to me.

"So what's the plan?" I ask her, a shiver of thrill running through me as our Leech schemes take on a new level. Meeting a prick Lord at a prayhall is one thing, but this is something else.

She turns to me and narrows her eyes. "It's a very simple plan, Sammy girl, couldn't be simpler. You wait here, and I enter, and dependin' on what my eyes see before me, I either kill them or secure them so you can come and have a natter, with all of your learnings, no doubt."

"I think I should come, too," I say firmly. It never gets easier to stand up to Alanna, but it gets less unnerving over time.

A quiver of a smirk crosses Alanna's tanned face. "I thought you were keen to avoid the violence and killin' these days, Sammy."

"There doesn't have to be any killing," I say. "I'm sure you're capable of securing a single sorcerer."

The thought runs through my head that even Alanna would most likely have a hard time securing Neuras Sinassion, who can read, if not directly, people's intentions from a few hundred yards away and also has a frankly unfair fighting style based on reading your thoughts. I remember Alanna turning the table on the Grays—Sinassion's old Shade army—when she fought them at First Gods, with a dying Daphnée at stake. How they stopped being able to read her mind—whether it was due to her singing or possibly her insanity—I was never clear on. Maybe he won't sense her coming after all, if it is him.

A lot of maybes.

Reluctantly, I concede. "Fine, Alanna. But don't kill, please. Even if it's Sinassion. He claimed to be our ally."

"I give you my pardons if I have a hard time believin' that the mage that caused so much havoc in the Twin War is keen to be our forever friend."

I take a bit of time to parse Alanna's words, as usual. "What's a forever friend?"

"A friend you have forever."

"I regret asking that."

I watch as Alanna creeps out from under the tree cover and skips toward the house. She's completely silent, and there's no window facing this way so she can't be seen, so it's not completely absurd that she's skipping, but it's still quite a sight. When she reaches the house, she hugs tight against it and pauses, as if considering something. It's currently five bells; we calculated that at this point in the middle of the night with it being so short the sorcerer would be asleep, assuming he is creeping round in the day. But would a sorcerer like Neuras Sinassion sleep? Is he even in? The uncertainties on this mission start to creep in on me, and as the adrenaline fades I regret coming.

I always overestimate myself, and one day it'll get me in real trouble.

Just as my doubts continue to give me a good walloping, I see Alanna pry open the shutters on one of the windows with her daggers, and then, despite the gap looking too small, she dives in, noiselessly, from a standing start, like a cat. Alanna would make a good cat, I ponder, though she'd use up her nine lives in a night.

Then I wait. Out here on the fringes of the city there is blissful quiet, punctuated by the occasional cry of a hawk who knows not to get too close to the city itself lest they find themselves shot down by an illicit crossbow by one of the Southwestfall gangs to purloin an unexpected couple of vials of some of the best blood around. I hear a haunting, pained screech from beyond the mountain line: foxes mating.

I hear no sounds of vampire-mage fighting.

I wait a little longer, and a chill runs through me as I start to imagine explaining to Daphnée that her love—for that is surely what they are, or will be, or should be, I've seen their looks—her love that survived Last Light and a battle with the Grays, the indomitable Alanna, has fallen to someone even stronger than her and all I did was stand behind a shitting tree.

Then, as I summon my wits and decide to follow in her footsteps to the house, it becomes clear as I approach the window Alanna jumped through that I will not mimic her athleticism. I can't even reach it, for a start. I inspect my surroundings. There's a crate behind the house, old and worn—empty, cracked bloodvials nearby suggesting it was from a previous inhabitant. I drag it inelegantly to the window, wishing I'd had more fox for this escapade, or convinced Alanna to supply me with some of the noble bloodstores. Then I clamber onto it and reach for the open window, pressing myself up and over the sill like a fish flopping onto the shore. I half fall, half land into a pantry room devoid of any food or blood containers, and I listen quickly for sounds.

A faint muffling?

Outside the pantry is a small passage with stairs winding up to the second floor, and I take these, my breath coming quick and my heart running wild. I try to creep up but I can't say that I'm as quiet as Alanna or, in fact, quiet at all.

At the top is another small passageway, dimly lit with one oil lamp, with two doors off it. I creep next to the first and listen. The remnants of my last fox vial make the noises quite clear in one room. The muffled sounds of someone, maybe trying to speak. I hang suspended for a second, half in a crouch, trying to work out the best move. I'm not as afraid as I should be, because of my faith in Alanna. But I'm not as confident as I want to be, because of my fear of the unknown.

Alanna wins.

I open the door and enter the room, which is lit only by the moonlight peeking in the window. For a brief moment, I see Alanna tied to a chair, rope across her chest, cloth hood over her head, sounds coming from her mouth, which means she's presumably gagged under the hood. My heart skips every beat it can.

But then my eyes catch up to the tricks of my mind and I realize it's a sorcerer tied to the chair; at least I presume so because they're wearing a sorcerer robe and they smell like one—even on cowblood a vampire can smell one of its own kind easily enough. But they're not wearing the colors of any of the sorcerer types; the robe is brown. I heave a quick sigh of relief at realizing that it's not the black that Sinassion wears—not that Sinassion would likely be found tied anywhere.

Then the dregs of my last foxblood clarify the shadows in the back of the room, which quickly form the shape of Alanna, leaning against a desk behind the tied-up sorcerer, tapping one of her emerald-encrusted daggers lightly against the wood.

"Took your time, Sammy girl," she says, face still in deep shadow, even for my Midway-blood eyes. "I think our guest is getting impatient, judgin' by the increasin' pitch of his moanin'."

"Wait, what?" I ask. "But I was waiting for your signal?"

Alanna steps forward a little into the pale moonlight, her face still impassive. "Signal? I don't remember discussin' any kind of that thing."

"But . . ." I pause. "How . . . how else was I supposed to know when to come?"

Alanna shrugs. "I normally just go by feelings."

I sigh. "Of course you do."

I look to the tied-up sorcerer.

"So it's not Sinassion then."

"No," says Alanna, tapping her dagger lightly against the hood, which elicits a louder muffling from within. "In many ways, not."

"What do you mean?"

Alanna starts the ghost of a grin. "Why don't you look for yourself."

I peer at the mystery sorcerer. "Is . . . is it safe? Who are they?"

"Would I be invitin' you to peek if it wasn't safe, Sammy?" asks Alanna.

Depends on the Last Light definition of safe, I think to myself, but I proceed anyway, and move in front of the sorcerer, then reach out and gently lift up the hood.

"Alanna!" I cry, not sure whether to gasp or laugh.

"What?" she asks, that hint of a grin threatening to grow.

"It's Sage!"

I stare at the unhooded but still very much gagged Quantas sorcerer, the leader of the Cult of Humanis, technically still the ambassador representing the Archmage, and the man who helped us uncover the truth about the Grays and, perhaps most importantly for the slight speedup of that treacherous heart of mine, the last person I kissed. It was a brief kiss, after a nasty one-on-one fight with Rufous Azzuri when I was sure we would never meet again. But still.

This is unexpected.

He looks much the same as last time I saw him: short brown hair a little more ruffled, three-day beard now more approaching a beard proper, his light-brown skin a little paler, his time spent out of the desert starting to show. His wide hazel eyes fix on me and for a moment I'm reminded that he has, for a sorcerer, something of the good looks about him.

At that point, with his eyes widening and his muffling growing louder, I realize I've been staring a little too long and he may want to be ungagged.

I dart forward and remove the cloth and he sucks in a lungful of air.

"And the rope please?" he says, clearly not entirely happy, nodding to his chest.

"I'll attend to that," interjects Alanna. "My knots are a bit on the complex side."

"I noticed," says Sage darkly.

"Sage . . ." I say. "Why . . . why are you here? I . . . I thought I'd never see you again."

I regret the words as soon as they leave, wincing at the drama of them.

He fixes me with a stare and smiles warmly. "Hello, Sam. It's good to see you." Then he stands and turns to Alanna, with the rope now free, and glowers.

"Do you want to explain yourself, Alanna?"

Alanna frowns and thinks for a moment. "Explain what?"

Sage's eyes widen. "Why you tied me up and gagged me and placed a hood over my head for the best part of a quarter hourglass?"

Alanna shrugs. "Better to be safe than sorry."

"What does that mean?"

Alanna rolls her eyes. "Calm down, mage. I'm sure both me and you have been all tied up in worse spots than that for longer. I gave you a moment of meditation."

"You gave me a moment of unwelcome confusion and mild terror."

"Exactly. Lots of different types of meditation there be in Last Light."

Sage raises a hand as I try badly to conceal my amusement. "Regardless, it's good to see you both. I imagine you want . . . an explanation?"

"As to why you never left First Light, and why you didn't tell us? Ideally, yes," I say. I wonder whether that came out harshly, but I realize now that the relief at seeing him has passed, I *am* feeling harsh thoughts. I've had certain moments of . . . missing him the last month. Regret at meeting such a kindred spirit and then parting forever. Possibly some consideration of that kiss. But all this time he'd been a half a glass walk away?

Sage has the grace to look sheepish, and then that old surety comes back. "Well, to be accurate, I did leave First Light, with Raven and Jacob. But I didn't make it far. I left them both in the Borderlands, and came straight back here."

"Why?" I ask, as Sage lights an oil lamp, and some of the shadows retreat. In the new light I see his robe is looking much worse for wear. As for the room, along with the desk there are a chest and a wardrobe. No bed; I assume that's in the other room on this floor. Which means he must have been in here, writing, or organizing things, at least, given that no light was lit. So not sleeping. No wonder he looks a little rough around the edges, although I'm not sure how much sleep sorcerers need. I don't know as much about them as I'd like. I'm starting to wish I read less on vampire councils my decade in the palace and more on the Desertlands. "Why didn't you tell us? Why all the secrecy? Why run about in the day?"

He considers this. "Well, for one thing, I was worried that Rufous and the new spymaster would be expending a lot of energy to try to find you, and me turning up could raise suspicion. Even if I'd been able to find you."

"Sage, it's *you*; you'd have been able to find us. And that doesn't explain why you're here."

"Aye, and I'm getting a little impatient, Sage mage," says Alanna, who has kept out of the new light, preferring to linger in the shadows. "Perhaps we should be gaggin' and tyin' you again."

"To be clear," I say, "we're not going to do that."

Alanna shrugs. "We'll see."

Sage sighs, and drags the chair over to the desk, then sits on it, facing us. "I can't tell you. I made a promise to someone. All I can tell you is that it is not connected to First Light or anything going on that you're involved in. But it's important. It's really important. And I will tell you when I can. That I promise."

"You know, I think meditatin' is much improved when the legs are bound, too, maybe we should try that," says Alanna from the dark.

Sage ignores this, then stands up from his chair and walks over to me, facing me. At first I think he's going to try to re-create our moment from the edge of the city, when my fist was still covered in Rufous's saliva and blood covered most of our clothes. A moment of uncaring passion, quickly abandoned in the sorrow of partings.

"Sam," he says, piercing me with his eyes. "You trusted me to help you when you went to the Blood Bank, do you remember? I gave you a random cube and you used it, though it could have been the end of you. And then I trusted you on the roof of First Gods to find us a way out of there."

"Well, technically that failed as we were then imprisoned, but . . ."

He ignores me, and his serious countenance stays. "We've been trusting each other since we met. Since the moment you recognized me and decided to bring us in on your secrets. All I'm asking for is a little bit more of what we've always had."

That was poetic, I'll give the frustrating mage that.

"Can you at least tell us what's happening in the Wolflands?" I ask. "With Jacob and Raven? What's been the reaction from the wolf alphas to the news?"

Sage looks away. "Jacob can't contact me, he doesn't know where I am. But he's safe with Raven. And I know he'll get the job done."

I squint, surprised to see him be so direct about his separation from the man he was tied to the hip with.

"You really did just abruptly leave him, didn't you?" I say. "This must be very important to you, what you're doing."

Sage lets that one go.

"Very well, Sage," I say, to an audible sigh from Alanna. "Go about your secrets." I nervously side-eye Alanna. "But I want to come here again." An awkward pause. "To discuss the city," I add quickly. "We could do with that deducting of yours."

A cloud covers Sage's face. "I . . . I need to be alone until I've done what I need to do here. I'm sorry, Sam. Once my business is concluded, I'd like to see you. But until then . . ."

A small pang hits me but I quickly smother it.

"Right. I see. Well . . . stay safe then, Sage Bailey. You've still got a lot of secrets to tell me." And before he can reply, I walk out of the room and, in short order, the house.

If he said something in parting, I wasn't listening.

# 3

# Atmosfear

If you see a Cloak, think.
If you see a Neuras, think not.
If you see a Kinet, hide.
And if you see an Atmos . . .
Run.

Anonymous vampire ditty

## Daphnée Hocquard

Alanna is looking at the scene before us, and so am I, except for when I get the chance to stare directly at Alanna. We are here, at the Blood Farms, to witness a revolution, or at least the very first stages of one, yet my mind is on love, not politics, and in my experience the former always bests the latter.

The weather is chill tonight; we are firmly into winter, and as I take much less of the noble blood than I used to, mainly taking Midway and often not magicked, I am feeling it especially hard. Except tonight I am on magicked fox, the very best of the Midway bloods (with gracious apologies to raven and boar), as my eyesight needs to be good. Our chosen spot to hide is in the shade of an awning from a storehouse a good hundred feet opposite from the gated entrance of the Blood Farms, far enough away to be witnesses and not participants in what is to come.

The Blood Farms themselves lie behind large cast-iron gates, a foot deep and twenty foot high. Beyond these, I know from a previous visit, is an enormous empty courtyard in front of a building that looks rather like one of the bank buildings in Centerfall: rectangular, symmetrical, lined with columns. But rather than vaults or offices, this is where all the blood barrels are arranged, ready for transportation across the city—to the Blood Market, to various Lords' abodes, to the Guard forts, to the Wall. And beyond this fairly unoriginal example of Old Mage style, I know, will be another building where the blood is poured into the barrels from large vats, and in a building behind *that* one, the Kinet sorcerers manipulate that blood deemed worthy of being magicked, ready to be placed in said vats. Alongside this building, I believe, though now we are talking of things I have heard but not seen, are the sorcerers' quarters and gardens and suchlike. And then beyond all these buildings, taking up by far the largest square footage of the Blood Farms, are the enclosures where the animals to be bled are kept. Bear enclosure, hawk aviary, snaptail pools, stag and fox and boar fields, all manner of animals from the Worn class to the Midway to the Noble. These Blood Farms have taken on an enormous amount of significance after Grayfall, since it has become impossible, or in the Scout Guard's case, astoundingly dangerous, to go outside the city to hunt new animals. Thus, the animal breeders have become some of the most important men of the city. Quite why so much effort has gone into breeding snaptails, though, I am not sure, although the new reports of the improved calm it gives compared to whale blood—not so soporific, still a mild amount of alertness when magicked—may explain this. And, of course, whale blood is even *harder* to source; unsurprisingly we cannot keep whales, so winged guard must fly beyond the northern mountain line to the sea mere miles beyond and kill them, which is as difficult and cruel as it sounds.

I am snapped from my reverie on what lies beyond my immediate sight by Alanna, who glances at the night sky and murmurs, "They'll be here soon, m'lady."

"Alanna, I am not a Lady—" I begin, but give up even as I say it. I have told Alanna numerous times that as I have lost my mansion and surely my place forevermore in noble vampire society, having been reduced essentially to the Worns I used to mimic so often, it is ridiculous to still call me *m'lady*. But when Alanna wants to do something, I find, she will continue with the doing of it till the Blood Gods descend.

"Remind me of the plan, then, Alanna," I say, taking the opportunity of my ex-first maid and now merely deputy looking up at the sky to inspect her. There is much dirt on Alanna's face; there often is these days as she spends just as much time conversing with the rebels as she does with me and my Leeches. As the rebels have slowly become aware of her formidable talents, which were previously mine alone to benefit from, she is much in demand with them. It means I see less of her, of course. Less of that perennially tightly tied-back ponytail; less of those knowing, sharp eyes and thin, permanent scowl-smile; less of that strangely tanned skin, strange for a vampire but common to survivors of Last Light. The less I see of her, I find, the less I go about my day with a spring in my step. For the truth is that I had thought we had come to an arrangement, a month ago, shortly before our fateful visit to First Gods, where on the roof of that cursed church we discovered the true, terrible nature of the Grays. We had said we would have words about what we are to each other. But then the great conspiracy of the city was loosed into the world, and I took a Gray bullet, and Alanna somehow—and the truth of this she refuses to tell me, as is her way—saved my life.

Then things progressed quickly, as things often do when they have been coiled like a spring for decades. The Leeches found a new home and now we work hand in glove more than ever before with rebels, given new life and purpose by the actions of Sam that brought down a First Lord and a spymaster. And in all of that maelstrom, in the wind howling at our back and demanding change, a change to all things, in all of that, the promise of what Alanna and I could be was lost, at least for now. I almost died, and all I have learned is to delay things further.

I fear I am a poor pupil of life.

"Well, first off, m'lady," Alanna replies, bringing me out of my veritable sulking, "the rebels will descend on the gates quickly, like scavenger gulls on a gutted fish. With a heady amount of their stores of noble blood in them, they'll break these gates and descend on the Blood Farms, where they will, it's hoped, quickly knock out the bloodguards—"

"Stop there, Alanna," I say quickly, used to interrogating plans. "How can they be so confident of this? With so much powerful blood stored here to fall into the wrong hands, there are sure to be a prodigious amount of guards. Our Leeches say fifty, last count."

"I have no qualms with such figures, m'lady. But the rebels have the greater numbers, and if the battle is quick and they have the element of surprise, the guards will not have had time to take advantage of the better blood available to them. We won't get all their numbers at first."

"And what of wings? The Flight Guard, even the First Guard. There is no wolfblood here for the rebels to drink to combat them when they arrive from the Guard forts, or the palace."

Alanna shrugs, her head turned back to mine, giving me a brief once-over as is her wont, which could mean affection or annoyance, it is hard to parse with her. "They will arrive quickly, it is true, and in terms of strength their wolfblood can hardly be matched. But their numbers are still low after those fevered events we were a part of, m'lady, and some will not yet be fully trained, more like puppies than hounds, and more to the point, the hope is that the business here will be done and overdusted even in the short space of time before the winged cunts arrive."

"And that business is?"

"Secure enough of the very best magicked blood—the type only bested by wolfblood—even just a few barrels of it, then scarper into the wind, and use that to mount an attack on the Guards' wolfblood stores before the Guards know what is conspirin' before them, and then when they have some wolfblood . . . the rebellion can begin."

I reflect on this plan. "And do you see any flaws in this set of arrangements you have so concisely laid before me?"

Alanna pauses. She is turned away from me again, peering into the dark, at the gate, barely lit by the moon, the large edifice of the Blood Farms' facade looming beyond it. "Maybe the better question, m'lady, is what I or we could do about it if there were. They seem very set on their ways. I did . . . introduce some doubts into their thinking but it washed off them like a saltstream."

"A saltstream being . . ."

"A very salty stream, m'lady."

I consider this. "I do not know why I asked, in retrospect. But Sam has expressed doubts yesterday, I believe?"

"She told me she did, yes. She felt that if it was this easy to clobber the Blood Farms, the rebels would have done it already."

"And what do you think, Alanna?"

"I think that they are correct to say that the Blood Guard, and the First Guard, are still somewhat in disarray, and the new way of thinking about the Lords and their clawed hold over this city is still restoring itself from the last month, so it does feel like this is a good time to be tipping up the apple cart and skewering the apples, so to speak."

I have never seen apples skewered, but I let it go. "However?"

"However, m'lady, I cannot but help think that if the Blood Farms are this vulnerable, then why do the winged cunts have to fly here? Why are some—"

"Not stationed here?"

"Yes, m'lady. Exactly. You know my thoughts, as ever."

I turn back to the iron gates of the Blood Farm, concerned at this line of thinking, and I feel a small chill descend on me, more than should be so with the fox still flowing through my veins.

"It would have been useful to get the thinking of Sage on this, now he is back in the city."

Alanna snorts. "We don't need his advice any more than we need a dance in the sunbeams."

I turn to her, eyebrow raised. "And when did you take such a dislike to the man?"

She lets that go, and I smile, knowing my Alanna. "I think it's very sweet of you being protective of Sam like that."

"I know not what you mean, my Daffers."

I think on it. "I agree with Sam that we should trust Sage. But I cannot help wonder why he would be here, why he would part with Jacob so suddenly and leave him in the Wolflands, and why he cannot tell us. I do not like secrets in the city. Would you consider, Alanna—"

"Following him? It would be my pleasure and then some."

I smile at her, and then turn back to the gates ahead, my mind returning to the imminent assault on the Blood Farms.

"There's something else about this plan, Alanna, something at the back of my mind," I begin. "I feel like it's there, some warning, but I can't quite . . ." I am interrupted by the sound of feet, many feet, hurrying from all around me, and though at first it is a sound that will be too far away to be heard by a Worn, soon it is loud enough for anyone on any blood to discern. Moments later, the figures responsible have emerged at all angles and immediately descend on the road before the gates.

They are all dressed the same, these figures, though I can see they are both men and women. They all wear simple brown linen tunics and loose-fitting brown breeches; many have dark-red caps on their head, and all the women's hair is tied back. The only thing separating them from the average attire of the Worn on the street, who very much favor the color brown, is that they are all wearing necklaces, and though I cannot see what is on the end of them, as they are tucked into their tunics, I know they will all be wooden-shaped vials, representing the smallest container of blood there is. Not everyone here will be part of First Light's last surviving gang, the Vials, the mix of thieves, smugglers, and cutthroats who are based in Southwestfall and have managed to so far evade the ruthless gang-breaking tactics of the First Guard these last hundred years. There will be other kinds of rebel dragged in for the biggest action since the days of Lightfall itself—but from what little I know of the Vials leader Hands Parker, she would have insisted on uniformity.

No sooner have they all arrived than they gather before the big gate, and a small crowd cluster before the heavy bolts keeping it in place. They ready their fists back, but then wait there as a figure walks toward them. She's dressed the same, but my magicked fox gives me easy sight of her face from here through the dark, and even with her cap and her bun-tied hair it is clearly the dead-eyed visage of Hands Parker herself.

I turn to Alanna. "Should you not be with them, Alanna? They appear as a small army, but I know you yourself to be one."

"No, m'lady."

I don't look at her; I keep my eyes on the scene before me, struggling as I am with the faint scent of Alanna's skin—mild sandalwood and dirt and some exotic flower I couldn't begin to guess of—going straight from my nose to the brain, enhanced with the fox, threatening to take me far away from here and straight into my fancies. Gods, I would touch her.

"And may I ask why?"

"You can ask, m'lady," she says, and I cannot see her face but I know there will be a hint of a smile, and I also know this is said not entirely to ward me off.

But before I can reply there is a tremendous sound of twenty vampires on magicked noble blood crashing against the gate, and the doors swing open, and both the destroyers of the cast-iron lock and the rest of the rebel mob rush into the courtyard. At this point, of course, the Blood Farm guards have noticed the rather obvious commotion at the main entrance, and thirty of them come rushing out of the building at the other end of the great courtyard, pausing beneath the columns of the facade briefly to survey this unexpected attack of Worns, before rushing on. Their crimson-red tabards look deep maroon in the barely lit courtyard gloom, and their faces appear a little taken aback by the sheer numbers before them.

"A good fifty to take on thirty, m'lady," murmurs Alanna next to me. "The numbers do appear to be favorin' the ones we root for." I nod.

"Yes, indeed. There will be more guards from deeper in the Blood Farms, surely, but if the rebels can win this small victory and rob some barrels stored in the building immediately in front of them, then they can be away before too many of the others arrive." I look to the skies. "And more importantly, before we hear the sound of wings."

"Yes, m'lady. This must not just be a sweet victory. It must be a short one for the ages."

As we watch, the Vials and the Blood Guard collide, both sides full-blooded, their nails elongated into talons, eyes blazing with recently taken good blood, virtually the same save for their differing uniforms.

At first it looks an equal fight, vicious blows descending on all. The guards are clearly well trained, and I wince as I see their vicious stabbing motions, some of which connect, spearing the arms or torsos of the rebels. But the Vials give as good as they get, and some guards go down as well. I see many using just fists, pounding the guards' faces with concrete hooks, and some of the guards are doing the same, powerful swinging hammer blows that they put all their strength behind.

Soon the numbers and the strength of the blood the rebels are on start to make a difference and more guards than rebels fall, either knocked out cold by the vicious blows or else woozy from blood loss. I note that those guards on the ground are left as they fall by the rebels, no final blows to try to take the head off or rip their body apart so no blood can restore them.

"Molly's orders, I imagine?" I ask Alanna, who, always in sync with me, replies immediately.

"Yes, m'lady. She has a lot of enthusiasm for avoiding Worns killing other Worns. Hands Parker sees them as betrayers, but old Molly knows we have to eventually get the Guard behind us."

"Well, thank goodness we have some moderation to the rebels," I reply.

A few more moments later, and all the guards are fallen, except for a couple who have run away, presumably alerting the others, although anyone not alerted by now and who is not hurriedly taking extra potent blood is unlikely to be much use in close-quarters combat anyway. Next, the rebels advance on the open doors of the first Blood Farm building. I cannot see inside from here—it is all shadows—but if what we know of the layout is true, the barrels for immediate transportation will be just inside.

Sure enough, moments later several of the rebels come stumbling out of the doorway with the barrels, only two per barrel—what would normally take ten Worns is a breeze on magicked noble blood. I idly wonder what they will be on; most likely bear, though magicked mountain cat is good also for strength, I believe.

And at that idleness I realize that I have stopped worrying.

"It appears to have proceeded according to plan, Alanna," I note, as a large wagon rolls up outside the gates for the barrels, which are now halfway across the courtyard.

Alanna doesn't reply.

"Alanna?" I ask, and turn to her, seeing that she is inspecting the sky. "Ah, looking out for wings. Still none yet?"

Alanna doesn't reply.

"Alanna," I add, the breeze escaping from my demeanor and the chill of winter returning, "I know you have a flair for the dramatic, but if you could do me the grace of words, then it would be most appreciated."

Alanna turns to me then, and stares at me direct, that look to the soul that gets me every time. "In Last Light, m'lady, that line you just said about it going according to plan was most unwise to be said at any times."

I laugh a little, more to dispel the growing sense of unease than any real desire to do so. "And yet, Alanna . . ."

"What do you feel, m'lady?" she asks, and, knowing Alanna to be most literal at most times, I take her at her word.

"I feel," I try, "a . . . charge in the air. As . . . as before a storm."

Alanna points up to the moonlit clouds. "And what do you see?"

I look up. "The clouds are darker."

Silence. She wants more. I decide to play, because I like her games; even in my tension do I like them.

"The clouds are vertical shaped, with a dark, anvil-like base."

"Indeed, m'lady. And what follows with such clouds?"

I turn back to the dark that lies behind the Blood Farm doors. "Alanna, you don't mean—"

My words are cut off by the low peal of thunder, a deep boom right above us, as soft rain falls when no rain was anticipated this night.

"Alanna," I say, my voice scratchy and rushed, "the thing I was thinking of before, at the back of my mind . . . I am afraid to say I have recalled it. That scheme that Sage Bailey constructed to help Raven rob the Blood Bank. He used a Cloak sorcerer, Cloak Kastillion, the most powerful kind in the war, remember? He was the one who created the illusion of the Grays invading the city. He was hiding among the bloodmages here in the farms, hiding among the Kinets' lodgings here."

"Indeed, m'lady, I recall, that was a sneaky revelation if ever there was one."

"But if the most powerful *Cloak* of the last few centuries can be secreted in First Light, then . . ."

Alanna turns to me, and grins, but there's gallows humor in that wicked smile and she knows it. "I think, m'lady, we might be suspectin' why there are no winged guard at the Blood Farms."

"Oh gods, what do we—"

My words are cut off by the first lightning strike, which crackles down from the largest of the dark clouds hovering directly above the Blood Farms and shatters the closest of the barrels being carried by the gate. Blood, sizzling and burnt, sloshes out across the courtyard, and the rebels carrying the barrels freeze. And then, like the rest of their companions, they turn and see a figure standing in the open doorway of the Blood Farm.

The figure is dressed in the cloak of the Kinets. Dark red with orange stripes. But their hood is down, and I see their face. It is a common sorcerer face in most respects, light-brown skin, light stubble, nothing particularly remarkable except for one thing. And though I was not alive in the Twin War even I know who it is, because that one thing is a lightning-shaped scar running from left brow down to right cheek, and they are grinning wide, with feverish eyes, not caring if they are recognized.

And as they stalk out of the shadow of the doors and into the courtyard proper, and raise their arms to the storm-addled skies, I recall the poem taught to young vampires to get them afraid of sorcerers, after the Twin War when a small number of the more powerful ones had caused so much damage.

> If you see a Cloak, think.
> If you see a Neuras, think not.
> If you see a Kinet, hide.
> And if you see an Atmos . . .
> Run.

And then he starts laughing, big peals of laughter, arms still raised, and a great ball of lightning shoots down and explodes the second barrel and the two rebels next to it. One moment they are there and the next they are not; instead, a great wave of bone and matter and blood crashes down onto the ground where they were, sloshing and mixing with the contents of the barrel, good blood mixed with bad, shards of indeterminable matter swimming in the tide.

The rest of the rebels—none of whom are stupid enough to fail to recognize, if only from war stories before their time, the presence of Atmos Reclantis, the most powerful weather mage to have ever lived—make a very quick and intelligent decision to run.

Most of them get within a few yards of the gates when Reclantis drops his raised arms a little and brings them closer, as if he is about to begin conducting an orchestra. Then he flicks his wrist and a thin bolt of lightning shoots out of the sky, entering the skull of the rebel nearest to the gates and exploding it. As the lightning grounds itself, the rest of the rebel begins smoking and quickly erupts into flames. Another flick of the other wrist, and another bolt lances down to the one who was nearest behind him; this time the skull stays intact and they simply become a juddering puppet as streams of sky fire course through them, small flames erupting throughout their body, a thin squeal coming out of their molten mouth that sounds as ghastly as a roasting pig. Then they fall to the ground, charred and smoking.

Reclantis's wrist actions increase in tempo and height now, and the bolts come down quicker in response, one every second, each one lancing a new rebel trying to get out of the range of death by sky. Soon half the rebels are stock-still, smoking, juddering, squealing, before once again collapsing to the ground as grotesque burnt-out carcasses. And all the time I see the Atmos laughing, enjoying himself, directing the orchestra of sky-wrought violence like the music is in his soul. I can barely wrench my face away.

I feel a hot breath in my ear, and I turn to see Alanna, her face next to mine. "We run. Now."

There is no room for doubt in the words, each one dropped like a sack of bricks at my feet, her eyes giving me violence, not the care they normally have.

"But he cannot see us here, we are far enough away—Alanna, they are all dying! We must see what happens."

Then Alanna grabs me roughly by the shoulder and spins me round to face her, and the shock of the touch, for she never touches me, and the shock of her face, for she never shows me such a furious expression, is almost as much a burden as the sight of the smoking faces of the dying rebels.

"We go now. Now!"

"Alanna, are you scared?"

I mean it not as judgment but it sounds it, and I instantly regret it, but it does not change her expression or her fury, and her grip on my shoulder tightens. Rather than question her anger—her seeming loss of that tight control of comporting herself, even in the most extreme situations—rather than question all that . . .

I run, run away with my Alanna, and I leave the rebels to smoke.

# 4

# The Passage of Blood

Round our way in the south of Dawn Death there were nothin' but swamp and the swamptails that came wit' it. We knew a bit 'bout the blood dealin' that went on in the city proper, with the nobles and stuff. But we never saw it. Or learned it. And then Grayfall happened and me and me ma made it to First Light. And now we live in Worntown and it ain't much more different from the swamp in most ways and we be just as ignorant as before about the city proper. There's just whole worlds of choosin' blood and getting it to places an' selling it and drinkin' the good stuff that we don't know an' will never know. And that's just how it be.

Anna Dupre, *A Worn Growing Uppe,*
memoirs written in pamphlet form by Redskill Fastpipes

## Sam

The Five Cuts smells just as strong as when I was there last month. When I'd just discovered that Daphnée was still alive, that my quiet life of hiding, barely a couple weeks old, was over, and I was led into that famous meeting of Molly Threetimes, smuggler; Hands Parker, gang leader; Redgrave, first man to the First Lord and, it turns out, inside man of the rebels all along; and then the final cameo, the former First Lord Azzuri himself—if I can still believe that happened.

If anything, the whiff of spilled blood and alcohol inside the inn is more potent.

As soon as I step through its doors, a light snowfall starts outside. The season has changed, for me more than anyone else. I'm not trying to worm my way into the Leeches while solving a murder anymore. No, I'm deep within the rebels of First Light, with the future of the city at stake. I'm still in the center. They still want me around.

I remember just a month ago when Rufous Azzuri, psychotic son of the First Lord, now the ruler of the city, was lying unconscious on the ground, defeated by my fist in his mouth, with the corpses of his First Guard all round him, and Sage and Jacob agog at my achievement. I'd decided then that I was done with violence, done with trying to better my station and save the city or whatever endless ambition coursed through my veins.

But that fire that I thought was dimmed? It was flared when I saw Lady Hocquard, Daphnée, in that alley, magically still with us, and now I feel it burn fast and fierce, no end to its wick. I'll have my revenge on Rufous for the death of my mother and father—a proper revenge, not just beating him in a fight. But taking his city from him. Not *his* city. It never was his. But I'll help these rebels, these Worns, and I'll save this place. I feel the hubris well up inside me; I'm not that foolish, but this isn't an old sorcerer stagetale and I'm not destined to be taught a lesson.

At the bar I order an ash chaser. Since I saw Alanna order one here it's been on my mind. The barkeep smiles at me, as if questioning my judgment.

"What's in it?" I ask, trying to parry his condescension with fake bravado.

"It's a secret," he says, pleased with himself. I inspect the shot glass, with its small ball of inky-black liquid suspended in the blood. I gulp it down, feeling the harsh chemical fire burn my tongue, and try not to grimace before him.

"Okay, then," I say, ordering another. "If I can guess what's in it—beside the blood, obviously—then you give me the coin back for it." I think on this. "And I drink for free the rest of this week." I might not be back again this week, but there is principle at stake.

He grins, still cocksure. "You're a funny one. A wager it is."

I stare at the black liquid, as if trying to discern its nature, but the idea that I wouldn't have immediately found out what it was after seeing Alanna down it the previous week is a nonsense. Knowing all the small details can save your life, as I've proved time and time again.

After a few moments of faked concentration, I smile at him triumphantly. "It's the juice of the buzzcatcher plant. Suspends itself in liquids. Deadly for insects, just harsh for us."

He gives me a scowl that says he doesn't like my knowing of that but he knows a bet is a bet, and he puffs out his cheeks and says, "Well it's a good week for you and your drinking habits, then."

"Hmm." I laugh. "Jacob would have liked that."

"What?"

"Nothing." I saunter off, or do my best impression of it, past the bar and around the blood drunk and, in some cases, completely tankarsed denizens of the Five Cuts through to the back and up the stairs to the corridor with three doors. I knock on the first one, the same as last time. The same knock, too—three quick, two slow, two quick—and when Molly Threetimes opens it, I see the leaders of the revolution sitting in the same spots as last time.

The round table is not covered in cards now; no one feels like playing anything. Sitting opposite Molly's seat is Hands Parker, Vials leader, the first time I've seen her since she was first introduced to me a month ago. Her expression is no different: that blank canvas, those dead eyes, those dangerous thin lips, the limp brunette hair currently out of the net and falling round her shoulders. The only sign that she might be feeling some intense emotions is her fingers, which are twitching, like wriggling blood eels, counting out the meter of her emotions that her face cannot.

Daphnée is here, too, sitting between Molly and Hands, her hair half bunched up in a ribbon of flowers that has replaced her carefully placed single flowers these days. Her face is plain of face paint; these days she is never adorned like the highest noble she used to be. Her face is also thunderous. Alanna is standing behind her, leaning against the blacked-out window, expressionless like Hands but mildly less psychotic.

Most of the rest of the room is bare, the shadows haunting its corners barely kept at bay by the weak oil lamps fixed to the walls. Two rickety chairs sit against the right wall, unoccupied, next to the side door that ex–First Lord Azzuri sprang out of last time. Against the left wall there is a freestanding blood cabinet that wasn't there last time, with large wheels fixed on its undercarriage. Both its doors are wide open, revealing seven shelves crammed with full carafes and bottles, and empty bloodvials snugly nestled in cotton-stuffed boxes, and rows of sparkling-crystal bloodflutes.

"Twin hells, Sammy, well, come in if you're comin'. Sort of makes the secret knock bloody useless if you just stand in t'open doorway gawpin' for anyone to see." Molly grins, and as she slams the door behind me I take in her blond-gray curls and her deep wrinkles, the kind you get at near two centuries that most would be ashamed of. But Molly isn't most, and I can't imagine the legendary Lightfall blood smuggler, the hero of the Worns of that dead city, ever feeling ashamed at anything. That said, her curls seem a little more unruly and the frown lines are showing even deeper than normal.

She strides over to the blood cabinet and grabs a flute so hard I fear it might knock into the others and send them flying, and then she taps her fingers on her lips as she chooses from the blood selection. "Hmm, let's see. I reckon I *should* give you plain hawk. Keep you focused for this next bit. But frankly that would be cruel, because it's a bit rough nonmagicked, and the crash would be harsh on you, you still with the memory of all that wolfblood you had in you not so long ago, more than anyone's ever had since the Twin War, I'd wager. So let's show you what the Midway bloods can do these days." She grabs at a small carafe on the top shelf, with MAGICKED C. scrawled on the label, and pours a fluteful.

She hands it to me. "Here you go, Sammy. That should do you for this meeting at least. Down it quick, now."

I do as she says—it's hard to resist a command from Molly Threetimes, I am quickly learning—and the clarity hits me almost immediately. The colors of the room stand out a little more, and I fancy I can hear a little more of the conversations down below. And my mind begins to race like a fox in a henhouse. "That's a Midway blood? Even with magick . . ."

Molly's eyes twinkle. "Ah yes, Sammy. That there is crow. An often-neglected Midway blood, but one that fairly leaps into the veins when these newfangled Kinet mages get to work on it in the Blood Farms. Those nobles are so occupied with the smugness of their own bloods that they've not even noticed how good the Midway types are gettin', almost under their noses. . . . That's always been their fault, you see. They never see the chance for progress in those they deem not capable of it."

"Their faults are my fancies," I say, enjoying the poetry of it even as I'm aware I have to thank the blood for that more than my mind.

"Do you want to go nip yourself a normal drink from below? Keep your hands occupied while we talk?"

"No, I'll be fine."

She nods, her round rosy cheeks full of the blood of her own flute. "Right, I forget, me. You're young. You don't have that need to be always suppin' on something." Her face darkens. "Wait till you get to my age and the urges start."

I'm about to ask about these urges but I remember the rest of the room, and I quickly sit down, between Molly and Hands. The small smile that's been playing on Daphnée's face as she watched my interactions drops and returns to her stormy expression.

"How many survived?" Molly asks, turning to Hands. "Out of the fifty who attacked the Blood Farms?"

Hands shrugs, her eyes barely flickering Molly's way. "A handful."

"Can you give me a number? These are Worn lives, dear. Endless lives snatched away." Molly's lips are pursed, and never has the word *dear* been so venomous.

"Seven."

Even Alanna's face registers that one.

"And would you say that was a good result?" asks Daphnée, lips thin, voice frozen over.

"I don't know, Queen Leech, would you say not knowin' that the Lords had the most powerful weather mage ever known in their back pocket was a good result for you and your Leeches?"

Daphnée's eyes widen but she doesn't rise to that. Maybe because she knows there's some truth to it, I think, with the added guilt of thinking it.

Molly drains her mug and sighs. "Well, that's put paid to that plan. Even if we found a way to defeat Atmos bloody Reclantis, the Lords know our aims now. And they know the rebels are active, and lookin' to strike. Everything gets harder now, not just that plan of action."

"It also puts us on the defensive I fear," says Daphnée calmly, whose face has not quite caught up with the new calm of her words, still shooting icy daggers Hands's way. "Rufous and the new spymaster will raid Worntown, looking for all the rebels. They will speed up the training of the new winged guard. They will reinforce, increase guard numbers. Get a grip on the city again."

"Exactly. So we try again. Different assault point, maybe. They're still weak. We just need more numbers," says Hands casually, as if she's talking about vials of slugblood not Worn lives. I get a chill just listening to her, like something is broken inside. She reminds me of Rufous, in a way.

They carry on talking, on that borderline between debate and argument, and as I sit there, my mind wanders. I think of my meeting with the First Lord, of how things have changed. I think of my times at the palace, finding rare silk dresses originally from Dawn Death in the wardrobe of a visiting Lady in the palace, daring myself to try them on, crying with laughter as I do a poor job of getting into it, and only later realizing that if I'd been caught it would have been sunburst for me for sure. For a moment I'm aware I'm leaving someone out of this memory, but it hurts to think of them, and when I try to do there's a cutscene in my head, of her falling, falling, screaming, and my head twitches to the right like I've been slapped, and my breath comes on a little strong—

"Sam, deary! Did you hear what I said?"

I snap to the sound of my voice, plummeting out of my nightdreams. Molly is looking at me, and so is everyone else.

"Sorry," I say, trying to catch my voice from the cavern it fell into. "Say that again, Molly."

Molly grins. "I was askin', Sammy, if you had any ideas."

I frown at her, and turn to Daphnée, who smiles at me, and I wonder if words between them have been had about allowing me to contribute.

"Actually," I begin. "I do." I sigh. I've had the idea brewing ever since a conversation I had with Sage a few weeks ago, sitting in Centerfall, watching the traders. But this might be difficult to explain, especially to the glass-eyed gangster to the right of me. "Well, it's all about the Invisibles."

"The Invisibles?" says Hands, who ironically has the most visible expression on her face since the short time I've known her, and that expression is one of pure suspicion. "The game the noble fucks play?"

I shake my head and gird my loins for patience. I don't know how many books she's ever read, but this could be a difficult one. The easy part is always doing the reading. The hard part is explaining it to the ones who never read.

"It's not a game," I begin, cautious as to the dangerous ground I'm climbing over. "It's a market. It's the same as the Blood Market really, except instead of taking possession of the blood, you take possession of the reputation of the blood."

Hands's expression doesn't change, which is fine, because it rarely does, but I see no light in the eyes, either, and I know I need to change tack.

"You buy the idea of the blood. You buy into its success. If a type of blood does well, you get more money, even though you never bought it. If it doesn't do well, you lose your money."

More blank looks. Even Daphnée is looking a little confused—I expect she thought I had a plan involving the Blood Market itself. I feel a pang of sadness that Sage isn't in the room, too. That smile he would make as I explain shared knowledge. Damn him and his secrets, he should be helping me. I sigh, and stand up. This might involve some pacing.

"Imagine," I begin, "that you're buying a vial of a new type of blood, except you don't actually buy one. You buy it in theory—an *invisible* vial. That way, you tie your money to the success of the blood without actually buying it. Whether you make more money for your invisible ownership depends on how popular the new blood will be. How much will be bought by the Midways and the Lords and the percentage of them who consider it good enough for a repeat purchase."

No one is interrupting me, so I assume I have a captive audience. It feels good. I feel important again. *That feeling that takes me somewhere good and gets everyone killed*, says a voice in my head, one that I told what feels a long time ago to burn in the sun.

"Let's say," I continue, "that there is a new blood on the market. A magicked blood, stronger than before. Now let's say that the experts in the Invisibles House decide that from the sounds of the new blood that has been created, it will be as popular as a type of existing blood that sells for five bloodcrowns per vial. So now a trader gives five bloodcrowns for the equivalent of one vial of blood—an invisible vial. If it turns out that this new blood really *is* more popular than the price it's been given originally, then your invisible vial of blood is now worth more than the five crowns you gave for it. You can keep your ownership of the invisible vial in case the blood gets even more popular, or you can sell it and take a tidy profit. Of course, if it turns out to be less popular, then you will lose some or all of your five bloodcrowns you started with."

There's a long silence as I wait for Molly's or Hands's expressions to go blanker. I chide myself even as I think that. How is Hands meant to know all this stuff? There is little time for this in the down and dirty world of Worntown. Maybe my love for books has made me a little unforgiving of those who don't want to know or *can't know* the rest of the world.

More silence.

*Or maybe not.*

"How do they know how popular it has been?" says Daphnée, grinning, breaking me out of my enforced purgatory.

"There are Worns who act as messengers and they collect the opinions of the merchants after the delivery of the new blood. A group of clerics then work out overall how popular the blood is on any given day. Then the popularity of the new blood is announced and the traders buy or sell their invisibles accordingly."

"This is . . . interesting," says Hands, her face giving me various ways of telling me that it isn't without ever doing anything, which is a curious trick. "But how does it help us . . . do anything?"

"Because," I say, giving the word a bit of space in an attempt to create a dramatic buildup, "we're going to . . . crash the market."

Hands frowns. Molly smiles. Daphnée begins to smile, but I see confusion interrupt it. I'll need to do a lot of work here.

"I honestly don't know what that means," says Hands, who is now looking bored and dangerous.

"Look," I say, pacing now, back and forth, wishing I'd asked Molly for some more of that magicked crow but fairly confident the rush in my veins that comes from excitement, not blood for once, will do the work for me. "Imagine if you're a Lord who dabbles in the Invisibles market. Or maybe a successful Midway. You've made a bit of money. You've got a taste for it. You're confident. You're *cocky*. There's a new coin-making game in town—well, a century or so, still new by the standards of those on the good blood—and you're getting pretty good at it." I stop pacing and turn to my audience. This is the part I need to sell. I try to recall all the books I've read on money. And the market. And the animal spirits that power them.

"Now imagine that you hear of a new blood. The experts in the Invisibles have got word from the Kinets at the Blood Market. It's good. It's magicked. The magick has made it more potent than before. The early reports from tastings at the farms are incredible. It's going to be priced well, priced high, initially. But not *too* high, because no one really knows yet.

"Then the rumors start. About just how good this is. That it's better even than people imagine. That they're not letting many taste it till it arrives on the market because they don't want to cause a rush, but that someone did taste it and they said it was like *wolfblood*."

Daphnée, who I'm fairly sure is beginning to see where this is going, smiles, running her fingers through her hair. "And I wonder who is spreading these rumors?"

I grin in return. "I couldn't imagine." I stop my pacing and sit down, turn my chair a little to Hands, who is the one I really need to convince, the possibly psychotic gangster who needs to calm down and follow the advice of a simple bookish Wornmaid. "Okay, so now the rumors are out. Everyone buys the initial price when it finally hits the market. Everyone thinks they're the only one who knows the secret. By the time some start to twig that maybe everyone knows, it's been bought and bought and bought. And we're talking huge amounts. The kind that make a difference. The kind of amounts you pay when you've been making small profits for years, getting more and more confident in the system, waiting for the chance to make some *real* money."

"Sammy, dear, I know you're havin' a good time, but maybe it's time to get to the point," says Molly.

I breathe. Here we go. "And then the market—the Invisibles traders—get the very first reports of the batch. And you know what? The rumors were *right*. It's incredible. It's potent. It makes your veins feel like they've been filled with the blood elixir of the Blood Gods themselves. It might not make you fly like wolfblood, but you'll feel like you could, so better stay away from any rooftops!"

"Sammy," says Molly, amusement verging on impatience.

"Sorry . . . point is, the market gets even more feverish. Now everyone is buying, less nervous at the thought of putting their coin on the line, and the price goes up, and still people buy, and now they're really throwing their money at it, trying to make some profit before it gets higher, *and they know it will get higher*."

I stop. I think I've earned one final dramatic pause.

"And then . . ." I stare at Hands Parker. "They find out that it's a lump of cow shit and the whole made-up thing falls apart and everyone loses everything."

For the first time, I see the inkling of something on the gangster's face. "And they won't be happy about that."

"No," says Molly, "they won't. Have you ever seen a Midway or Lord who's lost some money? It's like you've murdered their whole family." She stops then, and stares at Hands, a little aghast at her own words. Hands doesn't seem to have noticed. I make a note to ask about that later.

"But it's not the Lords who will really get angry, is it?" asks Daphnée, weaving threads of her own in the air. "It's the Midways."

"Yes," I say excitedly. "Exactly. The Midways. The ones who have enough money to try and play the Lords' game but not enough to survive it if it gets rough. They've been shit on all their lives, not as much as we have"—I glance at Daphnée here, the one noble in the room, wondering if she minds me including her when she was until recently among the elite, but she doesn't seem to notice—"but they must know that they are given a taste of luxury but not all of it, and I bet they hate it."

"We Leeches know their secrets," says Daphnée, "we *know* they hate it."

I nod. "Yes, so when a fair number of them lose life-ruining sums . . . it will not be pleasant."

Molly nods. "And it will be our jobs to ensure that that pleasantness has a nice and easy path straight into outright violence."

I pause at that. This whole thing was meant to avoid violence. Somewhere in my head, I start to see a body tumbling out of the sky again, face about to get remodeled onto the ground, and my fingers twitch, and I hope no one sees. "Well, not violence, but a . . . distraction."

Hands Parker nods. "We could use a distraction."

I grin, finally feeling that I might have the entire room on board. "And then you get your blood from the Blood Farms."

"Oh no," says Hands, staring at Molly, "we would go straight for the wolfblood stores."

I almost gasp at that. Things have escalated.

But then Hands shakes her head. "Nice story, girl. But this is all a lot of ifs and maybes. We can't deal in that." And then she's back to staring at the wall, as if that's decided. No. Not after all that. I turn to Molly, who's surely on my side now. To my internal horror, she has a look of doubt on her face.

"It is . . . a little more confusin' than I was hoping for, Sammy, dear. A lot of cogs there. A lot of cogs that need to turn and then rely on the whole blooddamn waterwheel collapsin' at the end of it."

I sigh. I didn't want to talk about books, I wanted to keep it to real life, always more convincing for people, but . . .

"There've been market crashes before," I begin.

Molly frowns. "I think I would have heard about them. There haven't been any in First Light post-Grayfall, and the Blood Market itself, never mind the Invisibles, has only really been around since after the Twin War. I know it well, Sammy, my smugglin' depended on it."

I shake my head. "I'm not talking about First Light. Or Lightfall.

I'm talking about Dawn Death." This is a bit of a risky diversion. Dawn Death, the southernmost vampire city, where the Centerlands touch the Swamplands, was a strange place little talked of outside of it. It was the Centerlands city pre-Grayfall with the most sorcerers in it. A curious mix of mage and blood, closer than in any other city. They formed their own cults, away from the Desertlands. Things went on amid the mists of these swamps that you would hardly believe, and there are lots of books on the subject if you want to look at them, not that anyone does. It sounded like Last Light, but a strange city you could actually visit. At least until the Grays put their touch on it like the rest of the Centerlands.

"In *A Treatise on Dawn Death* by Carmine Ceruli," I say, trying not to wince as I see Hands's vacant expression get a little more vacant as I bring talk of literature into the room, "Ceruli describes how they had their own small Blood Market, and it sort of worked a bit like the Invisibles . . . although with actual blood. A powerful mage manipulated it. Spread rumors that were too good to be true, just like the plan I've given you. A lot of people lost a lot of money. Some vampires went to war with the mage and his own Dawn Death cult. It threatened to get very violent, until the First Vampire Lord of Dawn Death intervened and restored the lost funds through his own pocket."

Hands looks unmoved. "A take from a tome, excellent."

I look to Molly. "It's a good plan, Molly. It uses all our strengths." I turn back to Hands, my desire for this to work outshining my fear of those dead eyes. "And unlike her plan, it won't get a bunch of rebels fried by a sorcerer." She doesn't even turn to me, which is not a good sign.

"I wish we'd had something of the sort closer to home we could use as a sign, though," says Molly, making my heart sink further. "It's just . . . it's just a lot, Sammy."

*No. This is how we do it. This is how* I *do it.*

I try to mouth the word, but I've used my shot. The room is not as convinced by the records of dusty volumes as I am.

"Why don't we think about it?" asks Daphnée, who turns her round, emphatic eyes my way and shoots me a look of kindness. Oh, no. Kindness. Next we'll have pity. And I know pity well. When your whole family has been killed, you get to know it very well and hate it all the same.

Then a voice from the shadows—always in the shadows—comes out.

"Sammy may have read the books, but I've lived the sorry tale," says

Alanna, and like everything she says I don't know what she means but I could hug her right now if she wasn't so terrifying.

There's a pause, as everyone waits for her to continue, and for a second I worry that will be it. That would be very Alanna. But then she clears her throat and wanders to the blacked-out window as she does, idly dragging on the blinds with her dagger, inlaid with emerald, glinting in the light of the weak oil lamps.

"In Last Light there was a strange thing found under the earth. There were a lot of strange things found under the earth in our city. . . ." She pauses, playing with the blinds a little, and for a moment I wonder if she's been distracted, but then she comes back to us. "But this was a mineral, and valuable, and . . . powerful. So everyone wanted it, and the market for it was high and wild, and made the whole place giddy for a while. But then it started to get robbed, you see, Last Light not being the safest of places to go at the best of times. Tiny streets, dark corners . . ." She turns back to us and I see the ghost of a grin. "I should know, I found myself in many of them, in my time."

I glance at Hands, and I'd swear that even that vacant morass of a face is betraying a little concern at where this wandering story is heading.

"So a market quickly started on this rock, and the prices went high. Then it was found that it hurt people, turned your skin over time to the starts of ash, just like the sun. Except this had been hidden by the Cidemis, one of the four powerful families of my city who controlled the rock extraction and distribution, you see, so it all came out at once, over one night. And fortunes were lost, and the panic that happened . . ."

She flips her dagger up into her palm as she says it, and rubs the emeralds in the hilt thoughtfully, deep into her past. "This was a much simpler market than everything Sam has just wittered on to you about the Invisibles, and yet no one understood it, and they didn't care that they didn't understand it. And when it fell, oh, the fury it caused, and the chaos . . . there was a spirit among those men of finance, something greater than themselves, something they neither understood nor could command, something that fed on itself, and for a few stark days it almost took Last Light down with it, down, down, down."

And then she flips the dagger up in the air, and as it falls, blade down, into her open waiting palm, she nudges it with a gentle caress and it flips over at the last minute, landing handle down. Then she takes that dagger and slams it into the table, much nearer Hands than Molly, and there's a quick beat of silence after the slicing sound of wood.

"So listen to Sammy, and let's be crashin' the whole bastard thing."

And then she walks out of the room.

Molly grins. "I reckon she got bored of debate."

"She knows how to make a point," says Daphnée, sharing the grin.

I turn to Hands and see resignation in her face. She doesn't like it, but she doesn't have to.

Twin hells . . .

I have them.

# 5

# How People Work

> There's a rift between us and the Midways and the Lords, and it grows by night. We're concerned with what you can touch. We craft and we trade things and we drink things and we care about people. Them lot? The ones that never age? They're fussed over the things that don't exist. The things you can't see. The concept of money. The idea of ownership in summat that only exists as you agree it does. Take the Invisibles. The name alone should tell you all you need to know. They're telling you it don't exist. The stuff they put their money into. And so they can do what they like, cos it was never there in the first place. But one day they'll regret that they don't care about things you can't touch no more. One day we'll make 'em regret.
>
> Thea Lyons, *A View from Worntowne*

## Sam

The walk back from the Five Cuts to the Leech house in Westfall is a long one, about an hour. I thought I would have Daphnée as company, but she rushed off in a cart to who knows where, full of plans for which Midways to get on side to start the rumors of the blood we'd need to get the wheels of our plan turning. Unlike the Lords, where almost all the real wheels of power are turned by men, at least in public, there are a fair few female Midways with influence—less than there were in Lightfall but still some—and there are several Leeches in there with connections to the Blood Market. I feel like it might take more, though, and I have a feeling I know who to go to about that, but I need to mull on it a little.

As I walk the rough dirt streets, which slowly get wider and better cared for as I go north and near Westfall, I think about how well my plan has worked. For now. It won't be enough to stop the violence that'll come when the market crashes and the rebels seize the wolfblood, but I'll work on that. For the time being, I have the means to bring the city a little closer to the revolution with the kind of chaos I'm in favor of: the one that doesn't start with violence, even though it might end up like that. The kind that doesn't get more people killed; the kind that avoids the bloodstains on all my schemes that I can't turn from, no matter how blind I make myself. There are cogs turning now, and I feel so *alive*, but I know that the highest point of that feeling is right before someone else tends to feel so *dead*.

And then, almost unbidden, I think about Sage, whose temporary accommodation will be coming up a little to my west soon, who I could just go and wake up if I wanted, or interrupt his insomniac study, more like. I could demand he tells me what he's doing here. Or I could spy on him. I could do a lot of things. But I won't be that woman distracted from my plans by a man; I won't be that. Even though I could say it's in the city's interest to find out what he's up to. Thing is, it is much, much more in mine.

Then I look up at the moon, almost full, surely no more than three nights away from its pomp, and I remember a night with more clouds, and the sight of something falling through those clouds, a person, a friend, and I gasp before that image is complete and turn to the rough timber buildings that line the street instead.

And that's when I see the figure following me, stalking parallel to me, darting across an alleyway that breaks up two houses, so quick I could almost tell myself it was a trick of the moonlight. But I've seen enough people in the shadows now—wolf assassins, First Guard, and whatever Alanna is—to know when someone is really there, and I trust my instincts and pick up the pace. I turn to my right, looking for a way to cut through to the next street rather than continue winding down this one, and that's when I see a flash of something on that side, too. I'm still on the magicked crow that Molly gave me prior to the meeting, the last dregs of it, at least, the last sparks in my veins lighting up my eyesight and my instincts, and so I wonder if whoever is following me has got careless. Or maybe I'm just paying attention properly for the first time in my journey and using my most recent blood properly.

I look around the rest of the street. It's almost empty. I think I know why. This road, Eel Tea Lane (ironically named, surely, as eel tea, or even eel blood, for that matter, is a delicacy you would never find in Worntown), curves west leading from Southwestfall to Westfall but taking a wider route; it ends up being quicker if you stay on it but now I'm close to the mountainside ringing the city, and most will be deeper in Serf-town this time of day.

Even so, I'm surprised that there's hardly anyone here.

And then I remember what else I know about Eel Tea Lane. *The Underworkings of First Light* by Rufous Lazuli, a Lord obsessed with the Worns, who knew even more about their dealings than the spymaster himself, who identified the western end as the heart of the gangs of First Light, specifically the only gang worth the name, the Vials.

Maybe it's the very last of the magicked crow, or maybe, since crow shouldn't be that great at workings of the mind, I'm just getting better at sensing danger, but something clicks into place. The dissatisfied look on Hands Parker's face, seeming in such contrast to her eventual agreement. The figures to my left and right. The way this blooddamn city works.

And then I run.

I run ahead, following the street round, trying to work out a path that won't take me left or right into where I'm now certain my stalkers are. As I run, the remaining few people on the street thin out further, until I can only spy the occasional beggar, crying for a vial or a bloodcrown, and the houses start to thin out, too, and I realize I've gone too far and missed the turning back north and I'm getting close to the mountain line, and that gives me a little hope of evasion, because once I'm out of road any chance of a pincer movement my followers were surely hoping to make goes out of the count. Then I wonder why they're waiting and why they don't take me now, and a voice in my head goes, *You defeated Rufous Azzuri in combat, Sam. You ingested more wolfblood than anyone has in a century, perhaps. Maybe people have good reason to be cautious about you.*

Thank you, voice. You're much more confident in me than I am.

Ahead I see the end of the road and the start of trees, and beyond that it's the great start of the Fang Tips, the western mountain range, soaring into the cloudless night sky, blocking First Light in and protecting it. *Good*, I think, *I'll lose them in there.* And then a follow-up thought: *I really hope there is someone to lose and your mind is not just going on you, Sam.* I kick that shit of an idea right out of my head and I focus on running, and as my breaths come harsher I realize the last of the crow is wearing off, and any physical advantage I might have is dying with the fading power in my veins.

Then the road ends and I scurry into the tree cover, and I stop to turn around and see if I can catch any sight of the figures. Nothing. The street I've just left is quiet, eerily quiet, and no shadows move. Just a plain canvas, the only sound my harsh breaths in the still winter air.

*Okay, Sam. Maybe you should listen to that voice—*

*Snick.*

I hear the sound of a knife being slid out from its sheath, but before I can react, I feel the point of it on the back of my neck.

"Very good of you to escort yourself into the woods, Sam," says the lifeless ashen voice of Hands Parker. "You should know that I can't sever your head from your neck easily with this knife, but I can hurt you, and that'll give me time to do the rest. So turn round slow. Nice and slow, now."

"What's the plan, then, Hands?" I ask, turning round slow, eyeing her long dank hair and emotionless eyes, and then looking down at the short, sharp blade now at the front of my throat. "I never make it back to Westfall, and everyone assumes that one of the new spymaster's lot finally caught up with me? Or Rufous and his First Guard? Or the Blood Guard? Do you think that would wash with Molly, or Daphnée—or Alanna?"

She cocks her head at me, and as she does so two figures come out from the trees around her dressed in dark-brown tunics, with visible necklace strings: more Vials like her. Three. Three for me. What do people think I can do? Whatever it is, it is much more than the sum of my actual abilities. I still remember the wolfblood in me. Surging through me. Making me not just strong and fast and quick-witted but making me *see* things. How the world really is. Stripping away the surface. Oh, to have a little wolfblood now. I can practically taste it on my tongue. The pure metal, with notes of earth. I would carve through these three, and then I wouldn't stop, I would run through the mountains, and I'd take on the Grays, I'd—

I'm aware I've missed Hands's reply. "What was that?" I ask, and the blank face frowns a little, and I feel triumph that I've forced an expression out of her.

"I said . . . they will believe it, because that's the times they live in. Violent times. My kind of times. The world belongs to those who do what they need to, Sam. Through force. And death. The only things they understand. Your clever plan to change the city is oh-so cunning. You could put it in a glass case and admire it forever." I feel the knife press in a little at my throat. "But this is the moment where they're weak, and I've been waiting for this moment a hundred years. And me and my Vials and all the rebels we can muster will show them how weak they are. This is not a time for you and your words." She sighs and turns to her accomplices on either side of her. "You got a little too fucking high on yourself, Sam, is what I'm trying to say."

Then her fellow Vials draw blades and ready them at either side of me. "Three on one is a quick way to kill another of our kind, properly, no chance of reviving with blood, but also without hurting them. I don't want to hurt you, Sam. You're just a bloody maid who got too far, and now you're in my fucking way."

As the knives close in, I ask, "What made you this way, Hands? To be killing your allies in the woods?"

Hands shrugs. "What do you think? They did." And she nods to the city behind me, and I know she's not talking about the Worns and the Midways.

And then, in the half moments as I wait for the blade, I realize that although I'm afraid, I'm not as afraid as I thought, and I can't help but wonder why. Is it because I'm tired of the guilt? Or is it because I'm tired of the ambition, that ceaseless roving thing that will never make me happy?

Even more so than when I was tied to a stake before the morning sun, I find myself surprisingly ready to die.

Arms pulled back now for the killing blows. Three sets.

I close my eyes.

*Snick.*

*Snick.*

I open my eyes. Even before the relief comes the laugh. "Alanna," I say. "One of these days you're going to get bored of saving me."

Alanna, who has a blade to the throat of Hands, shrugs. "At least you got my name right this time."

I turn to my left, and then to my right, staring at the two Vials who are on the ground, clutching in panic at the gushing blood from their opened necks, well, more spurting than gushing, really, little geysers of crimson splattering the nearby low-hanging branches. The wounds are deep, surprisingly deep for the slash of a simple dagger, not that anything Alanna carries is likely to be simple. They'll still be fine and healed after a while, but we have time, even if they have good blood on their persons.

I put my hands on my knees and crouch. My breath comes out in great heaves. My mind may have been ready to die, but my body doesn't know that. We stand there a few moments, Alanna holding her emerald-gemmed dagger to Hands's throat, me trying not to throw up.

Hands, who has not yet spoken since Alanna's appearance, finally whispers some words like dry leaves on the breeze. "You make quick and brutal work with just a dagger. What blood are you on, Alanna?"

"Hard to say," replies Alanna. "I lose track a lot of the time. Maybe something good. Maybe something not."

"It must be something good," says Hands, who is being pretty stubborn for someone with a knife at their throat.

"Must it?" asks Alanna, who, I am starting to realize, quite enjoys throwing more mystery up around her.

"So what now?" continues Hands. "Do you kill me, and finish my two comrades off?"

"I could do," says Alanna, who, in the gloom of these trees where the moonlight barely penetrates, looks almost wolflike, her eyes dark and her face taut and her body seemingly encased in shadow, like she could change at any moment. "Maybe I should do. Me and Sammy here have gone through a lot, and I would kill more important people than you to protect her at this point, I think."

Hands Parker snorts, or at least she makes a sound that could be snorting, because actual snorting would show far too much emotion for her.

"You care for her that much?"

"Maybe," says Alanna. "Or maybe someone *I* care for a great deal does."

"This plan will not work, Alanna. It will waste time, and we will lose our chance. They killed our children, they killed our kind. They got away with it. Would you have the bastards do so forever?"

Alanna shakes her head. "You've been on the streets for too long, buried in your gang, Hands. The world is more complex than any of your imaginings could comprehend. Sammy sees a lot. I have seen it myself. I think you need a little faith."

"I lost my faith a long time ago."

Alanna thinks on this. "Yes, if I'm honest, mine slithered down a blooddrain a good couple of centuries ago. Maybe we both need to change."

"Just fucking kill me, gods' sake."

"No," says Alanna, her voice falling low to a whisper. "I'm not going to kill you, Hands. You're going to keep on doing what you're doing, and we're all going to keep these schemes a whirlin'. And when Sam's plan works, you're going to do whatever you need to the Lords you hate so much, for whatever they did to you to make you like this. And we are all happy, in our own ways."

Hands's eyes slightly narrow. "And why would I do that, Alanna of Last Light? Why would I not just try and kill Sam tomorrow?"

Alanna grins then; Hands cannot see her grin but I know that smile well.

"Because, *Laura*—yes, I know your name. It is easier to not use our real names, is it not? We are similar like that—because you only have so many in your gang, big as it may be, and after a while, they may start to get a little fatigued at having my dagger thrust inside them."

"You can't be everywhere," says Hands.

"People have been sayin' that for a long time." Alanna sniffs. "Much good may it do them."

Hands laughs then, a couple of quick harsh barks. "Fine. Let this plan spool out. Let it bring the nobles to the ground. And if it does not, I'll ring round all my Vials and we'll see what a Last Lighter is really made of."

Alanna laughs, higher and longer than Hands did. "Madness and wine, Hands of the Parkers. Madness and wine." But she releases her knife, and looks at me.

"You can say something at some point, Sammy, if you like. This isn't a stage play."

I sigh. "Do you think one day I could have normal friends?"

She grins. "That's the spirit." She starts to walk off, and I turn back to Hands; she's not looking at me but fishing vials from her tunic, presumably to restore her guards, who are still slightly spurting on the ground, to enough fitness for the walk.

"So that's it?" I ask, running after Alanna. "We just leave them?"

Alanna doesn't turn back to me. "I thought you were trying to avoid death, Sammy."

"Well, yes, I . . ." Something hits me. "How did you know? How did you know to follow me? That I would be attacked?"

"Do you know why me and my Daffers get on so well, Sammy?" she replies, half striding, half dancing, as is her way.

"No," I reply, avoiding all the lewd answers that file into my mind.

She half turns to me then, a whisper of her previous grin returning. "Because we know how people work."

I can't help but smile at that.

"Speaking of people . . ." I begin.

"I don't know what Sage the Mage is up to," says Alanna, much quicker than I like.

"How did you know . . ."

Alanna turns and looks at me dead-on and says nothing.

"Fair enough," I reply sheepishly.

"I tried to follow him," continues Alanna. "After our little dance with him. He was movin' north. But then he vanished into all of the airs."

"Vanished?"

"That's the word I used, Sammy. Ain't no one ever gone puff into the air before me before. I don't normally lose someone like that. It was a first, actually." Her eyes narrow. "Not an enjoyable one."

"Interesting," I say.

"That's the word, Sammy. I heard about what he pulled against the First Guard, when you and old Raven were fightin' them. Turned into a big old metal man an' shot 'em all down. He's got a lot of tricks up his sleeve."

I let that linger in the air, dreaming of knowledge and other worlds.

"Oh, and one more thing, Sammy," Alanna continues. "When you're recovered from your almost death, and gots all your courage back, you've been invited to a meeting. One on one, like."

I frown. "Is this meeting with someone else who wants me dead?"

Alanna shrugs, face impassive. "Maybe. It's Vermillion Azzuri."

I give this a few beats to sink in. It never does. "As in the First Lord Azzuri? Well, old First Lord. I don't know what he is now."

Alanna grins. "He's one of ours now, ain't he? Not that I'll believe it for a good few moons."

"And he wants to meet me?"

"Repeatin' me is never a good idea, Sammy, unless you're of the desire to be me."

I let this lie for a few moments, imagining meeting with the man who tried to have me killed. His former first man Redgrave, it turns out, was a rebel spy, and claims to have converted the former leader of the city to the cause.

"Do you think I should go, Alanna?"

Alanna stops and turns to me, the waxing moon shining on her face. "I think you decided to creep along the moment I told you of your invite, Sammy girl, and that's why we get along, I reckon."

I don't know what to say to that, so we pick up the pace instead, the night's cool air icy on our skin.

# 6

# It's a Sinassion

> All sorcerers are orphans. Not just that, they have no family. They are born alone. Think on that. It explains much of their societal behavior: how strong the sects they join are, how much it matters that they so often stick to their own magick type. It explains the feverish devotion to a cause they follow; in the big sorcerer cities this cause is, sadly, these days, mainly furthering the politics of their own sects. But in the cults that are dotted around the desert wilderness, you can find fevered devotion and strong found family of the most curious kinds.
>
> Redfold Steelclasp, *A Vampire's Guide to Magick*

## Sage Bailey

The limestone quarry spreads out before me, a giant pit, an open mine of striated ringed sections patterned with white stripes, with a small lake at the bottom. The noon sun bounces off it, reflecting violent rays in kaleidoscopic ranges of harsh white. It's empty of vampires, not just because of the daytime but because since Grayfall it's been all but abandoned. Building and construction has almost ceased in First Light. There are no Kinets in the city to blast the rock out, for a start; the mages who improve the blood are hardly up to the task, having dedicated their lives to moving the smallest matter only. And the Lords are hardly going to spare their precious noble bloods or even wolfblood on building when they are busy hoarding them all. A civilization that ceases to build is set to fall; I don't have to refer to the tomes to conclude that. The Lords, no doubt, dream of returning to Lightfall soon, and are happy in the stasis, not understanding that the abandonment of progress has a way of eroding you from within.

I sit at the lip of the quarry, in the shade of a sprawling redoak tree, and ponder my situation.

Tonight I have, perhaps, my most important meeting in a couple of centuries. But I can't stop thinking about my completely unexpected meeting two nights ago with Sam. The manner in which she left, obviously hurt. The secrets I had to keep from her, after barely a month ago revealing so much of myself.

It's been a long time since I had to choose between secrets and my feelings, and my emotions have atrophied in that sense. But now I find my old guardrails melting a little.

I'm not sure I like it.

But I have to suppress my emotions, because I need answers.

And the figure who is hopefully in the vicinity has them.

*If it's answers you want, you could do worse than me, yes.*

I sigh, trying not to show the mild alarm of suddenly having a voice in my head. "I thought you didn't read my thoughts without permission." I choose to say it out loud, rather than think it. Sinassion must be nearby, unless his powers have increased suddenly.

*This does not count, old friend. You were practically screaming it. You must be more considerate of mind-readers if you wish to hide your thoughts.*

"You're the only mind-reader who can read thoughts without touching."

*Fair point. You must, then, be more considerate of me.*

"I think I'm being pretty considerate now, all things . . . considered. I left Jacob alone in the Wolflands to come and meet with you."

*For a good price.*

I leave that be, for I can't argue with it. He knows what I want most in the world, and he has me. "Are you going to reveal yourself at all, Sinassion? This mystery of yours was always a little tiring."

There's a pause then, no doubt as Sinassion plans his elaborately impossible entrance, and having mentioned Jacob my mind turns to him. Leaving him to go on to the Wolflands with Raven was not the fairest thing to do to him. Nor the wisest. But I understand Raven enough now to know he would not let any harm come to my deputy and my friend. And what else could I do? Sinassion had told me that the mortals were coming, and once he said that, regardless of how much I can trust him, my sights were always going to be set and my mind always made up. We are who we are, and we can never change, and we will always go where we must. I will always follow the quest for the truth, and to other worlds.

And right now this quest is all about one thing: Are the mortals coming back? Jacob and I have spent the best part of the last fifteen decades collecting evidence of their existence from around the Everlands, and storing much of it in the vast catacombs under our temple. That much is at least obvious to some outside the cult after I was forced to intervene to save Sam and Raven from the remains of the First Guard, with some of the mortals' technology. But we still don't know who they were, when they existed, where they went, and *why* they went.

Now Sinassion claims to have answers. Which is rich, as he was the one who abandoned my quest for answers. Right at the start of the cult. This is a fact I decided not to tell Jacob, too, and is more fuel for my guilt.

Some of those answers may also include why the Grays will not harm me or attack me. We know now that the Grays are Shades, Sinassion's old army, repurposed by the now dead Saxe and his conspiratorial accomplices to do their bidding and fake an invasion. They do not quite have the mind powers of their old leader Sinassion—who does?—but they are much more powerful than a Neuras, and I must find out why he taught them not to harm my kind. The Quantas kind. The magickless kind. The pitiable kind.

And just like that, Sinassion is before me, that old Neuras appearing trick.

*Greetings, old friend. I am glad you came.*

"I'm not sure I am," I say, staring at my old friend and history's greatest murderer, if war deaths count as murder. I continue to speak at him, unwilling to give him the grace of mind-talking yet.

His hood is up, but his face can still be seen, or at least it would be if it wasn't for the burning glow of his eyes, making it impossible to see anything else around them. To look at him is to look at twin suns, and though I once got used to this sensation, it has been one hundred and sixty years since I last saw him, and so I feel again as discombobulated as at my very first meeting. Are his eyes really burning orbs of light, or is this one of his tricks? No one has ever found out, and you'd get good odds at the betting halls in Luce at that continuing indefinitely.

*I'm sad to hear that, Sage. You once trusted me with the deepest secrets.*

"I did. But a lot of things have happened since we founded the cult. You led an army of sorcerers and turned a regional war between vampires and werewolves into an all-continental war and caused tens of thousands to die in an attempt to take over the entire land. Things like that."

*I killed soldiers. Who knew what they were doing.*

I snort at that. I'm too weary for a morality debate right now.

*You know I am still the same man,* he continues. *You know that I would not harm you, for instance.*

"And how do *you* know that?" I ask, suspicions roused. Most Neuras have limited mind-reading powers. Far from the subject, say a mile, they can, if they are well trained, sense the presence of a person in the vicinity. As they get closer, they may be able to sense emotions or the basest, most simple of thoughts. To read a mind properly, they must be touching the person. And you can train yourself, over many years, to resist this almost completely.

But Sinassion? He—and this is how I knew him originally; I dread to think what he is capable of sixteen decades on from when I last saw him, shortly before the Twin War broke out—he can sense minds and thoughts from . . . miles, that I know of. And when he nears you, he can read you like a book and speak into your mind, too, which is a strange novelty that he alone is capable of as far as I am aware. Yes, a rare few Neuras are trained to send messages from city to city. But it takes ten of them putting their minds together for hours to send a single simple message. Having a conversation in someone's head is impossible for normal sorcerers.

As for defenses against him? With training, great training, you can resist a mind as powerful as his from a distance, but once he is near you, or Light forbid he touches you . . . the best of luck.

He taught many of these skills to his Shades, now the Grays, which is how they created that strange Neuras combat style of seemingly being invisible, or at least never being in the same place the person is thinking of. But they never quite became him. He is alone in his abilities.

*I can see I have to reearn your trust, Sage Bailey,* thinks Sinassion, and I sense rather than hear the offense in my head. *It is a challenge I accept.*

He turns from me then and faces the quarry. We are in Northwestfall; the Fang Tips rise up to the west. To the north, a smaller range gives way to the sea, the mighty swell of the Endless Ocean, which must, I am confident, have an end. A little east of us is the Blood Farms. And south is Westfall, my hasty abode, Sam's new home. All around us, things are happening, the slow cogs turning, sometimes quickly, always inevitable. But here, under this tree, before this quarry, at this time of day, it feels peaceful. Not quite desert peaceful. But for now, close enough.

Sinassion sits on the grass beside me. I flinch for a second.

*Ah. You are nervous around me. I understand.*

"Do you? Last time I saw you, you had killed no one, to my knowledge. Last time I saw you, you were giving me an ultimatum."

*Yes, I remember that. We had different paths, I suppose.*

I laugh bitterly. "I didn't expect your path to lead to the murders of thousands of people," I reply. "That was a surprise, to be honest."

*And in my absence, you recrafted the cult,* he continues, ignoring me. *Rebuilt it after the War, with your fellow Quantas. It is rather poetic, I have to give you that. An entire cult filled with sorcerers who have no magick in them, dedicating themselves to a magick of a different kind. A long-gone race and their ancient secrets. I wonder what a therapist would say to that.*

"A therapist?" I'm unfamiliar with the word.

*Never mind. Before your time.* He's silent awhile. Then: *You feel bad about leaving Jacob. But you know what he managed, once upon a time. What he achieved. You know he is capable on his own.*

I let that one go. I have no desire to speak of my feelings about Jacob to him.

*Well. I suppose you want to know why I'm here.*

I turn to him, feeling a little anger growing in me. Anger is such a pointless emotion, and I have trained myself to discard it. As soon as you feel angry, your body is subject to the vapors within you—different in men and women, I have theorized, though ultimately following the same principles—and your reasoning becomes impaired, and you find yourself in a circular trap: the angrier you get, the less in command you are of the situation and the more cause you have to be angry. But I find myself uncharacteristically allowing the vapors to rise. Sinassion is a man full of secrets—if *man* can be a correct word for him, who really knows?—who enjoys dangling them in front of me. I can be patient with secrets when they are found with things in the ground. But with people who have knowledge more than me, who won't give me that knowledge? I find my patience wearing thin and my Lightdamn vapors rising up.

"No, Sinassion. I want to know why, shortly after you abandoned our cult, you went on to form an army and murder thousands, why you almost took the whole continent for yourself, and would have done so had not the wolves and bloods conspired to work together to stop you. I want to know what could have possibly justified that, and I want to know what that had to do with our cause, the cause of research and the cause of the cult, the one you professed to care about as much as me. I want to know if you feel bad that your Shades turned out not to be killed, but to have been repurposed as a genocidal army that went on to massacre just as many in Grayfall that died in the war. Because it seems to me you're responsible for that, too. I want to know whether your claim that the mortals are returning is true, and how you know that, and what you know of them that I do not, and how, after almost two centuries of exploring such artifacts of which you surely cannot comprehend, you still claim to know all that when I, cataloguer of so many mortal relics, do not. And maybe, *maybe* after all of that, maybe I want to know why you're here."

There is silence then, and though he stares ahead of him and I stay behind, I can still see a soft glow of the eyes from his side. I do not know if I should from this angle. But the glow is always there.

*I would say*, he thinks eventually, *that you should not have listed all those questions at once because I have already forgotten the first one.*

"LIGHT OF LUCE, MAN!"

*Calm yourself, old friend. Anger does you a disservice. I've not felt it, not really, for years. I do not miss it.*

"Do you feel guilt?"

*Now that's a good question. But let me answer a couple of your previous ones. Let's start with why I went to war.*

I turn to him then, see the glow of his orbs from profile. He smells slightly astringent this up close; he always did. Not unpleasant. But mechanical more than man.

*What plant is that?* he asks, pointing a tight-robed arm ahead of him. With his black robes, he's almost swallowed up by the shade, and it takes me a second to follow his arm to a small clump of herbs ringing the next tree along. They have small circular leaves with tear-shaped indents in them.

"The one with the tall stalks? That's takepast moss."

*It is very much not a moss.*

I shrug. "I didn't name it."

*It robs the memory if taken, yes? Funny to randomly see it out here. I wonder if the vampires know. Those Lords would misuse it if they did, I have no doubt.*

I sigh. "Stop delaying, Sinassion."

*Am I delaying? Or is it just . . . nice to talk to someone.*

I laugh. "You were never one for idle conversing."

*No, I suppose I wasn't. Too late to change now, I expect. Very well.*

He sighs in my head, and it feels like a gust of wind blowing through my memories.

*I left your cult, as I told you then, because you would not use the relics. You would only study them. You would not create an army with me. So I went off, without your help, and I created one of my own. I trained my Neuras army to become Shades, and I gave them such power as even I was surprised to find I could give them. And when the bloods had scored that great victory over the wolves at Extinction Valley, though weakened themselves through previous battles, and moved south to finish the wolves off entirely, I saw my chance. To strike when both were weak. So we fought, my army, and we would have won; we would have taken this entire continent, this entire land, for ourselves, had the bloods and wolves not overcome their mutual hatred and worked together, and had my own kind, all bar my Neuras, not turned against me.*

"I know all this," I growl, trying to put a leash on my impatience.

*Not from my perspective.*

"True," I concede, annoyed at the empirical fact.

*But here is what you want. The why. I did it, old friend, because there was a greater thing at stake. I couldn't watch anymore as blood destroyed wolf and wolf destroyed blood. Such a pointless waste. Such pointless trivialities. Not when there was a greater goal at stake. One with meaning. Something to give us hope in the great blackness of it all.*

I wait. I won't give him the benefit of acknowledging his dramatic pause.

*The mortals, Sage. They still exist; they have always been here, and I know how to get to them. We will never be free until we end them, and that is what I wanted. A continent united, united against the real enemy.*

"United under you, specifically."

He shrugs—physically; I see his robe go up and down, and I wonder if he allowed me to be pulled away from the magnetic draw of his eyes for a second just to see that.

*Semantics, old friend. I wanted to stop the killing, anyway. And create an army with a true purpose.*

"I see. So you wanted to stop the killing with a lot of killing."

*Actually, I tried. I do not particularly care if you believe me, but I did. I explained my case to First Lord Azzuri. Well, the previous one.* There is a pause. *Previous one by two, now, I suppose. And I tried to explain it to Archmage Revellion, the old fool. And the wolfpack leaders.*

"And they thought you were insane."

*Yes, they thought I was insane. I couldn't tell them exactly how I knew, I suppose. That probably did not help.*

"So then you tried to kill everyone."

*NO.*

His voice comes loud into my head, hard, like a wall of water crashing against the coastline, and for a second, submerged, I can't breathe. Sinassion has never shouted inside my head before, and I very much hope he never does so again.

*I did not kill any civilians. Not like the bloods or the wolves or all the mages who worked for the former. I killed soldiers, who had made their choice.*

"That's not what I heard."

*Well, then, Sage Bailey, you heard the lies of war, and I would expect better from you. I killed soldiers, and I did it to save more lives in the future. How many more pointless wars do we have in our future? I would have united us under a common cause. The last great fight. Against an enemy worth the name. And after that, peace, with the technology of the mortals.*

"You've always seemed bleaker than to speak of utopia."

He laughs then, bitter, dry, and still inside my head, but clear as any real laugh.

*If you could see inside my heart . . . but no matter. These are all things lost to time. I failed.*

"What then, assuming any of this is true, of my final unanswered question, Sinassion? How do you know the mortals are still here? Where are they? How do you know they pose a danger? How do you know they are returning?"

Sinassion gives me a long enough pause for me to feel the stupidity of my desperation. *There you go again. Asking all the questions at once. But I'll still answer these last ones. But you have to do something for me first.*

"Ambitious of you to ask a favor of me."

*You might have noticed I am not lacking in ambition.*

I sigh. "Go on, then. What is it, Sinassion?"

*I need you to help me with the Grays. I need you to get my Shades back.*

I let that linger in my mind for a second.

"Why did I know you were going to say that?"

As always, when faced with decisions, I think about my birth. All sorcerers are born as adults—adult males, bizarrely and frustratingly enough for those not enamored with wolves or vampires or those of the same sex—in a chamber deep in the capital Luce, and though none but the chamber guardians know what lies beneath it, it's presumed that it is some form of the Light that creates us, regularly, for reasons no one knows. I have an idea, but I barely have the evidence to prove it.

But I do remember my very first thought, before all the questions that sorcerers normally ask of the chamber mages.

*I want to know the truth to it all.*

And, unbidden, a memory slips in, of my home in the desert, my cult, years ago.

I'm playing with a relic when Brother Gulam walks into my study chamber, which is a generous way of saying a long worn table covered in parchment and tools and bits of mortal relic I feel safe having so near the catacombs. In reality I should only study relics down below, in the great network underneath us, and I do for the . . . larger items. But I have never seen any harm in bringing up the smaller ones for study in the more hospitable rooms above, and by hospitable I mean the air is mildly less stale and I don't have to walk quite as far if I need a fresh gulp of it.

Brother Gulam looks stoic and a little more tired, which is understandable given the news that I've just bestowed on all my brothers. We will have to work through the night to make the preparations in time for the following evening, when some assassins are expected at our cult home, trying to murder us or uncover our secrets, as usual.

This is no issue; sorcerers can go a week without any sleep, although the falloff in mental productivity is increasingly noticeable, and, as I have studied, beyond four days with nothing is counterproductive to any hopes of fruitful rationalizations. I have not slept in three days, and I am not happy. But the anxious vapors coursing through my body will take me through the next twenty-four hours.

"How has everyone taken the news, Brother?" I ask.

"About as well as can be expected. We are used to assassins, now, aren't we?"

I feel the haunting chill of guilt for those under me, and I wrap it in another strongbox and cast that into the depths of my mind, at least for the time being.

"Gather them all in the main chamber hall in half a glass, Brother. I will explain our strategy, and they will feel better then. No one will be hurt. The preparation will involve all of us, but the fighting will be on mine and Jacob's shoulders alone."

Brother Gulam nods and turns to go.

"One moment, Brother," I say. "Do you know what this is?" I ask, indicating the relic in my hands. It's a long, thin, stick-shaped object, only ten inches lengthwise by two wide and two deep, made of the same indiscernible material that most of the smaller relics are from, in fact. Light, virtually unbreakable, dull gray.

"That is not one of the relics I've had the opportunity to study," he replies, and I see that yearning on his face, that excitement, that *need*. For a second, I remember the old cruel ditty we give ourselves: *A Quantas born and a Quantas ever shall I be.* But right now, being a Quantas is not so bad for him.

"What do you think it does?" I ask.

"On sight, I cannot hazard a guess," he replies quickly.

"A very fair answer." I grin, satisfied. "The only possible answer without further study. Like so many of their relics, you could never conceive of its use without probing it."

Holding it in my left hand, I press an indentation down on the side, one which is not marked nor visible to the eye but only found with touch. Instantly a light shoots out from the tip that I am pointing toward the far wall of my study, and Brother Gulam leaps back from me toward the door, which is wise once you have become familiar with some of the more dangerous relics.

"I'm sorry, Brother," I say, trying not to laugh. "But this one is harmless." I shake it a little, and the light expands, turning from white to a deep blue, then a night-sky black, and then quickly expands further to fill the entire study—the walls, the ceiling, everything. Then I blow out the candles lighting the room and for a moment we are enveloped in black, not simply night black but the deep midnight of something else. Then, slowly, but increasingly fast, small white objects appear against the dark canopy, and the blackness turns to shades of purple and pink and even blue. The small white objects cluster in great swirls, or clouds, leaving other areas more spaced out and awash with the magenta hues. Some are small, some are larger; one has faint rings around it. It is a mesmerizing display, and it feels so real. I know not the effect but I am hypnotized. As is Brother Gulam, from the sound of his gasp.

To be a scholar of the unknown is to be serious most of the time but also, on occasion, to bathe yourself in the childlike wonder of your soul.

"Do you know what it is now, Brother?" I ask.

"It is a constellation of the stars above," he says. "But . . . it is not a sky that I recognize."

Lit by the starlight hues, I grin wide. "Perceptive, as I would expect, Brother Gulam. You do not recognize it because it is a view no one can see from our continent, at least. And I would wager from any continent."

Brother Gulam turns to me, shocked. "You think it is not from . . . anywhere?"

I nod. "That we know of. I have long suspected that the mortals came not from some yet-to-be-explored land across the seas, but from another world entirely. A world that has skies that look like this at night. I wonder if those who carried this were far away from such a world, and this reminded them of it."

There is a pause then. The pause goes on for a while.

"That is . . . a lot to be considered."

I sigh. "Do not consider it too much. It is a lot of conjecture, with very little evidence. I should not dally myself with it too much."

Brother Gulam reflects on this. "But it's in our motto, is it not? There are worlds beyond mine and things I have only dreamt to touch."

I nod. I like this. "Yes, you're right. We're allowed to dream ourselves sometimes, are we not?" Still holding the stick, I press the indentation again, and all the clouds and swirls and pinpricks of representational light slowly wink out, and then in a literal flash it is all gone. I put the stick down and turn to him.

"There is so much out there for us. So many centuries of discovery. Unlike the mortals, we can live to see it all. And I don't know about you, Brother Gulam, but I rather want to."

The memory fades, and I know as it does I will help Sinassion.

There are worlds beyond mine and things I have only dreamt to touch.

But right now, my dreams are going to require a little work, and those worlds seem still so far.

# 7

# The Lord and the Worn

The poor may roar like thunder,
And oh that we might blunder,
Through rain and shine to rise again
And make some richer better friends;
Still dreams are torn asunder.

Charles Battison,
*Worn Ditties We Have Loved*

## Sam

The abode that holds the former First Lord of First Light—the last First Lord of Lightfall, the most senior member of one of the most distinguished and long-surviving bloodlines that vampires have ever produced, who for some reason has asked to meet with me—is the kind of basic dwelling that an actor of the stagetales would be pleased as bloodpunch to own, but anyone with higher status would feel something had gone horribly wrong somewhere. A simple redoak two-story timber-and-thatch affair, it's tucked away in the back streets of east Westfall, far from where Alanna and I and all the artists of Westfall reside, but still not quite in the northern reaches of Westfall where all the richer craftsmen, stoneworkers, and bloodsmiths live.

As the door is opened by a maid with ageless, well-blooded skin and nervous, cautious eyes, I ready myself for the absurdity of what I'm about to put myself through: a meeting with the former ruler of the city in a house better suited for a man who sings about doomed lovers to a throng of bawdy Worns.

A small entryway with a mild smell of mildew gives way to a pitifully small receiving room that contains a couple of reclining chairs with the pale look of crestwood about them, a small varnished oval table, and a freestanding drinks cabinet containing a few flutes and some carafes of indiscernible blood. Last but not least, it contains a tall, fine-cheekboned Lord who had me strung up on a cross before the dawning sun.

"First Lord Azzuri," I say, immediately regretting the incorrect moniker and the respect it shows to someone who until recently was my enemy. And what is he now? I'm unsure. He killed Spymaster Saxe out of revenge for his son's death, and tried to kill himself, but Redgrave saved him and spirited him from the palace safely into the ignominy of Westfall, into hiding. Is he an ally now, or just a man who's lost it all?

He moves quickly from his position next to the fireplace so he's standing before me. As he examines me, he strokes the long beard he's grown. I do him the courtesy of examining him back.

His hair is long now, almost to his shoulders and roughly combed, and when you combine that with his beard he could, in bad light and if you had bad Worn eyes, pass for a Midway who worked in some manner of the Westfall arts. His frilled shirt, cheap purple jacket with some token curlicue, and pale, worn breeches help with this. Very stageboards. But if you've ever seen the First Lord before, properly stared at him, then you can still see that aquiline nose and fine cheekbones. The perfect pale glow of his skin belies the fact he's still on the noble bloods—some things you can't give up however hard you fall, I suppose—and so I imagine he stays in the shadows a lot at the moment.

"Samantha Ingle," he says eventually. "The girl who almost burned it all down."

I don't like the use of *girl* but I have much bigger blood to clot.

"*Almost* being the word there, Azzuri." Well, look at that. I appear to have found some courage. From the slight smile that creeps onto his scruff-covered face, he doesn't seem to mind me switching to his choice name or the way I'm talking.

"Yes," he says, sighing. "Redgrave told me how you could have killed my eldest but chose not to. I imagine he will be keen to keep that secret for eternity."

"Your son is a psychotic, evil bloodstain, and maybe I should have ended his pitiful life there and then, but I was thinking of the city." I thought he would fight that description of Rufous, but he just shrugs and moves toward one of the chairs.

"He is, on reflection, not my favorite of my sons. My realization that I liked the dead one considerably being the reason I am here, of course." He pulls out a chair for me. "Please, have a seat, Samantha."

"Sam," I say reflexively, sitting down in the preferred seat and awkwardly tucking my legs under the narrow table, struggling to not let the oddity of this scene swamp me in its blooddamn weirdness.

He smiles. "Sam it is. Would you like a drink? I don't have quite the range I did at the palace. But I still have some of the nobles. Perhaps some bear? Always an all-rounder, bear, I find for a conversation that could go anywhere." He grins at me then, and for a second I see it as a threat, but then I detect something more. . . . Is he nervous? Of me?

"I'm surprised you can still get blood like that," I say, taking the flute he offers and swirling it around a little, letting the scent of the bear free, as Lady Hocquard, sorry, Daphnée, would do. I consider declining him, standing up for my fellow Worns against the offer of noble blood, but my time when I had half a wolf in me—the blood of Raven Ansbach, to be precise—still lingers in the memory, and my body has cried out for better blood ever since. "It's not like you can just walk into the Blood Markets and purchase some now."

"Redgrave has secret stores stashed away," he replies, sipping at his own, now sitting opposite me with his long legs awkwardly squashed under our tiny shared table.

"And just because you have to be one of us doesn't mean you want to give up the good stuff," I say, once again marveling at the gall of me. A few dress-ups and blackmails and suddenly I'm whiplashing the powerful. Did I always have this in me, or is this a mask I wear, barely covering the real me?

Azzuri laughs, a dry, windswept thing that sounds like it came from the same crypt his son's ashes are kept in. "Yes, you call me out for a hypocrite and you are right to do so. I claim to be working against my own kind and yet I refuse to give up their finer habits. But look at it from my perspective, Sam. I have the entire city looking for me and Redgrave, just as they no doubt seek you out, too. Is this a good time to wean myself off the finer bloods that accompany the mind's reasoning, or give me the zest I need to work with you and your . . . colleagues?" He has a little trouble over that last word, reflecting what I imagine is a little trouble his mind is having with associating with a bunch of Worntowners.

"Do you really believe that?" I ask. "Redflare Dustcap examined the noble bloods in his treatise. I've read it twice, it's that fascinating. He concluded that the noble bloods were, compared to the others, by far the most addictive."

Azzuri puts his flute down and leans forward to study me closely. "And do you think that something that puts us in our natural state could ever be considered addictive?"

I don't answer that; I reckon it has more strength floating in the air.

We stare at each other a few more seconds, and then that thin aristocratic smile makes a return and he leans back, apparently satisfied. "I think you are as intelligent as Redgrave said you must be, if you want the truth."

The last thing in the Everlands I want from him is a compliment, so I decide to move on. "Why am I here, Azzuri?"

"I doubt I can get you to call me Vermillion, can I, Sam?"

I let that go, too.

He sighs. "You are the beating heart of whatever it is we need to do to stop my fellow Lords, Sam. Not Molly Threetimes, not the extremely scary Hands woman, not even the redoubtable Lady Hocquard and her Last Light fiend, impressive as they are, even though half are Wor—" He sighs. "I'm sorry. Old habits die hard."

"You misspoke. I believe you meant prejudices." I grip my flute of bear hard, feel its mix of strength and confidence and clarity inveigle itself through my veins, giving me the confidence I dreamed of in all those years in the library reading of the world-movers, fantasizing of one day being one.

He simply nods. "Perhaps I did. My point, however, is that it is you who powers this, though you may not have realized it yet." *Oh, I have, Vermillion Azzuri*, I think. *That's partly the problem.* He continues, "You put the torch to the blaze when you found the note my youngest left. You assembled your companions, the mages, the Leeches; that then brought the wolf to you, and then you were instrumental in everything that happened. They say you fought alongside Raven Ansbach, the most powerful wolf there has ever been, and defeated my First Guard. You almost, and perhaps should have, killed my eldest son. To put not too fine a point on it, it is you that I see at the center of this unlikely alliance, and it is therefore you I must get to trust me."

"That may be a stretch, Azzuri," I say. "Your son killed . . . someone close to me . . . and you almost had me burned at the stake."

"Yes," he says, sighing, pushing back some stray locks of that strange new hair from his face, and reaching for the blood cabinet behind him. "Which is why I think we need another drink."

## Vermillion Azzuri

Samantha Ingle is still in my receiving room, if that is what I must call it—a mere cupboard this would be back in the palace—and as I inspect her I reflect on how I used to have twenty visitors to my study quarters a day back in my old life, but now I have Redgrave and apparently this Worn girl, who seems to have as much planning in her as half the old councils I used to oversee. We have had three drinks, and somewhere along the way she made a decision to trust me.

"So let me get this straight," I begin, after I have plied her with some hawk, magicked, too, for this is a complicated plan. She sips it more freely than she did the bear. She is getting a taste for things, and I cannot say that I blame her. "First, facsimile reports are sent out by the Invisibles House that a new batch of blood is, in fact, more remarkable than all that have come before. This is boosted by the rumors spread by Leeches. A market frenzy is begun on the new batch, like nothing that has come before. Then more facsimile reports come through that the blood really is that good, and the price on the Invisibles goes up again. Then the truth comes out and the whole thing crashes. Midway violence erupts, the Lords are distracted, and you and your rebels . . . well, yes, I suppose *our* rebels now, attack the main wolfblood stash at the Southfall Blood Guard fort. The fight for the city begins in earnest. Have I understood the essentials correctly?"

Sam nods, taking another sip of hawk, her flute almost half empty. "That is it, more or less, yes, First Lo—yes, Vermillion." She pauses then, and runs a hand through her hair.

"I see. It sounds like you have all this planned extremely well."

"Well, maybe, but this plan, it is . . . ambitious. A lot of things could go wrong."

"This is normally the way for plans to take over cities, yes," I observe, and she gives me a look in return I would normally have been graced with from Daphnée. The protégée is learning.

"There's two parts that are particularly difficult. The creation of the first rumor that the new batch we randomly choose from one of the new Blood Farm batches is unusually potent. Then the fake reports that this rumor is supported by evidence once the blood has started to go out to buyers and the initial opinions of it come in. Both these parts need Lords, not Midways. They are the key to it all. A Lord at the Invisibles House, ideally, maybe on the Blood Market Council as well."

I frown. "And what makes you think they would help?" I ask, feeling a sense of intrigue here, lancing through my blood vessels in time with the hawk, making me sweat a little in my palms.

"I have been in the Leeches long enough to know that there are Lords, not just Midways, who are . . . not happy with the direction of the city. Ones who would seek a new direction, more like the one Lightfall was going in. Ones who are horrified by Saxe and his machinations. Who dare not speak of them to the Midways, but who feel in their gut that it's wrong. Daphnée cannot reach them now, not with her exposure. But you can. You can recruit them to the cause."

I blanch at this, taken aback by the confident call to arms. I rub at my beard, my itchy, dirty thing that is the cost, among others, of my sins.

"Samantha. Please, consider this: If Daphnée is exposed, how exposed would you wager that I am?"

Sam shrugs. "I'm sure you and Redgrave would find a way. I suspect you both were good at that, in your time." She grins, eyes blazing with a little bit of hawkblood and a little bit of gusto.

I pause, and then, to partly my own surprise as well as hers, I bark out a great booming laugh. "I will get you your Lords to help. I know who they are, and I know how to convince them. What I cannot do, Redgrave will ensure."

Sam looks a little surprised at that, at the ease of my agreement.

"Anything else you would ask of me?" I inquire, increasing the ripple of shock on her face.

"Yes," she replies, with the look of someone playing the card game Tascuza who seeks to double down on the advantageous hand that has flown into their grasp. "If this plan works, then even though the rebels will have the advantage, once they've robbed the largest store of wolfblood in the city, there'll still be a lot of violence to come. Bloodshed not seen since the Twin War, at least in the sense of two armies fighting rather than the massacre of Grayfall."

"I would agree with that, yes," I say. "But you, Sam, you do not want this violence, do you?" I ask.

"No," says Sam, who knows that I know what she wants and, I would wager, knows what I want in return. Such is the dance of two intelligent people talking, inspired by the blood we are drinking, having become acquainted just enough to be considering forming a tentative sense of trust.

"You would see a decisive end to the rebellion right there, would you not? A takeover without bloodshed."

"I would," says Sam.

"And why is that?"

Sam grimaces at me. "Why wouldn't I? Fewer dead people is normally good, in my experience. War is normally bad."

"You've never experienced war, Samantha."

"But I've read about it."

"Hardly the same."

"You've not read enough books, then."

I grin at this. The last time I enjoyed a back-and-forth this much was with Sage Bailey, the sorcerer. I wonder who rubbed off on whom.

"Have some more hawk, girl, and then tell me the real reason." I nod to the decanter, and she eagerly obliges.

"I do want a peaceful takeover, as much as possible, because I don't want the city to burn," she begins. She takes a sip and steadies herself, and then she locks eyes with me, and for a brief second I wish this brave girl had been my daughter, instead of the cold, disinterested thing languishing at the palace with the rest of my family, whom I will never see again. A terrible thing to think, but these are terrible times.

"But," she continues, "I also want it because of *me*. I'm . . . tired of being the cause of people dying."

I frown. "Who has died because of you, Samantha?"

She turns away, her voice falling into shadow. "Everyone. My mother was at the market because of me, when your eldest son saw her, and then returned to our house. I, at the age of eight, needed a book that was there. Demanded it. All the events that followed, all because of me. My sister tried to join the palace maids because of me; I didn't listen to her wishes for a better life than orphans on the street and so she chose the worst way out. And then there was . . ." She stops then, and I notice her twitch her head a little. The words do not come.

At first, I do not know what to say. I feel a great pain, scuttling its tiny legs across my nerves. I do not know if things like this would have haunted me so once upon a time. But I know what my youngest son would have felt. I feel him beside me now, my kind, empathetic dead son, whom I failed, and I hear his whisper across my neck, and I feel myself feeling the pain he would have felt for her. A tear thinks about forming in the back of my eye; it never comes, but it pricks my vision nonetheless.

"I would wager very few, if any, of these things were you fault, Samantha," I say, as kindly as I can.

"If words could make me believe that, wouldn't I have believed them years ago? I've had kinder confidantes than you," she says, not hiding the sharp tone, and I, with the ghost of my dead son in my periphery making me soft, am wounded by the unexpected barb.

"I expect so," I say, clearing my throat. "Very well then, Samantha. Tell me how we avoid bloodshed."

"You speak to all the Lords and more senior Midways. The ones you can really trust. You don't tell them the details, you just get them ready. When the time comes, we need as many as we can. The ones who control First Light's Blood Guard. The ones who can turn the guards away from all the prevailing Lords and for the rebels. I reckon most of the guard will favor the rebels anyway, but it's their offices and the Midways that you need as well. They'll take direction from certain Lords. Especially the guard on wolfblood. The Flight Guard. Both in the city and on the wall. If they can be convinced to switch sides, it's over. Once all the ones on wolfblood and their stashes are not in play, the real danger is gone, and the rest can be talked over."

"Apart from the First Guard," I note. "The ones being trained, the replacements for the ones you and Raven killed. The new ones will be loyal to my eldest. Loyal to Rufous. He'll have made sure of that."

Sam shrugs. "Alanna has plans for them."

I grin. "Do I want to know?"

She just looks at me.

"Very well," I add. "I will speak to these figures, who can help you usher in a peaceful takeover. In fact, I know of one man who can do most of the work by himself."

"Can I know this man?" asks Sam.

"Not until I have turned him," I say, neglecting to mention that one of her old party, the sorcerer Jacob, has already met with him.

There is a silence then. We both know what is coming, but we are both also comfortable enough in our own skin with each other—in such a short space of time, which I find a little remarkable—to enjoy a little silence, a little sipping of fine blood, a little appreciation of the thoughts it opens up in our minds and the renewed appreciation of life that it gives us.

"Here is my price," I say.

"Peace is not price enough?" Sam asks, attempting a scowl even though she knew exactly how this would play out. "Or how about revenge against the people who did that to your youngest son?"

I leave this be. She knows my answer. I give her that respect, and I give her that grace.

"When the new world order arrives, by peace if we get this right, it must include the Lords. Those who have not embraced the way of Rufous and Saxe, may he rest in the twin hells, and the new spymaster and all the Lords who scurried around them when the conspiracy was revealed. Not to mention all the Midways, who are the hub this city revolves around. That psychopath Hands Parker, who leads the Vials, who has the same look in her eyes that my eldest does, she would have them all butchered, I have no doubt, the Lords at least and, I wager, a good amount of the Midways.

"Molly Threetimes, she was adept at compromise in Lightfall pre-Grayfall, and I have nothing but respect for her, but I know she has soured a little on that idea, and the shock of the true horror of the conspiracy I think was the chaser there. Daphnée would, I imagine, be less willing to make this a city run by Worns only, but she is partly made of a fuel and fire I know you have seen, and I do not know her, really, and I suspect that thing of hers, Alanna, has a hold over her.

"So, of the key players in this picture, it comes down to you, Sam, to promise to help me usher in an order of compromise, where the better Lords can still play a role and not lose everything. Which is, of course, the quickest way to your bloodless coup, because I hardly think any Lords or Midways, even sympathetic ones, could be persuaded to assist if they know that in the aftermath they will lose any form of control over the city."

"And you think I can agree to this?"

I shrug. "I know you will agree to this. It is the only way to ensure peace and the least amount of deaths possible. It can't just be Worns who lead the new city. You know this. It's the price of peace."

Samantha gazes down her flute at the deep-crimson hawk, a slight shimmer in the outer hue betraying the magick alteration. She cannot disagree.

"Regardless of my agreement, I know I can't get the permission of the rest in advance."

"You do not need to. If the plan works, it will be your plan that swung the city, and you will have all the power. Power is a pendulum. It will swing your way, if only for a while, and you can carve it in your own image."

"With you helping with the fine details of it, I imagine." She locks eyes firmly with me.

I smile. "You feel gamesmanship in my words, still. I understand. I am no innocent player here, but I am not Saxe. I have . . . other motivations now."

"Such as?"

I pause. I wonder whether to speak of such things. I have given a lot to Samantha already, put much trust in her, though nowhere near as much as she will have to put in me. But this next part . . .

"Do you know what was remarkable about my son?" I ask.

Sam is not expecting this, and she frowns, and then quickly recovers. "No," she says, putting the vial down and crossing her legs.

"He did not care who someone was. In society, I mean. I have had a lot of time in this past month to . . . read certain of his writings I found, and I . . . I understand his principles. He believed that people should not be judged on the rank they came from, either way—Worn or Lord—but rather judged on what they did for no benefit of their own, when the pressure was on them. He was fascinated by what he called the 'true soul' of a person. That is why he painted so prodigiously. Worns, Midways, Lords. It is one of the reasons he was such a traveler. He knew that the lottery of someone's birth and the influences of the society around them constrained them in some ways, but he was fascinated by what happened when those constraints were taken off and they could truly choose for themselves. He . . ."

I pause. I realize I am saying thoughts that I have not fully formed yet, and this is neither the time nor the place. "What I am trying to say, Samantha, is that I know how he would have formed a future for the city, and this is it. I find myself learning of a new characteristic of his every day, and they are all . . . they are wonderful, Sam. They are. He was a unique person, a wonderful person, and I didn't see it, I never saw it, I . . ."

I stop. I do not want to cry. I cannot cry, not yet. I will never stop.

"I am stalked by the ghost of my son, Samantha, and he calls out to me of how things may be. I could not save him, but by the gods I will serve him."

She takes a little time to digest that, and then she nods.

"Very well, Vermillion. That's good enough for me."

Redgrave looms behind me, and I turn, my strangeness at his absence of moustache still not fading. Sam's flute sits empty on the table.

"That went well," he says.

"I see you were listening, Redgrave," I reply, a hint of a smile on my face. "Where were you this time?"

"I was half a street away, pretending to inspect some rather suspect *nuevo mage* art in Redstair Brushmore's gallery."

I nod. "On the magicked stag again, then, to hear so well. Your reserves do seem endless, old friend."

Redgrave gives me a knowing look, a look he has been perfecting much more since it turned out that he has been allied with the rebels all the time he has known me. Our power balance has somewhat considerably shifted to me relying on him to evade detection from my eldest son and the new spymaster and every Lord who wants his share of the reward for me. To his credit, he has given no indication that he is enjoying this unexpected reversal of our relationship. Most of the time.

"I have been preparing for eventualities for a while, Vermillion. We will be on the best blood for a good while longer."

I nod. "And you don't see it as hypocritical?"

He shrugs. "You did not in that conversation with Samantha."

"I was rather stretching there."

Redgrave smiles. "No zealot like a convert."

"I'm sorry?"

He rubs his clean-shaven face and smooths down his short, neatly cut hair. I am very jealous at the lack of adornments he needs on his face. He was able to go invisible by shaving it off, not putting it on. "What I mean, Vermillion, is that you have jumped quickly to the cause, following in your son's footsteps, following his beliefs, and all the guilt that comes with that for everything you stood for. But you should relax a little. There'll be plenty of time to prove yourself soon. A few good bloods won't harm anyone."

"Hmm. Well, if you insist. I do fancy following up that hawk I just shared with Sam with a little bear."

"Have a Midway. Ocelot is in fashion. It will do you good to mix it up."

"Oh, so I do have to refine my tastes, Redgrave?"

"No, you just have to not decimate my stores in a month."

I laugh. For a second, I am back in my study, in happier times. Or were they ever happy? I find my memories in flux.

"That went well, then. With Samantha," says Redgrave, taking a seat where she sat, but not pouring himself a flute. I suppose he won't need any for a while, with the stag in him.

"Yes, it did. She wants peace, I want peace. We have similar aims."

"Hers probably featured fewer Lords in them."

I grunt. "She does not know them I like do, Redgrave. Does not know there is some good there. But if my son can have thought so, too—my son who practically worshiped the Worns—then I know it is necessary."

Redgrave nods. "I agree. I sometimes wonder if it's just because I have spent so much time among your kind, though."

"My kind?" I ask, frowning. "You sound like the most rebellious of the Worns."

"Come now, Vermillion. There is great ocean water between us, no matter our friendship."

I think on this. "A little less now, though, would you not say?" I ask, more hopeful than combative.

Redgrave smiles. "It's certainly a start."

I venture further. "Do you think, then, you will ever tell me your tale? I find myself having known you for two centuries and thinking I had the measure of you, yet seeing there is a great valley of unknowing stretching out before me."

"I do not like talking about myself, Vermillion. You know this. I prefer to get on with the work before me. Things in the present. Besides, it is very boring. I do not have the tall tales of Molly Threetimes. I was never a particularly uproarious rebel."

"Really. Yet I do not even know how old you are, Redgrave. How do I know you were not around before even there was much of a class order to rebel against?"

Redgrave smiles and sighs. "If we thread the needle on these plans ahead, if we change the city, then we will sit down and I will force myself to outline my tedious past to you, Vermillion. Is that good enough for now?"

I grin. "It will do, yes."

Redgrave nods. "So back to Samantha. Now you just need to work on your side of the bargain. Find those who would prepare the way for when the crash happens and the rebels take the wolfblood stores. Find those who would smooth the way to the new order."

"Exactly. I already have some ideas. A few names."

"How many?" asks Redgrave, and I see that flicker of an idea on his face.

"I see where this is going, Redgrave. I will say something, and you will tell me how that something could be better."

"I would never presume such a thing," says Redgrave, smartly looking away. "It just occurred to me that there is a large attachment of risk involved in you seeking out all these hopefully friendly faces. You could be seen by the new spymaster's whisperers, or recognized by the Guards or anyone. More worryingly, frankly, you could put your trust in one of these figures you have in mind and then be betrayed, and then all the rebels are forfeit."

"When you put it like that, old friend, there is a large element of risk, yes. But I can hardly stay here. These must be face-to-face conversations. It will take persuasion. And I fancy I am a better judge of character than you think."

"I have no doubt," replies Redgrave, his voice suspiciously full of doubt, "but what if I had a better idea?"

"A better idea?"

"Yes. Not a number of figures. But just one. One man who is so trusted by the Blood Guard, and most Midways, and no doubt a number of the Lords you were thinking of approaching, that should you get him over to the side, he could, with just his word, prize the city apart like a flower, ripe for the rebels to relieve it of its pollen."

I ponder this. "I'm not sure that analogy went entirely the way you intended it, Redgrave, but color me intrigued. One single man, you say?"

"Indeed. One man to take a city."

"Oh, Redgrave. You do like your drama. And who is this man?"

Redgrave grimaces, or at least as close to a grimace as his carefully composed visage will ever get to. "I'm not sure you're going to like it. . . ."

# 8

# Je Ne Regrette Rien

I came across a wondrouse thing, in a deep cave yesterday. A small cube that does not break and feels oh so funny. I could not make head nor tail of it, and I showed it to my husbande but as usual he did not want to know. But then when I was in the fields behind our house I took it with me and oh! The most wondrous music suddenly came from it, like a fiddle but even more mournfulle. It happened while I was thinking of my old long dead ma too, and feeling sad. I will not showe it to anyone, they would be scared of such magick, surely sorcerer kind, and maybe I would be punished.

But I will take it out into the fields every day and it will be my delighte.

Tess Bentley, in a long-lost diary, circa 200 AL, Shadowfall

## Sam

I can't rightly say why I'm back here, now, of all times, when I'm on the cusp of shepherding in a revolution (or failing worse than anyone has ever failed at it). Maybe it's the emotion of Azzuri still ringing in my head, his desperation to make it up to his son. Maybe it's the intensity I feel in the air, like the city knows something's about to happen. Or maybe I just miss talking to him.

But whatever the reason, against his wishes, I have returned to the house where Sage Bailey is staying. And this time I'm not leaving without some answers.

It's five bells, the middle of the night, and if his pattern of moving about in the day is still correct then he'll be sleeping or working. I try to creep up, doing a bad job of impersonating Alanna, and then remember I have nothing to fear, so I walk a bit more brazenly toward the front door. My senses are strong tonight; I took a good couple of bloodflutes of boar from the Leeches store—magicked boar, so twice as good, boar being better than fox, I reckoned, as it has some aggression to it along with the clarity; the Midway version of the noble blood bear, I suppose. Part of me was worried I'd lead someone—maybe one of the new spymaster's whisperers or, worse, one of the winged First Guard—to Sage's door. But if they knew where I was, then the Leeches would already be taken, so I think I'm all right. But you never know. In this city, that's all you *need* to know.

I stop at the front door, alarmed. Alarmed because it's open, the cold winter air shrieking in. Open is a very bad sign. Open is the last thing Sage would want, given he's in hiding. I stop, and tense, and listen, and smell, all my blood heightened. I think—it's hard with the scent of the mountain air all round me—but I think I can smell someone inside, someone sorcerer. Maybe Sage. I can't scent any other vampires. But I can't be overly confident on just boar. Sundammit. I should've risked the noble bloodstores. I'm getting overconfident.

Speaking of overconfidence, I decide to creep in against my better judgment. Sage saved my life, after all. I owe him. Although I also did save his. We should tot our debts up sometime.

The downstairs passage continues before me, lit dimly by an oil lamp, turning to the right at the end where the stairs are, and the window I clumsily fell through last time. I see no signs of a struggle or anything untoward. The downstairs doors on either side of the passageway are closed and, I find when I try, locked. I smell dust and little else down here, the faint scent of mage still there, but most likely upstairs. I continue to the turn, and then face the stairs. I tune my ears . . . nothing. Wait. A creak? Most certainly a creak.

I think of Sinassion again, those burning eyes, those black robes. Then I think of a winged guard on wolfblood, waiting for me upstairs, crouched down, wings folded. I shiver. I forget myself.

I am Sam Ingle. I almost brought their entire city down around them.

There you go. The boar gives me confidence as well, it seems.

I creep up the stairs like I know what's coming, and then on the turn I make out the same room Alanna and I saw Sage in last time. There's no light. I don't need it on magicked boar. But I still can't make anything out except the clear shadows.

Another creak.

And then I see him. Sage. Walking into view from the hidden part of the room, walking toward the door. I go to cry out a greeting, but then I stop, as something's wrong. Very wrong. Sage's eyes are rolled back into his head, and his arms hang limply down to his sides. He's more shuffling than walking, dragging his feet toward the door. He stops and stands there, swaying slightly, whites of his eyes still showing, and then slowly turns around and shuffles away from me, out of sight again.

"What in the twin hells," I mutter, feeling a chill run through me despite the recently taken hot blood still in my veins. "Godsdamn this," I add, then I leap the remaining stairs and barge into the room, immediately relieved to see that it's just Sage in there. Shuffling Sage, walking away from me.

"Sage," I cry out. Nothing. Cloak Caspantion in his *Materiale Reflections* wrote that the definition of insanity is doing the same thing twice and expecting different results, but just because I read a lot doesn't mean I absorb it all, so I ignore that advice and try again. Still nothing.

He turns to me, though, and shuffles nearer. I hate the way his eyes look, and I hate the nothingness in this clever man, always in command, of his brain, at least. I get some fire in me, and I grab him, shake him, and I shout, "*SAGE*."

And then, just like that, the life drops out of him and he falls to the floor, his head whacking unceremoniously off the boards as I gasp in shock.

He comes to a short while later, after I've picked him up—my boar blood strength fairly easily handling his slim, tall frame—and deposited him on the single bed in the other upstairs room, which other than the bed itself and a chest of drawers is just as sparse as the previous room. I light the candle on the chest, for his sake, and watch with concern as he looks at me in groggy alarm and then rubs the side of his head.

"Ah, yes," I explain. "That was, uh, me."

"You came back." His eyes look tired, and his hair and beard even more unkempt than a few nights ago.

"I did, yes." I pause. "I didn't expect to see you so . . ." Another pause. "Actually I've no idea how to describe that."

Sage closes his eyes, at first I think in annoyance, then I realize that it looks more like sadness. When he opens them again, his expression is tense. "I can't tell you, Sam, just like I can't tell you I'm here. I feel . . ." He searches for a word, uncharacteristically. "Bad. I don't like keeping secrets from you. Actually, I'm surprised how much I don't like it. I have this need to tell you everything." He clears his throat and sits up quickly in the bed. "That sounded stranger than I intended."

I smile and decide not to make his awkwardness worse. There's an unsaid thing here: the kiss, the kiss with unconscious Rufous next to us and all the ashes of the dead First Guard in the air. The kiss with the knowledge this was a final goodbye. I feel like I want to mention it, but I don't want to be that person caught up in fleeting moments of madness when the fates of bigger things lie in the balance. So I stuff that memory of something good among all the blood into the recesses of my mind. "You want to tell me everything? So tell me everything."

"I made a promise, Sam, to someone who was once a good friend. Their secrets are not mine to tell. Not yet. If everything goes to plan, I hopefully won't have to keep you in the dark too long. But please know, I wouldn't have . . . abandoned Jacob if it wasn't important. If it wasn't . . . I just couldn't see any other way. I didn't know what to do."

I sigh at this. I made a promise to myself to come in hard, to be firm, to demand he explain himself. But I didn't expect his . . . vulnerability, I suppose. And I can't actually fault his reasoning, if it's the truth. Sun-dammit.

"Can you at least spare a couple of moments to talk about other things then?" I ask.

Sage grins at me. "Well, I'm not going anywhere."

I narrow my eyes. "Technically you were going somewhere. Just very slowly, and banging into walls and things."

"I'm glad you've not lost your wit now you're the great savior of—" Sage looks at me, concerned. As he should be, because I am sniffing, sniffing hard, and cocking my head to hear better, my face a rictus of fear.

"I—I can't be certain," I say, standing up quickly. "Some of the magicked boar is starting to wear off, but . . . I think there's some blood-guards nearby. Winged guards. Maybe . . . First Guard? Oh gods."

Then my attuned ears hear the slow beats.

Sage can't hear yet, but I see him nod, unquestioning, and then he leaps out of bed, rubbing his head a bit as he does, and he darts to the wall and starts to remove some of the plaster in front of the stone.

I look at him confused, wondering if the knock on his head was worse than I thought. "You need to go now . . . they'll be here any moment. Sage, you need to *run*." I think on this. "Also, I need to run."

"There's no other house for a good quarter mile from here, Sam," says Sage, still fiddling with the wall, "and little cover until we get a good way into the mountainside. If they're so near you can hear them, they'll see us running. We have to stay here."

"And do what?" I ask, the beat of wings now clear to me, threatening to take me back to a moment I don't want.

*I see the shape falling, and it's not my friend anymore, it's . . .*

"They can smell us, Sage. And hear us. They'll be on wolfblood. The wings are a clue."

Sage turns back to me, and to my shock I see a grin on his face. "Jacob, is that you? Or do I just inspire sarcasm from everyone . . . Aha, here we are." He has revealed a hole in the stone wall, and he reaches in and takes a cube from it. It's a metal cube, smooth and light, the size of a large die. Not any metal you would find in First Light. It has no markings and no etchings on it.

I immediately recognize it. Sage gave me such a cube when I went to spy in the Blood Bank, and it knocked a Midway out and stole his short-term memory. He used another cube to save me and Raven when we were slowly being overcome by the horde of the First Guard, turning him into a metal man with a frankly unfair set of weaponry on him. Weapons from the mortals, which he had brought with him from his stores of ancient relics in his desert-cult home.

My heart spasms with relief. "It's the one with the bullets, I hope."

He glances at me while caressing the cube gently. "I'm afraid not. I only brought one of those with me to First Light and there aren't many to begin with. This is more . . . defensive."

At that moment all my fear is forgotten and I want to ask him . . . I want him to fill me in on everything he knows about the mortals, these strange relics he has, how long he's been finding them, what they mean, what they *could* mean. I want him to give me the knowledge I didn't find in a library, the kind that takes me to new lives, the kind that only those who are truly curious ever find out. I want time to stop, just like it felt like it did when I drank all that wolfblood, and I want to spend eternity in this moment here, finding out the truth of things and seeing if it can make up for all the pain I've had to feel.

Instead, the moment is broken and I say, emotionless, "They're here." And then I sniff again, and I feel a flash of something cross my face: primal, terrified fury. "He's here. *He's* here. He's come as well."

Sage nods, jaw clenched. "Rufous Azzuri. Your new First Lord."

My fists unclench and clench, and my fangs and claws try desperately to lengthen, seeking the better blood absent from my veins.

Sage crosses the room to me then, cube in one hand, and to my surprise uses his free hand to grab mine. "Do you trust me, Sam?" he says, face close to mine, mimicking the stance we made just before he lost his mind enough to kiss me.

"For my sins, I do," I say. "Maybe it will be my undoing."

"Not on my part. But if you trust me, then you need to hold on to me. And not make a sound. And—and this is the most important—by the Light of Luce, Sam, *do not let go*."

Then, as I hear the sound of a heavy body landing on the roof, and more landing outside the house, and as the front door bursts open downstairs, Sage throws the cube into the air above us and clicks his fingers, and as he catches it I grab hold of his waist and we freeze in that position, like dancers mid-stride, faces inches from the other, breaths held.

As far as I can see, nothing has changed, and I go to speak, but Sage's eyes widen, and I still my tongue and hold on to the mage as footsteps I recognize and a scent I recall come up the stairs.

"Mage, mage, Sage the mage. Come out, come out, you little cunning fuck."

Rufous Azzuri, new First Lord of First Light, turns the corner at the top of the stairs and faces me directly, as the bedchamber door is open. For a terrible moment I feel caught, on inferior blood, holding the man he is clearly after with no weapons to defend us. But he stares right through me as if I'm not there, though he sniffs, then turns to the First Guard behind him. "He's definitely been living here."

I stare numbly at him, then back at Sage, still inches from his face. His eyebrows are raised at me, as if to confirm this is actually happening, which I'm not quite sure it is; I still haven't fully rejected the possibility I've finally lost my mind after everything that's happened.

Back to Rufous: his shoulder-length blond hair, shining with the luster that only a regular infusion of wolfblood can give you, frames his face, that regal, arrogant, perfectly symmetrical, freshly shaved, high-cheeked psychopathic face with the vibrant blue eyes that are entertained and mildly insane in equal measure. He wears the red-and-gold velvet tabard of the First Guard, the edges lined with blue and some tiny gems twinkling from the seams, which tells me he's made some changes to the uniform and, unsurprisingly, vain ones. Under the tabard is simply a short-sleeved undershirt, which means his arms are exposed and the strong, near-invincible wolfblood skin shines. His wings that got him here, most likely all the way from the palace on a hefty dose of wolfblood, are furled behind him, leathery, veined things held close together, a blond streak of wing fur just visible from here. His fangs are long, just like his claws. His eyes blaze. He took a lot of wolfblood, not just for wings. He must have expected Sage to have weapons again.

Alarmingly he ignores the first room and stalks toward the bedchamber where Sage and I stand, mid-waltz, apparently invisible. These sorcerer cubes, I swear to the Blood Gods. He eyes the room, where there is notably nowhere to hide, and thankfully doesn't start moving around it, because Sage and I, though invisible, are still very much here, my body backed up against the wall, Sage's slightly herby (not in a bad way) breath on my face. Infrequent, calm, quiet breaths. To Sage's credit, he's not scared. Probably using some kind of arcane technique, knowing him.

I am not so trained, and I try to summon all my courage to the sticking place, and remind myself that last time I met this sick bastard, I defeated him through the simple tactic of shoving my arm in his mouth, albeit I was on an ungodly amount of wolfblood at the time. But when I try to summon the bravery, all I get is the sound of wings in a cloudy sky, and the plaintive, dying cries of—

"He's not here, is he?" says the First Guard behind Rufous, a smaller man with a thin moustache and an air of queasy obedience to the blond prick.

Rufous seems to stare straight at me again, and for a moment I think we must be caught, cube or no cube. But then he frowns and looks away. "He was here recently. His mage stench is strong; it lingers. . . ." He sniffs again. "Oh, and it gets better. Our dear friend Sam the palace maid was here with him. Rutting as the rebels they are, how romantic."

He spreads his arms out. "This is wonderful news, my First Guard," he booms. There's only a couple more in the house that I can hear, but on wolfblood the ones scoping the perimeter outside will be able to hear him, too. "We can find them both."

"Should we post one of ours to wait for them?" asks Moustache. For a moment my calm breath hitches, and I imagine myself trapped here, unable to leave the house. I look at Sage, whose eyes haven't left mine, I notice (neither of us is invisible to the other; *fascinating* mortal magick, I think, already wishing to learn), and I wonder if there aren't worse outcomes than that.

Rufous barks a laugh. "I'm not wasting one of the First Guard on fucking watch duty. We'll send some of the wings the Blood Guard can spare to hide in the mountain forest line till they come back. We have the advantage here. Make sure there's no signs of our arrival. Use these wolfblood senses to check for threads and such that need replacing. That fucking mage no doubt has tricks of his own to tell for intruders."

He pauses then, and says, almost to himself, "They think they are noble, these who scurry away throughout my city. But I will expose their hypocrisy just as I will expose their organs to the air." And then he laughs and turns to Moustache. "You know what I love about wolfblood? It makes you sound bloody sensational."

Then he and his kind are gone.

We wait till the remnants of the boar blood within me have told me that they have indeed flown away and none have lingered outside, and then, with a final look at each other that could say a lot of things if we had time, I take my hand off his waist and he lets go of my hand.

There is a pregnant pause, or an awkward pause, if you like.

"You need to go, Sam. There'll be guards back soon." He sighs. "I need to go, too."

"So that's how you evaded Alanna when she tried to follow you after we met. You went invisible. A suit made of metal and an invisibility cloak. Or however it works. There's no end to your mortal relics, is there?"

"There very much is an end to them, sadly, at least the ones we've found, or thankfully, given their power. And this"—he gestures to the cube—"can only be used for short periods. But seriously, Sam, we need to leave." He moves around the room, collecting his few belongings: a spare robe, some herbs I don't recognize. He retrieves two more cubes from the recess in the wall. He dashes into the other room and comes back with his notes, parchment tied with string.

He stops when he sees the look on my face. "Sam?"

"I hate him. Rufous."

Sage nods. "I know."

"Not just that. When I saw him, it brought back . . . It made me feel . . ." I shake myself. "Now is not the time. You have to go."

"I'm sorry, Sam."

"Where *will* you go now?" I ask him.

"I have some similarly abandoned houses I have scouted in case this occurred. Nearest is in Southwestfall, about a quarter mile south from here. Not quite as nice as this."

"I mean if you're going to carry on walking round catatonic it's not like you'll mind," I point out.

Sage flashes me a grin. "Fair point well made."

I sigh. "You're really not going to explain that bizarre moment, are you? I came for answers and I leave again with nothing."

"I'm aware my debt to you is growing," he says.

"And you're not going to tell me where you end up now, are you?"

"No," says Sage. "But I promise when my business is concluded, I will find you and do what I can to help your revolution."

"An invisibility cube could come in handy."

Sage grimaces. "You just want me for my cubes, don't you?"

"I think that sentence is the strangest one you've ever said."

"You haven't been paying close attention to my sentences then, have you, Sam?"

We laugh then, like we're not both caught in plans beyond our control, running headlong into events that may kill us both. We laugh like we trust each other, though the secrets are growing, if anything. We laugh like this is nice.

Because it is.

And then I leave him to his fleeing, not having got what I came here for, but not regretting it.

Not in the slightest.

# 9

# Tears for Fears

It is notoriously difficult to locate survivors of Last Light. Those known tend to stay in the shadows. Did they have plans when they arrived in the Everlands in 450 AL, the survivors on that single ship, fifty years before Grayfall? If they had, then the events of Grayfall have surely put a crimp on such plans. So we must take clues where we can, from those we know or have heard of. For example, none of them are happy, or joyous, or in close relationships with others. Whatever it was they went through, whatever it was they saw has made them tough and secretive and, surely, shadows of what they once were.

Quantas Questol, *The Mysterie of the City of Secrets: A Thorough Analysis of Last Light*

## Daphnée

On the top of our Westfall abode, in a rickety attic that stretches across the whole floor, with timber beams arching up past our heads and small motes of dust landing every time a particularly heavy mountain gull rests on the thatched roof . . . here we plan to bring the city down. Around the entire attic walls are pieces of parchments, filled with lots of small writing and many arrows enthusiastically drawn; most of them from Sam, a few from Alanna. They have been working together on the plan the last two nights now. Two nights is a ridiculously small amount of time to execute such a complex web of rumor and intricacy that aims to create such a disarray that the most valuable safe house in the whole of the city, the wolfblood store of the Southfall Guard fort, will be, at the very least, a little more vulnerable to a concerted heist. But with every day, the new First Guard grow stronger, more used to wolfblood, and the spymaster extends his new grip on the city. And every day Rufous comes closer to doing something extremely stupid in the name of protecting it or, in his fevered imaginings, most likely getting revenge on some Worns, *any* Worns.

So two nights it has been, fueled by magick stag, of course, using up much of the reserves we have and may need. The problem is, though hawk is good and any magicked noble blood will set the brain to do a month's work of tasks in one night, nothing short of wolfblood compares to magicked stag. Alanna and Sam have been downing it on the hour, imbibing it like it is cow. And the result, twinned with their remarkable brains, of course, has been nothing short of remarkable.

Sam's plan has come into being. It has been given life. And I see her come to life, too, some of the hesitancy of the last week or so being lost, some of the confidence going back into her. Now she has Azzuri behind her, willing to help us, she has relaxed a little, seeing everything going her way. I am still not completely certain what price he got from her for all his help. Sam assures me it was nothing, and I believe her; he is a man grieving, I think, and eager to help, at least so says Redgrave, and I trust that man.

I am so proud of Sam, and constantly astonished by every new achievement. I am also afraid, and not a day goes by I don't remember how confident my daughter was, right up until the moment she lost all her lifeblood through a gaping hole in her throat. But if I let my fears escape their vault inside me for more than mere moments, I would never have done the things I have done. Let them fester. They will not take hold of me, I know it.

And now, with the papers of this plan of ours surrounding me like stagetale notebills dotting the streets, glued to the walls and the literal rafters in some instances with a sticky substance from a mage plant in the Desertlands, I stand before twenty of my finest Leeches who live in this house with us. My mansion family reduced to an attic.

They are my best girls, and they will be the start, and rumors will fly from them like sparks from a well-fed bonfire.

"Listen up, ladies," I begin. Their whispers stop and they all turn to me, standing on a chair at the front of the attic, very aware my head is almost touching the top rafter.

"Here is what we have so far, and here is what you will do, my Leeches. We know the blood we will use. It is otter. Magicked otter. A new Midway blood. Our Leechmaid in the farm tells us it is coming out next week. It is perfect; what with all the confusion around what the Kinet bloodmages can really do and the rarity of a new blood, the chance for rumor is rife. There is a Midway sympathetic to our cause in the Invisibles House, a lesser administrator, but she will fake the report from the Blood Farms telling of its potential. Your job now is to go and inform all our Leeches—whether in Midway or Lord residences, in tradeshops or mansions, wherever they may be—that the rumors start now. Then, when the initial report is given next week, this will give meaning and succor to the whispers, and it will take wing. Insinuate itself throughout the city. When the first reports come back from the tasting, and that is faked, too, the effect will be like nothing there has ever been in the city. Everyone will buy. But that is not your concern. For now, you are my voice, and you are my whisper. Together, my girls, we will show the Lords that we do not need a mansion to wreak our will through this city. What do you say, ladies?"

I stop, slightly breathless. I do not normally make such speeches. Sam's ambition must be rubbing off on me. I eye my trusted girls, the core of the Leeches, those who have been so wronged or scarred that the sun would sooner grace all vampires with its love than one should betray me. They stare back at me, also mildly surprised at my vim. Then one shouts, "Lady Daphnée!" It's a title that makes no sense, as I was Lady Hocquard, but strangely fits now, and I feel a flush of something—I hope pride. And then the rest join in. For a few moments, the attic unwisely echoes with the shouts of a title I never had but seem to have earned.

I would never cry before my girls—I cried before my own girl, dead in my arms, and that was the last time—but if I could, I would shed tears aplenty now.

"Right," I say, quickly moving on before other thoughts can consume me. "Alanna will give you the notepaper with all the details about the blood and what you shall spread about it. Read it, commit it to memory, then burn it—all of it. Even the smallest scrap still on your person could doom us."

Then I hop down off my perch and my ladies scarper away, my Leeches, not to suck the blood of the city but to give it new life, or at least a new conversation topic.

I turn to Sam, who has been in the corner, watching the proceedings with what appears to be awe. Or it could be fatigue. "You have worked well, Samantha. My gods, you have worked well. Now we wait till next week. You should get some rest."

She nods and turns to go, but then turns back. "Do you think it will work, Daphnée?" she asks.

"I believe she is now Lady Daphnée," says Alanna, deadpanning from the shadows as is her wont.

Sam grins but then turns back to me.

"I think it is as good a plan as I have heard in my time," I reply. "But it has so many moving parts, and relies on something we have always been able to steer but never fully control: the whims and passions of men."

She nods and a look of panic flashes across her features, so I step in again.

"But fear not, my remarkable Sam. I suspect that men, as in so many things, are as predictable in their market fancies as all their other ones. I just hope you are ready for the only thing scarier than failure."

"What's that?" asks Sam.

I sigh. "Success."

Sam has departed for some well-earned rest, and it is just me and Alanna in the attic. Alanna is inspecting the floor, where some small packages—a plan of our own, noticed by no one except us—are secreted behind a beam.

"I asked Sam if her plan would work, Alanna," I begin, a little nervously, "but more pressing is whether *our* plan will work. To take care of the First Guard."

Alanna looks up, and there is something in her eyes. "It is a plan straight from Last Light, m'lady. Those plans do not fail. Besides, now we know from Sam's visit to Sage that Rufous, the shiny-haired prickard, is keen on coming on jaunts with the First Guard, even now he's First Lord, well, it is a gift we cannot look away from."

"I'll take your word for it, Alanna. If we could keep Sam out of it, too, though. She is not ready to hear of any violence, even against the First Guard. Actually, especially not them, as it was she who, along with Raven, killed all the last ones. I'm not sure how all that violence has rested with her. She says it is half a dream, gone with the wolfblood. But she cannot mention her dead friend, Beth, have you noticed that? Even when her topic of avoiding death comes up, it is always half on her lips, never fully broached."

Alanna nods. "I wonder if her ambition and her plans are sometimes a way of putting a masking face on her pain. It is often the way. But it is of no concern. Let her focus on her own spinnin' and webbin' and plannin'. Just as long as she knows not to be here when it happens. Just me and my schemin', that's all I need on that day."

"And me, of course, Alanna," I say, gently.

She looks at me, and that's when I notice she has not crossed the room to me. Normally the first thing she does when we converse is to reduce the distance between us, though never touching (well, hardly ever touching; I still recall her shoulder grip on me as we watched Atmos Reclantis fry the rebels). But there is half a room between us, and so I cross it myself, and I wonder whether with her off the leash, as it were, our roles are not sometimes reversed these days.

"I will be there with you when we do this, Alanna," I say. "The First Guard. I will be there, yes?" I try to hold her eyes, and for a second I have them, striking, hazel, sharp like a honed blade, but then she turns away, and her hand instinctively goes to where her knife is, her way of telling me of her unhappiness better than any words.

"It should just be me, m'lady. It is too dangerous."

"Compared to what?" I say, louder than I would have liked. "All the endless danger we have put upon ourselves these last eighty years? Come now, Alanna, since the moment I met you we have danced with peril and seen it exhausted far before we have been."

"And yet my appetite for it has been reduced, m'lady," replies Alanna, still turned, hand still poised over her pocket.

"Can I ask why?" I say, cautious. This is new ground for me, trying to prize some semblance of feeling from her like blood from a dry joint.

"You can ask, m'lady, but the answerin' . . ."

"I wish you'd stop, Alanna," I say, striding round to face her again, to challenge her avoidance. And then, feeling like it might be the most daring thing I've ever done, I reach out and I lift her chin up to face me, and for a second her eyes widen in shock and her lip curls in some expression I cannot fathom, and my fingers rest on the underside of her chin, and we are trapped there, frozen, a scene rendered in time like the fossils of house-size cats found deep in the Fang Tips. It goes on for an age, and then I pull my fingers back, now warm from the touch of her skin, but she holds her face there, the same angle, and she fixes me.

"I'm not your Lady, not anymore. I am Daphnée. Call me by my name, Alanna." And then, a little anger—or something, some fuel to the fire—pours out of me. "*Call me by my name.*" And I almost shout even as the shout itself gets lost in the attic beam, and I immediately feel foolish.

Alanna has not moved, has not taken her eyes off me. Her lips have opened slightly in a half O, and there is something in those sharp eyes I have not seen before.

"But that's not my name for you," she says softly. "You are my Daffers."

I pause, slightly taken aback. "Daffers?" I ask.

"Yes."

I smile. "I like that. It is very you. I have never heard it before."

Alanna reaches out then, and for a moment I feel afraid, because for all my feelings for her, she is a foreign thing, a dangerous thing, and I half wonder if she would bite me in half before ever touching me properly, not that it diminishes my feelings for her.

But she does not go for her knife but for my left hand, and she grasps it, and I gasp at how warm her fingers are, not unpleasant warm, not clammy warm, but glowing, and I grasp it back.

"That is because I have never said it before you. Except one time. But you were busy then, so busy were you and you did not notice."

"That does not sound like me," I reply. "What was I busy doing?"

"Dying. You were busy dying."

She lets go of my hand then, and her head drops, and the moment passes, and I miss the warmth already. "You were dying on the roof of that sundamn church, you were dying in my arms, and I carried you away. I carried you away from there, time not on my side. I ran from that place, and all the time I saw in my mind's eye all the ways in which you would crumble, all the hows and the whys and the wherefores of the ways you would fall apart in my hands, and it was like there was a chorus of harpies in my head, screamin'. And I felt something I've not felt for so long."

Her words are coming quicker now, and as her Last Light lilt grows heavier, I have to concentrate on picking out every word.

"I felt *fear*, my Daffers. So much fear, grabbing at me, pulling me down, down, down. I ran so hard and I made it, but only just, and you came so close to dusting in my arms, *you came so close*." She is growling the words now, spitting them out, and she looks up at me again and her eyes are wild, gleaming, and her fangs have lengthened and I can see them properly, poking over her lips. "I almost lost you and I feel it now,

I feel it hard and I can't . . . you don't understand, I can't." She stops and turns away from me, and with her back to me she squeezes her fists.

I give her a few seconds and then, tentatively, I put a hand on her back. "I am sorry, Alanna. My Alanna. I am sorry you felt that." I leave it there, feeling her warmth again, reluctant to be without it.

"You do not understand . . . because . . . I have given you nothin' in all of the worlds to help you understand," she says, still turned away from me, me still pressing my fingers against her like I seek to push her away, when the opposite is all I wish to do.

"You can give me something now," I say, delicately as I dare.

There is a silence, and then, "I was not always who I am today, in Last Light, I mean."

I already know this, though I know not the details, but I am wise enough to not say anything and let the moment spool out.

"I was . . . more normal once. And then, things happened, all of a whirl, and to become the one I am now . . . to see the things I saw, to do the things I had to do, I . . . put certain things away. I am not afraid, I am never afraid. I have nothing to lose. The world is a dance, and I steps all the way through it. All these things had to be true, m'lady, *my Daffers*, until such a time as I met you and then more than ever such a time as you almost came to ashes in my arms."

Another pause. The dust beams in the attic dawdle through the air, spotlit by the moonlight; far off a crow caws; a cart trundles down the street; I see a spider half leap, half scurry from one beam corner to the next. The world and I wait for my love to confess herself.

"But if I am to feel fear again, and the loss of things, and all that hijinks and emotions, then what does that make me? Because I can never be who I was, and the thing that I am now cannot do what they must and be so open to that. So who can I be?"

I think on this. I want to pry more, to finally find out her past. To get her to tell me everything she was, everything that happened to her in that damned city, partly out of selfishness, the selfishness of curiosity, partly out of love, because she needs it. But we are not there yet. We may never be there.

"Alanna," I say carefully. "Listen to me. You can be anything you want. You are not a slave to this thing you think you have become. Your past is not a place you can never return to. You are remarkable, and you can be fierce and you can be you. If being my . . . friend . . . gives you such pain, such fear at what may happen to me, and if it is unbearable, then do not be in my company. It would give me great pain, but it would give me greater agony to see you suffer. But, perhaps out of inner selfishness, I feel this is you trying to return, and you should not hide from fear. You are not one thing, Alanna, you are many things, and I want to know them all, and I will be here for you always as you learn how to live with them." I pause. "And, if it makes you feel better, I have absolutely no intentions of almost dying again."

I take my hand away, and I wait for her to turn back to me. I wait and I wait and I wonder if she has frozen in time, my own relic, my own love caught in her emotion. But then she revives herself from her frozen tableau and, without looking my way or turning my way, she stalks right out of the attic, leaving me alone.

Moments more pass and I stand there.

Then, my senses still on fire from my foxblood, I notice a small droplet of water on the floor where she stood.

A single tear.

# 10

# Father's Night

> The worst thing I saw in Grayfalle? Let me tell you the worst. It were the children killed in their parentes arms. Mothers holdin sons as they died. Fathers holdin daughters as they crumbled into ash, trying to get a last good looke at them before they were gone into the wind. Goin from griefe to tryin to get all their ashes up before they blew away. There is no worst sight than that and there never will be. I hope them that did it burn for ever.
>
> Andrew Peloquin, *What I Sawe in Grayfalle* (pamphlet collection)

## Azzuri

I sidle next to the man who Redgrave thinks can change the loyalties of half a city on his own, and I ready myself for what may be the most stupid thing I have ever done (though I feel that list is rapidly expanding at immeasurable speed), which is to put Redgrave's and my lives in the hands of someone of high rank who could very easily have me arrested momentarily.

Before I speak, I glance around. The market is quiet for a Vialsday, two days into the working week, and the stalls have few customers. Then again, the Moon Market is rarely that busy. It is located roughly on the border of Southeastfall, the (slightly) less dangerous and run-down half of Worntown, and Eastfall, where most of the better-off Midways live who are not in the business of construction or the arts like their Westfall compatriots. As a result, it is frequented both by Worns and Midways, although more the former as many of the Midways of increasing status and wealth in the redbrick townhouses just north of here look down on such mixing and such a place. But some people still come here, for the Moon Market sells items of strange curious interest, no blood . . . just other things.

And one of those people is the man standing next to me, the soldier of legend, in the war at least, and a man who now occupies one of the highest and most respected posts in the Blood Guard.

Commander Tenfold looks much like he did when I last saw him, as I was markedly not apologizing for the loss of eight of his men to the Grays thanks to my ill-advised trip outside the wall to go to the place where my son was killed.

"Well met, Commander," I say, and to his credit he does not show any sense of alarm but carefully puts down the sprig of herbs he was inspecting and turns to me. Thankfully the stall owner, a small, deeply lined, gray-haired Worn thick with beard and long straggly hair, is deep in conversation with another customer, and so I remain unmemorable.

That said, I see Tenfold immediately recognize me. My hair is long and unkempt, my beard is increasingly voluminous and taking on a life of its own, and Redgrave made sure to apply a thick coating of grime to my face to really hammer home the impression of a Midway whose career on the stagetale boards has taken a nosedive thanks to a presumed overliking to bloodwine or bloodale or anything with alcohol in it. Even my family would not recognize me, I wager, unless they were on the finest noble wine and could take a smell of me or bother to use their eyes and senses properly. And my opening words were thick in Midway drawl, at least as much as Redgrave taught me.

But Tenfold knows. I always knew he was a clever bastard.

"First Lord," he says, to his credit, thankfully, and I feel time slow to a crawl. Redgrave made two gambles with this plan. One, that Tenfold does have the influence he thinks he does. Two, that he would want to use that influence to help me. And three, and the one most pertinent to me now, that he wouldn't immediately scream of my presence.

Realizing that we are alone for the time being—and making a perhaps unwise bet that none of the new spymaster's whisperers are secreted in this random market full of blood good enough to enhance their hearing—I slip off my Midway tones and speak as myself.

"Are you going to apprehend me? Or call for guards?"

Tenfold laughs. "Not for the time being, you bloody fool."

I must look startled at the insult, as he continues.

"Oh, I can say what I want now? No offense, Azzuri, but you're not my ruler anymore, and you're not exactly a sight to be intimidating anyone, not less a soldier."

"You think of yourself as a soldier?" My old presumption that I can ask whatever I want to whomever I want as ruler coming back to me even in my most perilous of situations.

"The war never ended, Azzuri. Different enemies, same war. If you can't see that, maybe it's good you don't rule anymore, no offense."

I let that one go. He has a lot to be angry with me about and I am not in much of a position to defend myself.

He sighs. "Right, I expect you'll be wantin' a proper conversation with me a little more private." He turns and points eastward. "There's a park over that way. Small thing. Barely worth the shitting name. But it's good to get some quiet sometimes."

I nod, and as we leave the Moon Market, my head still turning anxiously, half expecting guards to rush me or the sigh of a whisperer's cloak to rush by in a window somewhere, I ask, "Do you not walk with anyone?"

He gives me a sneer. "You mean do I make some poor bloke follow me round all the time doing fuck all? No, I do not."

I grimace a little, realizing that though I have no status anymore and he does not owe me any respect—in fact, he is already showing me far more respect than I expected by deigning to speak to an outlaw—it is still quite a thing to get used to a former subject speaking to me in that way. I quickly right myself.

"I respect that. You always did things your own way, Commander."

He chuckles and scratches the beginnings of late-night stubble on his cheek. "That's the start of what I see will be a lot of lubing up to come."

A cobbled path stretches from the east of the market between a row of houses, and we follow that; up ahead I see a small gate that leads to a smaller dirt path lined with trees, which opens up to a wider circulatory route.

"This is the park you speak of?" I ask, nodding ahead.

"It is, aye. I used to walk it with my daughter, when we came to First Light to visit my wife's family here. They lived nearby. They weren't that fond of me, so we'd spend a lot of time here, just the two of us, walking."

"Your daughter . . ."

"Died in Grayfall."

"I am sorry."

He lets that one go.

"And your wife?" I ask, as we cross through the gate. I see there are three symbols etched on the gate. Claw, moon, tree. The symbols of the wolfpacks. I think on the name *Moon Market*, and I wonder at the connection there. There is so much history of my own city I still do not know, I realize.

"She left me several decades before Grayfall. Shacked up with a wolf. I don't blame her. It wasn't easy to be married to me. Devoted to my work and my daughter but rarely to her. It's not easy to be married longer than a century, especially when you're married to me."

I marvel at his forthrightness. Perhaps he has so little opinion of me now that he thinks he can just be honest. I think about my own wife. Whether she misses me. Whether I miss her. It was always a cold form of marriage, political, originally, then some love creeping in, but stilled by the passing of the decades and the demands of ruling. Are any of us happy in love in this city?

By this point we have come out of the path and into the wider park, and for a second I am taken aback by its simple beauty. A circular dirt path follows the park around, lined with sycamore, maples, chestwoods, and I even see a couple of redoaks, unusually. The parkland itself is mostly lawn, bifurcated by a smaller path that leads to the center, where a thick cluster of trees towers over several benches. More benches line the main route around. It is small, it is true, but there is something perfect in its moderation, and I feel immediately at peace here, more so than I ever did in the more lavish, heavily featured and sculpted palace gardens.

I listen and hear the high trills of the nightthrush, the only songbird we are likely to hear in the night, and the lower bass of an owl. On the last vestiges of the magicked hawk I took recently—desiring its intensity at the expense of my peace of mind—I fancy I spy a bat roosting in the central cluster of trees.

We take a left turn on the path and stop at the first bench we come across. Just a washed-up stagetale actor and the commander of the most respected guard unit in the city.

"How is the Scout Guard?" I ask, tentatively probing what comes next.

"Let's cut the cow shit shall we, Azzuri," he says gruffly, leaning back onto the chair. He reaches into his jacket pocket and takes out a small pouch with several bloodvials in it, and quickly downs one. "Even on magicked Midway, I still start to feel the cold as winter draws in," he says by way of explanation. "What the bloody hell is up with that, do you think? Do I feel it more after a couple of centuries, or am I just getting bored with feeling normal?"

I let that one go, as it seems to me more of a way of a complaint than conversation.

"It's clear to me why you're here," he continues. "The official story was that you were kidnapped by the rebels, did you know that? Yes, I suppose you do. They killed Saxe and spirited you away. Makes them look a bit foolish, letting that happen, but then I expect they had the excuse of that supposed Gray attack on the city."

"Supposed?" I ask, intrigued. I know now that that was Sage Bailey and his Cloak associate providing an illusion for the wolf Raven Ansbach to rob the Blood Bank. Once I was entrusted with that information, I really knew that I was to be trusted overall. Redgrave's word really meant something with the rebels. But though confusion over why the Grays never properly attacked is rife across the city, I did not expect Tenfold to be so condemnatory of the official excuse.

Tenfold chuckles, short of much mirth. "Yes, *supposed*. I've been a soldier or guard or whatever the bloody 'ell you want to call me for long enough now to know when an enemy is an enemy. And that was no enemy. More spirits than anything else. If it wasn't an illusion, then the Grays have suddenly got a lot less good at killing folks. And they never fucking got past me and my men on the wall, I'll tell you that much. And I don't appreciate all the talk of us not doing our jobs properly."

It hasn't occurred to me that Tenfold would have had his pride wounded by that. This could be something useful to work on.

"Which leads me to think that something else has been going on," he continues. "And that you being kidnapped by the rebels was probably horseshit. And now you turning up like this, well, it's obvious. You're one of them, aren't you? You fucking turned. Or maybe you were always one. I don't know. It's all games to you lot. One big fucking game of secrets and lies, while my men pay for it." Anger flashes across his face then, and I'm reminded of how tall he is, and how broad, and even though I'm on the vestiges of superior blood, his body strength and his magicked Midway blood would, in most likelihood, be more than enough for him to incapacitate me, especially given my notable lack of combat experience at any point ever.

"And what do you think is going on?" I ask.

He bellows at that, properly loud, and for a second I am alarmed at the attention it draws, but no one else is in this park; he has chosen well, and I fancy that his laughter dies harmlessly on the night wind.

"I haven't given any more thought to it, and nor will I," he says. "How can I be expected to figure out the machinery of you lot? I care for my men, and I protect them as I can—much good you did with that, you careless bastard who cost me eight of their lives—and anything else can go piss in the wind."

"I think you do yourself a disservice, Commander," I say, carefully. "You are not simply a charge to the men in the Scout Guard. Though you are not commander of the entire Wall Guard, you may as well be, given your reputation and how the men listen to you over anyone else. More than that, you have the respect of all the guard regiments in the city. They remember you in Grayfall, marshaling the retreat. I did not realize . . . your daughter . . . it makes what you did even more remarkable. They remember what you did in Lightfall, as commander of the Southern District Guard, helping to foster seventy years of peace and make that city thrive. But most of all, I suspect, they remember what you did in the war, when you were just a captain. How many men did you save that day, in the Battle of Shadowfall, when the wolves broke through? How many through your actions?"

"It weren't just me," he replies, low.

"How many?"

He shrugs. "Three battalions or so."

I nod. "Fifteen hundred men, thereabouts. When your commanders were dead. It made you legend."

He snorts. "I was no legend. I was shitting my pants as an entire regiment of wolves came to rip us to pieces up our rear."

"Well, you obviously shit yourself a lot more composed than me."

He turns to me properly for the first time, and I see him grin. "You're a funny one, Azzuri. Go on, then, what do you want?"

I pause. I thought this would take longer. I thought I would have to dance around, engage in the subterfuge. But I realize, now, that I am in surprisingly safe territory with Tenfold and that I can simply speak my mind. For a moment, a voice in the back of my skull asks whether I should maybe have befriended more men like him and fewer backstabbing, conspiratorial Lords in my time as ruler of the city. But Captain

Hindsight can, to coin a phrase Tenfold would be proud of, bloody do one.

"Very well, then, Commander. Here it is, the full carafe for you. The rebels are going to do something. I hope you are not insulted if I say I cannot entrust you with the *what*. But when it happens, and you will know when it does, I want you to use your power over the guards of this city—and by power you know exactly what I am talking about, your *legend*, though you would deny this term—to rile up the guards against their ruling Lords and to join the rebels in taking the city, as many as possible, anyway. If enough are roused, it can be done almost bloodlessly. Get enough of the sympathetic Midways and a few Lords on board—and yes, there are some—and the city can turn almost overday. You can have a new ruling body, more like Lightfall—more radical, certainly—but better for your men than . . . my surviving son and the cadre of Lords that surround him now."

Tenfold puffs out his cheeks. "That is quite a transformation you've had there, Azzuri. Straining to light the tinder to everything you built. Someone really shoved some firepowder up your arse."

Yes, I think, they did. Someone who died before I knew what my city really was. Someone I never really knew.

"But why," asks Tenfold, "in the bloody twin hells would I help you, even if I could, when I would be risking all my men's lives on a whimsy and a lost cause?"

"Because I now know that your daughter died in Grayfall, and so I know you'll want to help me when I tell you this next piece."

His face goes granite stern at that, almost like he is hewn out of rock, and he clenches his fist at his side, and I can see, without me telling him, that he already knows. He has sensed it, maybe like everyone in the city; he has sensed the lie at its heart. Or maybe not, maybe he is just far more clever than I give him credit for and he really has understood the lie of it. Either way, the rage is there seemingly before I tell him.

But I still tell him. I tell him everything, everything that happened before Redgrave saved me. I tell him of how Saxe and his cadre of Lords faked the death of Sinassion's shades and turned them into Grays, with the impossible weapons found under the ground. I tell them of Grayfall. Of how after it they sought to keep everyone afraid while they built up their stores of wolfblood with the excuse of a made-up enemy.

When I am done telling him, he has moved from stone to a deep shade of red that makes his fiery hair light by comparison, and for a dark moment I fear he might explode.

"My daughter," he says softly, the whisper of the fuse before the fire-powder blast.

"Yes," I reply. "Your daughter. Murdered by the Grays, by my fellow Lords, with so many others of your comrades. Of our kind, Worns, Mid-ways, and even Lords."

He reflects on this. Then he stands up quickly, turns, and picks up the bench we are sitting on. I only just manage to jump off it before he has raised it up in his arms, and tree-trunk muscles straining, he arcs it up into the air, where it sails on a fast-descending parabola before landing forty yards ahead in the middle of the central cluster of trees, smashing against the first one with a splintering crash that echoes through the crisp late-night winter air. The tree, I am impressed to note, is fine; the bench is not. A clash of two woods.

Then he turns to me, face still red, fists clenched, fire in his eyes, and for a moment I think that I'll be smashed to pulp just like the bench. But his breath slows, and bit by bit the feral rage in his pupils slithers away.

I try to show him my composure is not disturbed. It is a great effort.

"I was just thinking how I wanted to sit on a dirt path," I say.

He grins then, not a smile of warmth but one acknowledging me nonetheless.

"Do you know why you are still able to talk with me now?" he asks, keeping the slight grin on but getting a bit of that feral back into him.

"No," I reply.

"Because no one who was responsible for that would be that stupid to tell me that piece of news face-to-face."

Unless they were pulling off a most daring double bluff, I think, and decide to keep that witty comment to myself. "So you believe me?"

"Course I believe you. Look at what you are now. Plus that entire story rings completely true to what I expected of that bastard Saxe and half the bastards you used to rule alongside."

"Rule *over*," I correct him.

"I think that story shitting disproved that, didn't it?" he says, lying down cross-legged on the path next to me.

"Fair point," I say. A cold winter breeze rattles through the park. I feel it slightly, which is how I know the hawk is wearing off. The dull fall off the hawk, thankfully short-lived, spreads through me, putting a temporary pall on the world. Maybe that is why the next thing I say does not quite have the vim I intended. "So you will join me, and the rebels. Use your influence, give us most of the Blood Guard."

Tenfold stares straight ahead. "No. I won't."

"But," I say, confused, sure that I had him after that display with the bench, "they killed your daughter."

He nods, still avoiding my eyes. "Aye, they did. And I'll find my way to killing most of them that arranged that, if it takes centuries, which if I'm not too bloody foolish I will obviously have. But my daughter, she that filled me heart every hour of every day, is dead. But my boys—my Scout Guard, my Wall Guard, all the guard I know in the city, hell every one that does his duty every night for little thanks from you and your lot—they are alive. And I won't get them killed for listening to me. I had enough of that last month with your little fuckin' excursion beyond the wall."

"But . . . like I said, it will be bloodless, they won't stand a chance. . . ."

"Oh, and you know that for a bloody fact, do you, Azzuri?" He whips his head to face me then, granite face cold, mouth curled into a half sneer. "You who were so sure in ruling the city but a couple of months back, only for it to turn into shitting ash between your fingers? You're so sure that this marvelous plan will come to pass? Or will it be me and my lads again, paying the price like all wars?"

"It's not a war, it's a revolution," I say, knowing as the words peter out pathetically that I have already lost him.

He waves his hand at me. "War. Revolution. It's all the same. We dance to the fiddle and we get fucked by the piper."

"I don't know . . . I have never heard that before."

He shrugs. "It's a saying."

We stare ahead of us for a while. Across the lawns, on the circular path opposite us, a Midway walks across. I can see it is a well-dressed sort of Midway, maybe a banker, though having not taken good-enough blood recently I cannot quite make out the exact features. He saunters along, clearly enjoying the last hourglass of the night, and then disappears through another park exit to the north.

"Tell me about your daughter," I say, not knowing where this is going, but feeling my way there anyway.

"If this is some fucking new attempt . . ."

"My youngest boy is dead, and it kills me every hourglass. I'm a dead man walking. I would not use your daughter like that. I just . . . I just want to hear."

Maybe it's the crack in my voice or my words, but Tenfold turns to me sharply, studies me, then turns back.

"She was . . . eleven when she died. Still my child, but you could see what she would become. Brave as anything, she'd run round the city ramparts while I commanded Southwatch in Lightfall. Curious, too. Wanted to know everything. Don't know where she got her thirst for knowledge from, couldn't have been me, certainly not her ma. But she cried hard, too, animals mostly. Hated to see them suffer. Not a great outlook in our world, but I loved how bloody kind she was. It was a different world to me and my fighting past. When I was with her, the world was gentle, and I wasn't this fucking giant with blood on my hands over three godsdamn centuries. I was the father to the best . . ."

He stops then, and looks to the right, and I hear his breath hitch.

Then he turns ahead again, composed. "You say it kills you every hourglass, thinking about your son. It still does me, thinking about my daughter. Maybe not every glass, but still most, when I'm not distracted anyway. And it hits fresh every time. A century hasn't cured that. I doubt ten centuries will."

I leave that be, give it the silence it deserves.

"At least you didn't fail as a father," I say, after a while.

"Don't be sundamn stupid, Azzuri," Tenfold says back, brusque in his voice. "I didn't save her. Ain't no worse failure than that."

"That's not true and you know it," I reply quick, maybe quicker than I would have liked. "But you definitely did not fail her in life. Not like I failed my youngest. I had no idea who he really was. I had somewhat given up on him. We had not spoken in . . . too long when he died."

"Such is often the way," Tenfold says. "If mine had lived, I'm sure I would've disappointed her."

"No, you would not," I reply. "You don't have to associate with you for very long to know that whatever faults you pin to yourself, you were and would always have been the very best of fathers to your girl."

He looks down and does not say anything. He knows I do not know that, or at least I do not know him well enough to know that. But for now, I suspect, he is content enough for the charade.

"I, on the other hand," I continue, "failed that boy all his life. I chose to believe it was his failure, not mine. It is only after his death that I discovered that he was not spurning me or the family. He was doing greater things than I could imagine, and being a far better person than I could ever conceive."

A grunt and, perhaps, a laugh from Tenfold. "You don't need to tell me that," he says.

I frown. "What do you mean?"

"Oh," he says, a little surprised. "I assumed you'd know. That fucking cheeky bastard of a mage Jacob knew well enough when he accosted me in the Rushes, so I thought you and your bloody spies would. We were friends, your youngest and me. Not lifelong blood pals, but frequent enough friends over the last few decades. We'd drink together."

I leave that in the air for a while, because I do not know what to say. I try to picture them together as friends, that barrel of a man used to being around the rowdy guardsmen all his life and my slim slip of a soft-spoken son, the painter, the writer, the traveler, the dreamer. I cannot, frankly, do it.

"I . . . did not know that. Clearly I am still learning so much about him. What kind of things did you talk about?" I ask.

Tenfold looks at me, really looks at me, squinting his eyes. Perhaps once upon a time my mind would have interjected some tiresome gibe at this point about how nonintellects like him, big bricks of men, always squint as they are forced to think, but even as I reflect on that I feel a little loathing at myself, or at what I once was or what I partly still am but am starting to not be. Because Tenfold may not be the reading or studying type, but he has already proven in many ways to be far more wise than me.

When his examination has concluded, he turns to stare ahead again. "You really are changing, aren't you, Azzuri? No assumptions that we were anything more than friends. No lazy feelings about your son, that just because he liked male company in that way that our friendship would be more than that. No panic, none that I can tell, and I'm good at reading men just as you were good, on occasion, I suppose, at ruling over them." He sighs. "Good for you." He runs a hand through his short sunset hair.

"We talked about everything," he continues. "It might not seem like we had much in common, but we both knew our city, and the Worns—which I used to be, and still am really, despite my rank—and we knew the misery of it. And the joy of it, too. He told me about the stagetales, and I even started going to the Sunsphere on his recommendation. I saw that big one a few back, *Sinopia and Carminia*. Bloody tragic, had everyone soppin' around me. He told me about the poorest Worns out near the western Fang Tips, and I had some of my men send them some provisions. He told me of his travels too, just before Grayfall. I've never been to the Desertlands, but he had. He was a great storyteller. And he told me of his paintings, and he showed me them sometimes, too. He would have a canvas on him often, a small one, and he'd whip it out of his jacket. I'd rarely seen art before, and I grew to love it. There's a portrait stall at the Moon Market. It's one of the reasons I like it."

He stops then, as it occurs to him that my face is buried in my jacket. He gives me the grace and the space to recover.

"I am sorry," I say. "It is just . . . hearing someone speak of him like that. It is . . . something."

"You've got nothing to fucking apologize for," he says, louder than he may have intended. "Least, not for that."

"He was a good person, wasn't he?" I say.

"One of the best I've ever known," Tenfold replies. "And I've known some bloody heroes. He helped a lot of people in the city, when he wasn't busy with his arts or his dreamin'."

"Yes," I say. "I've been finding out about that. Slowly but surely."

"He drew me a painting of my daughter, too. From my descriptions. It was her, as well. The spittin' image. Right there and then, I would've taken a Gray bullet for that lad."

A bell rings out, clear and high, against the sky. Others join it across the city. Fifteen bells. One bell to lightfall.

"Right," says Tenfold, "I reckon that's us, don't you, Azzuri? Unless you want to be continuin' our reminiscing with the sun in our face."

"I wouldn't mind that, to be honest," I half whisper to myself.

"What's that?" asks Tenfold.

"Oh . . . nothing." There's a pause. Tenfold seems reluctant to move. I think he feels like me, that we were caught in something then. Something necessary. Something that conversations rarely go to.

He turns to me then. "I spoke a bit harshly when we met, Azzuri. Whatever the hell kind of a man you were before . . . I think you're turnin' into something different. Don't bloody ask me what that means, because I'm about done with talking and I need sleep and then soldierin' and guardin' in that order, but just . . . don't go back, you hear me, Azzuri? Don't go back."

I nod, and go to reply, but then on impulse I reach into my jacket inlay pocket—a pocket that didn't exist when this worn Midway jacket was procured for me by Redgrave but that I had sewn in—and I shove a bundle of papers at him, tied with string.

"Take these with you, Tenfold."

He studies them suspiciously. "What are they, Azzuri?"

"Some writings of Red's."

His eyebrow raises. "You calling him by that now?"

"Yes. It was the name he chose. It fits better than the choice name I gave him."

He nods. "You're right about that. You nobles and your fuckin' color shades." Then he takes the papers off me. "What's in them?"

"Writings on the city. On its people. On what he was doing. What he wished for the future. What this city could be and should be. What's important. What is not. I know you cannot help me and the rebels, and I understand. I judge you not a single bit. But seeing his vision, I think in a way that would help, too. I think you will like it, if you knew him so well."

Tenfold thinks for a moment. "I think I will, yes. But don't you need them?"

I shrug. "I have . . . lots of others."

He stands up then, and places the papers in his own jacket. He looms over me, still on the ground, and for a moment I think he will just walk off. Then he turns, and I see he wants to say words. Maybe he wants to say sorry for my loss. Maybe he wants to tell me how he enjoyed reminiscing about my youngest with me.

But a man as sharp as I now see Tenfold is knows that it is not in the moments like that where the meaning is to be found, but in the moments that do not seem like them when you are in them. Like the conversation we just had, sitting on the dirt in a park.

So he walks off, slowly, tired, but not in a bad way.

I watch him till he is out of sight.

Then I quietly weep into the soil.

# 11

# The Sound of Wings

Please, I am begging you, do not go forth with this scheme, this Invisibles. One of these days it will be manipulated so badly by someone with terrible intentions, just as it was in Dawn Death. If you are not careful, it will bring a whole city down.

Redscroll Flutecap, minutes of the 275th meeting of the Lightfall Bloodshares Council, 452 AL

## Sam

We wait on the Westfall side of Centersquare, the three other ladies and I, first bell hardly gone. Centersquare, the vast yet constantly teeming plaza, is the beating heart of Centerfall, the home of the pinnacle of First Light culture in the Sunsphere and the Blood Canvas and the heart of its trade in the Blood Market, and the focal point for its finance in the Crown Bank, the Blood Bank . . . and, most importantly for me, the Invisibles.

The air is bitter and cold tonight, but I won't be feeling it at all, as Molly has plied me with magicked hare, a rare Midway blood but one that gives you some of the alertness of hawk but without the penalty once the effects have worn off. "I thought you could do with a bit of a rest from that," she said, maybe referring to the last two nights' fevered planning I've had, downing hawk vials, putting together the plan that will either fly or fail tonight. Alanna tasked herself with organizing the Leeches, their comings and goings the next night, when they were to help spread the rumors of this new blood. Meanwhile I calculated how the market side would work.

"So explain it me one more time, Sammy. Just so I know what we should be seein'," says Molly Threetimes. She's wearing a tightly wrapped brown shawl over a large gray tunic, and I can see her feeling the winter chill a little. I know that though she drinks greatly, she tries to stay on the Wornblood when she can, and maybe it's that or maybe it's her age that's making her feel it. Come to think of it, a talented smuggler like her should never really have aged as much as she has in the first place given the opportunities for good blood she must have always had. I make a note to myself to ask her about that.

"So the new batch of blood we're using has been delivered from the Blood Farms to the Blood Market now," I say, nodding vaguely in the distance to where, hundreds of feet away to the Northfall side and barely visible in the night, the soft lights of the Blood Market can be seen. "That means it can now go on the Invisibles roster officially."

"So traders can start buying shares of it," she says carefully.

"Yes, exactly," I reply. As the best smuggler in Lightfall, I did expect Molly to be more versed in the Invisibles, but I suppose blood trading and the actual Blood Markets are a world apart. The Invisibles is a new thing, barely over a century old, and there was no need for her to find out about it in the new world of post-Grayfall First Light. It's funny that the thing that will bring down a city if I—if *we* have our way is something no sane, normal person has taken the least bit of interest in.

"Now, here's the key bit." I turn to Hands Parker as I say this, because I desperately want her look of cynicism, as much as she ever shows emotion, to be wiped off that blank face. If she finds it awkward that she tried to kill me and was then humiliated by Alanna, she's not showing it. Speaking of Alanna, she's not here, but Daphnée, who completes our foursome, hasn't mentioned why.

"If our Leeches have been doing our job, then rumors of the blood will be flying around. The traders, both Midway and Lord, will have heard it on the street, in their homes. The Leech sympathizers in the Midways should have made this easier, too." I nod to Daphnée as I say this.

"Yes, Sam is right," she confirms. She pushes a pale hand back through her bunched-up hair as she says this, almost dislodging the single white flower there peeking out of it. She looks distracted. "We have got a Midway woman who has managed to make her way onto the Blood Council subcommittee. And a clerk for the Invisibles Committee. They should have worked their magick, I expect."

I nod. "So that's that side. But we also need the initial information about the blood to be good. Not good enough to match the rumors—that would arouse suspicion, people wondering why a Midway blood might be as good as wolfblood itself. But enough to suggest that it's better than normal. That's where Azzuri comes in. He and Redgrave have a Midway on the Invisibles Council—sympathetic, one that can be trusted—and they've asked him to amend the information. It should all be there."

I point to a large maroon-colored tent pitched on the Eastfall side. Through the opening, dimly lit by oil lamps hanging off the tent poles, I see piles of parchments neatly arranged on a lengthy wooden table. Mostly men—although I see one woman there—are studying these closely, making notes with quills on their bits of notepaper. They're dressed neatly: finely stitched jackets, good linen breeches, shining boots. Blood traders. You can practically smell their confidence.

"That's where the blood traders go to find out new information about the new blood that's made available from the Blood Farms. With that confirmation and the rumors, we should see a rush to buy at the Invisibles."

Now I point to the building at the Southfall end of the square. A long, rectangular limestone-and-marble affair, designed in the Old Mage style similar to the Blood Bank and so many of the buildings built in the last two centuries. It has rows of symmetrical windows, with blue-and-red pediments over them. The central portico entrance features plain-topped columns with a frieze running above them, depicting carvings: thin containers of blood crossed over each other like swords. The sigil of the Invisibles. At the moment, hardly any traders are walking beneath these columns. It's still early.

I look back at the assembled ladies. Hands Parker makes a sound of a dying hawk and then spits a large glob of phlegm somewhere to the right of me. "So we should be seein' a big rush of finely dressed fuckers descend on the . . . Invisibles." She says the last word with barely disguised distaste, someone thrust into a world they hate and don't want to even think about. What did the nobles do to her? Her hatred outshines all ours.

"Exactly," I say.

"Unless Azzuri was lying to you." Hands fixes her funeral eyes on me. "Taking advantage of the maid."

"Hands," says Molly, visibly annoyed. "We're this far into the plan now, dearie. May as well see it through. I trust Redgrave with my life. He's done as much for our cause as you and me, maybe more with the life he's had to pretend. If you don't trust Azzuri"—she looks at me almost apologetically—"or our brave Sammy here, at least trust him."

Hands shrugs. "Fine." But her eyes keep their distrust.

"Right then, our Sammy," Molly continues. "How long do we have to wait? I'm not saying I'm not already keen for a little dram and a sit-down, but I'm not sayin' I'm not, either."

"It should be soon," I say, trying to keep my nerves down. I have a lot riding on this. If the rumors of the most powerful new blood since Grayfall don't start the rush to buy I've wagered they will, then the plan is over already. Hands Parker will no doubt try to kill me again, and if she doesn't, I'll have to watch her throw more bodies at the rebel cause to get slaughtered, knowing that it was my failure that did this. My failure. Just like—

"Sammy," says Daphnée carefully. "Are you all right? You went a bit . . . far away there."

"Yes, yes . . . just . . . much on my mind. I should also say that everything I said is just the first phase."

"Sorry, *phase*?" says Molly. "You sound like Alanna, darlin', you can't just make words up."

I laugh, wishing Alanna was here. I used to find her presence terrifying. Now I find it reassuring. Might be something to do with the fact she's saved my life twice. "Actually, it was Alanna who used that. Some old Last Light word. Means the first part of a plan."

Molly goggles at me. "Why not just use *plan* then?"

I shrug and grin. "What would Alanna say?"

"Fair point, dearie, carry on."

"So the first . . . phase . . . is the initial buying of the Invisibles. Which is hopefully big. And then in six bells' time, in midevening, comes the second phase. That's when the first reports come back." I turn to the Westfall side of the square to point at another large tent. There's no long table and no parchments in this one. Just a bell on a rope hanging down from the tent, and a Midway in a tall stovepipe hat and long moustache and fancy ermine-lined jacket with curlicues of red and gold thread round the lapel and sleeves. Behind him are several vampires that look like Worns, with dull-brown jackets, who are listening to others who have raced from across the square to the tent. Every so often they turn to the behatted Midway and whisper something in his ear, and he scrolls something on some paper with an elaborate gold quill.

"There are Worns who act as messengers and they collect the opinions of the merchants after the delivery of the blood. They race back here, and inform that announcer, who declares the current popularity of it.

The traders buy or sell the Invisible shares they already bought earlier in the evening accordingly."

I see Hands frowning, and I rush to explain before she can try to pour cold water on me again. I've explained this, multiple times, but it needs explaining again, clearly. I struggle not to smile. That sounds like something Sage would say.

"If you're wondering why that won't harm us when people drink the first batches of our chosen blood and find out it isn't what they say it is," I say, cutting Hands off just in time, "that's because of Daphnée." I nod at her, and she doesn't register me for a second, distracted. Something's not right, but I shovel the concern down underneath all the other compacted stress.

"Oh, that's kind, Sammy," she says, "but it was your idea, too."

"It was literally your idea," I say.

"Well, I suppose . . ."

"Oh, by the twin 'ells, end this polite nonsense now or I'll leave you all for the tavern," cuts in Molly. She may not be addicted to the finer bloods but, I'm coming to realize, she has a bit of a taste for the spirits that can go in them.

Daphnée grins at me. That's a bit more like the old her. "Well, it occurred to me that the best way to make sure those reports reflect our false rumors rather than the true results of the initial home tastings is not to try to create facsimiles in the homes of Midways and Lords but rather to swap them after the fact. We will pay the boy runners who take the reports from homes to here, and swap the true reports for ones that a couple of my scribe Leechmaids prepared."

Molly nods, impressed. Even Hands looks satisfied.

"That's wickedly clever, Daphnée," says Molly.

"Thank you, Molly. Alanna will be waiting for the boys later on this evening near the square to make the swap."

Molly blanches. "When I said it was clever . . ."

Daphnée tries to contain her smile but it escapes one side of her mouth. "Do not fear, Molly, dear. She will not scare them . . . too much."

The waiting over the next half a glass is awful. I never knew time could crawl so badly. Not even in my decade at the First Lord's palace—

trapped in a life of drudgery part of me feared that, for all my plans, I might never escape from—not even then did I feel time like this. In the last ten weeks since I found Azzuri's note, time has sped up, a life of eternity feeling like eternity has decided to squeeze into a season. You can feel the sense of things moving in the air; it's like the whole city knows it. When you're immortal—and I'm cribbing the words of Neuras Sondallion in his philosophical musings here, but it fits—your mind adapts to decades of leisure (of the inactive kind, not the enjoyment kind) as you know you don't need to rush, you have centuries not just decades. But then periodically it's like we forget we're immortals and moments in time go *fast*. Like a juncture. It feels like we're here now. A whirlpool of momentum, careering us somewhere we know not where.

Except now. Right now it's sundamn slow. Just my reputation and, maybe, my life on the line.

Everything's fine.

"Seems quiet to me," says Hands, nodding to the Invisibles, which is still notably missing any larger-than-usual crowds, and the marquee where the blood reports can be found, which is even more notable for the lack of frenzied traders.

"Patience, Hands," I say, a little more cockily than I would normally talk to her, but I survived her murder attempt so I reckon that gives me license to talk like that to her on occasion.

I turn to the square. Nothing.

Well, not *quite* nothing.

Off to the Eastfall side, where most of the Midway blood traders would come from, I see a few blood traders wandering across. Is that slightly more than you'd expect at this time of night? It's hard to tell. A couple groups here or there. If I was actually on hawk, not hare, I'd be able to peer farther into the gloom, but no. . . .

"This is interesting," says Daphnée. I'm not sure what blood she's on, but it must be a good one, as she's peering into the Northeastfall side of Centersquare, where all I can see is night shadows.

"What?" asks Hands skeptically.

"A large group of Lords are coming, something in a rush, too."

I think on this. Lords can trade, too, although often they'll send Midways in their place. They could be going to the Blood Bank, of course, or have other business here. Maybe they'll turn off to the Blood Market.

"They're heading toward the marquee where the reports are now, I think," adds Daphnée.

Something leaps in my veins.

I turn back to my Eastfall crowds. They have gotten bigger. As they loom out of the darkness, I see a wide mix of Midways. Some well-dressed, clearly well-heeled traders, but also some who look like more trade-based Midways, rougher jackets and fewer hats. That's interesting. The more popular a blood is, the more wide an array of Midways try their hand at the Invisibles.

"Oh my," I hear Daphnée say.

And that's when it happens. Almost at once, the two crowds converge in the square before us. The Lords and the Midways. Guided by haste, impatience etched across their faces, they stride toward the tent across the square where all the reports are kept of the recent blood batches. The traders already studying them look askance at the crowds descending on them in mild alarm, and suddenly close to three dozen traders, noble and Midway alike, are frantically attempting to view the parchments and papers that will hopefully confirm the rumors they've been hearing the last night or so about the new magicked otter batch.

Then, to my great surprise and to Molly's evident amusement, one of the Midways, a broad-shouldered, large-moustached blond trader, loses his temper with one of his colleagues studying the reports in front of him for too long, and pushes the offender to the side. His colleague does not take well to this, and shoves him back, harder, baring and lengthening his fangs as he does, and Big Moustache falls to the floor on his arse. A couple of Lords deep in study on some notes across the table look up in surprise at this and reprimand him, and though it's a bit too far for me to hear the response on my blood, I know it's not a good one. One of the other Lords, a six-foot-eight beast of a noble with unusual girth for his class, takes umbrage at this and rounds the table to defend his colleague to the Midway, overstepping his grounds and his class, and grabs him by his jacket lapels, lifting him up and throwing him smartly outside the tent.

At that point I lose track of the exact particulars as the space inside the tent turns into a brawl, with fists flying, fangs lengthening, and, in one Midway's case, even some claws lengthening a good few inches, something that should only happen when real injury is intended. It only lasts a few moments, though, as a couple of other Lords and Midways quickly intervene to pull the fighters apart and shout some sense into them. Then, calm is more or less restored, although I can see a lot of distress in the rest of the trader crowd.

I turn to Molly, who's laughing, great belly laughs, enjoying the sight, her need for a drink long forgotten. "Bloody men, eh? Don't matter the class or the location, never far from a brawl."

"Rare sight here, though," adds Daphnée, a curious expression on her face.

I smile to myself, hesitant to say what's on my mind, aware of the put-down that Hands Parker will have ready if I show too much optimism for my plan. I carry on watching as the crowds, having satisfied themselves on the reports, turn to face the Invisibles building. For a moment, I see them look at one another, pondering on what they've read. On all the talk of the blood that we and our supporters have faked, the promises of greatness, of the money that comes with it. I see their minds working, and I can almost sense their thoughts in the air, a great miasma covering me in their sweaty little ideas: *How much money can we make? This could be big. We must act fast.*

There's a moment I sense, not something that can be put into words but something instinctive, something lingering at the back of the mind, when the thoughts of the individual become the thoughts of the crowd and the seeds of a collective fever grip them. I remember then, too, the words of Sage, when he was at my bedside, just after the Blood Bank, not so long ago yet long ago still, telling me about the future, about enlightenment and all the knowledge that will come to this continent. And I wonder if this moment, too, is a part of it, a prelude to the time when the fever of crowds over invisible things will start wars and change continents just as much as the old wars.

And then all my thoughts give way to a great smile as the noblemen and Midways alike, separate in their classes but united in their greed, start to run—run, not walk—to the great column-lined entrance of the Invisibles building, all decorum forgotten in their haste to buy a share in the blood, in *our* blood, now.

"Animal spirits," I whisper, voice half lost in the wind that scurries across the square.

"What's that?" Hands asks, watching the running men like me, blank expression gone, genuine surprise in its place.

"I said . . . I think there's a chance my plan might work."

Daphnée sits herself down opposite me in a thick padded chair, one of the few in our Westfall Leech abode that doesn't feel like it's designed to prod every part of you into submission. A memory flashes into my mind of her reclining in a grand armchair next to her ornate fireplace in a mansion half a city away. For all her fire and poise, she doesn't suit these quarters, but you'd have to bleed her half dry to get her to admit it, I expect.

"You must be happy, Sam," she says, gently sipping on a small flute of fox, no magick. Her chosen blood for every occasion. I miss her pendant. A foxy lady drinking fox and wearing fox. *Calm down, Sam. You're practically delirious.*

"No time to be happy yet, Daphnée," I reply. I've long got past the point where I have to concentrate to not call her Lady. I have to remind myself sometimes that she's the leader of the Leeches, the Queen Leech still. She seems to be welcoming the shift of power, too. I wonder why.

"There's so much that still has to go right," I continue. "The first batch of reports later tonight, the facsimile ones Alanna will put into the hands of the messengers, have to be well received. There needs to be another buying frenzy that happens after that. We need this blood to be in the Invisibles portfolios of hundreds if not thousands of traders by tomorrow, when the real reports show up. When the truth that it's not some remarkable new contender for wolfblood but simply a standard Midway is revealed. We need that panic and dismay to turn into violence. The kind that distracts the guards enough to steal the wolfblood from under the their noses."

Daphnée smiles. "Ah, Sam. My thoughtful, cautious Sam. You are allowed to enjoy the small victories, you know. It does not mean you are chancing fate at the bigger one." She downs her flute and puts it on the small side table next to her, then fixes me with one of her absorbing stares. "You have a lot invested in this plan, do you not?"

I'm a little taken aback by her shift from casual talk to piercing eyes, and for a moment the words are caught in my mouth. But I'm not the ingenue anymore, so I quickly recover.

"We all do, don't we? If this fails, it's back to Hands Parker's idea of revolution. Throw bodies at it until Rufous gets furious enough to bathe Worntown in blood."

"True," she concedes. "But I can see a different need in your eyes, Sam." She pauses. "You desperately do not want to see anyone hurt, do you?"

For a brief moment, I see a night sky, and then the sound of wings. "I'm a bit tired of the death we've been around, yes."

Daphnée considers this. She goes to say something, then stops. Eventually, she settles on, "All that violence. You and Raven. Killing the First Guard. Fighting Rufous twice. You have not really had a chance to reflect on it, have you? Or . . . talk about it."

I frown. "Talk about it?"

"Yes," Daphnée says. "What it was like. What it has done to you."

"In all honesty?" I say, stretching my legs out a little and wishing I had joined her on the fox. "I don't think on it much, and, as bad as it sounds, I'm not even sure I was affected by it. I was on so much wolfblood at the time, that it almost . . . wasn't me doing it. It's hard to explain, but it was like the wolfblood was . . . rationalizing it even as I was doing it. Telling me what it was, what life is, that this doesn't matter . . ." I pause, realizing that I'm trying to explain the absolutely inexplicable. "Sorry, it's . . . impossible to get across what that much wolfblood does to you. It's . . ."

"No, it is fine, Sam. I think . . . I think I understand. Well, not understand, but I believe you. You are strong when it comes to that kind of thing, I think. Stronger than me."

I can't help but laugh at that. "I doubt that, Daphnée. I doubt that very much."

"No, it is true." She reaches behind her head and unties the hairnet she's kept on since we were watching the traders an hourglass ago. Her hair falls out, completely wild, completely unkempt. It feels like her fall from Lady is complete, but she's still glowing and still utterly beautiful; by all the bloods, is she beautiful. I can see why Alanna is so completely in love with her. I'm not that way inclined, and she represents something completely different to me that makes the thought strange even as

I think on it, but I can see that if I *was* that way inclined, then it would be easy to become completely obsessed.

"But I think there is something else bothering you, Sam," she continues, pouring herself another flute of fox from the silk-lined carafe on the side table. "Why you don't want anyone to get hurt. Why you are so taken with a bloodless revolution."

I wait for her next words, the sounds of wings at the back of my skull getting louder.

"Have you cried for Beth, Sam? Properly?"

My reply is instant. "Of course I have." *Have I? I remember being sad.*

"It wasn't your fault, you know."

I nod, slowly. "I know that."

"Do you?"

I pause. I wish I'd taken blood. "Of course. It was Rufous. He killed my parents, as good as. And then he killed . . ." I let the words slide.

Daphnée nods. "But you didn't kill him. Do you regret that, Sam?" Her eyes are calm, and she has a gentle smile on her face, but she's leaning forward, toward me, expectant.

"No. It was the right thing to do. For the city. The deaths that would have happened if another Azzuri had been killed . . ."

"Yes, you are right. I cannot fault that reasoning," she says. "I wonder though . . . I wonder if you did not kill him because you blame yourself, not him."

I laugh at that, too loudly. I can hear the wings so loud now. My hand twitches, and I wonder if she notices.

"Like you blame yourself for your mother and your father and your sister. Because you think everyone around you dies, and it is your fault, and you deserve it. So you must never let anyone get hurt again."

I don't reply to that. I barely hear the words. Somewhere off in the distance, something lands on the ground and snaps. It sounds like bone. Up above, the beat, the beat, the beat of wings.

"How is Alanna?" I ask, clawing my way back into the present.

Daphnée stares at me awhile, and then she says, quietly, more to herself, "I'm sorry. I—it's not that simple, is it." Then she reclines back in her chair and swirls her flute around, staring into its contents. "Alanna is fine," she says. "Right now, I imagine she is preparing to scare those poor messenger boys into delivering the right blood reports."

"So everything is . . . well?" I ask, tiptoeing my way around this line of conversation like a field buried with firepowder.

Daphnée smiles, one of those amused smiles that threaten ice just under the surface. "Sam, my dear, we could be here all night if you proceed like that. I do not bite, you know. My friends, at least."

*That remains to be seen*, I think. "You looked concerned earlier. At the square. You've looked concerned for several days, but even more so then."

"And you know me that well?" asks Daphnée.

"Yes," I say, confident and meaning it. "I think I'm starting to, just as you're starting to really know me."

She smiles then, a proper smile, no ice. "You mean it, don't you. You are concerned. You are a good girl, you know that, Sam?"

I give that one a miss.

"Oh, to the twin hells with it," she says. "You know my feelings anyway. Our feelings, I would like to think. You do, don't you?"

I nod. "I really do."

She laughs then, sharp and loud. "Ha! That obvious?"

"Well, it's not hard. You just have to look at your face or Alanna's face when the other speaks."

"I thought you found Alanna's face uniformly terrifying, Sam."

My turn to laugh now. "Most of the time, yes. But not when she's looking direct at you. Never then."

Daphnée sighs. "I fear I have been selfish, Sam."

"I highly doubt that."

"No, no, it is true. Alanna has . . . suffered things that I could only dream of, I suspect. Or at least seen things. I fancy myself to have suffered, with the loss of my daughter. But things happened to her that were so bad . . . they changed her. She wasn't always like that, like . . ."

"A riddle in an enigma, who sounds like one half the time?"

"Yes, ha! That is a good way to put it. Her terrifying nature, her ability to . . . kill many people quickly. The things she can do that cannot always be explained, like when she jumped off the roof of First Gods, carrying my body, and was unharmed. The ways she speaks, even the way she thinks. Do not get me wrong, I am not critiquing her; how could I, when it is her, in that guise, who, as you have so adroitly spotted, I love dearly, in the romantic way?"

She pauses. "I have never said that out loud before." Her voice is quiet, like she's just discovered some great secret, and she puts a hand to her cheek, as if to check she is still there.

I smile. I almost want to go over and hug her, but that's not quite me and I don't know if she would like it, frankly.

"The point is," she continues, "I think she has had to put some parts of herself in a box to become who she is now, and lock that box, if you get that meaning, and maybe some of that was giving herself to another, and the vulnerability that comes with that."

I think on this. "She can't be scary Alanna and mysterious Alanna while also being romancing and courting Alanna."

Daphnée nods, twirling the flower in her hair in thought. "Yes, I suppose that is one way of saying it." She sighs. "And there is me, threatening to break this shell she has had around her. All because I cannot keep my feelings to myself." She looks away from me then, and clenches her fist. "So utterly stupid."

We're quiet then. I stand up and walk over to the worn brown sideboard in the corner of the room, and open a drawer, where some flutes are haphazardly stacked. Not exactly the careful arrangement of the mansion, but these are different times. Below me, I hear some Leeches arrive back from their various errands, darting around, their boots clicking on the thin floors. I walk over to the side table next to Daphnée and pour myself some foxblood from the carafe. She doesn't mind. More signs of how our relationship has changed. I remember how frozen I was when we took eel tea in her parlor but a couple of months ago. Then I return to my seat and sip the blood. It hits me straightaway, as it often does after a few hours without blood. I feel my eyes go red and my skin lightly flush. Fox is subtle, neither calming nor agitating, but it readies you nonetheless. It tastes herby, too, for some reason. I lean back in my chair, embracing the warmth, and stretch my limbs out. The room grows hotter.

"Have you considered that she has been just as keen to respond to you?" I ask eventually, after Daphnée has patiently waited for me to adjust to the blood. "Have you really made all the . . . suggestions?"

Daphnée thinks on this. "Well, now you mention it, I suppose she has been the one to say a line or two to me. . . ."

I nod. "Well, there you go. So don't you think that while a part of her might be finding this hard, another part of her is willing to risk it?"

Daphnée shakes her head and briefly shuts her eyes. "You should have seen her last night, Sam. It was like she suddenly had the weight of the Everlands on her. I have never seen her lacking control like that, or so . . . not exactly emotional, but threatening emotion. I do not want to break her."

"But maybe she wants to be broken."

Daphnée doesn't reply to this, but the thought has landed, and I sip my fox, satisfied.

12

# Grave Situation

> Oh cousin! My brother Vermillion has come across a most amusing new find, this Redgrave, a Midway. He assures me that he is most useful to him and do you know it, I think he is right! The man is most polite and seems to know everything of Lightfall that could be useful. I quite see why Vermillion is thinking of making him his first man. He seems to have come from nowhere to have quite the influence! A shame he is but a Midway too—that moustache makes him look rather dapper.
>
> Sinopia Azzuri, in a letter to her cousin, dated 400 AL

## Sam

I sip my flute of bearblood in Vermillion's receiving room, and realize two things.

One, bear is addictive. If I never had to have hawk—never needed that racing of the mind, that edginess, which you can get with magicked stag or maybe others but good luck having that all the time, so the anxious edge of hawk it is—then I could get used to sipping bear half the time and Daphnée's fox the other. I am getting a taste of the good stuff, and my own words to the man I'm sitting opposite come back to me, about whether this is a good thing, a natural thing, or something else. And somewhere sitting at the edge of my thoughts is the call of the wolfblood, the true blood, and how it felt to have half a wolf in me.

Two, I now think of the old First Lord by his choice name. Azzuri out, Vermillion in. And this is the fourth time I've been at his new abode in a matter of weeks.

Both these things could do with some study, but more pressing matters abound, like bringing down a city.

"You expect news, I assume," says Vermillion. He's dressed in a plain shirt, no edging or rubies or curlicue. His roguish Midway affect has gone. His hair looks even more unkempt than usual, and his eyes look tired. He looks like a man without sleep forced to play his rested self in a stage play.

"Actually," I reply, "I first wanted to say thank you. Your influence with a Lord or Midway or two at the Invisibles or the Blood Bank must have had an effect, because the parchment work on the blood batch we chose was perfect. Even better than we'd hoped with just the influence of the Leeches. Everyone thinks it's the one they've been waiting for. The blood to close the gap between the very best that isn't wolfblood and wolfblood itself. You should've seen the rush to buy. We've been hearing more rumors in the hours since, of Midways and Lords alike investing small fortunes in it, hoping to capitalize on the first day of trading. And right now, the first reports are being received of how the blood has been received by its early buyers in the first tasting of it—reports written by us, of course—and that frenzy will continue. It's a fire burning through the city, burning in men's hearts, you can *feel* it, the infectiousness of it, threaded through everything, ready to take it all down, you can almost *taste*—" I stop. "I'm sorry, I'm . . . getting carried away. I just . . . can't believe it's working."

"No," says Vermillion, leaning forward suddenly, eyes fixed on me. "Do not apologize, Sam. Never apologize for that. You are doing something many have tried in centuries past. To change a city for the better. And you are doing it your own clever book-learned way. Embrace your vitality." He smiles so widely then I can't help but smile back as I grab the carafe of blood from the side table.

He raises one eyebrow. "But maybe embrace it by not drinking all my bloodstores at once."

"Oh . . . I'm sorry, I . . ."

"That was a jest, Sam. A jest. My gods, am I so dry . . . ?"

I shake my head while quickly pouring my second flute before he changes his mind. "Actually, for a Lord I think you can be mildly witty on occasion."

"Ah!" He laughs, leaning back again. "I will take that, I daresay I will take that half compliment." As quickly as it arrived, his joyful expression slinks away again. "But you might not want to compliment me when I tell you of how I have failed, Sam. Failed in the next part of the plan."

I say nothing to that, but my hand grips a little more tightly on my flute. The slow beat of wings is heard somewhere, rhythmic, ceaseless.

"I had the perfect person to go to," he continues "who would have had the influence to turn the entire guard, or most of it, at least, our way, if this plan of yours had worked and the city was vulnerable and distracted. I was . . . I was so confident he would listen. But though he did listen, and though I . . . I do not blame him, he refused. I cannot guarantee you your bloodless revolution. I am so sorry, Sam."

*Whoosh.* The wings fly lower, and if I listen hard, a broken thing starts to fall. But even as I listen, I see the pain in Vermillion's eyes, hear the desperate guilt in his voice.

"Do not apologize. I asked much more than what was possible." I put my flute down. "Do not apologize, Vermillion."

He looks down, at his frayed shirt ends and his dirt-covered hands, and he smiles a little. "I do not deserve that, but thank you, Sam."

"It was hard, wasn't it?"

"What was?" he asks, head still down.

"The conversation. With this . . . person. It took a lot out of you."

His reply is a half whisper. "You have no idea . . ." A little louder. "But it healed as much as it scoured me." He looks up then, eyes a little brighter. "But you know, Sam, just because one figure won't be pulling their strings in our favor, it does not by any stretch mean that things cannot change by themselves. Once the guard and the Worns all see the revolution beginning proper, with the wolfblood stores robbed, and once they see the eruptions throughout the city . . . I think you'll be surprised at how quickly the careful illusion the Lords have cast over the city falls apart. What happens when fear gives way to hope and possibility."

I hesitate, my old malice against him slipping from its prison. "Really, is that what you told yourself when you ruled? Or did you spin a grimmer story?"

A smile creeps across his face, more like the expressions when we were first sparring in here, and I am glad, because although apologizing and encouraging is, maybe, part of him now, it isn't all of him, and if I'm getting close to someone I want their wholeness. I don't want to force them into something new.

"Yes, you're right. I was much more skeptical of such things. But then I saw the lies the city is built on, gossamer thin, and now I see how quickly what I helped build can fall apart. . . ."

He pauses, seemingly unsatisfied with his own answer, then continues. "And you must remember, Sam, that you only knew me when

I ruled this city. But I ruled Lightfall, too, at least for the vampires. The Lords had less purchase there; the lines were fluid. That is why Molly and her smugglers and rebels made such progress. Why, I suppose, Saxe and his kind justified the awful choices they made to end that city. It was only in the shadow of Grayfall that I told myself that we must be firmer, and that there was no accommodation to be made anymore, tight rule for the safety of the city. I still did not consider myself cruel, and I never exercised cruelty myself, but I let Saxe and my son and all those have their run of it, and turned my eyes away from them, and spun my bedside tale to myself that it was this or calamity for the city. Ultimately, I was afraid. One proper conversation with my son could have robbed me of that fear, I see that now. It is something I will have to regret for the rest of my days."

"But it wouldn't have. You were too stubborn. Stuck in your ways. With the Grays around, you would never have shifted. I've read enough of leaders in my books to know that. Only in your son's death did you come alive. He had to die for you to see."

I worry then I've gone too far, been too honest. I mean the words to help, but so rarely does the balm actually do the healing.

He nods though, and smiles, and my chest loosens. "Sharp as ever, Sam."

My next words come easy to me. "It doesn't matter if your plan failed. To recruit your . . . person. I will still honor my side of the deal. About the Lords . . . *your* Lords, the few who understand, playing a role in the new city, if by a miracle we get to that point. They should have the opportunity to show . . . how is it your son put it? Their 'true soul.' We will need their wisdom."

"Sam," he says, successive words failing him.

"Not that it will be easy to get this past Hands and Molly, so thank you for that challenge I have coming my way. It would be easier to get a suntan I'm sure, but I got this far, didn't I?"

He grins. "You did." Then he raises his glass to me. "I will not let you down." For a moment, the role reversal, the power shift is so stark it stuns me, roots me to the spot, throws me out of time itself, and leaves me unmoored. Then the spell is broken by Vermillion looking down at his glass, then at mine. "One more?"

I automatically go to say yes, but then I remember what night it is and that I can't just sit around drinking noble blood, as much as, still to my surprise, I really want to. For a dangerous moment, I wonder at the true reason. Underneath his scraggle he is still handsome, in an austere, keep-the-poor-down kind of way. But no, there is none of that flame in me. None of what flickered for Sage. It's something else. A sense of what I haven't had for a while. Not just a friend. Though he looks the same as me, timeless due to his blood, he is much, much older, and so it's maybe no surprise I feel . . .

The flicker of my father, my dead father, comes through my mind, hugging me, keeping me safe, and guilt lances though me like a boil.

"I should go," I say quickly, standing up. "Lots still to prepare. And tomorrow night is when the true reports come in. The rebels will be waiting for the signs of chaos. The Flight Guard leaving the guard forts. Everyone distracted. The chance to rob the wolfblood stores." I breathe out. "The biggest night of my life, I suppose."

Vermillion Azzuri smiles and raises his flute to me as I leave. "The moment of truth. I have every faith in you, Sam."

I want to believe him, but oh, the ceaseless sound of wings.

## Azzuri

After Sam has left, Redgrave comes sidling in, from wherever he has been listening from this time. I wonder if she would be offended if she knew he heard everything. I do not think so. I think she would expect it. She seems to get sharper by the night, that one. It is wonderful to watch.

"She's right," Redgrave begins, taking Sam's chair again.

"Which part? She seems to be right about everything. To think she was cleaning my carpets for a decade when she should have been administering to my city."

"I'm right here, you know," he says, barely disguising his smirk. Now his moustache has gone it is much easier for me to notice how almost everything he says is accompanied by his deadpan half grin.

"Well . . . ah, obviously you would have done things together. The perfect team. The—Blood Gods, what the bloody hell am I talking about, Redgrave? I am so tired!" I chuckle to myself and put my bloodflute down. "Maybe enough of that."

"Yes, I notice you didn't tell her that yours had wine in it."

"She probably guessed from the fact there were two carafes. She's very . . ."

"Yes, yes, I know." Redgrave breathes out theatrically. "She's very sharp."

"I am becoming a bit tiresome, aren't I?"

"Becoming?" says Redgrave, pouring bloodwine, and this time carefully disguising his expression. "But no, actually I . . . I am enjoying watching you grow . . . close with her. I did not expect it, truth be told, I thought the hate would be hard to overcome. It is refreshing. If I can be frank for a moment . . ."

"For a moment?" I reply quickly, getting my own sparring in despite my fatigue.

"Touché." He grins. "But seriously, it was hard to watch you all these decades drift off from your actual family."

I go to say that he is my family, too, not by blood but undoubtedly so, but I hesitate. He would take it as awkwardly as I would, I suppose. Plenty of time for that.

"Your wife you grew cold with, or she grew cold with you," he continues. "Rufous . . . have you ever been warm with him? Then there is your daughter, not that her turn to the cruel was your fault. Watching you with Sam was the first enthusiasm I have seen in you in at least a century."

"Suns, Redgrave, there is frank and there is—"

"If this goes wrong, we may all be dead tomorrow. You'll have to forgive my tongue."

I shrug. "Fair point. You are forgiven. But you have also fallen into a trap of your own making. If we may be dead tomorrow, and if this is the time for frankness, then I want to hear your story. The truth of it, not these hints. Who you were. Why you came to the rebels, and then to my side, in such a convincing deception. Out with it, man." I point a wagging finger at him. "No excuses this time."

To my genuine surprise, he shrugs and stretches out on his chair, then nods. "Very well. Why not? If I grow boring, please tell me."

"A few fine witty replies to that crossed my mind."

"I'd expect nothing less." Then he drains his flute, and nods at the side table. "But I want a drink first, and from *your* carafe please."

Bloodwine supplied, he starts to speak.

"I was born in Dawn Death in 310—"

I almost interrupt him immediately, I am so shocked. I do not know why. Lots of people lived in Dawn Death, the second-biggest city of the Centerlands after Lightfall. Sitting just above the southern Swamplands, it was home to people who liked their freedom; it had the most mages of any Centerlands city, and they lived in cautious harmony, interrupted by the occasional bloody battle with the vampires there. It was an anarchic place, a place of chaos and much invention and strange events as a consequence. But I suppose I just struggle to see careful, restrained, planning Redgrave living in this raucous bloodstain of a city, the unpredictability of which sometimes spread to my own city of Lightfall, forcing me to confront it.

"—and I soon learned the consequences of poor governance and even poorer uprisings," Redgrave continues, immediately answering my premature imagination. "The vampire Lords who ruled there ruled capriciously, to say the least, hoarding blood for themselves, much more so than Lightfall. They warred among themselves, too, not to mention the various sorcerer cults in the city. As a result, when I was but thirty years old, there was an uprising by the large population of Worns there and Midways, although Midways had little access to the best blood, so they were more like Worns, I suppose. These rebellions were poorly planned, the rebels addled by the earliest attempts at magicking blood."

"There were Kinet bloodmages as early as the 300s?" I ask, incredulous. Blood magick had only become known in the late 400s, I had assumed, only a couple of decades before Grayfall, and by Lightfall mages.

"Indeed. But dangerous and ill-advised. It made those who took it more aggressive than normal. Between that and the inherently chaotic nature of the rebels, the uprising was vicious and bloody. Both sides hired sorcerer cults, so the resultant civil war literally leveled Dawn Death. It was the neutral sorcerer cults who intervened and brokered a tentative peace, not being enamored with living in a city of dust. But by that point I was not enamored with living in the city at all, so I moved to Lightfall."

I notice he hasn't mentioned his family, but I decide not to press him for now.

"In Lightfall, I . . . applied myself. I found a city of relative order compared to Dawn Death and, appalled by the behavior of the Lords in my birthplace, I found more to like in Lightfall. . . ." He stops then, looking at me cautiously.

"I am not offended, Redgrave, carry on," I begin. "Hold on . . . were you talking about me?"

"I meant in a more . . . general sense. Not individuals."

"Ah. Good."

"However, if I was to specify individuals, I'm afraid . . ."

I put my hand out. "No, generalize is good, thank you."

He does another bad job at suppressing a smile, and carries on. "However, at least it was more orderly and less cruel. And the rebels, when I found them, were orderly and more careful, too. They weren't anywhere near as organized or powerful as they would be a few decades later in the 400s, after the war, and all the changes they would bring about to modernize the city. But I saw the potential. To my surprise, they also saw the potential in me . . . but not to work with them. To work *for* them. Be their eyes among the Lords themselves."

I nodded. "Well, they were right. You fooled me for gods know how long."

"Two hundred and one years," he interjects quickly. "That's how long we've known each other. Since 399."

I raise an eyebrow. "You remember it that well?"

He smiles. "Vermillion, how could I forget? My life changed the day I met you. I finally had purpose."

"The purpose to turn me to the rebels." I nod, half smiling, half, I suppose, a little grumpy. He is right, but that still does not change the fact he deceived me all those years.

"You make it sound like I was using you," says Redgrave, attentive to my subtle mood change, as ever. "And, in a way, I was. But really, Vermillion, I was trying to change you. I never saw you as a tool. I saw you as someone who could rule a city, and one day change it. If you do not believe that, you never knew me at all."

"Do I know you?" I ask, genuinely unsure what the correct answer is.

Redgrave looks down at his bloodwine, which I notice he has drunk even quicker than me. For maybe the first time ever, I see what I might call sadness on his face, if I had any other sorrowful expressions of his to compare it to. "If you don't know, then I'm not sure anyone ever has. You have been in my life for so long. I have not maintained many connections with people." He looks up then and quickly wipes the morbid expression away.

I feel immediately, desperately guilty. "Redgrave, I—"

He laughs. "It is fine. You see why I was reluctant to tell you my past. One slip of the tongue and we lapse into maudlin drama."

I sigh, still wanting to make amends for my unthinkingly cruel words but realizing the moment has passed. "I fear that, Redgrave, is the story of my life. At least recently . . . But wait a moment. You have skipped over so much. I want to hear it all, Redgrave. What of your family? That is what I want to know. I know how you came across me. I may not have recalled the year, but I remember the moment. That bloody boring testimonial dineblood for the Midway who ran the Blood Market in the Southern Quarter, do you remember? You were introduced to me, and I, still getting used to my father's new demands to introduce myself more to high society, was out of my comfort zone, so you immediately warned me who was the dullest of the Midway tradesmen there and whom to avoid in conversation."

Redgrave smiles. "That was not hard, to be fair, Vermillion. All I had to do was point to everyone in the room."

"Ha! Indeed. But seriously, your knowledge was astounding. And it always has been. You know of everything and everyone. But I am getting distracted again, damn you. To my point: What of your family?"

Redgrave sighs and puts his empty flute on the table, carefully dabbing some blood on his top lip away with a small square cloth he procures from his jacket pocket. "That is for another time, Vermillion. There is only so much of the past anyone should share. Besides, it would not be as revealing as you hope. Honestly, much of it is in shadow now. It's funny, is it not, how your past, when you start to near three centuries like us, becomes another land. One that begins to seem so distant that you cannot be sure you ever lived it, or even if you had, whether you can stomach the remembrance of it."

I reflect on that a little. I am not sure I feel the same, but my life, until recently, has been an unbroken line of family, and duty, and clarity. But I see in his eyes that the past has separated from his present, and I wonder how a man living a double life who has so cleaved himself from his origins can ever hope to seek peace the more the centuries roll by.

"I am not sure, Redgrave, that this much bloodwine drunk is meant to make us this maudlin."

Redgrave grins. "Then let us put my past aside and talk of tomorrow, and the rebellion, and the future, and maybe getting a bigger place that has more than one room to sit in." He glances at the empty carafe meaningfully.

"Redgrave, my oldest friend," I reply, lifting my mildly intoxicated self off the chair to search for some more wine, "now I believe you are talking sense."

13

# Revolution, Part One: Born This Way

What, my love, of this talk of a smugglers' confederacy? And all that will come after that? They say the next thing is that the Worns will take the city proper. That Lightfall will become a Worn paradise. But to this I say fa! Fey! Ho dinkum! It shall never be.

For Worns, my darling, will always fall to their base instincts. They have no patience, as they know that they age, and so they must rush to get things done.

They have no discipline, for they have never been asked to shoulder any great responsibility.

And they have no love for each other, for if you offer them the chance for good blood, they would surely rip each other apart just as they seek to do to their betters.

So let us end this talk! We Skyes are not afraid—let no Lord be so either!

Marina Skye, in a letter to her husband, dated 485 AL

## Sam

From the top of Fourth Gods, the biggest prayhall in Worntown, which lies on the eastern edge of Southwestfall, you can see fairly far. Not as far as from the top of First Gods, of course, the biggest prayhall in First Light and the place where I learned what it was to have half a wolf in me a mere month and change ago. But it's still the best place to stand if you want to see all the way to the main guard fort in Southfall.

The key point to know about Southfall is that there's not much in it. Just the Blood Road, stretching from the city gates north all the way to Centerfall. I know from various history volumes that this is on purpose. When First Light was built the vampires got a little tired of the damage caused by various city breaches by wolves and mages, back in the bad old days when battles seemed almost a daily occurrence, before the big cities were built and temporary peace reigned, at least until the Twin War. So they emptied Southfall of everything except room to fight and, crucially for us, the city's main Blood Guard fort.

The fort sits halfway between the city walls and Centerfall, just off the Blood Road itself. It consists of four piles of three-story buildings arranged around a central courtyard and parade area. On the northwest corner and southeast corner two tall outlook towers stretch up high.

I know, thanks to Leeches, that on the southern end of the courtyard are stairs. I know that those stairs go down to a series of thick doors, each with a guard posting and each with progressively more potent bloodstores behind them. Behind the final door, six inches of bronzed iron, is the biggest store of wolfblood in the city.

It's a store that the rebels are going to rob.

But first, my plan has to work.

I turn to Hands Parker on my right, who is squinting at the faint outline of the Guard fort half a mile away. As usual, her face is devoid of any kind of expression you'd expect to see on a normal face. I realize that if still she wanted to kill me, she could just push me off the parapet. Maybe it's only the presence of Molly Threetimes on my left stopping her.

"So run me through it again, Sam," says Molly, "and then let's get some bloody blood up here. If it was any colder I'd have icicles for tits."

I pause as I consider that image. "Well, right about now the real reports of our blood will be hitting the market, and, if Azzuri's and Daphnée's people on the inside are correct, then the biggest one-day Invisibles buy in history will vanish up in smoke once everyone discovers that the blood is not, in fact, the Blood Gods' gift to vampire kind, almost as powerful as wolfblood, but in fact a very ordinary and not particularly potent Midway blood."

"And then chaos."

"Yes," I say, trying to project some confident into my voice. "And then chaos." I decline to say what that chaos will consist of, because I don't know, and no one knows. But it doesn't need to be one thing or another. It just has to be enough to draw away as many of the guardsmen as possible from the fort to tackle whatever disturbances are caused in the city when a fair few Lords and, more importantly, a good chunk of Midways who can't afford it realize they've lost everything.

Crucially, it has to be enough to distract the twenty-strong Flight

Guard, the unit of the Blood Guard allowed to take wolfblood and fly. Once they are far enough from the fort, then all wagers are off.

"Hands, do you have everything ready?" asks Molly.

"I do." She sniffs.

Molly turns to her, a patient look on her face. "Could you elaborate on that, Hands, dear? Good to know we're all on the same page."

Hands shrugs and clears her throat. "Once we see the Flight Guard fly off and a good number of the guardsmen leave, then me and my Vials and your rebels will ride on over there, quick as you like, and sort out the guard still there, and get some of us that wolfblood."

"Sorry, ride?" I ask.

Hands stares at me. "Yes, ride. Horses. The less time it takes the better. We don't want the remaining guards to have more than a twelfth of the hourglass to prepare for us. Even on the best magicked noble blood reserves we have, we can't be quicker than a galloping horse. Maybe the same speed if we really try. But we want to have enough energy left to fight the guards."

This is the most I've ever seen Hands speak, I think. She's clearly in her element here.

Molly interjects. "And there's no way we can sneak up on them?"

Hands shakes her head. "They put the fort there for a reason. Nothing around it, a mile in each direction. So horses it is. Is that fine with you, Sam?" asks Hands, in a tone that tells me just how serious she considers my approval.

I'm not sure why it wouldn't be, since I'm not going, I think, but I just say, "Yes."

"Oh and speaking of fighting the guards, Hands," says Molly, "we're knocking them out only, yes, dear?"

A long silence. "Yes," replies Hands. "Unless they make it hard on thems—"

"*Hands.*"

A longer silence. "Whatever you want, Molly. Whatever you want."

"I do want, dear. And it is appreciated. Well, now we just wait."

"Yes." I sigh. "Now we wait."

Now we wait for my plan to succeed or fail. There will be violence on the guards at the fort. I can't stop that. But no deaths. What happens next, though? When the rebels have the wolfblood and have equal power to the Lords and the Blood Guard? Because that can go two ways. Maybe, despite the failure of Azzuri's attempts to secure his man on the inside, the guards will fall in line with the rebels. Maybe most of the Midways will, too, and maybe even a few Lords who see the bloodmarks on the wall. Maybe the bloodless revolution can still happen.

Or maybe it will be hard-fought chaos and death, and guts and fire, and broken things and families split, and a city's worth of blood will be spilled in my name, just like . . . I stop, not wanting the wingbeats to come. Not now. I need a clear head. I need a clear heart. I need to hope for the best.

"You know, Sam," says Molly, wrapping the red shawl she's wearing tight around her and rubbing her hands together. "I remember when I was your age. Best part of two centuries ago now. After the Twin War. I was young, and I was ambitious. And I hatched one heck of a plan."

"I know," I reply. "The Worn uprising."

"Ha! I should have known you'd know your history. You know how it went then."

I don't want to say it failed. "It . . . left a mark."

She grins from ear to ear. "You're polite, Sam, and I like that about you. Could do with a bit more manners around my way. But we didn't take over Lightfall like we wanted. And a lot of us got killed."

"I hope there's a *but* coming, Molly," I say, suppressing a smile.

She gives me a devilish side-eye. "You better believe it, girl. About three decades later, I led the Smugglers' Confederacy. And without hardly any violence, but a lot of cunning, we met with the Lords and we made a bargain, better blood at better prices for all, and until Grayfall it stuck, and the city started to change. But my point is that we couldn't have done it without the sense the city had from that failed uprising that there was somethin' in the air. Without the confidence that gave the Worns, even in our failure."

I frown. "Are you saying it's no matter if this doesn't work?"

"No," Molly says, carefully. "I ain't saying that, Sam. Bad things happen if this doesn't work. I won't blow smoke up you, dear. But whatever happens, the efforts you've gone to, my bloody marvelous clever dash of a thing, they will have changed the city, and the city remembers." She breathes out and rubs her hands together. "The arc of history is long, my dear. Remember that. Now let's get some flasks of something up here before I jump off the parapet just to get warm."

Three bells comes and goes and nothing much stirs from the guardhouse gates that we can see. That's three turns of the hourglass since nightfall, with a distinct lack of signs of chaos. Some guards come in, some go out. No large detachments. No sign of the Flight Guard being called to use their precious stores of wolfblood.

I begin to get concerned.

A little while later, a rebel comes running up to the roof where we're watching, various blood drinks now firmly in our hands (in Molly's case she holds a tankard while another backup mug waits for her on the floor beside her). She's a short, athletic-looking Worn, her ragged blond hair sticking out in tufts from a cap that doesn't fit. Jane Brown, if I remember.

"A bit of noise from the markets," she begins. "Honegull just came in here from one of our own that way. Bit of a scuffle near the Invisibles. Not sure what it's about. Few of the Guard intervened. Nothing major yet, sounds like."

Molly nods. "Thanks, Jane." She turns to me and Hands. "Could be something. Could be nothing."

A little while later another one comes running onto the roof, holding a small bit of parchment in her hands. A man this time, ginger-haired, lanky, two big front teeth, bit of excitement to him.

"Best read this, Molly," he says, handing it over.

Molly gives it a quick glance, peering at it in the gloom. "By the suns, I should've put some hawk in my ale, not ocelot. Writing's blooddamn tiny." She gives it to me. "Sam, you're always on the noble bloods, you Leeches. What does it say?"

She's right. My night vision is perfect, thanks to the vials of hawk I have on me. Daphnée made sure I was supplied. I'm not sure I could have lasted on this roof without it. She offered fox, but as much as I'm impressed by that kind, this is a time for the old classics, and the edginess of hawk it was.

"There's . . . It's strange. It says there's a commotion up in Northeastfall."

"Northeastfall?" Hands looks over, her comatose waiting state suddenly enlivened. "Fucking Lord territory?"

"Yes, outside . . ." I gasp. "Outside Lord Sapphiri's mansion. Some Midways traders. Complaining outside his house. A hundred of them, it says."

"Hmm," says Molly, "I wish whichever Leech of yours wrote that had been a little more clear. Complainin' could mean a lot of things. Still, it's interesting."

It's more than interesting. Lord Sapphiri is the Lord of the Blood Markets. He's on the First Council. Probably the third most powerful Lord after Rufous and the Lord of War. To go to his actual house . . .

They must be raging.

And then I hear something joyous.

"Wings!" cries Hands, who has resumed her lookout as Molly and I puzzle over the message. "All of them."

I drop the message on the roof in my haste and rush to the parapet, squinting with my hawkblood eyes at the Guard fort half a mile ahead of us.

And I see a wonderful sight. All twenty of the Flight Guard, wolfblood surging through their veins, the strength of a thousand vampires in their cohort, beating their great wings in the cloudless moonlit sky, heading east from the fort. Great leathery, veined wings, carrying them fast away from us and away from the fort.

For a moment I recall another set of wings, and a chill grabs at my spine.

But then I shake it off, and I see dozens, perhaps hundreds, of guardsmen pouring out of the fort gates. It's hard to tell how many, as the gates themselves are shielded by some trees immediately outside and the path it takes the guardsmen leads them round the corner of the fort east and then straight out of sight.

But it must surely be most of them, leaving a skeleton detachment at the fort itself.

I hear Molly whistle, eyes worse but able to see enough, and I hear Hands dryly chuckle to herself.

"I didn't know you could laugh," I say, without thinking.

She turns to me, abruptly quiet. "There's a lot of things you don't know about me, Sam."

I let that die in the air, and I turn as more runners arrive on the roof.

"More honegulls from Northeastfall," babbles the blond girl quickly, out of breath, the same one as before, cap now gone, hair sticking up everywhere. "There's . . . a proper riot outside of Sapphiri's now. The Midways have gone mad. Not just his, too. The Lord who chairs the Invisibles Council. His mansion, too." She takes a beat to get some breath into her. "And honegulls from Eastfall. The Midway townhouses. The ones belonging to those on the Invisibles Council. And even the Blood Bank. Other Midways. Traders, businessmen even. All rioting."

Molly turns to me and grins. "Fuckin' hell, dear." She shakes her head, searching for the words. "Fuckin' hell."

I grin, not even trying to hide my triumph. "I told you, Molly. Animal spirits."

Two streets behind Fourth Gods, in a vast outbuilding owned by the rebels, a hundred horses await us, having been walked over from all round the rebels' various haunts in Southwestfall two glasses before. Hands's horse appears to be a proper thoroughbred, distinct from the others. I don't ask her why because there isn't time, but I have a moment to inspect its shiny midnight-black coat, its large, expressive eyes, its long, sloping shoulders, its fine-boned legs with small hooves—

"Sam, are you going to stare at that fucking horse all day or are you going to climb on her back?"

Hands stares at me, a flash of impatience on her dead face.

"What's her name?" I ask.

"Hooves," she replies, not even giving me a hint of any deadpan.

"Hello, Hooves," I say to her kind face. "Please don't throw me off."

Hooves does not throw me off. We speed out from under the long shadow of Fourth Gods, out from Worntown to the vast expanse of Southfall and the Blood Road. Behind us are two hundred more, a mixture of Vials and rebels, all galloping as fast as their mounts can go against the chill night wind that whips fierce against us in the vast openness of this part of the city. It's an astounding sight.

As I cling on for dear life, I can just about hear Hands muttering to her steed, whether words of calm or encouragement I don't know. As for me, I'm not ashamed to say I close my eyes; there's something infinitely more terrifying about flying across the open road on the back of a horse built for racing than there is flying myself through the night sky, steering the currents on great leather wings. I can't explain it, even to myself.

But it's only half a mile, so the ride is over barely before it started, but as we go to slow down, the fort looming ahead of us, I see the guard in the westward tower cry out. On my hawkblood eyes his red tabard is clear against the night, as is his pale, pink face. There's no disguising what we are, and we knew the alarm would be raised quickly. To my surprise, the guard is quick to raise a crossbow resting next to him, aiming it at somewhere in the masses of riders. But, barely slowing down, Hands reaches one hand into her tightly wrapped tunic and retrieves a small throwing dagger, and with just a quick pause to think on her flight path, she throws it up what must be eighty feet, and it sticks into the guard's torso.

"Bloods!" I shriek.

It's not enough to hurt him much at that height, but he drops the crossbow, and by then we're at the gates.

We both jump off Hooves, the riders arriving behind us. The gates are wrought iron, huge and strong, twenty feet high. Built to withstand vampires on everything but wolfblood. Beyond, some guards have assembled. But not many. Fifty at most. I was right. The main companies have left for the east of the city. This will be an easy and bloodless fight. Euphoria surges through me.

And then Hands reaches into one of Hooves's saddlebags and takes out a cork-stoppered carafe. She gives it to me. "This," she says, "is all the wolfblood we have in the Vials or the rebels. All of it."

I look at the carafe dimly. "Oh, I see. You're going to drink it and break the gates open."

"No," says Hands, cocking her head at me, eyes vacant but with the first sign of passion in the night in her voice. "We are. Half each. We need two to break the gates, I reckon."

"No," I say, panicking, "no . . . I . . . I don't want to be on wolfblood again, thank you."

She shoves the carafe at me. "Not a choice. You can handle it. You had half a wolf in you last time. Now unless you want those guards beyond the gate to have the time to get a few crossbows and start taking potshots at us, please fucking drink it up or I will actually kill you this time, and there's no fucking Last Lighter to save you now."

I squeeze my eyes shut and try to drown out the beat. The beat of wings. Then I open them. "Fine. But tell me what made you into this." I wave my hand up and down to indicate all of her.

"What? What the fuck are you taking about."

"What made you into this?" I repeat. "Did they kill your family, the Lords? Did you lose them all in Grayfall? Were you tortured? What did they do?" It's not a fair question, even for the terrifying Hands.

And then, for the first time since I've known her, I see a genuine smile flit across her face. "They've never done anything to me. I just hate them all on my own. And I was born this way."

And then, not knowing what to do with that, I breathe out and then down half the carafe and shove it back to Hands.

*Hello, Sam.*

I didn't expect the voice of the wolfblood—which is my voice, I know that—to hit me so soon.

*Ride it out.*

And as the blood surges through me, hot currents lighting me from the inside, I feel my mind expand and my skin harden.

It's not as much as I had before. It's not half a wolf. Which is why I'm not contemplating the point of my entire life, perhaps, like I was on the roof of First Gods with Grays all around me. Or maybe I'm used to it. But as all the tiny hairs on my body stand on end and my eyes blaze and my breath gets light as my lungs expand, and wings start to form on my back, I laugh, knowing that I missed this feeling and knowing that this won't end well for anyone who tries to stop me.

I turn to Hands, whose skin is glowing—is that what I look like?—and whose long, lank hair seems to be radiating soft bioluminescence. Her fangs have lengthened into long needles, longer than mine, and her nails are thin talons. She looks as terrifying as I feel holy.

"Now," she says, her voice having gained some extra layers of bass and alto.

I nod, and we turn to the gates, all the rebels now off their horses and gathered behind us. I wonder how long it will take us to break the gates, and instantly I calculate it.

Not long, essentially.

We run into them, shoulders raised, and the great clang of hardened wolfblood skin and the strength of fifty vampires in each of us almost shatters them on first blush. Next time we do a run-up, which is unnecessary, but we are both enjoying it, embracing the initial rush, the initial promise that *time is yours and time is nothing, you can be anything and you can do anything, as long as you remember what time is.*

*Not now, Wolfblood me*, I think, as we collide with the gates a second time and they simply snap off their hinges inward, the guards within scattering. One has had the foresight to fire a crossbow, but the bolt clatters harmlessly off my skin. What few guards seem to be there dissipate, and the way is clear.

Hands turns to the rebels. "Wolfblood stores. Now!"

I smile, but my wolfblood nose tells me something is wrong before we hear it. I smell pine from within. Too much pine. Godsdammit, what is pine? What do the wolfkind smell as that again?

*Ah.* Excitement.

And then the guards that were hiding from sight round the corner, all five hundred of them, give or take, emerge from the side, arranged in infantry columns ten deep, with a line of crossbows, surely a hundred or more, at the front.

I hear the gasps of the rebels behind me, but from Hands's ethereal face I can tell her wolfblood mind has instantly told her what's happened the same as mine. It is pretty simple, after all.

The guards didn't really leave. They came out the southern gates and went back in the northern ones, out of sight.

They baited us.

And even with two of us on wolfblood, two hundred rebels against five hundred trained guard on magicked noble blood—and I know they will have had time to down that—are not enough. Not when they have those crossbows.

The wolfblood knows we've lost.

As I digest this, and I see Hands's contorted face try to accept it, one guard walks out in front of the first column. The four blood droplets stitched onto his epaulet tell me he's a commander. He has short brown hair, and a lean, muscle-jawed, and clean-shaven face, and last but not least, a look of vast superiority.

"Commander Cyani," he says, "at your service." Well, look at that, a noble in the infantry guard. "You are clearly outnumbered. If you surrender now, you will be spared sunburst."

"How?" I ask, my voice twice as loud as his and the strange, layered timbre of it so strange that the first column of guardsmen recoil briefly in shock. They obviously don't hear the Flight Guard much when they down wolfblood.

He raises his eyebrow. "How? Standard protocol, darling. You really think the fort would be left barely manned at any time, when it contains enough wolfblood to bring the city down? No, in the event of . . . disturbances across the city, the new rule—and you can thank the new spymaster Cabalti for that—is that we make sure there's enough here, in case it's all part of a plan. And, look at that." He gestures triumphantly to all of us. "It was."

*He will die soon, in a future war*, the wolfblood tells me, and I never know if that's the strange hallucinatory properties of it talking or, maybe, it just sees time a different way.

*Focus, Sam.*

"Besides," he says, "I'm sure the Flight Guard are more than capable of dealing with a few annoyed Midways. There may be only twenty of them, but just one could take on fifty without breaking a sweat."

I sense a little lemon on the air as he says that, which I know for wolves is fear, and I realize that some of the guard have heard that it's a lot more than just a few annoyed Midways. And I wonder if they've overplayed their hand with these numbers when the rest of the city is in increasing uproar.

Not that it helps us.

"So what's it to be, ladies?" says the commander. "Death, or surrender?"

Surrender, of course, will mean death. I don't need the wolfblood to know that.

I look at Hands, and she looks back, and the knowledge there is nothing we can do but die hangs heavy in the wolfblood air.

## Daphnée

While Sam and Molly and Hands and the Vials and the rebels and all those remarkable women, and some men, I suppose, get ready to change this place forever half a city away, I am standing in a Westfall attic with my love, whom I have not spoken to for two days since our awkward and painful encounter in this very room.

I have thought on what to say to her a great deal, even as we planned to change the city. I have thought on how to ameliorate her pain, how to address her fear that having feelings for me would threaten everything she has become since Last Light fell, everything I suspect she had to become during Last Light. This hard thing, this tough thing, this possibly half-insane thing, but, as I tried to tell her, in the most beautiful way—I want to make her see that it is not a binary choice. That she can thaw the shell around her a little and still be her terrifying unknowable self. That she can have her sweetblood and eat it.

But I do not know how.

So I stand politely as Alanna makes some preparations. Soon she will carry out her mission against the First Guard, that trained company of twenty or so Lord vampires commanded by none other than First Lord Rufous Azzuri himself, that twisted little boy in adult's clothing. Their predecessors died in a hail of mortal bullets from whatever the sorcerer Sage had become, after being thoroughly contested by Sam and Raven Ansbach. Now they will face a reckoning.

Whether or not Sam's plan succeeds or fails, one thing is for sure. The new First Guard, barely trained, will go the way of the old one today. And if Alanna and I do not make it, then that is the way of it.

*No.* I sigh. Not Alanna and me. I know what I must do.

"Alanna," I begin. Alanna has her back to me, crouched down, tapping the floor.

"Alanna," I try again. On second blush, she turns, guarded, but doesn't get up. With her pointy, thin face, angled but gorgeous, and her tied-back ponytail, and her suspicious, sharp small eyes and thin smile ever eager to curl up at the corners, she is capable of mesmerizing me even as she scrabbles around in the dust in a stained tunic.

"I . . . I know you don't want me here," I continue. "I desperately want to be by your side. But it is not fair." I breathe out quickly as the words leave me, surprised I managed them. "So I will leave you now, to be who you are. But Alanna, darling, my Alanna, if you do not survive this, then I will find your spirit whether in the Bloodhalls or elsewhere and oh, the sharp words I will certainly have . . ."

I have to break off then, because I have started to cry. How embarrassing. There is nothing bad with tears, but there is a time and a place, and what we are about to do for the city is so much more than anything just here in this room.

"I am a pitiable mess, Alanna. I will see you soon."

And I start to walk out, but at the doorway I hear a soft "No."

Desperately hoping it was not in my imagination, that I have not started hearing voices to go with my sadness, I whip around.

Alanna is off the floor—I never heard her get up; that's my Alanna—and a slight smile plays on her face. I dare to hope.

She moves toward me and stands before me. We have had so many moments like this. I suppose, in a way, they are how I have measured my life ever since my daughter's death. Things happen, and time happens all around me, but these times are when it all freezes and life *really* happens.

"My Daffers," she says, and forms a strange O with her lips, like a child considering something with clotted blood trapped in their mouth. I almost want to laugh.

"Yes?" I ask patiently, trying not to smile.

"You would leave me alone, would you, with the guilt you would have if I died, all in the name of respecting my wishes?"

I think on this. "Yes."

She nods. "I do not deserve you." Then she sighs. "I was a princess in Last Light. I was one of *the* princesses, I was. One of the princesses of the four noble families who founded that place. Everyone knew me . . . I was very innocent. Very obsessed with beauty. You, my Daffers, would have chuckled all nights and all days to have seen me."

I do not know what to say to this. I am completely and utterly stunned.

"Then," she continues, "some things happened, *all the things*. I'll not go into the peculiar and the curious details now. Maybe I'll have to very soon. But what I want to tell you now is that many of my family died, and I saw them die, and I was almost killed, too. And I learned, with a little help, I learned to be a very different Alanna. And I got my revenge, in ways even you, my strong, hard Daffers, would get all of the nauseas at thinking about. And then I discovered some more secrets of Last Light, and I changed even more, in all kinds of ways. And I was a spy for a while, and an assassin, too. And I killed many. And then Last Light fell, and most of the remaining people I cared about fell with it. And when I got on that last ship out of Last Light, the only ship there ever was, with the few who made it out, my transformation was complete, and I suppose my mind was a little gone, and I had become the Alanna you see before you. Not Alanna of Last Light—not really. Not the person who could love and be loved. Just Alanna."

She reaches out her hand then, and strokes my chin. "But if you can bear it, because it'll be strange, and if you can bear me, because I'm even stranger, then I will try and be both. It may not work, but it'll be fun, perhaps, and I promise I'll run before I ever hurt you in any way."

She breathes out then, flustered with that speech, and looks away.

I want to scream in delight, but I laugh instead. "Alanna," I say, "are you embarrassed?"

She looks back up at me then, a little red in those odd tanned cheeks. "Maybe, my Daffers. See, I'm changin' already. Will you still have me?"

"Oh, Alanna. My Alanna, my princess of Last Light. I've wanted you since the moment I first laid eyes on you, my wondrous, terrifying, beautiful thing."

And then I grab both her hands, her hot, glowing little hands, and I lean into that mouth, those lips that haunt my thoughts, and I close my eyes because if I keep them open I might ruin it by hardly believing it, and then . . .

*"OH, LADIES!"*

We both freeze.

"*OH, LADIES!*" cries the voice again. "Come out, come out, wherever you are! We won't hurt you, much. But we will definitely hurt you if you stay in there."

It's the high, confident, unstable singsong of Rufous Azzuri, and I can't suppress a shiver at it.

Alanna turns from my face—godsdammit, what a time—and races to the small triangular window that gives us a view from the attic to the main street a good ten levels below. I quickly join her, and I put my palm on her back. For my reassurance, assuredly not hers.

There, standing like he has just purchased the entire street, is Rufous Azzuri, arms outstretched in welcome. His long blond hair flows, his pearly white teeth shine as he grins, and his boyish, cherubic face conceals, as usual, the dark within that horror of a mind. He wears the red-and-gold doublet of the First Guard, which by now you would think would be too shameful to wear, given their failures so recently against Raven and Sage and Sam, but this is a man I suspect who does not understand the first thing about the contours of shame.

A few yards behind him are the rest of the First Guard, eighteen of them, at least. Like Rufous, they wear the red-and-gold tabards; like

Rufous, their furred, leathered, veined wings rest behind them, twitching every now and again.

I look left and right down the street. It is empty. I am on magicked fox, so I can see very well, and I see no curious faces in windows, either.

"There you are!" Rufous beams. "Come to see the commotion. I am afraid we have cleared out this area," he adds, seeing my furtive glances. "It is just us now! Privacy is very important, don't you agree?"

Alanna is stock-still behind me. I keep my hand on her glowing back.

"But," he continues, raising a finger, "speaking of privacy, I am afraid there has been a rather unfortunate breach. One of your lovely loyal Leeches." He pauses, chewing on the words. "Bit of a tongue twister, that! Lovely loyal Leeches . . ."

I narrow my eyes. Perhaps it is my imagination or my contempt, but he appears to be even less inhibited or sane than last we met.

"Anyway, one of your bunch of cunts got a little tired of the life of running round in the mud listening in on people prattling, so she came to us with a rather tantalizing proposition!"

He gives a big wide smile then, and pauses for effect.

Somewhere far off to the east, I see the wings of another vampire. Interesting. Events are happening elsewhere, perhaps.

I wonder if we will live to see them.

"Aren't you going to ask me what it was? No? Very well, then. But I must say this is turning into somewhat of a monologue. I thought you were meant to be the society wit, Lady Hocquard . . . oops, you're not a lady anymore! My mistake. It's so hard to keep up with you these days."

"Whether I'm a lady or a nothing, one thing is always consistent, Rufous. You are boring and you love the sound of your own voice, and I feel a little sorry for you. You are a child who never got to be an adult."

I feel Alanna quietly snort beside me.

Rufous's grin gets wider, but I see something break in his eyes.

"You're right, Hocquard," he says. "I have been stringing the moment out. So let me put it simply. One of your stupid bitches ratted you out for a better life, and here we are to fucking end you, you annoying whiny shits. Is that concise enough for you? Oh, but don't worry, I won't end you right now. I want you two lovers to have a final moment together. It will be facing each other as I torture the twin hells out of you, but still. It will technically be a moment."

I nod. Then, with my most polite noble smile and a flash of my own pearly whites, I say, "Very well. Come and fucking get us, you embarrassment of a man."

I turn to Alanna then as Rufous's First Guard take to the air toward us, and I smile. "This is it then, is it?"

Alanna nods. "Something for the road, perhaps, m'lady?" Her mischievous smile widens. "I jest. My Daffers. You're my Daffers now, ain't you?"

I grin wider. "Always and ever, Alanna of Last Light."

I move closer. Alanna stops me. "Not in front of the street, Daffers. Though I respect the peccadillo."

I laugh and pull her away from the window, to the far attic wall.

Alanna pulls something from her petticoat and drops it on the floor near to us.

And then, with one hand free and one hand around my neck, as wings reach the attic window and heat starts to bloom, she pulls her head toward mine and locks lips with me, and it's gentle at first and I fall into it, but then she pushes hard and I reply, and the taste of her is so sweet that nothing else really matters, now and evermore.

I feel her drop the lit match in her hand onto the trail of firepowder beside us. And then she pulls the lever hidden in the wall recess next to us, the one meant to drop us through the floor all the way to the tunnels dug out beneath the house, safely away from the explosion designed to be the end of Rufous and his First Guard.

Nothing happens. The lever fails.

I pull away from her kiss. "Alanna . . ."

Alanna shrugs. "It was always a risk, my Daffers. I regret nothing."

And then, before I can think on what to do next, she guides me back to her lips and I realize that I, too, regret not a bit of it.

A few beautiful moments later the entire street explodes and everything goes orange.

14

# Revolution, Part Two: It's Not Your Fault

> Sammy! If you reade this, then be sure to cum straight to the horses stabulls. I have a righte funny thing to show you! It will cheer you upp.
>
> Beth, a palace maidservant, in a note to Samantha Ingle, her best friend, circa 590 AL

## Sam

At the gates of the Guard fort, as throughout the city riots break out that will soon be mollified by the Flight Guard, Commander Cyani stands staring at us, patronizing us with his expression, his body language, even his scent, which is soft, earthy, grassy, complete calm. The aroma of a man who knows we are beat.

I turn to Hands, who is trembling a little, but not out of fear, I know that.

I sigh. If my plan is to fail like this, I'm not sure I deserve to live. I certainly don't want the guilt of seeing all the punishment to come on the Worns. The beat of the wings in my head and the far-off scream of a far-off friend would make my life seem like a living death anyway.

*She died because of you*, comes a faint wolfblood chant.

"I don't want to be captured," I say to Hands.

"Obviously I feel the same," she mutters. Then something occurs to her and she turns to me. "You got us all killed. But you're a fucking bold one. And I'm glad I didn't kill you."

I think on this. Even with the wolfblood in me, I know it to be a lie.

"No, you're not."

She barks out a laugh then. "Clever girl." Then she points at the commander. "At least let's kill him before the end."

"Yes," I say, letting the anger in me overtake my senses. "I think we can do that."

Then, as the crossbows on the front line are raised, and as the guards begin to sense our decision, Hands turns round to her people.

"Fuck the Lords," she says, her voice twice as loud and twice as deep as it has any right to be.

As final words it's not the most poetic, but it'll do. The rebels and Vials ready themselves on the fires of their blood, nails lengthening, teeth sharpening, blood pumping. They knew what the risk was. They are ready to bleed. At the front is the girl with the untidy short blond hair. I thought she would stay behind. I didn't realize she would fight.

I got her killed, and maybe that's what leaders do.

As I turn back to face the guards, suppressing all the distracting, hallucinatory whispers of the wolfblood—*You can't die if there is no future. You will survive in some form, you know this*—I think on how this ends, and how inevitable it was. A maid can't change a city with a plan and a wish. No matter how many books she's read. That's not how it works.

I think of Molly's words. About the arc of history. Will the city remember? Will First Light remember the stand we took? Will things change in some way at some point in some place?

Or was that cow shit and nothing will happen, and I'll just end up a few passages in another history tome read by some overambitious maid just before lightfall in a palace somewhere in a century's time?

Ah, well. No one can say I didn't try.

Hands and I scream then, at the same time, unified in our blood, and we start to run. And then, because our hearing is better than anyone else's, we stop.

Because the sound of hooves is coming our way, and coming fast.

Commander Cyani hears it now, and he shouts, "Incoming, ready!" Not that his men could be any more ready, but he had to do something.

I turn and look into the night, crystal clear on my wolfblood eyes. I could see a mile from here on my blood.

But I don't need to.

Because riding right toward us, mere moments away, is Commander Tenfold of the Scout Guard, and he rides with all his men.

My wolfblood mind makes five connections in a row, and I shout out to the rebels, who have turned to take on this new threat, "*HALT*."

They listen to me.

Tenfold comes to a stop just behind the rebels. He has the black tabard of the Scout Guard on, but over it is steel chest armor.

The Scout Guard are the only ones who wear armor, for they are the only ones who go out into Gray territory. The effect is awe-inspiring, and I see it on the faces of the guards in the fort.

Tenfold's face is granite, hewn straight from rock. His short orange hair blows slightly in the wind. His face is grim and solid. I know immediately he is Azzuri's one, the one he spoke to, the one he had hopes for.

Behind him, his men, all dressed the same, all looking as rough as the rocks of the Fang Tips, stare at our scene impassively.

"Well met, Commander Cyani!" shouts Tenfold, and, knowing what I must do, I bellow, "*CLEAR A PATH*," and beautifully they do, the rebels parting like the Northern Sea to let him through. On his dark-brown horse, a First Light thoroughbred more than the equal of Hands's mare, he slowly clops down the path I have made for him.

Hands stares at me. She knows.

Commander Cyani also stares, confused. His initial relief overcome by perplexity at why Tenfold has just so casually ridden through the rebels.

"Well met yourself, Tenfold," he says, and I hear the dismissiveness of the absence of Tenfold's title in those words, and I smell the brief flare of metal—anger—on Tenfold, quickly abated. "You have come in time to support us with these rebels! But are you not needed on the wall?"

Tenfold shakes his head, his jaw still tight. "No. My Wall Guard brothers are quite up to the task. We are the Scout Guard. And tonight, we are not scouting." Then, immediately dismissing the commander, he turns his head to the ranks of the guardsmen lined up behind him.

"All right, you lot. You all know me. I'm not a man given to long speeches. Those of you who served under me in the war know that. I see a few of you who I commanded in Lightfall, too. My old Southern District brothers."

I see a surprising number of faces in the guards nod at this. Tenfold, I am reminded, the wolfblood instantly bringing forth every mention of him I've ever read to my mind, is a living legend in armor.

"Well, I only have one thing to say to you now. The city is rebelling, and me and my boys are on their side"—he gestures to us and the rebels—"and not on the side of the ones who only see fit to give you the good blood when you're about to die otherwise." At this he points to Commander Cyani, whose face has turned from outrage immediately to shock and fear, the passage of steel to chalk to strong citrus on the nose almost comical in its speed.

"There's lies the Lords have told you about the Grays," Tenfold continues. "And they'll come out soon enough, I expect. But until that time, all you need to know is that the Midways are in uproar. The rebels are here and poised throughout the city. Me and my boys are ready to fight anyone, and my Wall Guard are with me, too. So if you want to fight brother on brother and friend on friend, then go right ahead. But I know you, lads, and I reckon you're ready for a better master."

There's a pause then. Nothing sounds in the night air save the shriek of some animal in some tree in some place.

"Well, that's it," says Tenfold. "That's all there bloody is. Let me know quick, lads, because even with the blood in me, I'm freezing my bollocks off out here."

I see the guards turn to one another. I see them think. I do not see them think hard. Because would you fight Tenfold? Or would you follow him?

Vermillion Azzuri, you beautiful bastard.

And then, one by one, the front line drops their crossbows.

Commander Cyani takes one look at this and, to his credit, does the only sensible thing in the circumstances. He turns and runs, back into the fort, across the courtyard, heading for the northern gate. I see Hands raise her dagger and squint her eye to aim, but I grab her arm.

"No." I go to say that we don't kill people running away, but I know that won't work on Hands, so instead I say, "Guards are Tenfold's prerogative now. Let him deal with them."

Incredibly, that works, though it comes with a hint of a glower, and she sheathes her blade.

As the guards start to lose their formation and mill around, unsure what comes next, and as Tenfold's men slowly ride into the fort itself, the commander trots up to me.

"Tenfold," he says curtly, nodding.

"Sam," I reply, nodding back.

"Yes, Azzuri told me all about you. Remarkable. Remind me never to get on your bloody bad side." Then he turns to Hands.

"Hands Parker," I say, introducing her. "Leader of the Vials."

Tenfold snorts. "Huh. Glad I've been on the wall and not in the city having to deal with you lot."

Hands's impassive face doesn't react. "You'll have to deal with us now."

Tenfold's lips twitch, maybe to smirk, but he doesn't reply to that.

"Why?" I ask him, before he can move on.

He considers this. "Azzuri."

I nod. "Vermillion's words really got to you."

"Oh no." He shakes his head and pulls out some tied-together parchment from his saddlebags. "Not the old man's. His son's. The dead one."

I must look a little confused, even on the wolfblood, as he adds, "He wrote about how a city should be." He shrugs. "And I liked it."

And then he rides on.

But as he passes into the fort courtyard, he turns back to me. "Oh, one more thing, Ingle. Heard the First Guard, that bastard Rufous and his boys, were heading to Westfall. Where you lot are based. Pretty quickly. Might want to check that out."

I turn to Hands. She shrugs. "Well, fucking go then."

And, panicking, the wolfblood in me deciding now to whisper predictions of doom, I concentrate and feel my wings sprout and expand from my back, skin stretching out into muscle and cartilage and fur and bone.

Then I leap into the air and head west, to the sound of my own wings.

I have Westfall in sight when it happens.

I've been flying well, the movements still in my memory. The last time—the first time—I had wings was after downing half of Raven Ansbach's blood on the roof of First Gods. My tenuous flight then took me, fairly successfully, from there to the dome of the palace. What happened next was less than successful, but about that part I have no complaints.

And now, it all comes back to me, but even better. I beat my wings when I need to, soar on the currents when I don't. The wolfblood makes all the calculations. A large part of me never wants to come down at all.

It's all very peaceful, in fact, and I even forget the claustrophobic panic of the original reason why I was flying: the sighting of Rufous and his First Guard heading toward Westfall.

But then the tall, rickety, chaotic pressed-together streets of Westfall heave into view, the larger townhouses to the east and the Sunway stagetale building to the left of that. But my area, the Leeches' house, is straight in front of me. I start to register the winged figures below.

And that's when the explosion happens.

A great ball of gas and fire rockets up into the air, and the house—no, half the street—I had my wolfblood eye on is immediately hidden in the blast. I'm still flying head-on when it happens, and the sound wave hits me, buffeting me in the air, and shortly after the heat of the blast itself overcomes me, almost scorching me, forcing me to land on the street below.

As I run toward the devastation, I'm enveloped in a great cloud of bitter smoke rolling eastward my way. I don't cough; my wolfblood lungs will filter this out and a thin protective film immediately covers my eyes so I can still see. A wolfblooded vampire is prepared for all occasions.

But for a few moments, as I finally reach the scene of the explosion, all I can do is stand and wait for some of the smoke to clear, so thick is it.

And when it does, I see the calamity that has been wrought.

Half the street is a crater. Small fires burn around the perimeter. In the middle of this crater is the scorched, visceral remains of the First Guard. It's hard to tell most of their corpses from any standard vampire, so blackened and scattered they are: an exposed torso here, a charred eyestalk there. But the burnt stubs of wings, like leathery pieces of meat a wolf might slaver over, give it away.

It comes to me then. Daphnée and Alanna's plan to destroy the First Guard and, more importantly, the new First Lord of First Light.

Not a plan they were ever likely to walk away from.

I drop to my knees. The wolfblood makes my shock and grief numb, and tries to empty it out completely. *You knew them, that was enough. There is no past, so you know them still. They were never really here.* But the sadness cuts through. I gasp.

Someone puts a hand on my shoulder. I spin round. It is Vermillion Azzuri. He squeezes it gently. The billowing dust clouds have rendered his black beard and wild stringy hair gray. An insight into what he would look like if he ever had to age.

"I heard my . . . son was flying over here with the First Guard," he says, and then glances mournfully around. "Daphnée?"

I shake my head. I cannot smell them. Daphnée's rose-lily perfume and Alanna's sandalwood aroma would be clear to me on this nose.

He doesn't say anything but squeezes my shoulder harder.

"I suppose my eldest son . . ." he says, his voice hardened.

I shake my head and indicate the body parts.

He nods. "Good." He contemplates this. "That is a terrible thing to think, isn't it?"

"You won't get any judgment from me," I reply.

I see Redgrave walk up behind him. He puts a hand on Vermillion's shoulder. Shoulders are really getting a good feel today.

Azzuri's head hangs low. "I have no sons now."

"The news is spreading like forest fire," replies Redgrave. "Tenfold has rallied the guard to our side, Vermillion. You helped change the city. You have no sons but you may still have a legacy to be proud of, you hear me?"

I see Azzuri turn to Redgrave, and smile, and begin to say something.

And then I see, through the smoke, a thing diving from the sky above. A thing with wings, horribly burnt. With strands of scorched, burnt hair stuck to a blistering, pus-filled face. Blond hair. I go to scream a warning, but as I do the figure bunches up into an arrow shape and flies straight through Redgrave, and back up to the sky.

As he goes, I hear a half-strangled cry through horrifically burnt vocal cords. "Miss you, Father!" and then the freak from the sky, the somehow still-breathing Rufous Azzuri, is gone.

I turn back to see a picture of stark carnage. Redgrave's entire chest is gone. Not injured. Gone. Blood leaks faintly around the edges of the hole. A tube of something or other squirts idly into the air. He stands for a couple more moments, then falls to the ground. Azzuri drops to his knees by Redgrave's side, his face a rictus of shock.

I go to say something and then I stop. I hear a beat. Strong, powerful. *Whoosh, whoosh, whoosh.* I can hear it above me, and someone laughing, too. The wolfblood in me amplifies the sound rather than mollifying it. I go to make a noise, make a sound, but my throat has seized up and I can't speak. I back away from Azzuri and what remains of Redgrave, but it's not him anymore, not at all.

It's a sack of bones and flesh and twisted skin and exposed muscle. There's a face in it somewhere, but it's not the face I knew. There's an eye hanging out and teeth concertinaed together like a smashed piano, and a nose completely broken out of joint.

"*Betthhhhh,*" I moan softly, trying to reach out but unable to move, unable to reach my best friend dying in front of me once again.

*Whoosh* goes the beat of the wings above me, and they feel so close, and that laugh is ringing in my ears, straight through my brain; the laugh is thunder in the skies.

"*Bethhhh*," I choke, the word puncturing my mouth even as I spit it out, needlelike.

And then the one remaining eye opens, and I see Beth's still alive, just, and her breath whistles out of her mashed-up mouth like a breeze through wind chimes, and I gag.

"Oh gods, Beth. Oh gods, I'm sorry. Oh gods."

And I try to move but I can't, it's all frozen, nothing I do can change it, and I moan and I gag but she still looks at me.

And then I feel a hand on my shoulder, sharp, strong. "Come back to me, Sam," the voice says, soft, feminine, gentle. "Come back to me, dear, oh my Sam, come back to me." And I ignore it and reach out to Beth, one-eye-staring Beth, my Beth, the one I couldn't name, the one I failed, my Beth—

"I've got you, Sam. You're safe."

And now the hand is gripping me hard, and I feel an embrace, too, an embrace that smells of rose-lily and the hint of foxblood. I'm hugged hard, and as much as I want to reach out to Beth, that scent takes me back, takes me back, and the vision of bone and heaps that used to be my best friend recedes, slowly, and I make one half-hearted attempt to reach out to her, but it's gone.

Then I turn round, and as the fog in my vision clears, I see the face of Daphnée Hocquard, white flower in her hair, tear in her eye, calm smile on her face.

"You're safe, Sam, do you hear? Now come out of those horrors and into the light."

And there's something soothing in that voice, but commanding as well, and finally the beat of wings goes away and the laughter dies, the wolfblood giving me reality back as quickly as it helped drag all my fears into the world.

"How?" I ask, my voice still faint, seeing all of her now. She's covered in smoke and dust. But she's unharmed. There's not a scratch on her.

"Oh, Sam," she says, stroking my hair. "You think Alanna would let me die? She . . . well, I'm not sure what she did, but it saved us from the explosion, and now I think we have a few questions we need to ask of her, once I've thanked her in my own very slow and—very pleasurable—way."

I stare at her, and she raises her eyebrow at me.

I laugh. "About time," I say. And then something occurs to me, and my memory returns, and I spin round to the real sight that my guilt-hallucination of Beth masked.

## Azzuri

I cradle the body of Redgrave, trying to look at his face, not the destruction of the rest of him. His face is spotless somehow, even as everywhere else is blood. His eyelids flutter.

"Oh gods," I say, putting my hand on his cheek, which is cold, so cold. "Oh gods," I say again, uselessly.

"Listen to me, Redgrave," I say, panicking, willing his eyes to open. "Listen to me, old friend. No, no, no. That's not right." I stroke his cheek again. "Not old friend. *Best friend.* You're my best friend. And you're family. You've always been. I love you, do you hear me, Redgrave?" I shake him now, desperate. "Godsdammit, man, you hear me? You're my best friend and I love you."

But he's gone, and he was gone before I said any of my words.

My own heart drops out of me then, and I bow my head, and I give in to the pain.

## Sam

I crawl over to Vermillion, who has hung his head, still holding what remains of Redgrave. A soft moan comes from his lips. "*Nooooo.*" Over and over, like a banshee from a child's tale.

I reach him and I grab him and hold his head to my breast. He doesn't try to stop me. "It wasn't your fault," I say. Still he moans.

"It wasn't your fault," I try again, and I squeeze him harder. "It was them." I point to the sky. I mean to point at the now-escaped Rufous, or maybe I mean all the Lords who made the Grays, who manipulate this city, or maybe I mean all the nobles who hate the Worns. "It was *them.* It's always been. You were never them."

Still he moans.

"It wasn't your fault."

He breaks then, great rasping sobs, and he holds me back, his hands around my back. He weeps on me, heaving, wailing. His hands dig into me.

"It wasn't your fault," I say, stroking his hair as he cries.

"It wasn't your fault," I say, each word a balm.

"It's not my fault," I say, rocking him.

"It's not my fault," I say again.

And then I break, too, and as I hold him, tears flowing down, intermingling with his, weeping to match him, I croon it over and over again.

*It's not my fault.*

A glass later, I sit on the side of the crater. In the streets behind, the fires caused by the explosion are being put out, one by one, by the Westfall community. The smoke has largely gone now, whipped away in the unforgiving winter-night gales. My wolfblood still rages strong in me, but slightly dimmed. It will last until the start of nightfall tomorrow if I am lucky, though much diminished. I drank half a carafe, not half a wolf, this time.

So many things are happening, and having started them I should be part of them. A city has been turning as I sit here. But I'm not ready to wade back in yet. Vermillion has taken Redgrave's body somewhere. I wanted to go with him, but he shook his head, seeking to be alone. Daphnée, who should also be orchestrating things, is sitting next to me, hand in mine. Alanna lingers a few feet behind, giving us space. Daphnée said the Leeches weren't needed for the rest of the night, that this was Tenfold's turn to make sure the city was rebel-held by night's end. I don't believe her. And I'm grateful.

I want to ask her about Alanna, about how they survived the firepowder blast completely unharmed, but I don't want to disturb this silence. I've let something out of me, and for the first time since Beth died I feel calm. Restful.

The silence is disturbed anyway, as Molly lands beside us.

Lands? I turn and see her draw her wings in. She sees my look of shock and smiles. "I'm only on it for tonight, don't you worry, Sammy, dear. I've not gone and got myself above my station." She laughs. She looks a little less gray, too. Aging of a Worn can be completely reversed, if you drink enough good blood for long enough. But I know she won't. It occurs to me then, my wolfblood brain giving me the insight denied to me before, that a smuggler like her could have been on the Midway bloods at least regularly enough to not have aged the last couple of centuries. She didn't have to do this. She didn't have to age.

Maybe she knows something the rest of us don't.

"You'll never believe it, ladies," she says, taking in the scene of devastation before us calmly. "Bloody 'ell, Dee. What have you done here?" She laughs. "Never mind, you crazy doll. I'll ask later. But you'll never guess what's happened."

There's a pause. Daphnée and I wait expectantly.

"You're meant to say, 'What?'" Molly adds.

"Molly, darling, for the love of the Blood Gods, please just tell us," says Daphnée, grinning at me.

"Well, you're no fun, dears. Anyway, it's the Lords. They've . . . gone."

I frown. Daphnée frowns. I think of words. "What do you mean . . . gone?"

Molly shrugs. "I bloody well mean gone, don't I? Tenfold's rallying cry went round the guards quicker than a skybolt, and the whole city guard immediately pledged to us within an hourglass. A few companies, the ones loyal to the Lords or their Lord commanders, held out, but other than that, the whole bloody lot! And then . . . well, then we heard from the Wall Guard. That some Lords were fleeing the city, through the Fang Tips–gate side. Except it weren't just some Lords. It were the whole bastard lot."

"I'm . . . I still don't . . ." I try to use the wolfblood, but my wolfblood brain is as stumped as me.

"Best we can figure out, they must have always had a plan like this," continues Molly. "For if the whole city turned on them. They left before we could do anything. Killed a couple of Wall Guard, I'm sad to say. But not many. They were just concerned with fleeing."

"So who has actually . . . left, Molly?" asks Daphnée, voice still thick with shock.

"Well, let's see, we're all trying to work it out, but it looks like . . ." She takes her fingers out and counts on her hand. "All of the Lords and Ladies and their families, bar some of the very few loyal to Azzuri. Then there's some of the Midways. Not many—most turned our way after the Invisibles crash—but still a good few of the stupid bastards, maybe a fifth? Hardly any Worns, I'm pleased to say, save some servants I suspect didn't have much choice in the matter. But most of them will have to do their own fucking work from now on. They took some bloodstores, not all of them, only those that they could take with them in a hurry. Got some wolfblood, too, but only the stores in the palace, so that won't last them forever. Although . . ." She pulls a frown.

"Go on," I say, wolfblood impatient, sensing bad news.

"They took all the fucking Kinet mages with them. So, beyond the stores left behind, they'll be no more new magicked blood going forward as long as they're gone. Although that skybolt-spinning Atmos sorcerer fuck guarding the Blood Farms was seen going with them, too, so at least the Blood Farms are free for us. We can get Midway and noble blood. And we've still got the wolf criminals. They're safe and sound. So we got wolfblood, too. So fuck 'em."

"But . . . where are they . . ." Even as I ask it, I know. The Grays are theirs to command, so they can go anywhere in the Centerlands.

Where would you go?

"Lightfall." I sigh.

Molly nods, a grim look on her face. "Aye. Welcome back, Lightfall. But Sammy," she continues, grabbing me by my shoulders. "Wipe off that sad look, my dear. You fucking did it. We have the city. *First Light is ours.* And almost no one died!"

For a second, I bow my head, thinking of Redgrave. But the guilt is not mine. Not anymore. I know where to place the blame. So I smile instead, and I say, "You're right. Well, almost. *We* did it." And I smile at my ladies, my ladies of the revolution, glowing in our various bloods.

"And now," I say, heaving myself up, "I'm going to sleep for a godsdamn eternity." I turn to the devastation behind me.

"Probably not here, though."

# 15

# All My Possessions for a Moment in Time

At the end of the night, my dears, I only have one question for you: If you were to face your end, now, with your friends around you, even if all your goals were not met, would you feel at peace? Would you feel you had done all you tried to do, even if it didn't work out in the end?

If the answer's no, then bloody try harder.

Molly Threetimes, in a speech to the
Southern Chapter of the Lightfall rebels, circa 447 AL

## Sam

I'm woken by a knock on the door to my chamber. A lot of things happen in my sleep-addled brain then. First I'm unsure where I am, and I look to my right in panic, expecting to see Beth. Old habits. Then, when it comes to me that she's not there, and I'm in my sleeping quarters in Westfall, I don't feel the tight panic that any thoughts of Beth have roused in me this last month. Just a quiet sadness, of a time gone. Not a time I missed, except for her. And in the realization of that comes a feeling of lightness. I feel empty, in a good way. Cleansed. Sobbing will do that to you. Sloughing off your guilt—the stupid parts, anyway—will as well. Somehow, I'm the most tired I've ever been but the most refreshed and awake. Which is a good job, because it worked. And almost no one died. The city is . . . the city is *something*. No one's sure yet. Maybe today we find out what yesterday's events have reaped for us. Maybe I find Sage. Maybe everyone is together again.

I think all of that in a moment, but maybe the moment was a bit too long—I still feel the wolfblood in me, distracting me, speaking to me—because the knock turns into the door thrust open and there is Daphnée, in her day gown, hair wildly trailing behind her. Her face paint is half applied—I see she's returning to her former face now there's Lords playing a part with the revolutionaries, I think, and instantly dismiss that thought to the judgmental cellar the little shit came from—and she's half shouting at me.

"Sam, dear, get up, no time, we have to go. I let you sleep in, after last night, it's almost one bell, but oh, I shouldn't have done, what a time, I—Sam, it's bad." Her face is pale, even more than her natural look. "Godsdammit," she mutters. "Daphnée, compose yourself." She breathes out, and she transforms in an instant. Gone is the panic. Here, in a moment, is the woman who strode into a room little bigger than this one and changed my life forever but a few weeks ago.

It's quite a trick.

"Sam, we have just received a honegull from Tenfold. Rufous has breached the walls somehow. In the day. With some Grays. He has taken some Worn children hostage. He is demanding you come or he will kill them."

*Did you think it would be so easy?* says the wolfblood, half mockingly. *Recall how life goes.*

"Where?" I ask, using the blood in me to suppress the fear.

"Southfall. Between the Guard fort and the wall."

I leap out of bed, and I focus on my back, feel for them.

"Some of the wolfblood has worn off. I don't have wings."

"That won't be a problem," says Daphnée, turning behind her, where a winged bloodguard waits impatiently but politely, wings out but down. "Do you need some blood?" she asks, holding out some vials.

"No. The wolfblood is still strong enough in me."

"Yes." She smiles. "I can still hear it in your voice, and see it in your skin and eyes." She stares at me a moment, almost rapturous, and a part of me thinks *I could be this way forever*. Yes, sure. You and whose wolves?

I breathe out. I think of the last time I faced Rufous. Full of the wolfblood, just like now. Confident. Ready. But that time it was a battle between me and him. It was personal. Now, there is a city on a knife edge. Between what it was and what it could be. Those moments in immortal history where everything changes on a dime. I don't need the endlessly pretentious whispers of my wolfblood brain to tell me that.

Now, I can't make it personal.

I have to make it something *more*.

When we arrive at Southfall, that great empty strip of the Blood Road that goes from the Guard fort all the way to the city wall, that place where Sage unleashed the illusions of the Grays so recently, one thing quickly becomes clear.

Tenfold's message wasn't quite right.

It's not some of the Grays here.

It's *all* of them.

My winged guard lands gently a few hundred yards from the horrific sight. Next to me another guard lands with Alanna, and then soon after more with Daphnée and Molly Threetimes. To my left, in front of the ranked masses of all the city's guards battalions, is Commander Tenfold, and next to him a disheveled but alert Azzuri.

As Tenfold comes rushing over to us, I try to make sense of what I see before me. Blocking the Blood Road, in what my wolfblood mind quickly calculates is twenty lines of fifty, are an army of Grays. A thousand in total, I estimate. They stand silently, hoods covering their faces in the early evening starlight, the torchlight along the Blood Road itself casting strobing shadows where their expressions should be. Next to every single one of them—a mortal gun raised to their head, one arm held by the Grays—is a child. A Worn child. A terrified Worn child, each one between five and ten years, each one shocked into silence. I can see every single one with my wolfblood eyes. And every single one will never be the same again. Gods, I hope that's just the wolfblood talking.

In front of this spectacle, straight from the twin hells, stands Rufous Azzuri, proud and tall, his leathery, golden-hued wings stretched out, casting great arced shadows in front of him. His hair flows freely, blond and slightly curled, and his full lips are parted in a great toothy grin, his fangs half elongated. His wide, innocent eyes take everything in. His red-and-gold doublet—still wearing the First Guard uniform despite their death (for a second time, I think evilly)—is covered in thick layers of blood and guts and matter. I smell the stench of him from here. It's vampire blood, and on my wolfblood nose I can smell it's male. I can smell how scared they were in their last moments. Strong steel and a hint of the pine of the excitement of a battle that must have been extremely short-lived.

Even before Tenfold tells me, I can work it all out. Except for one thing.

"Ingle," Tenfold begins, running a sweaty hand through his thick red mane, addressing me like a soldier, which I like. Or the wolfblood likes. "Somehow, he flew over the fucking wall. In the day. Carried the Grays in where the mountain meets the wall, it looks like. One by bloody one, as far as we can tell. Enough to rout the Day Guard, at any rate. He . . ." He pauses here, to compose himself. To his credit, it's only a flicker. But I smell the deep, deep flowery scent of sadness, half rose-lily, half rose itself.

"He took them by surprise. Obviously. They didn't expect the Grays behind them. With those weapons . . ." He slices a hand through the air. "It was like Grayfall. It's too early to tell but we think he's killed most of them. Then we presume he opened the gate, let the other Grays in. It's all the Grays, Ingle. All the fucking Grays. They snuck into houses, stole children. I was awake, at the Southfall fort. We didn't see or hear anything. I should have been there. I should have been at the wall. . . ."

Azzuri is behind him, and he puts a tender hand on Tenfold's shoulder. "And you'd be dead, Commander. And of no use to us now."

Tenfold gives him a side glance that could mean anything, and carries on. "Anyway, all he's said is that he wants the leaders of the revolution here, now. And you. He was very particular on that point. The man next to him is the new spymaster." I turn and look again, and see a small, almost shriveled man, short dark hair, clean-shaven, cold, blinking eyes. Young but something old about him, almost like a Worn. He is so inconsequential-looking that I completely failed to notice him the first time. "His name is Cardinale Cabalti." He sees all our raised eyebrows and nods. "Yes, grandson of the original. One who founded this blasted city. He may not look like much but he's just as cunning as Saxe was, and colder, in a way."

"Oh, you can say that again. Not surprised to hear he was one of Saxe's cabal. Hideous little bastard," says Daphnée. She's kept her composure after that snapshot of her when I woke, but I can smell the tinge of metal underneath, threatening to get out. Next to her, Alanna rubs her daggers thoughtfully, one in each hand. She looks like she might be about to race into battle with them, but as if anticipating me, she smiles grimly.

"I think an army of Grays might be a little too much for the old girls," she says, and it takes me a moment to realize she's talking about the weapons whose handles she is calmly rubbing.

I look to her left, where Molly and Hands stand. Hands is as furious as I've ever seen her. "Trust men to guard the city. The Vials should have been on the walls."

"And all your fucking gang would be as dead as mine," replies Tenfold with the force of a cannon, lips pursed.

"Right," I say, impatient to end where this is going. "Let's go and speak to him then, shall we? Not the first time we've faced him."

"You hear that?" says Molly, loud, so the first line of the nearest of Tenfold's battalions can hear. "The same girl what beat him last time is ready to wallop him again."

That draws smiles from them, but it doesn't change the chill frost in the air, part winter, part lingering dread. Everyone knows this is the end of the game, the last spin of the dice gone to the enemy.

No one's ready to admit it yet. They don't have the cold truth of the wolfblood inside of them, I suppose.

*On such moments do continents spin*, chimes my wolfblood self, as if on cue, and I take that cryptic line with me as I march up, with the ladies of the revolution next to me, as well as Tenfold and Azzuri. We stop about fifty yards in front of Rufous.

We face each other, the nascent revolution and the army of the damned.

Rufous's grin grows even wider as he sees me.

"Samantha!" he cries. "Samantha of Ashfall Lane." His smile drops and he looks round furtively. "Between you and me, we really need to stop meeting like this." Then he chuckles to himself and wipes what looks like brains off his tabard. "I had a moment of revelation, last night, as I picked the brains of my First Guard off me and regrew the scarred remains of half my flesh." He lifts up an arm and moves it in a sweeping arc that encompasses our front line. "I keep underestimating you all. Just because you are . . . you, doesn't mean you don't keep coming out with some interesting moves. I underestimated you, Sam, and I ended up with your arm down my throat. Slightly too intimate, that, if you don't mind me saying. Invite me to dinner next time."

I leave that be. The faces of the children in front of me keep me quiet. I have to let him talk. The longer we have, the more chance we have.

"But you didn't kill me, Sam. And those two . . . *cunts*," he says, pointing at Alanna and Daphnée, letting his real face into view for a second, "they failed as well. Ultimately, when it comes down to it, none of you are ruthless enough to do what a city needs. Not the jumped-up Worn commander who couldn't keep me out of his city for a night." Tenfold's eye flickers a little, but otherwise his granite face remains impassive. "Not my pathetic sire who, I have no doubt, wept for his servant as I flew away with his heart." Vermillion, too, shows no emotion. Those tears we flushed out together have done us well. "Not the women who, typically, thought they could bring a city to its knees without violence. You don't have what it takes. You don't have the blood of centuries in you, the class to know what to do with it. You think yourself better rulers, yet look how quickly I bring you back to my feet. Lay the hypocrisy of your dreams at you."

"Whatever you have to say to me, or do to me," I begin, carefully, choosing to speak now because I can't stand any more of that fucking speech, "you can do it now. I'm here. We're all here. You don't need the children anymore."

For a moment, a dreadful, awful moment that stretches out through time, echoes through it, a mischief is alight in Rufous's eyes, and I fear what he's about to do. To show us all. Show us all how powerless we really are. His arm moves, and for all the boldness in me, all the wolfblood, all the certainty I feel in who I am after last night, for all that my world starts to fracture as his arm comes down.

"Ah. . . . Fair enough," he says. "I just wanted to get your attention, to be honest. I'm a bastard, but I'm not that much of a bastard," he says, lying. Then, louder, "*Grays, release!*" In one united motion, the Grays release the children. They all stay there, stunned, then one runs forward toward the first line of soldiers, determined, fast, and that breaks the spell and suddenly they're all running. The front line of guards breaks and guardsmen run out to them. By this point, Worns have assembled far behind them, some held back, and though they're out of sight, on my wolf ears I hear the frenzied gasps and tears of the mothers and fathers who have managed to make it here as they embrace their children. I switch my focus back to Rufous, and see all the guns of the Grays fixed on us, the front line.

"I think—" begins Rufous.

At this point, Spymaster Cabalti, who has been listening to Rufous's gloating speeches with an increasing twitch of impatience on his half-haunted face, cuts in.

"The mathematics of this are very simple, revolutionaries," he begins, his voice austere, cold and clipped, centuries of breeding distilled to velvet monotony. "This Gray army can run through all the Blood Guard quickly with minimal, if any casualties; those of you who recall Grayfall will be well aware of this. You will surrender immediately. The city will return to how it was before the unfortunate events of last night. Those responsible will be allowed to live if we can do this quickly and reasonably and those of us outside the city walls can be within them again this same night." He sighs and adjusts his winter jacket. Even with noble blood, it must be cold outside the city, or else they're limiting tonight the blood they drink in case they don't get the city reserves back. Interesting.

"There may, of course, need to be a demonstration of penitence before the city crowds. So one person may need to be sunburst. I will allow you, however, to decide—"

The words of Spymaster Cabalti are unfortunately interrupted by his head being suddenly separated from his body. Blood spurts from the hole where his neck should be. Rufous holds his head in his hands and studies the twitching of his eyes for a second. Even on wolfblood, I feel a shiver of horror run through me.

"If anyone asks," says Rufous, as his spymaster's last seconds of consciousness drain from him and his eye movements cease, "he fell in the battle to get into the city." He thinks for a moment. "You might have to pretend there was an actual battle to get into the city." Then, both hands still around Cabalti's head, he throws it as hard as he can behind him. On wolfblood, the throw is far, the head arcing back as far as the eye can see in the gloom. Well, most eyes. If I squint I see the head land half a mile back, and I hear the soft squelch as it opens up on the ground like a half-rotten gourd. Some droplets of blood from the head's flight land on one of the Grays, who either doesn't notice or doesn't care.

"Right, now it is just me, I have a new plan," says Rufous. "I don't know about you, but I'm tired of spymasters and their elaborate thinking that always goes tits up, if you pardon the Worntongue."

"Rufous," says Azzuri softly, just loud enough for his estranged son to hear.

"*I DON'T WANT TO HEAR ANYTHING FROM YOU, 'FATHER,' UNLESS YOU WANT ME TO GET THOSE CHILDREN BACK AND RIP THEM LIMB FROM FUCKING LIMB IN FRONT OF YOU.*"

Vermillion doesn't react to this. He just nods slightly and goes silent again.

Rufous cricks his neck a little and breathes out. "Sorry about that," he says, the quick flash of unconstrained rage that had contorted his face for a second being replaced by his lion's beam again. "Family, eh, what can you do? As I was saying, I have a new idea."

"If anyone has a plan," mutters Molly to my side, "it's getting very close to the time to bloody do it."

The silence that follows tells me everything, although I already knew it. There's no getting away with it. My wolfblood mind has gone through the options. With those Gray guns trained on us, with a near invincible army before us, there's nothing that can be done but play out the scene with the deranged noble before me.

Not everything has a solution.

At least one that you want to hear.

"The new plan is as follows. I kill everyone who led this . . . whatever this pathetic thing was. Right now. No last words. No mercy. No sunburst. Just bullets now, and then you die. Then I take back the city, and I try and keep the killing to a minimum. I'm not a monster, after all." He grins wider. "Although you ladies really keep making me want to be one."

He stares at us all, lets us acknowledge it. "If you run, not that you'd make it with these guns and these Grays, then I'll kill all of Southeastfall just to make a point. Die now, and you can finally do something useful that actually saves people instead of throwing them into a new fire."

Ah, I think, guilt. It won't work anymore. With the satisfaction of knowing that there's nothing that can be done, I start to laugh. His smile drops immediately.

"It doesn't matter how many tough words you say, Rufous," I add. "We'll never think anything of you. And you know that, deep down, and it will haunt you long after you've killed whoever you want." I laugh again, my voice tinged with the blood of the wolfkind, echoing across the wintry road. "The more blood you get on you, the more stupid you look, has anyone ever told you that? No, I suppose they haven't. Pity. You might have turned out to be less of a disappointment."

I see one eyelid on his noble, perfect face flicker, and he goes to shout something, lip quivering. But then he composes himself, and instead he bellows, "LISTEN, MY GRAYS."

"It is fine, Sam," whispers Daphnée, a soft voice beside me, holding my hand, her other in Alanna's. "You did more than anyone could ever have done. My daughter would have loved you. *I* love you."

I turn to my right, and I see Vermillion Azzuri smile at me. Gaze not on his son. Gaze on me.

Then I look ahead. I look into those guns, loaded with red bullets, red for vampires, red for our death. The color that gives us life will now rob it from us.

"READY," comes the gleeful voice of the man who caused my parents' deaths. Not *me*. I stare into those guns in the chill winter air and I think of them, and my sister. I think of Beth, now that I can, now that I am able to properly. I think of all the good times I had with her, in that worst of places.

"AIM."

The wolfblood in me takes over then, and it shows me, once again, that nothing matters, that time itself is an illusion. No past, no present, no future. Everything that has ever been is all here at once. When you see it like that, all you can do is stop worrying about the big things and look at the small things. The things that really matter.

I look left, then right, to my friends. My new family.

I feel, maybe for the first time, at peace.

"FIRE!"

16

# Just When You Thought They Were Dead

The Blood Road is well named. Not for the blood that vampires take—but for all the blood that has been spilled on it in the history of the Everlands.

Rufous Lazuli, *The Underworkings of First Light*

## Sam

"FIRE!"

*Do not fire.*

The second command comes whispered, half in my skull, a split moment after the command of Rufous. So soon after that I see the fingers on the triggers of the Grays trembling, caught between a certain act and a sudden reversal.

*Put your guns to your side.*

For a moment, the Grays do not move. Rufous looks confused. But he's not turning round. I turn to my side. Confusion reigns on the faces of everyone who, a moment ago, was ready for death. But they're not looking round either, for the source of those sinister tones, those hushed syllables, half shadow, half resounding bass at the depths of my skull.

On my wolfblood, it's made obvious: They cannot hear the voice.

But I can. Me and the Grays. My mind is different now, I suppose.

Finally, no longer able to resist the voice, the Grays slowly lower the weapons.

Rufous screams, apoplectic. "What the fuck are you doing! Raise your weapons!"

*It has been a long time, my Shades,* continues the voice of Neuras Sinassion. I knew it was him the moment he spoke. Even with the wolfblood making me my best version of myself, his is not a voice you forget.

And then, to me only, *Hello, Sam. The wolfblood suits you. Give me a few moments, if you would. This is going to be hard, even for me. I'm not sure I'll survive it.*

The wolfblood me, me with everything ramped up to ten, knows exactly what he's going to do. I just . . . I just know. It is obvious. I have seen it, a few days ago, after all.

I sense some movement to my side as it dawns on Tenfold and his soldiers that the opportunity is there.

"Don't move," I cry out, and even though it makes no sense, the timbre still there in my wolfblood voice and the urgency of my voice halts them. I look round to see if I can see Sinassion. Of course I don't. Even if he was near I doubt he'd be visible, but he doesn't have to be near to do this, does he?

*Good luck*, I think, meaning it just as much as I mean anything, and whether he hears me or not I don't know, but the next moment the Grays have lifted their guns.

For a moment I hesitate, wondering if I've made a terrible mistake, missed the window to do something. If maybe this is a cruel trick from Sinassion, or perhaps the wolfblood has finally broken my sanity. (*What is sanity?* asks the wolfblood.)

And then . . .

*Drop your weapons.*

*Turn around.*

Everyone except the slowest of people have cottoned on now, the gist of it, at least, even though they still cannot hear Sinassion's voice. Rufous is staring in horror, disgust on his face, wings spread now, caught between fight or flight.

A pause.

*Forgive me, my Shades. My friends. I'd hoped to have more time to save you. All I can do is stop you killing again.*

Another pause. I can sense the words, more words to be said. But they never come. *Now run. Out of the city. Don't stop till you are outside the walls.*

And they do.

Rufous flies away as soon as the Grays begin to flee the city. Maybe someone could have stopped him right there and then, taken wolfblood and flown after him, but everyone is too confused at what is happening. Only I have the voice of Sinassion lingering in my skull, after all. The wingbeats that haunted me so recently sound pathetic as they quieten to nothing, a man heading back to Lightfall having bungled his play. I watch him shrink to a dot on the horizon, and the remains of a weight slough off my shoulders, dead skin freed.

Everyone mills around, trying to gather their wits. In the last few moments, I've explained as best I can what happened, and that we're probably safe for now, and this was relayed to the guards by Tenfold, who are busy securing a perimeter and moving out to establish patrols. Above me fly some winged guards, presumably to check the Grays have actually fled the city, and to close the gates and secure the city before the now-rebels-themselves army of Rufous and the Lords and Midways can come in, not that they would be much good against the entire rest of the city without their Gray protectors.

And that is when we see them. Walking out from the shadows of some trees that line the Blood Road. The sorcerer in black, hood up, burning eyes that mesmerize. And the sorcerer in green, hood down. The man who I held in an invisible embrace not but a few nights ago. The man, it turns out, who had been consorting with Sinassion in secret. Tenfold gives the command and a hundred crossbows are raised, and he cries out, "HALT WHERE YOU ARE."

They both stop, a hundred yards from us.

"The balls of him," mutters Molly from my right.

I assume she's not talking about the man I kissed but the most notorious sorcerer in all the Everlands. But it applies to both, I suppose.

"Before anyone does anything rash," shouts Sage, his fragrant Desertlands accent a balm to me, even as I quell the sense of betrayal, "can I remind you that the man next to me just saved you all." A pause as he takes in the weapons aimed his way, and the shocked faces. "I feel it's extremely important to emphasize that."

"Better the devil you know," I hear Alanna mutter to my right, surprisingly coming to his defense.

"Yes, my Alanna, but how well do you know him?" sighs Daphnée.

"How do we know it's not a trick or a bloody illusion?" asks Tenfold.

"Did what just happened feel like an illusion?" shouts Sage, carefully. I like Sage a lot. I missed Sage, even in the last two nights, a lot. But in that moment I suddenly remember that his manner may not be ideal for standoffs.

"Oh, damn this for a bloodfuck," I say, striding forward. No one stops me. Wolfblood has that effect.

"Sam!" I hear Daphnée call out, but I am already halfway there, crossing the empty road to the sorcerers, ignoring the bodies to my left. On my wolfblood, I hear the whine of the stretched crossbow strings, their soft hum. I feel the racing heartbeats of the assembled onlookers. Not Sinassion's, though. But Sage's. Not nerves, though. Something else.

*What are feelings in this world?* cries the wolfblood.

Not now, wolfblood. Now I get to see a friend again.

I march up to Sage and Sinassion. I stop before them. Sage looks uncharacteristically nervous. I take in his messy fringe, his still-tired eyes, his now outrageously unruly beard. I don't want to be angry with him, I want to request that he shave, but he's making it hard.

I half turn to Sinassion. No voice is in my head. His arms hang loosely at his sides, and though I can see nothing beyond the burning eyes and the hood, I sense a quietness, an absence of something.

Sage sees me looking. "That took a lot out of him. In more ways than one. I . . . I thought for a moment it had killed him. He is with us, but not with us. He'll be recovered in a while . . . I think."

I consider this. "You're in quite a lot of trouble now, you know. Appearing with a man that most of the city knows as the most wanted man alive."

Sage nods. "It wasn't meant to be this way."

I return the nod. "I know. He's been practicing mind control with you, hasn't he? Making the jump from mind-reading to puppet mastery. That's what I saw the other night when you were walking in a stupor, mind gone, across the room. He was practicing on you, wasn't he?"

Sage's eyes widen. "Sam, you are—"

"On wolfblood? Yes. I can't seem to keep off the stuff. It really makes connections very quickly."

He studies me properly then, looks me up and down. "You took almost as much as last time, I see. Last night, was it? You're still . . . glowing a bit. Your voice is still . . . ethereal."

I roll my eyes at him. "You know how to compliment a woman."

To my satisfaction, he blushes a little. "But I didn't mean that. I meant you're . . . incredible. You would have worked it out without the wolfblood. I wish I'd met you years ago." He stares at me then, as if we aren't being watched by half the city. Even on wolfblood, I feel a blush coming on.

"Sinassion was meant to have more time," he adds, quickly changing the topic, "but then you turned out to be incredibly effective at the art of revolution."

"Not just me," I say quickly. "So he wants his old army back? To get back to his ways?"

"No. Not at all. He wants to free them. Reverse what was done to them."

"And you believe him."

"It's complicated. . . ."

"I bet it is."

"Sam, I can tell you're angry."

"Actually, I'm not. The wolfblood in me tells me that anger would be pointless now, would waste time. Honestly, if everyone was on this stuff I think life would be a lot simpler." I remember the way the wolfblood speaks to me. "And possibly a lot stranger."

"Well, that's good at least."

"When it wears off I think I'll be quite angry with you, yes."

"That's less good." A beat. "But you trust me?" Sage's eyes narrow, and a look of genuine concern comes across his face. For a moment I study him. Sage is confident normally, with a touch of arrogance. Now he seems vulnerable. He really does need my trust.

I sigh. "It makes no sense right now to trust you, even if Sinassion was telling the truth when he spoke into all our heads on First Gods, claiming that he had nothing do with the Lords' conspiracy. He's still the man responsible for the second half of the Twin War. And you've been working with him to make him more powerful. And you never told me that you knew him. So lots of reasons to not trust you at all." I pause. "But I do trust you, implicitly."

A look of pure relief passes Sage's face, and for a moment I think he's going to hold my hand, just like the other night, and I'm glad he doesn't, given who's watching, but I also regret the lack of it. "Thank you, Sam."

"It's not a good thing, though. It's a sign that I'm a fool."

Sage keeps my gaze. "Join the club."

"Right, well, we better get a move on," I say. "Not sure how long we can just stand here talking. A lot of people are going to want answers."

I pause. “They’ll take Sinassion into captivity, you realize. For a while at least.”

Sage nods. “I know. Him saving everyone probably isn’t enough to overturn everything else they know of him.” He turns to Sinassion, who looks literally like a dead man walking. “He won’t try to stop them, at least. He isn’t there at the moment.”

“They might imprison you, too.”

He shrugs. “It might give me time to shave, at least. If you could pass me a razor through my cell bars.”

I grin. “I’ll see what I can do.” My smile leaves my face. “But it’s time for answers.”

Sage turns to Sinassion. “I was hoping to get them from him. But I’ll tell you everything I know, Sam.” Back to me, piercing me with those hazel eyes. I don’t shy from them.

“No more secrets,” he adds.

## 17

# The Art of the Deal

One question I am always asked by vampires and wolves about our own kind is: How powerful could sorcerers ever get? In theory, or worse, in practice. Could a Kinet actually move mountains? Could an Atmos make it rain over a whole city? Could a Cloak make an illusion that spanned the world?

But what of the Neuras? I ask. Be more wary of them. I heard a story once, of something most sinister in the southern reaches of the desert. A small community of vampires, wolves, and sorcerers, where it was said the residents were controlled by the Neuras among them. Not mind-read. Controlled.

Ridiculous, you say.

But not impossible, I reply.

Cloak Kiscantion, *Tales from the Desertlands*

## Sage

Nothing is usual about this scene: not my setting, not the audience, not the topic.

The setting is a grand Westfall townhouse, one of the biggest in the district, nothing compared to the Eastfall Midway townhouses but nothing to be sneered at either: redbrick and slate and wide and proud, unlike the jaunty, narrow constructions of much of that quirky district. Lady Hocquard, or Daphnée, as I must call her now, apparently, informed me that it was abandoned in fairly quick order the previous night by one of the Midway traders who decided, perhaps due to some of their business dealings, that their fate lay with the Lords fleeing the city. I asked on my (heavily escorted) way here why they were not in the palace now it was empty, and Sam shrugged and said that the revolution began in Westfall and what came next should stay there, at least for now. I wondered what the remaining Lords and Midways will say about that, but I decided not to express that thought.

In a receiving room on the second floor with fancy paneled walls of knotted pine, I sit in a straight-backed redoak chair with a velvet cushion, Sam on a similar chair opposite me.

"This is nicer than where I thought I'd be put." Sinassion, still catatonic, though standing, was escorted to the jail in far Eastfall where the wolf prisoners of First Light are kept. I was worried I would join him.

Sam shrugs. Her wolfblood has begun to wear off now. I slightly miss it. She looked ethereal, glowing. That said, I am not opposed to how she looks normally. "You might still end up under guard. But I said I want to talk to you first. And Daphnée still trusts you, I think. She hasn't forgotten your help."

"Well, it was not much more than a month ago, so I'd be concerned if she had."

"Probably not the best time for wit," Sam says, though she looks like she might be concealing a smile herself.

I nod, making a mental note. After being around Jacob for too long, I find myself a little more careless when jests are made.

"So, Sage, tell me everything. And I'll see what we can do about convincing the rebels not to throw you in with Sinassion."

Sam has a slightly mischievous look on her face as she says it, and I know she trusts me. Our trust was earned in our time, though I seem to be doing my best to try to stretch it to its greatest extent, experimenting with when it will snap. And though I am sure she trusts me, there is a slight distance between us now; I can feel it. So many secrets my life has been defined by them. But at what cost?

Time for some honesty.

"I started the cult with Neuras Sinassion. The Cult of Humanis. It was just him and me, at the beginning."

Sam looks shocked, as well she might.

"I feel it's pertinent to note that Sinassion had not tried to conquer the continent or killed anyone to my knowledge at this point," I add.

She still looks shocked.

"I started the story too early." I sigh. I shift in my seat and try again. "My life began in Quantile, after I was born from the chamber . . . you know of this?"

Sam smiles. "Basic sorcerer knowledge. Do I look like a library beginner to you? Sorcerers are born as adults in a mysterious chamber. The first thing they're told is what type they are." She pauses. "It must have been hard to be told you were a Quantas."

"It was," I say, not wishing to make this too significant a part of my tale, for many reasons. "It was a cruel beginning, to be told I had no magick in me. None that anyone could see, at least. As a Quantas, I naturally moved to the city of Quantile, where most of us dwell. It's not a thriving place, nor one of much ambition. A lot of bitterness, as you can imagine. Moreover, the rest of the sorcerer world are . . . not kind to Quantas."

"I know," says Sam, quietly, and I wonder, as always, just how much she has retained in her brain from ten years of dedicated library time.

"I spent a long time in Quantile very alone. I felt robbed of a life, of the gift of magick. I sensed the disgust and the pity and everything else from many other mages I came into contact with. It scared me, it burned me, it enraged me, long before I fell to reason, like all of us now. You would think we would bind together in Quantile. But it is a lost place, and there is no unity there. We drown the longer we stay, hating ourselves and thus hating all around us. So I sought meaning, meaning in this land, meaning in this world, and all I found was ignorance. Or misdirected curiosity. I . . . hardly ever think about those days now. I put them in a box, and I leave them alone."

Sam gives me the grace to be silent for a few moments.

"But eventually," I continue, "what saved me was that I had this desire to learn, to know everything—"

"I am shocked."

"—but couldn't think of the best means to achieve this. I began to travel, though this was well over two hundred years ago, a few decades before the Twin War broke out, so the land was not safe, and tensions were getting bigger. That's when my fascination with the myths of the mortals took form—I'd always been interested, but I saw evidence and tales of ruins on my travels. Not enough to unearth things properly, but enough to know this could be my calling. But then, through a series of diversions, I became an inquirer in Luce, the capital. I'd shown skills in assisting various sorcerers on my travels, and word got out, and I got the chance to solve the serious mage crimes that perplexed the Archmage. It was controversial, given the fact I was a Quantas, but I somehow survived the tricky politics for a while."

"I'd love to hear of your investigations," says Sam, eyes bright.

"Well, I—"

"Not now."

"Ah . . . Fair enough. Anyway, as satisfied as I was putting my mind to such crimes, I wasn't fulfilled, ultimately. I felt the need to follow where the mortals may have trod. And so I left, and with more planning this time, resolved to do it properly. And that's when I met Sinassion."

Sam leans forward.

"He wasn't a notorious villain at that point, obviously. Hadn't tried to conquer the land with a deadly army and all that. He was just a standard Neuras, albeit a quiet one, and of course he still had those strange glowing eyes that stop you ever properly seeing his face. But he wasn't as . . . sinister. He didn't use his powers much; I wasn't even aware he could do more than a normal Neuras at first. He didn't even wear a black robe, just the normal Neuras colors. I met him in the desert, and we shared our fascination with the mortal myths and our need to know more. And so we began the cult in the desert. It was just the two of us at first, though we still called it Humanis from the start. We were—"

"Pretentious?"

"Ambitious," I reply, giving Sam a mild glare. "We had so much we wanted to know, and quickly. We soon found some others . . . we weren't Quantas only, then. And we went looking, and excavating, and unearthing, and learning. We began to find the kinds of things that you've seen, and much more. It was breathtaking. It felt like the start of something golden. The path to true discovery."

"And then?"

"And then . . . Sinassion . . . changed. He grew weary of the learning. He said with the things we had found, we could use them to take control. Take power in Luce. He said I could improve the lot of the Quantas. He said once in control, we could find out all the mortal secrets, set everyone to the task. He became . . . intense. I just wanted to learn, not take power. We couldn't reconcile our differences, and the next thing I knew he had left. To his credit, he didn't try to take the relics from the cult. He just left. The cult floundered without him; I floundered without an equal. It fell away, just before the war. Next time I saw him, it was from safely on a mountainside, watching his Shade army lay waste to a vampire battalion. And that's my story, Sam."

As much as I can say for now, at least.

Sam mulls this over. I study her eyes, her mouth, what she does with her hands. I'm looking for signs of warmth. I want her suspicions to be gone. I need all of her back. I need her.

I also think I need to calm down and regain some rationality.

"I can see why you've kept this all to yourself," Sam says eventually. "Hard to tell people you were best friends with history's most notorious sorcerer."

"Well," I interject. "That's a bit unfair. I'm not defending him, but he only ever killed war combatants, and there have been some truly horrific sorcerers in history. There was one, Atmos Rasassion, who shot skybolts at children for fun, and . . ." I stop, take in Sam's expression. "Not the right time for a story?"

"What do you think?"

"Point taken."

"Does Jacob know?" Sam asks.

"He doesn't." I think on my deputy, and I feel guilt, and concern over whether he is, in fact, safe right now, in the Wolflands. And I feel simple longing for my best friend. "I began the cult again, after the war, when I found Jacob, someone to bounce ideas off. As far as he knows, that was the original start of the cult."

Sam shakes her head. "You and your secrets, Sage Bailey. And what of now?"

I sigh. "Sinassion spoke into my head when I was with Raven and Jacob, only a few hours after leaving you for the Wolflands. He told me that the mortals were returning; he claimed they were coming back, though he explained little else. So I came back here, where he still was, to get answers. And he had, as is usual for him, a price to pay before I got them. He wants to save his old Shades—the Grays—save them from the Lords. They are broken things, their minds having being tortured into obedience. He feels he owes them freedom. And he had a solution."

"Mind control," Sam says, her breath stilled.

"Yes. I didn't know he could do that. Or at least that he was learning it. I've never heard of a Neuras being able to control people, as opposed to just reading minds. But he was."

"And he was practicing on you."

"Yes, hence our awkward meeting last time."

"Sage Bailey, master of reason, his mind a palace, allowing someone else to take control of it."

I clear my throat, avoiding her stare. "It was not . . . pleasant. But I . . . need to know what he knows, Sam. I *need* to. You must understand. I know you do."

Sam smiles and nods. Her blue eyes fix on mine. Those eyes could be a fine thing to get lost in if I had the time. "I understand. For my sins, I understand all too well."

"He needed more time, though," I continue. "To perfect it. To get them properly free. But then your revolution turned out to be a stunningly quick thing. A phenomenally clever plan, Sam, by the way, I have to hand it to you"—Sam mimes a bow—"but it meant he wasn't ready, so he could just about force them to leave the city, though it remains to be seen how much that has taken out of him."

"And so you still don't have his answers about the mortals."

I close my eyes briefly. "No, I do not." I open them. "But I have a plan."

Sam raises her eyebrow. "You thought of a plan already? On the walk here?"

"I did."

"Well," says Sam, smiling, a more warm smile now, like the conversations when we first met. I feel excitement in my belly. "That's a coincidence. I thought of a plan, too."

I lean forward, and I take her hand, and she doesn't resist, and I smile, and so does she, and then I say, "Samantha Ingle, would you like to combine our plans?"

The audience in the receiving room on the first floor of the townhouse—bigger than the one Sam and I were in previously and measures more ostentatious—is a half mimicry of the old team, shorn of Raven and Jacob, of course. Alanna lurks, not quite in the corner shadows this time but right behind her Lady's armchair, which is progress, I suppose, and a sign of something, their much warmer body language with each other indicating what that something might be. To their right, on one end of a long red padded chair, is Commander Tenfold, still in uniform, shock of red hair all frazzled, who looks surprised and a little irritable at being summoned from his attempts to secure the city after Rufous's breach to hear the words of a mage.

On the other end of the long chair is the most unusual member of this gathering, the old First Lord Azzuri, who was always so smartly dressed and so austere, albeit with a little bit of life and charm about him compared to some of the other dreary Lords, but now looks like the wine-cheered lead actor of *A Midwinter's Bloodflute*, the stagetale that came rolling through the Desertlands once, many, many years ago. His ragged beard, his vibrant mauve shirt, his muddy boots. By the Light, the phrase *how times change* hardly captures this one.

The room is completed by Molly Threetimes, on an old pine chair next to Daphnée's, one that looks too worn to belong to the room and, I suspect, she dragged in from somewhere to bring some of the Worn humility to this admittedly ridiculous townhouse. Her fellow rebel and obvious psychopath Hands Parker is absent, I am pleased to note, no doubt ordering her gangs around the city.

And then there is Sam, of course, sitting next to me, in front of the white plaster fireplace, facing the rest. She is putting a lot of her recently earned reputation on the line for me here. I find myself desperately wishing not to disappoint her and even more desperately wishing I was alone with her again.

"Right. Where do I start?" I say, by means of preamble.

"I could give you a few suggestions, if you like," says Alanna, face unreadable. I wisely choose to ignore her and begin to tell them everything I told Sam, my origins apart: of Sinassion, and his aims, and my history with him.

When I am done, there is one of those long silences that are impossible to decode and agonizing to be a party to.

"Well, bugger me," says Molly eventually, her thick Southwestfall brogue breaking through the awkwardness like a mallet through a glass window. "That's a lot to believe, boy. An' even if we believe you, you're still bosom brethren with the man with more blood on his hands than a bloodvatter."

"Well, I haven't been, uh, *bosom brethren* with him for a long time. And he didn't have any blood on his hands when he was with my cult. But yes, I agree it's . . . complicated."

"Actually, Bailey, it's very simple," says Commander Tenfold, stroking his chin. "We've just put Sinassion under lock and key in the same kind of cell we keep the wolf prisoners in. But unlike the wolf prisoners, we have to have two guards outside his cell at all times, in case he does his mind-reading, and especially now it seems he can take control of people. And then we have two guards a couple of passages back, whose job it is to look out for the two guards guarding him. And then we have a whole company of Blood Guard on standby, just in case that doesn't work. So what I reckon I'm saying is that you've been runnin' around the city I now have to protect with the man who it takes a bloody ludicrous amount of men just to keep under lock and key."

"Even if he recovers, he won't be a threat."

Tenfold grimaces. "Well, forgive me, Bailey, if I treat that advice like a trickle of piss in a rainstorm."

I try to parse how exactly you would treat such a thing before I realize I have bigger matters at stake.

"Look, ask Lady . . . Daphnée," I add. "She was there on the roof of First Gods with me when Sinassion spoke into all our minds. Told us he had nothing to do with Saxe's plan or his old army being turned into the Grays."

"That's true," says the Queen Leech, twirling the white flower in her hair thoughtfully. She looks very different without all her Lady trappings: her clothing, her face paint. I thought she might return to it now the city is, I suppose, hers, but if anything she looks more like Alanna than I've ever seen her. "However," she continues. "It does not take away from what he did in the Twin War."

"Nothing worse than what the vampires did to the wolves," I say darkly. "Better, if you consider he only killed soldiers."

"I'm not here to defend the Lords and their battles, darling," says Daphnée coldly. "Just reminding you of whom you consort with."

"Indeed," says Azzuri, sipping on his bloodflute, eyes narrowed. "Time does not take away the pain of my friends that sorcerer killed."

*And how many friends of the people in this room did your regime kill?* I almost go to say, but my trained techniques of anger restraint hold me back, just.

I blow my cheeks out. I had assumed, in my arrogance, that I could take the proverbial stand myself and defend my actions in front of this tough crowd, who have just won their city only to see history's bogeyman appear in it. I, not for the first time, may have overstated my abilities. I turn to Sam, who has been patiently watching me, and I throw off my vanity and I plead for help with my eyes.

Sam nods imperceptibly at me, and I understand in that moment that she knew I would do badly but that I needed to try. By the Light, is she perceptive. Something moves between us, and I know she has the floor now.

"Don't trust Sage Bailey," she says, pointing at me. I slightly regret giving her the floor. "You've no reason to. Well, you have a little reason, because it was his plan that helped Raven Ansbach break into the Blood Bank and find evidence of the terrible crime Spymaster Saxe and his cadre of Lords had committed against us all. And it was his assistance of Sinassion that enabled him to force the Grays to leave the city, which is why we're all talking and not ashes blowing away in the wind." She gives a beat to let her quiet edge of sarcasm hit its mark. "But regardless, you do not know him well enough. So don't trust him."

She looks at everyone in turn then, jaw set, eyes unblinking. Her wolfblood is all but gone but she is still ethereal. "Trust *me*."

She looks directly at Daphnée now. "Trust the maid that you saw fit to bring in to the Leeches. The one you trusted to hold the match you set fire to the city with."

Now Azzuri. "Trust the woman who came to you and gave you a chance when you deserved none. Who saw the pain of your guilt and your grief and how it had made you a new man." She looks at him, kindly, softly, and he looks back at her with . . . with the same look. Something has happened between them, you don't have to be a tiresome purveyor of body talk like myself to see that. Things really have changed around here.

Then she turns to Molly. "Trust the maid who gave you the plan that took the city with hardly any bloodshed. That stopped your daughters and your family and your neighbors from being cut down in the street by them that hate us."

Then Tenfold. "Trust the maid who put Azzuri on the path to you and gave your city back so your Blood Guard brothers didn't die in vain."

And finally, Alanna. "Trust—"

Alanna puts her hand up to stop her, the dagger she was playing with dangling from it. "I was on the mage's side to begin with, Sammy. But you can say somethin' bold if you want."

Sam smiles and turns to the rest. "If you trust me . . . you trust him. It's as simple as that, and there's nothing more to say."

Another silence then. Then Tenfold laughs, a great booming laugh, a guffaw. And points at Sam. "And *she* was cleaning pisspots and bed-sheets for ten fucking years? Bugger me, I'm recruitin' maids into the Blood Guard from now on, I'll tell yer that for free!"

Molly turns to him. "You should be doin' that anyway. And barmaids. Time to get a bit of sense into that big cockfest you're running."

Tenfold blows out his cheeks. "The winds of change, eh?"

Daphnée cuts in. "So what now, Sam?" She smiles, and their gazes meet, and there's a subtle exchange there. I'd almost say a mother proudly handing over to her daughter, if I wouldn't wince at the simplicity of the analysis.

"Well . . . it's not up to me to say what we do about the Lords that fled now," she begins. I'm not so sure about that, and I'm not sure she is, either. "But . . . Sage has a plan. *We* have a plan."

"And I have a deal to make." I look at Sam, who is slightly wincing. "I probably should have waited till we say the plan first," I add quickly, wondering if I will ever regain my reputation for incisive thinking after the remarkably bungling efforts I'm making before this crowd.

"From arguing why he shouldn't be locked up to making deals," grins Molly. "The balls on this one."

I am ready to let Sam take over, but she is looking at me with a *good luck* stare, and I sigh and wade forward. "First Light has just been freed from the Lords. But First Light's problems are not over. Even if you can keep peace with this new alliance of Worns and some Midways and the few Lords remaining, and avoid any kind of civil war, you have an unavoidable issue looming."

"The Lords who fled," says Molly grimly.

"Yes, exactly," I reply. "They are flailing now, especially after Rufous's failure and his impetuous murder of the spymaster, which I'm sure won't go down well. They will need time to regroup in the Centerlands, in Lightfall. Secure their own city. Turn the place they killed back to life. And for now, they will be low on wolfblood stores, just the ones they managed to grab with them when they fled. They have most of the bloodmages, it's true. But magicked blood doesn't give you wings, only wolfblood does. And they don't have the wolf prisoners to get new batches of it. They'll run out eventually."

"Yer not tellin' us anything we don't already know, boy," mutters Tenfold, who I realize too late probably isn't enamored with me treading on his territory.

"But they have the Grays," I continue quickly. "And that is everything. You can't rely on Sinassion to keep pulling that trick over and over again, even if you trust him to do so. They will come back to the city for war, come to reclaim their city, and when they do you'll need allies."

"The wolves," says Daphnée.

"Exactly," says Sage. "You all know your city better than me. You know you can't take on a Grays-and-Lords-and-some-of-the-Midway army, even assuming they don't find a way to get more wolfblood. Or at least, it would be too close to call."

"I see where this is heading," says Azzuri. "You are offering to go to the Wolflands and seek a vow to fight with us should it come to that."

"Exactly. I will secure the wolves as allies."

"And in return?" asks Molly. "What's your price?"

I clear my throat. "You guarantee Sinassion's safety. No sudden decision to execute him while I'm gone. And then you allow me access to him. I need answers from him about the mortals. I want what he promised me." I put my raised palm out, seeing a couple of my audience going to speak. "I know most of you don't believe me about the mortals. But I believe. And I want answers."

"Thought you were going to ask for Sinassion's freedom for a moment then, Bailey," says Tenfold.

I shake my head. *No*, I think. *Not yet. But when I return with the wolves at my back, you'll give me that, you'll see.* I try to shy away from my arrogance, but I believe it, and I mean it.

Daphnée narrows her eyes. "But Raven will be promoting our cause already, surely? And your man Jacob is there." She thinks on this. "Well, as I said, Raven will be promoting your cause. What more can you do?"

Sam speaks before I can. "I don't know if Raven can get us the wolves. I . . . I've read a lot on the wolfkind. They will not want to be drawn into a war, especially after the massacre of Extinction Valley, and I'm not sure Raven would want them to be. I'm sure she would be glad to roam the Centerlands, picking off Lord after Lord, and help in that way, maybe get some other wolves with her. But if you want someone who can argue our case to the wolves, and put together a strategy to win them over"—she nods at me—"this is the man."

"No," says Tenfold, then points at Sam. "That is the woman. She just turned the tide with us about Bailey here. I'm sure you're all clever and knowledgeable and can do a whole lot of thinking, mage, but Sam has the way with a crowd, I think we've all just learned that. She can convince them. You want your deal, she goes."

I see Daphnée raise her eyebrows in alarm. "Absolutely not. We're not sending her into wolf territory. I forbid it."

"I also would not allow it," says Azzuri. He clears his throat. "I apologize, I forget I am not ruler anymore. I mean, I would thoroughly discourage it."

"Nicely done, that," mutters Alanna from the shadows.

I look to them both, the Queen Leech and the ex-ruler. Does Sam see it? The panic in their eyes? The care they have for her? They, who have lost so much, their children, but found something in its place.

"Also," cuts in Molly, "you're in command of the Guard, Tenfold, not bloomin' everything, so don't be quick to be makin' those decisions on your own, all right?"

I turn to Sam, and I know, because I feel I know her now, I can read her, maybe not as much as she can read me but still strong—I know she's split. I see the excitement in her eyes at having the responsibility of bringing the entire Wolflands to our side. Her ambition burns from her, especially now her guilt over Beth has gone; it glows more strongly than she did on wolfblood, even. But she also doesn't want to leave her new family here, and the city she has steered to freedom. Even if I didn't read people so well, I would see this. I understand her even more than I understand Jacob.

I think we might be the same.

Then Alanna, as she so often does, decides it.

"Tenfold is right. Sammy brought this city down down down, and now she's got somethin' else to do. She's a weapon, big and scary, like it or not—if you haven't seen that yet, I don't have words for you. And she'll come back in one piece. Raven will protect her, and if you think this mage wouldn't jump in front of a foamin' wolfy for her then you're not readin' faces like you should. We're fighting. To survive. We're all pieces on boards. And it ain't our time to die. Not yet, anyways." She turns to Daphnée then, and says, sotto voce, "I'm sorry, Daffers, but you know it's true."

That's the most I've ever heard Alanna speak to a room, and after her Last Light lilt has faded away, her audience thinks on her words in thoughtful silence.

"I'm going," says Sam. "Hopefully not for long. We'll make our case, then we'll come back."

Daphnée looks away, lips thin, eyes pained, but she doesn't object.

Sam turns to me, and she says, as if she can make it so, "We'll come back."

# PART II

# Quoth the Raven, Evermore

18

# Welcome to the Wolflands

Wolves are not the same as us. You can have a conversation with them, you can observe their seeming emotions. But they do not share our values or our beliefs and you only have to watch the way they act with one another to observe that. Do not extend the same empathy you use for fellow vampires to the wolfkind. Do not fall under their spell, or fall for their forest cunning. Do not ever do that.

Carmine Ceruli, *A Treatise on the Real Wolfkind*

## Jacob

**One Week Ago**

I'm inside the most important castle in the Wolflands, though you'd hardly know it. The room I'm currently sitting in, along with Raven Ansbach, is one of the many windowless antechambers to the Great Hall, and it's pretty sparse. There's no upholstery on the worn wooden chairs. There's no wolf insignia on the walls. Aside from the torches in their sconces, there's nothing of interest. Just high walls that lead to a vaulted ceiling that clearly no one could be bothered to gild. Even a sorcerer's temple has a little more thought to it than this. A vampire Lord would piss out the contents of their last bloodflute to see such plainness.

Raven catches my subtle look of disgust and flashes me a thin mouth full of large teeth that I think is her way of showing annoyance but could just be her preparing to eat me; it's hard to tell. "We are wolves," she says. "We live in forests. Did you think we would give a shit about interiors?"

"Not really," I reply. "I just thought the home of the most important wolfpack would contain some, you know, furnishings."

"There are about five hundred wolves in Pack Ansbach. Only a hundred of them live in the castle environs. It is mainly for show. For the times when vampires and sorcerers used to come here. If we had our way, most of us would live in little more than a hut, if not the forest outright. Anyway, why do you care, mage? It hardly affects your drinking schedule." Raven shifts on her seat as she says this, which suggests to me that investing in comfortable furnishings might be a pretty universal requirement after all.

"That is a very reductive way of looking at my complex personality," I reply. "But if you must know, my drinking schedule has been quite seriously affected by the limited cellar on offer here. Mainly the fact there's no cellar. Just a lot of bottles of Wolfsbane whiskey, which may as well contain wolfsbane itself given their quality."

"I'm sorry your stay in the Wolflands has been so below expectations." Raven's lethal smile widens.

It *has* been below expectations, but still, I can hardly complain, as it's been a lot quieter and a lot less lethal than my recent stay in First Light. I arrived in the last vampire city two months ago with Sage to solve the murder of First Lord Azzuri's son. That led—in a twisty, fairly terrifying series of events during which time I was almost killed by a notorious sorcerer, shot by Grays, and executed by vampires—to the revelation that the Grays that had decimated half the land and kept us all to our respective corners of the Everlands were in fact a personal army of a bunch of Lords, who wanted to create a villain to keep the poor down and get a ton of wolfblood into the bargain. I think those were their motivations, anyway. Sage is always better on the details.

After that series of alarming and robe-wettingly horrifying developments, it has, if I'm honest, been nice to do absolutely nothing for the best part of a month—even if that nothing comes with a poor choice of liquor and a lack of both women who don't seem like they might eat me and any notion of thick mattresses.

At first I was fairly livid, however. Mainly at Sage, my oldest (and possibly only) friend, who had abandoned me at the start of our journey to the Wolflands, muttering some cryptic nonsense about needing to rendezvous with Neuras Sinassion; you know, the most dangerous sorcerer in the land whose claim that he had nothing to do with the Gray conspiracy was lacking a lot of concrete evidence. Sage had never abandoned me like that before. It was obvious he was keeping something about Sinassion from me. The sting of betrayal has gone deep in me, searing my insides, only mildly helped by the terrible spirits I've been imbibing and sometimes throwing up.

I'm still angry, but mostly I'm just impatient to see how the wolves in charge react when they discover that not only have their wolf criminals been handed over to the vampires to be bled for their blood on false pretenses for the last century, but that all the wolves who died at Grayfall were literally killed under the orders of vampires, a fact I'm sure they'll react to with a great amount of calm, I don't think.

As for me? I just want to fade into the Lightdamn background again. I was the jester in this story, my part in the most recent tale limited to plying some information out of a drunk soldier and convincing Sage to step in to save the girl he was mooning over, which he was probably going to do anyway. Sage is the hero; I'm the one who keeps them chuckling and gives some moral support when needed (with quote marks around the word *moral* on occasion).

Anyway, seeing Raven's displeasure at my moaning, I decide to change topic to save my arm.

"I notice you're clothed," I point out, pointing to Raven's outfit, which is stretching the definition of an outfit somewhat by being a loose collection of furs carelessly tied about her person.

"Ashen likes formality in his castle."

"Hmm," I say, sensing a sore spot and deciding to stay a good few miles away from it. "Very well," I venture instead, "so what's our plan?"

Raven squints at me with those small feral eyes of hers, pushing some of her jet-black hair from her eyes, which has all the use of an empty cask as it falls right back there. "Our plan?"

"Yes, our plan. What we say to Ashen Ansbach, your alpha and *definitely not the alpha of all the wolves, you have explained this to me in great detail so please don't do so again* but quite clearly your leader in all things but name. I feel like we should definitely have a plan."

"We tell him what we know."

"Oh, right, thank you. Glad I asked." I look behind me, hoping that in the intervening period since I last looked someone has decided to add a liquor cabinet to the piss-poor room, but alas not.

"I am an Ansbach," Raven continues, clearly sensing (or in her case most likely smelling) my cynicism. "Ashen is my alpha. I do not need to strategize a conversation with him. Wolves are honest, in our fashion. You can leave the politicking to your kind and the bloods."

I don't think anyone is honest when it comes down to it, but I decide it's probably not the time to be arguing such things. In fact, in the month I've been a guest in the Wolflands, there's not been much arguing going on at all. Raven has been out of the castle most of the time, hunting the forests of the Ansbach territory, familiarizing herself with it, I suppose, after years in the forests around First Light, while she waits for Ashen to return. I've barely seen her.

Meanwhile, I've been recovering from the memories of First Light in my own unique manner, by combining drink and cards in ever inventive ways. Most wolves have steered clear of me, not used to mages in these parts, obviously, though a couple of them have deigned to drink and game with me. I was surprised at first that a whole month could pass before the most important wolf returns to his home, but Raven said he was doing his annual forest run (she may have called it something more specific, I wasn't completely listening) and nothing comes before this for wolves. I said, yes, but surely there's a way of contacting him when, for example, the most important news of the century pops up. She replied that there is nothing so important that it can't wait a couple of weeks. This and many other things make me realize that wolves are not like sorcerers or vampires at all.

"So how much longer, Raven, do we have to wait for—"

"RAVEN!"

The doors to the Great Hall swing open and one of the largest specimens of the wolfkind I've ever seen strides through. He must be at least seven feet, probably more, a good half a foot taller than Raven, at least. He's a lot wider than her, too; whereas Raven is lean, tight muscle, this wolf is muscle wrapped in fat with a noticeable belly. But the extra weight doesn't spoil; it adds to his power and the sense that he could throw me through the wall if he chose, and maybe a few more behind that one.

He's covered in a fur gown, which I'm quickly discovering is what wolves wear when they feel they should be wearing clothes. The sigil of the Ansbachs is stitched into the collar: a full moon with some kind of plant half covering it. I know it's the sigil because it's shading everywhere in this castle; they may not like furniture but they're fine with symbolism.

The final clue to his identity is his face: red cheeks, lively, friendly eyes, and more importantly, a thick, deep beard as dense and unruly as it is ash gray. The color gives it away. If this isn't Ashen Ansbach himself it's a Lightdamn impostor.

"Ashen," replies Raven, moving to greet him. I'm reminded that wolves really don't give a shit about titles. Choice names only here. She pauses before him for a few moments, and neither speak, and I brace myself for some social awkwardness.

But then she grins and hugs him, and he hugs her back, and this bear embrace continues for a while, and halfway through they pause in the hug to push their faces against each other. For a moment I think this has taken an unexpected and very interesting turn, but there's no kissing, and I realize that this is the wolf in them, the equivalent of dogs mushing their muzzles together in greeting. An awkward amount of time later, the wolf greeting is over and Ashen turns his jovial features my way.

"Sorcerer. Welcome to Ansbach castle, and to the Wolflands. I'm sorry I wasn't here when you arrived. I was deep in the woods; my wolf run took longer than usual. Anyway, I'm here now, so why don't you join me in the hall, drink some ale, and tell me the bad fucking news, eh?"

I smile. This is certainly a different conversation to the last time I sat down with an immortal leader, First Lord Azzuri. Weren't too many *fucks* in that one, as I recall.

The Great Hall is well named. Vampires still wouldn't be impressed, but what the wolves lack in fine design they make up for in huge castle rooms that go up for days and great stone walls built to last covered in fine tapestries that look like they took years, not months, to stitch. A great fire roars in the central hearth, the flames giving off more than just heat but a slight whiff of the forest, earthy but fragrant. Raven notices me smelling it, and says, "Nosegreen. Grows near the northern coast. Classic wolf trick. Takes the edge off that muddy dog smell."

We follow Ashen to a long brown table set in the center of the hall, covered with dishes of what I hope is animal meat stewing in gravy and vegetables and large flagons of what I am really hoping is ale.

Ashen takes a seat on the fireside side and beckons us to sit opposite.

As I sit, I try to remember the basics of what Raven has patiently tried to get across to me. That Ashen isn't the alpha of all the wolves, not really. Wolves are made up of a series of separate packs, ruled—in a sense, and a Lightdamn confusing one at that—by alphas. But, crucially, none have dominion over the others. There are wolf rights and wolf laws, which are shared but are still the sole prerogative of each pack when it comes to the administration of them, or something. I think I'd definitely lost sobriety at this point in the telling. The key point is that the only exception to this strange way of ordering wolf society is that when foreign affairs are discussed—when it comes to bloods and mages—the wolves do look to a leader. That leader is Ashen. There's good reason for this, and I need to ask Raven about that story one day.

Speaking of Raven, she is now slouched in the chair next to me. "Ashen, this is Jacob, the Second Brother of the Cult of Humanis, and along with his first, the diplomatic point guard of the Archmage himself while in First Light."

"Basically the one who does all the shit your First Brother can't be fucked with, correct?" Ashen grins, as if I need another reminder that we're not in the company of noblebloods anymore. "How is life with Raven treating you?"

"She saved my life, so I would say fairly well," I reply, still slightly stunned by the formality of Raven's opening and the reminder that I'm still technically representing all the sorcerers, albeit memorably badly.

"Yes," Ashen says, "she's useful like that, is old Midnight."

"He saved my life, too, so on balance I would say these cult mages are more capable than they look," says Raven, expression fixed.

"Oh dear." Ashen grins again. "She won't like that at all, Jacob. Won't like that at all!" He chuckles to himself, then smooths out his beard, which seems the most pointless activity known to mage. "Right. That's the boring shit out of the way. Now let's get down to it. I want to hear what's so important there's the first bloody sorcerer in my castle for a century."

There's a slight pause. Then Raven nods. "We are fucked." Then they grin at each other, as if the fate of the entire continent is a fart of a dog by the fire. "But I think it is best explained by Jacob. He has his leader's way with words."

I turn to Raven, trying to work out if she is mocking me. Her face gives nothing away.

"Okay," I begin. "I suppose we're doing this. Essentially, the rub is this. The Grays are Shades, the old Neuras army of Neuras Sinassion. They were not killed as we were all led to believe, but secretly kept alive by a small group of Lords, led by Spymaster Saxe. They were turned through torture, I think, into weapons to be commanded. The bullets they were armed with were found in an underground store shortly before Grayfall. We don't know where they come from."

I turn to Raven at this point, and look at her impossible-to-read expression, her thin smile and hair-covered eyes. She doesn't contradict me, even though she knows from the evidence of her own eyes and Sage's First Guard–massacring metal suit that the Cult of Humanis are keeping a lot more than mysterious relics. She heard me when I told Sam that we hoard mortal weapons and strange tools to keep them out of others' hands, and to study them. She must have made the connection that the bullets can only be of mortal origin. That said, Sage and I haven't come across the Gray bullets before, so in a sense I'm not lying. In a very measly sense that's probably not invited to many festivities because it's such a little shit.

"Anyway," I continue, "Saxe used these Shades and their weapons to carry out Grayfall, to make vampire society into the pathetic, class-respecting rabble you see now rather than the bolder kind that had been brewing in Lightfall. And, most importantly for your lot"—I remember who I'm talking to and clear my throat—"for your kind, their actions meant they could get an endless supply of wolfblood to hoard from yourselves, or rather your wolf criminals, under the lie of one day taking the battle to the Grays, with wings rather than feet."

No one speaks for a few moments. I see Ashen breathing heavily, clenching his fists, and I'm a little concerned. I don't want to find myself in a room full of angry wolves for many reasons.

"*Mi thcil sed sednom*," says Ashen, repeating the words stitched into his robe below the moon sigil. I don't know Wolftongue—a language barely used by even the wolfkind anymore, except for their old mottos—but I know enough about the wolves to know the famous motto of the Ansbachs. *By the light of the moon.* "Great Wolf. I should have expected it from the kind who would do what they did at Extinction Valley, but this . . . it is something else. Something only the twisted dreams of the highblooded could have come up with. Great moon, this is fucked. But tell me, Jacob, to what end would the wolfblood have been used, which we gave them with such simple hopes?"

Raven takes over at this point, clearly having had her fun of putting me on the spot. "Saxe never elaborated on the conspirators' ultimate plans. I imagine it would have been to make a fakery of the defeat of the Grays at some point, then use the stores of wolfblood to attack us, imprisoning enough to give them endless supplies, with which they could reign supreme and remake the continent in their image."

Ashen nods and tears off a large leg of what might be rabbit in front of him. He rips the flesh off it, throwing the bone into a bowl behind him without looking. "That sounds like them. Domination, control, victory. It is all they know. You would think wolfblood would teach them sense. It must be in them, then, not the blood."

Before I can ponder this unexpected spot of philosophy from someone spitting out gristle, Ashen hits us with a series of follow-up questions. Raven takes most of them now, me having done my job, it seems.

Eventually, Ashen pauses and squints at me. "I have one more question. It may seem less diplomatic than you're used to, so forgive me. But wolves are direct, as you've no doubt already noticed. It is simply this: How can we trust you, and trust you're not working for the noble-bloods?"

I think about this. "It would be a strange move to be working for them while so boldly incriminating them, wouldn't it?"

Ashen leans forward and studies me. "We learned at Extinction Valley that there's no level of bizarre cunning that the bloods and the mages cannot sink to when they conspire."

This is the third time Extinction Valley's been brought up. I know enough to know it was a huge battle halfway in the Twin War that didn't go so well for the wolves. From the very start of that great stupid war, which ended the best part of two centuries ago now, the bloods and wolves had been fighting smaller battles and invading cities and skirmishing and genuinely giving each other bloody noses with no real momentum swing to either side. Throwing away lives with nothing much to show for it, thus it ever fucking was.

Eventually both sides got tired of this and, if my extremely bad memory for history is right, they met in a valley nestling between First Light and the Wolflands. One ruddy great battle. I feel like some sorcerers might have been involved on the vampire side, too. And I also remember that after it, the wolves were pretty weak and the vampires might have swept east and then south and all the way through the Wolflands if it hadn't been for the intervention of Neuras Sinassion, the crazy bastard, who thought that this was a good time to try to take over the Everlands himself with his creepy mind-reading army and was so good at it that the vampires were forced to work with the wolves they'd only just walloped in the valley.

I have a feeling, though, that I might need to ask Raven more about the details of the battle itself if the wolves are going to bandy it around constantly like the first lay they ever had.

"Well, look," I say, trying to summon the courage I did when getting information from Tenfold in his lair, too. "You seem like a no-nonsense fellow. A good judge of character. If you think I'm a spy for the nobles, then kill me and add me to those plates of yours." I nod to the meat selection remaining in front of him that's not been reduced to bones.

Ashen grins. "Not a bad answer. Although I'm not the one who'd kill you," he adds, eyes shifting ominously to the notorious assassin seated next to me. "Raven, old friend. What do you say? I will take your word."

Raven stretches, as if she's come out of a nap. "Everything he has said is true. And you can trust him."

"Do you swear it?" asks Ashen.

"By the bloodmoon."

Ashen nods, then rubs his hands together, which is like two birds' nests mating. "Well, that is it, then. I will assemble the Outside Council to decide on the next step."

"Hold on," I say, my surprise coming out of me quicker than any sense of my surroundings, which I will definitely blame later on the strength of the wolf ale. "What do you mean, the next step? What is there to decide on? The bloods literally killed thousands of wolves on purpose, through the Grays at Grayfall. You've been trapped in the Wolflands for a century, fearing death by Gray if you venture out into the Centerlands, and all this time the enemy you feared has been controlled by the vampire Lords!"

"Jacob . . ." Raven growls.

"No, no, hear me out for once," I reply, genuine anger surging in me now. "You signed a pact with the vampires to give your criminals over, so they could store their own wolfblood. . . . But if it wasn't for the Grays they needed that, then what do you think they were storing up for? To fly around for a bit for a jest? Aerial wanking? They were saving it up to destroy you utterly, surely? Finally kill you all, a great winged army, like they've been trying to do for countless centuries! If that's not an act of war, what is? I mean, you have to destroy them now, right? I never thought the bloody wolves would shy away from a fight!"

Ashen doesn't reply to this for a while. He doesn't seem angry, more thoughtful. He picks some unidentified meat from his beard and chews on it thoughtfully.

"Have you fought many battles?" he says eventually. "Slain many foes? I smell you, and I get a mix of chalk and soft metal, concern and fear ebbing and flowing through this conversation. Yet you who can barely handle us would counsel me on war? I've seen war. So has Raven. We've smelled it up close, the sense of death and the true smell of fear, which is iron, richer than blood. We've stood in the light of the moon and seen such desolation that would make you cry for generations. So if we do not immediately jump to war, you should think on that and ask why."

I gulp. "That's me told, then," I reply, and I see Ashen's fierce expression turn into a grin and feel a tiny bit bolder even as a little stream of piss threatens to leak out of me. "I don't mean to offend," I add, "but I've seen the workings of these Lords who conspire this up close, and they're more dangerous than you can imagine. I promise you that they must be stopped, and quickly. I swear it by the bloodmoon."

There's a long pause.

"That only works if you're a wolf, doesn't it?" I say eventually.

"Yes," replies Ashen, locking eyes with Raven, "it only works if you're a wolf." He smirks and reaches for a final limb of some indeterminate forest animal. "I like your fire, Jacob." He swallows it whole, then spits the bones out behind him, once again straight into the bowl. That's some talent.

"But heed my words on war," he continues, "though war may be coming nonetheless. Even if I wanted to, however, I could not make the decision here. I must assemble the Outside Council, for matters that concern other immortals. All the alphas of the other packs will meet here, at Ansbach castle, in one week's time, assuming none of them are on their wolf runs and thus not contactable. I will put the problem to them, and we will devise a solution, whether that is war or some other form."

He takes a moment to drain his ale, wiping his hand across his mouth, which does little to soak up the beer on his beard. "That is the wolf way. We do not decide decisions on the whim of one. That's for bloods. We of the forest know better than that."

I nod, sensing the meeting is over. But Ashen seems to think twice about getting up, and stares at me.

"Cult of Humanis," he says after a while. "That's where you're from, isn't it? The cult who believe in the mortals as fact, not myth or fancy fable." I must look surprised, as he laughs and says, "I might look like I drink and fuck and sleep all day but I do read, Jacob. So tell me, because I don't often get chances like these to learn new things. Where did they go, in your opinion, and who were they?"

I pause. "You're curious?"

Ashen shrugs. "If I'm to trust you, mage, I need to know you're not a madman. We're the only ones who are allowed to howl at the moon. Sounds fair?"

I consider this, and what I can tell him. Unlike the vampire Lords I doubt he'd be that keen on raiding the cult if he knew what was contained beneath it; then again, I think as I recall some of the relics, maybe he would. Well, as long as he doesn't ask *how* I suspect this. . . .

"I think the mortals existed once, long ago. When our ancestors were beasts, before the Great Intelligence, when sorcerers, vampires, and bloods became fully conscious and civilized. I think they had a great civilization, of magicks and artifices we can only dream of."

Ashen studies me carefully, stroking his empty cup. "And where did they go then, this great civilization? Just up and went, did they?"

"Well . . ." I clear my throat. "I should say with some emphasis that my leader Sage Bailey does not agree with me on this. But I think something bad happened to them. They killed themselves. Destroyed their civilization. Almost like we all did, in the Twin War, if you think about it. But with greater magicks, so they made it permanent. Doesn't matter how advanced someone is, sooner or later they find a way to fuck it up. It's inevitable."

Ashen raises his eyebrows. "Cheery bastard, you, aren't you? But not necessarily wrong. You're wiser than you look, at any rate."

"Thank . . . you?"

"So what were *we* then? Their pets? Before the Great Intelligence, I mean."

"Actually, I think they created us," I said. "Maybe as some experiment." I clear my throat again, already regretting this. "I should add that Sage also doesn't agree with this."

Ashen nods. Then he leans back and stares at the ceiling and closes his eyes. For a very awkward moment I wonder if he's fallen asleep. Even Raven, who's been watching our recent interactions with not a little measure of amusement, looks briefly confused.

Then his voice comes out, softer than before. "I've spoken to one or two wolves over the centuries—the few still around from that between time, that age of who-knows-how-bloody-long between the Great Intelligence and that stupid vampire dating system begins—who claim to have been alive *before* the Great Intelligence, or whatever the moons it was. I never believed them. They can't seem to remember anything about it, which isn't that helpful. But the older I get, the more deaths I see, the longer I lead . . . the more I think about our past. The more its secrets start to nibble at me and disturb my dreams."

Then, so suddenly I jump myself, he leaps up out of his chair, much quicker than his bulk would seem to allow him, and beams at us. "Right, that's it. Enough moping. Raven, we will talk soon, yes?"

Raven grins. "You can count on it."

"Then goodbye. I have a pack mate to greet who I've not seen in a bloody age. And some washing of this stinking fur to do!"

Then he's gone, leaving us with his food and drink and the strong odor of gristle and fur.

I turn to Raven. "It's just a formality, yes? They'll decide on war, then those vampire-Lord fucks will be sorry."

Raven gives me a faraway look. "Maybe. But if they do, what then? How do we wolves fight the Lords and the Grays? Our numbers are smaller after the war, never mind Grayfall. To go to war could be the end of us. There is no good strategy here, short of recruiting every single sorcerer to their side, too."

"But if they don't, then the vampire nobles will keep building up their wolfblood, and then no one will be able to stop the ruthless little pricks."

"Unless the Worns rise up."

I snort. "With whose army?"

Raven shrugs. "Well, then, there are no good outcomes, Jacob. The players are arranged, but the game is rigged. There may just be blood ahead, much of which I will shed."

"You're quite depressing to be around sometimes, you know that?" But try as I might, I can't disagree with her.

"How do you think that went?" I ask Raven. It's been a glass since I watched Ashen gnaw his way through a series of different forest animals and announce the Outside Council instead of outright war. Now I sit on a bench in the castle gardens, newly made, I assume, as I can smell the wood as if fresh from the forest. I didn't think wolves would have gardens, being all about the wild. I thought that was a vampire thing. I'm quickly learning that despite having drunk my way through the best part of two centuries I know as much about wolves as I do about the place I was born. Cock all, to be more specific.

"It went as well as could be expected," replies Raven. "You didn't offend anyone, and Ashen decided to summon the council." The Midnight Assassin is standing behind me, two paces to my right. Raven has the strange habit of never sitting next to someone but lingering in the background, giving the impression she could slip into the shadows at any moment. I suspect that's the point. Or maybe I'm just an annoying person to sit next to. I do tend to spill whatever I'm drinking, occasionally, on whoever's next to me.

I stare at the herb garden spread out in front of me. Takelily, chalkweed, and wolf parsley dominate. Other herbs I can't name are spaced beyond them in neat little rows. I even see some mageweed, which I'm surprised at because, as the name suggests, it's not what you'd expect a wolf to be growing. Beyond the herb garden is what looks like a rose garden, great tall varieties in all the colors: red, blue, green, and mixtures of all. Beyond that, in the center of some artfully cut concentric circles of grass, is a fountain spewing over an arrangement of smooth oval pebbles. It's impressive if you like that kind of thing.

"All Golden's work," says Raven, referring to Golden Ansbach, Ashen's wife. Or pack mate, as Raven would no doubt remind me with a scowl. "She likes such things. Not so much a forest wolf, she."

"That sounds like a criticism."

There is a long pause while I try to work out if I've annoyed Raven or she's just left my presence. I stare determinedly at the herbs ahead, refusing to play her game and look behind me.

"Wolves are not like mages and sorcerers," she replies eventually. "We do not judge one for being not quite like the rest."

"I'll believe that when I see it. In my experience, wherever there's a group of intelligent beings, there'll always be some who make a minority feel unwelcome."

"So cynical, mage."

"Ha!" Beyond my better judgment, I cackle out loud. "This coming from you. I have been in your company quite a lot, you know."

"Yes," replies Raven, "I have noticed."

There is another long silence, then I venture another line of conversation, hoping it's not into the wind. "Ashen will convince the other alphas to act, won't he?"

"Perhaps. Perhaps not."

"But," I add, readying myself for trying to understand wolf things,

"Ashen is their leader. Not normally, you've explained this to me a thousand times, please don't start again, but for the purposes of external matters concerning vampires and mages. Other immortals. So he has the final say over what to do, yes?"

"He's the alpha who makes the ultimate decision for the Outside Council."

"Yes. So their leader."

"No. The other alphas are not beholden to him. He must respect their wishes."

"But he makes the ultimate decision."

"The decision that all have agreed upon."

"But what if there is no agreement?"

"Then he makes the decision for them."

I pinch the bridge of my nose, wishing for a flask. "But you just said—"

"If they have decided that nothing has been agreed upon, then he is still respecting that by coming to a decision none of them have agreed upon."

I contemplate this. "I hate you."

I sense her shrug behind me. "I would recommend not trying to understand us, sorcerer. At any rate, you have assumed Ashen would want war himself anyway. You heard him in the meeting, did you not? I know you listen, even if it seems you are with the drink most of the time."

"Yes, I heard him, but I thought he was just making a point. I mean, he's Ashen Ansbach. *The* Ashen Ansbach. Didn't he save you all in the battle of Extinction Valley? The great shading battle that almost finished the wolves off for good in the war? The one everyone seems to name-drop round here? He knows how dangerous the vampires are. I mean, Light of Luce, surely he wants revenge, if nothing else?"

Raven sighs. "I think the problem here, mage, is that you do not understand the lessons we took from Extinction Valley."

"And what are those lessons?"

"Not now."

"Fine, grumpiest wolf in the land. Just tell me this, Raven. Do you feel the same? Are you skeptical against war?"

"What do you think?" For a second I assume she's being rhetorical—sarcastic, as is her way—but it sounds genuine. The first time Raven has ever asked me for my opinion. I'll take this as a sign of progress.

"I think you hate them," I reply. "Vampires, that is. The nobles, at least. I think you're barely controlled anger dressed up in fine clothes. I think you want revenge. I think you want blood. I think you would wage war on them, and Lightdamn the consequences. I don't know how many years you've kept yourself as a coiled spring, but one day you'll snap back and there'll be a shitload of death as a result."

I let her think on this. "That is not the most stupid thing you have ever said."

"Thank you."

"You know," she continues, "Ansbach castle, and our lands round it, used to be known by another name. Before the Twin War. We called it Moonfall."

I think on this. "I like it. Sort of a twin to Lightfall. Or Shadowfall. Very much a theme I'm picking up on."

"Exactly. And that is why no one calls it that anymore. Once the vampires almost killed us all, we did not want to think we were anything like them. Because, ultimately, we are not."

There's more silence. I'm sure she's gone this time. But then: "You know, Jacob. When you challenged Ashen. That was . . . surprising. I considered you a drunken coward. But that was unusually brave. Or foolish, one of the two. But it surprised me."

Finally I turn, confident in looking her in her endlessly shadowed eyes. "You just called me by my actual name for the first time, do you realize that?" But now she's actually gone.

*Sigh.* That makes sense.

19

# Extinction Event

> There used to be eight packs, once of a time. One was massacred centuries ago, and is almost forgotten now. Three more were completely eviscerated in the Twin War, two alone at Extinction Valley. Then a new pack was born after the war, the Stubbes. So only four of the old packs are left, five in total. I am one of the oldest wolves left in the Wolflands. I can remember a time of all eight. All of us thought ourselves invincible, that the Wolflands would remain as it was. But now? Now I am unsure if my pack will last a century. Life seems to get more fragile as the centuries go on. Is this what they call progress? It has a funny flavor, if so.
>
> Treemoss Soissons, *Me and the Pack*

## Raven

**One Week Later**

I scan the Great Hall, trying to control the waves of scents hitting my nostrils, the result of a fair amount of new wolves having arrived at Castle Ansbach for the Outside Council meeting. You'd think centuries of being a wolf would give you control over being in their presence, but the fact is that wolves do not have the habit of meeting in large gatherings, even in their packs, and when they do it is almost always outside. Hardly any packs have a castle like the Ansbachs and even fewer have a great hall this size to hold a large group of wolves in. Controlling the attack on my senses in this room is like trying to hold back the tide with a fucking snaptail at your back. How are the rest doing it? I look to my right as a wolf server brushes past me, clutching a tray of tankards, almost brushing me and eyes widening in alarm when they see how close they came to spilling it on me. Ale and spirits. I am tempted to take some myself, but I need to stay sharp, with so many new scents and old wolves around me. I should be relaxed in the heart of my pack. But despite what I say to Jacob repeatedly about wolves not being vampires, I know that this century has not been like the last and the one just beginning will be even less so.

I breathe in heavily. Try to separate the odors from one another. Unthread them, and calm them so they're not overpowering. I unpick a thread of soft decay from a group of wolves hugging a bench in the western side of the hall, chewing over some meat. One of them is feeling lustful, then. Lust is a rotting stench for wolves, unless the lust comes from one you lust for back, in which case it takes on the aroma of warm honey. I turn to the center table, packed with carousers. It is hard to distinguish anything from the general scent of soft wood, pine, and some alder, which comes from adrenaline and excitement, and there is a lot of that here. After all, how could there not be? The Outside Council is not often called. Once a decade, perhaps. It used to be more, but after Grayfall and the Pact—after the wolves agreed to send their criminals to the vampires to be bled for wolfblood in the hope of powering an army to take on the Grays—little has needed to be discussed.

But now the alphas of the four other packs are here: the Stubbes, the Morbachs, the Gevaudans, and the Soissons. There used to be more than five packs, of course. But then Extinction Valley happened, and a century and a half later there are still only five; all the survivors of the others filtered into the remainders, and the Stubbe pack was formed to take in some more. Around five hundred wolves in each pack now. Including the packless, that's barely three thousand wolves. Our numbers reduced to a third, and Grayfall didn't help with that, although that was worse for the bloods and mages.

Perhaps this is why Ashen is so reticent about war. He has a long memory, almost as long as mine. As the centuries pass, we decline, not rise, and the only guarantee with war is that you will have less of your kind at the end of it than at the start.

I consider the room some more, wondering where to start. I know Ashen will want me to be diplomatic, make words with some of the other pack alphas. Huddled round a corner table in the western recesses of the hall, I spy Bronzed Morbach and his two underwolves, separate from the others. Each alpha brings, by tradition, two unders with them to a council meeting. Normally one is a good fighter—not that they need this; we are not bloods and do our violence in the forest in fair fights, not secretly in the shadows. The other underwolf is normally their closest, most trusted advisor.

I decide to avoid the Morbachs for now. They are the closest of the packs to the manner of vampires; being the nearest to them in geography, they take after some of their customs and used to side with them in various dealings in that strange time of peace between the end of the Twin War and Grayfall. You can see the influence of the bloods in the finer furs they wear: thinner, with silk draped off them. Utterly ridiculous for a wolf but completely what you would expect from the first wolves to move to Lightfall and embrace the mix of cultures that metropolis provided.

I turn to the east of the hall, where several card tables have been laid out for those finished eating, and I see Berry Gevaudan and her underwolves, playing, by the looks of the ring of pairs taking up most of the table, a game of Moontide with a couple from my pack. Berry's bright summer fruit–blue fur stands out even from over here. The Gevaudans are traditional allies of the Ansbachs, respectful of the balance we've always tried to strike between aggression and calm. They are our mirrors, in many ways. But I am reluctant to talk to them. I have killed or recaptured four of their kind since Grayfall, all escapees from First Light. I did what I had to do to maintain the peace; I doubt they will understand. I lose friends as the centuries pass.

I realize with a sigh that I am not made for the conversation; I am made for the hunt. And there is no hunting to be done here. I am irrelevant.

"Standing moodily in the corner? Must be none other than the Midnight Assassin herself."

That voice dripping with half-congealed slime, making your day worse by the hearing of it. It can only be one wolf.

"Silver Stubbe," I reply, not turning round, making him move in front of me instead. "I wondered when you'd appear."

"Well, I don't drink that much, as you know, Raven. The carousing isn't really for me. I have other things to attend to." He adopts a sly grin as he says this, and I take him in. Silver Stubbe reminds me of Ashen, in the sense they are true opposites. His long argent hair flows freely down to his shoulders, so bright compared to Ashen's dusty gray. It is carefully brushed, I see, in contrast to Ashen's. Where my alpha has a round face, capped off with an amiable grin, Silver's is all high cheekbones and a long slender nose and close-together eyes with a thin, knowing smile, like he's busy writing down the things he will say to others about you when you're gone.

You can, perhaps, get a feeling of how little I like him.

"I am awash with anticipation to hear why this council has been called," he continues.

"I am sure you are," I say, hoping short replies will speed me through the long months this conversation could go on for.

"Do you think, Raven, that it will be about the large number of escapee wolves who have come from First Light? The ones hunted down by you, and sometimes killed, simply for the crime of wanting to return to their beloved homeland?"

"Straight to it, then," I reply, glad that he is not delaying the fight.

"We shouldn't be bleeding any wolves for bloods. You know this, Raven."

I take a small step toward him. Just a small one, with the potential for large ones to come. "What I know is that after Grayfall, we signed a pact. We give them our criminals to be bled. They fight the Grays for us, when they have enough wolfblood. Fly over the bastards and give us our continent back. And when I say 'we' signed it, I mean you did, too. Unless that was your identical twin making a paw mark in your own blood."

His eyes dart sideways and he sniffs, no doubt thinking of another line of attack.

"Always defending, Raven. Always defending the bloods. No matter how low we go, no matter how much we subject ourselves to their form of 'justice' or their one-sided deals, you can always rely on the legendary Raven Ansbach to take their side."

"The wolves being subjected to them, as you put it, are those who murdered cubs, or raped, or killed in cowardice. I am fine with that."

"They are still ours. You know, I remember you in the Twin War."

I gird myself for what is coming. Everyone always fucking remembers me in the war.

"I remember you biting the heads off the Crimson Battalion, ten, twenty, thirty. I remember they could barely land a claw on you, even on the wolfblood. I respected you then."

I try to remember Silver back then, but fail. I know that he was an underwolf in Pack Gevaudan. Outraged by the peace that followed the war, the peace between vampires and wolves, he formed his own pack, the Stubbes. It has only been done once, and done by him. It began small; most of the Stubbes were born after the war. They have procreated well and now equal the other packs. And they all share Silver's desire for revenge against an outcome very few were there to witness.

"I imagine this is the part where you mention Extinction Valley," I reply.

"And why wouldn't I?" he says, his stretched smirk now twisted into a sneer. "The great Ashen Ansbach, savior of the wolves in the valley, except really he sealed the doom of the rest, didn't he? And then sold their memories out by making peace with the bloods after the battle."

"We did not have a choice. If it had not been for Ashen's actions and the Ansbachs, there would not have been any wolves left at all after Extinction Valley. The moniker is a bit of a clue. We were devastated. Reduced to a third of our number. Besides, you may remember—although most of your infant pack will have to read it in the pastscribers' tomes—that Sinassion and his Shades threatened the entire continent. We had to work with the bloods. At least they brought peace."

"Ah, yes, and what a peace." Silver runs an angry hand through his hair, although whether true or performative anger you can never quite tell with him. "What a peace, restricted to one corner of the continent and obliged to bleed for the bloods!"

I go to make the point that it was the Grays that did the restricting, not the vampires, and then I remember what I know now, and I inwardly balk at how Silver will react when Ashen delivers the news of who the Grays really are and who they are controlled by. It will make his prowar argument fairly well for him when he finds out what the bloods have done to us.

"I don't feel restricted. I feel at home," I say instead, feeling a low growl build up in me as I tire of the words. "We would all be happier if the Stubbes would appreciate what they had."

"Be grateful, you mean? To who, you? Always fancied you for a messiah complex, Raven. I am not grateful. I am ready to fight for my kind."

"Spoken like someone who has only seen one war and lives with those who have seen none. Where were you in Extinction Valley? At the back of the wolf lines, keen to escape when Ashen led the retreat?"

Silver takes a step toward me, and then stops, correcting himself. He is angry, but he is a coward. Sometimes a moment is all you need to have your suspicions confirmed.

"Do you know what I find curious about you, Silver?" I ask, taking advantage of his belly-showing, as wolves say. "You talk with such anger. Such passion. But you do not smell angry. There is surprisingly little citrus on my nose."

Silver shrugs, not expecting this line of attack. "I am in control of myself. You could learn a lesson or two on control, from what I know of your past. You have a habit of killing people first, and never asking questions later."

"No," I continue, grinning a little, letting him see some canine. "I do not think it is control. I think it is an act. But the question I always wonder is, who are you acting for?"

I walk away then, before he can reply. This will annoy him, and my grin grows wider at the thought.

## Jacob

I put down another pair, face down, hoping the wolf opposite me won't guess I don't, in fact, have two moons. Moontide is not a complicated game in terms of the amount of rules. At least I seem to be following it despite having mostly emptied my flask of Wolfsbane whiskey, but it does rely on bluffing a lot; half the game is calling someone out when you think they've faked a pair. It's a game of luck and bluff and calling out bluff, very different from the complex vampire card games. It's funny that it would be a game played by wolves, surely the least prone to lying of the three immortals, but maybe that's why they like it the most. They won't stop bloody playing it, anyway.

As I wait for the other player to react, I glance around the antechamber, seeing if any new wolves have escaped from the boisterous chaos of the Great Hall to ply the card trade in mildly calmer surroundings. I say mildly because it's pretty clear when there's drinking and carousing around, as wolves seem to abandon any pretense of subtlety or caring about how their heads will feel in the morning. At least it's less crowded in here; there's only a couple of other games being played, but which wolves from which packs are playing them I can't tell because, I've come to realize, the furs they wear in person form are mostly the same. Sorcerers and vampires share a great affinity for getting their cocks out, sartorially speaking, showing off their status with their finery. Wolves do not. I am starting to warm to these mud-smelling freaks.

"Hmm! You are slowly improving, mage," bellows the beast hunched over a stool across from me eventually, and, I would say, testing the stool's ability to remain one. He is definitely an alpha. It feels like I'm playing a giant bush or some kind of foliage. The main reason for this is that the wolf is green. All the wolves in Pack Soissons have various shades of green fur, I've been told between rounds. The one I'm playing, the alpha Verdant Soissons, has the deep forest green that you'd expect from his moniker. It's quite the sight. Green fur is not something you get used to quickly. Especially when you were minding your own business among a frankly intimidating number of wolves when Verdant came and asked for a game with you, and then proceeded to play. He seems friendly enough, very much like Ashen in size, face, and friendly manner. I just wish there was one part of his body that wasn't covered with shading green.

"So why are you here again, little mage?" he asks, his voice deep and rasping, like it's coming from someone trapped inside him. "Not that I mind, it's fun to play Moontide with a sorcerer. There have not been sorcerers here since, well, since Extinction Valley, I suppose. They were not very popular after that! I wondered if I would ever see one again, to be honest."

I shrug. I decide it's best not to tell him what he's about to find out tomorrow. I've had some whiskey but I'm not tankarsed enough to have the massive bulk of Ashen breathing down my neck. "I'm here with Raven. We came from First Light."

"Ah, say no more. I will not pry. I don't want the Midnight Assassin on my arse." He winks, then downs his ale. "She is not as fun as we are."

"I don't doubt that. So, uh, Verdant," I begin, trying to distract him from the long run of bluff pairs I'm currently putting together, "I notice you have a tree stitched onto your fur." I point to his fur robe, to the sigil above the heart, where underneath it is written NETTAHCS SED SEMAUD. Just like the Ansbach motto, that's an easy one even with my poor Wolftongue: *the shadow of the tree*. "Ashen Ansbach has a moon. You have a tree."

Verdant looks at me. "Ah, mage, do you not even know the basics?" He puts his cards down (in the process showing me has a moon and a vial of blood rather than two vials, the shading liar) and points to the roof of the antechamber we are in.

"The Ansbachs have the moon. Just like the Gevaudans. The Morbachs and the Stubbes have the claw." He beats his chest. He is a very performative wolf, I am coming to realize. "But *we* Soissons view the forest as our guiding principle. We are not just forest first, we *are* the forest. We belong to it more than we belong to other wolves. We do not stray much away from it, and we fight only for it. When we die we will become part of it, as we always were. Forest first, forest last." He grins.

I must look confused, because he pauses, and starts again. "Wolves do not have gods like vampires. They follow three things: the moon, the forest, or the claw. The moon represents thought, the reflection on what we truly are. The forest is the idea of spirit, of how we are not simply ourselves but are part of something greater. And the claw represents our beast instincts, and the joy of giving in to them and thus finding peace. Wolves follow all three, but different packs feel fidelity to one or the other. This shows in the choices we make, the way we comport ourselves and the lives we lead. We are forest. The only one left. There used to be more, but those packs are gone. We seem to be low on packs these days." He looks sad for a second, and I see a lot of blood-spattered wolf history in that sadness.

I take a few moments to reflect on this before I reply. I knew that wolves didn't have gods, but I thought that just meant they were as beasts, mindless in what they thought of the things we can't touch or, as a drunk Quantas friend I had back in Quintile long ago once said, the things that haunt us just before we slip into our dreams. But this? This sounds like a whole wisdomsphere, the kind of annoying hokum that Sage studies for hours on end. I am impressed. Wolves have depth. And I have a good run of uninterrupted cards. I place them down in front of Verdant triumphantly, when a shadow appears before him.

Verdant turns and half jumps. He goes to say something at the shadow but thinks better of it and, with one look at his two underwolves and a grin at me, slips away from the card table.

"Hey," I call out after him. "I had five uncalled bluffs! That's a moon groat and some Shadowfall spirits you owe me!" I turn to the newcomer—to Raven. "I'm beginning to notice you have an effect on people."

Raven looks down at the growing collection of silver and gold coins on the table next to me. "And you have an effect on their cards, it seems, mage."

"I don't cheat," I reply, "I keep them drinking and lull them into not trying. You should try it sometime. It's called being companionable."

Raven doesn't reply to this, but lingers.

"Was there a reason you came to find me," I continue, "aside from ruining my good run?"

The fur she's wearing tonight is all black, which is why she seems so shadowlike. It covers most of her chest and reaches down to her calves. The Ansbach moon is stitched in white on it. I suppose this would be the equivalent of a noble vampire's ballroom dress. A slightly more trimmed fur is the best the wolves can do.

"I didn't need to look for you," she notes. "I can smell your decay from here."

"Wait, what . . ."

"Never mind." She stares stubbornly into the distance for a while, and as someone who has spent a lot of time around people who do not wish to be at social functions (well, one man), I recognize the signs. But there's something more. I know people; at least, after this much moon ale, I've come to think I know them.

"You may as well tell me what's on your mind, Raven. It's not as though I've got a lot of friends here to go telling secrets to."

Raven side-eyes me, then spins round to face me properly. Her dark tresses cover most of her face, somehow giving me all her attention while making her unreadable at the same time. It's a very Raven move.

"I am concerned about the council tomorrow."

"Concerned?"

"Yes. Concerned that Ashen, my alpha, may not be safe. The Outside Council has not been called for a decade now, and things in the wolfkind have . . . begun to become less civil than we are used to."

"'Less civil' sounds like a fakemoniker."

"A fakemoniker?"

"Ah, sorry, a vampire term. What I mean is that by 'less civil' it sounds like you've started to shading 'hate the tits off each other.'"

Raven shakes her head. "No. Not that bad. We are still not like you mages. The majority of the packs are still content, or at least civil with the others. But a couple, like the Stubbes . . ."

"Stubbes?" The name rings a bell, possibly because it might have come up in Verdant's recent explanation of wolfpack lore, which I wasn't really sober enough to soak in, to be honest.

"Yes. The youngest pack, the first new one to be formed ever. Formed after the Twin War. Their alpha is Silver Stubbe. He's been growling a lot in the last few years about the Pact, about giving our criminals to be bled to the vampires. What seems like necessity to us appears capitulation to that Silver moontwat. All based on animosity about the supposed wolf capitulation after Extinction Valley during the Twin War."

I think on this. "From what little I know of that, didn't you have no choice? Extinction Valley had wiped your numbers out, and Sinassion threatened you all, so you had to ally with the bloods and sorcerers to fight him?"

Raven stares at me. "That is not what little you know, that is *all* you know of that, isn't it?"

"Don't start," I say, nervously thumbing the moon cards that I will never get to show off to keep myself afloat in the standard confrontational conversation of Raven. "Sage is gone, I don't need another nagger. Anyway, you keep promising to fill me in on this important Extinction Valley."

Raven ignores my comment. "The Stubbes are the classic youngsters with a grievance. They would seek war for pride, having not had enough years to realize the true cost of it. Silver is doing his best to whip them up. I do not know what his motivations are, but they are not emotional, I can guarantee that."

"And how do you know that?"

Raven simply points to her nose. I forget that whereas I use my nose to tell me where frying meat can be found, wolves use it for, well, everything.

"Then there are the Soissons and the Morbachs."

"Ah, that rings a bell. I've met the green fellow here. Verdant Soissons. Don't know about the other one. Hard to keep up with these endless names."

"There are literally five packs," says Raven, and who knows if that's an angry smile or an amused one peeking out from her midnight curtain.

"Just tell me."

She sighs. "The Morbachs have their territory in the northern Wolflands, east of First Light. They're closest to the vampires. Despite being of the claw, which would traditionally make them loyal to the wolves, they developed over the last couple of centuries an affinity for some vampire culture. Dress like them sometimes, that kind of thing." She grimaces, not hiding her disgust. "It makes me want to do bad and bloody things to them."

"Shocking, that, you're normally so peaceful."

"Whereas the Soissons," she continues, ignoring me as usual, "live east of them, in the northeastern forest, and keep to themselves, but Morbachs are infringing more and more into their territory and that is causing problems."

"Ah, I see. Wolf territory disputes. Wait, I thought there were no fixed territory lines. Don't you just all run around happily in the forest on your wolf runs, having a shading great time?"

Raven gives me a deadly look. "Wolves can run freely throughout the whole Wolflands. In ones or twos, of course. The forest is ours. That is our right under wolf law. But large numbers roaming, no species could tolerate that."

Hmm. Maybe wolves aren't so superior to the rest of us after all. I decide not to verbalize this thought to Raven.

"Anyway the Stubbes, who as I hope you have gathered now are nothing but shit-stirring trouble, are taking Morbach's side. They cite the affinity of two packs of the claw, even though the Stubbes want war with vampires and Morbachs have ingested some vampire culture. I suspect their real reasons are more sinister."

"So these three packs have been at each other's throats? In your case, literally, I suppose."

Raven shrugs. "It has not come to a serious confrontation yet. No wolf rights have been officially asserted. Nothing to trouble the Outside Council, but . . ."

"You think it could change?"

"Yes. I think it could change."

"How quickly do you think it could change?" I ask, glancing over Raven's shoulder.

"Why do you ask?" replies Raven.

"Because those are two very angry-looking wolves behind you."

As she goes to reply, I see her nose twitch, presumably encountering the kind of emotions you get when people are about to start fighting. As she turns, a flagon whips past, narrowly missing her head and my shoulder, though loosing a fine shower of ale onto my cloak, the annoyance of which is muted by my temporary terror at the scene before me.

If you are not used to wolves, aside from trying to sleep with them when they visit faraway desert cities, then a wolf fight is quite something, especially when you're in close proximity to it. When sorcerers fight—normally Kinet on Kinet or Atmos on Atmos, given that the other two magicks aren't normally conducive to sparring—it's serious but not that scary up close. But being two feet away from the tornado of fur and claws in front of me is enough to make me leak some piss had I not, thank the Light, already relieved myself shortly before.

The two wolves fighting before me had been in the background during my card game with Verdant and my conversation with Raven. They were on separate tables, but I spotted them eyeing each other occasionally. I thought maybe they were flirting, which shows that I need Raven's nose or Sage's body talk, because it's clear now they were gearing up for a scuffle.

The male is tall, Raven's height rather than Ashen's, but shares the Ansbach alpha's large figure, half fat, half muscle, except with an emphasis on muscle, like Ashen but slightly gone to seed. His whole body, for they're both naked now, of course they are, is covered in thick brown fur, and his beard seems to envelop his face, being the most unruly example yet I've seen of the face fuzz. I can just make out small angry eyes.

The woman fighting him is short, surprisingly so for a wolf—I'd say, at a guess, around five ten, but if you think I'm good at guessing heights then you've mixed me up with the wrong sorcerer. Her hair is green like Verdant Soissons's but with whitish-gray strands running through it, and she's slim, even slimmer than Raven, and less toned, even wiry. She has a good body, a thought I have the decency to roll my eyes at, but then I notice to my side that another wolf at the table parallel to me, female, is ogling her the same way as me, and there's nothing like seeing the opposite sex leering, too, to make me judge myself a little less.

If I had to wager on a victor then I would say surely the massive slab of hair and bulk opposite, but as they circle each other, growling and extending their claws between swipes, I see the pure hate in the female's eyes and I decide to put a halt to my imaginary gambling. In fact, she's the first to make proper contact: she ducks nimbly away from a hammer blow of a fist from the fur beast and swings an uppercut to his chin. I don't know what she's made of, but it's more than she appears, because that's some blow, and he reels backward. Then she extends her claws, sharp nails suddenly becoming bearlike claws, and swipes across his belly. The blood spray hits the wall behind him; I watch it as it goes past, wondering inanely if a vampire watching these proceedings would leap out of their seat to lick up the precious stuff.

This new liquid development does not seem to bother Fur Beast, however, as he simply growls louder and goes to swing both club-like arms above his head, presumably seeking to pound her through the floor and into the caverns below the castle, by the look of his veins standing out. She dodges in time to avoid the main blow—he is fast for his bulk, but she is faster—but catches a glancing blow on the shoulder and half falls to the floor, angry spittle coming out of her jaw, which is . . . getting longer? That's when I look at his jaw, too, and I see that both of them are elongating, then shifting back, like someone is moving time back and forth; one second their snout is hairier and fangier and the next it is back to their normal mouth.

I look to Raven, expecting her to end this now, or at least explain why in all the five magicks only their mouths are transforming into wolf. But she simply watches, her own muscles tensed but doing nothing.

She turns to me, as if sensing my question. "It is their business. As long as it keeps to this antechamber and does not disturb the Great Hall, I cannot interfere."

By *cannot* I presume she means that she's tied by some wolf pride about letting people fight it out rather than any general reluctance to get into a fight, because you do not have to be associated with Raven Ansbach very long to know she's not shy in that department.

Meanwhile, having evaded most of the floor-pounding, granite-hewn blows raining down on her from Fur Beast, the green-and-white-haired fury before me decides to take a different tack. She swipes at his ankles, and as more blood spray jets out, uncomfortably close to my personal space, Fur Beast lets out a proper howl, and I see his snout extend again, but longer. Then his face begins to change, too, and a strange swirling surrounds him in the air. I taste metal on my tongue, and his whole body starts to contort with the air around him, and I see he's becoming more wolf than man.

"And that's enough of that," I hear Raven say, and she strides into the fight, and with one hand whips it into the neck of the changing wolf. For a moment her own arm's submerged in the distortions in the air, the shimmering cyclone of whatever the shade you're meant to call a wolf change. But then the shimmering ends and the strong taste of burnt steel on my tongue lessens and the fur beast returns to man, not wolf, holding his neck and trying, not particularly well, to breathe.

"No fights in wolf form. Not in here. You know this," says Raven, face close to his, voice low but containing all the hints of violence you'd expect from a Raven who is not about to be disobeyed. Then she turns and faces the female and says, "Are we done?"

For a strange hot second a look of vitriol crosses Green-and-White's features and I wonder if the small ball of fury is going to take a swipe at Raven herself, but then she sighs, turns, and spits some blood to the side.

Raven starts, "Badger . . ."

Badger interrupts her. "We're done, Raven. Just like half my fucking pack territory, if those Morbachs have their way." Then she laughs, a strange high cackle, downs a nearby mug of ale, and stalks out. Meanwhile, Fur Beast has recovered enough to glare at Raven.

"The fucking nerve on you," he begins.

Raven cocks her head left, as if properly studying him. He doesn't seem so intimidating anymore, panting, still rubbing his throat, visibly weakened by the canceled change. Still, not someone I'd insult in close proximity.

After an awkward silence has passed, Raven smiles. "I don't need much nerve. Just enough to face you down, Hawk Morbach."

For a second he chews over that and I wonder whether he's going to make a messy meal out of it, but then he grabs his furs from the table and stalks out of the antechamber.

I look around. During the commotion, the other inhabitants have skulked out—wiser than me, clearly—and now it's just me and Raven. Raven sits back down at our table, and I join her. She doesn't say anything for a while but studies the scratches in the tables intently. There's lot of scratches in the tables. They're not varnished like vampire furniture and it's probably a good job.

"Let me guess . . ." I say eventually, because awkward silences are more Sage's territory than mine. "Those were the underwolves of packs Morbach and Soissons, the ones here to back up their alphas? I heard what the female said, about the territory, the dispute you were just telling me about, right? Will they get in trouble with their alphas?"

Raven shrugs. "Unlikely. But still, fighting at the Outside Council meet-up. Unheard of. I mean, I expect that kind of behavior from the Morbachs, they are of the claw, and that under you just saw clearly is not as vampire-cultured as his alpha, more like how the Morbachs used to be. But Badger? A Soissons fighting? They are of the tree, they are . . . well, as peaceful as wolves can get."

"She didn't seem very peaceful just now. She seemed like she never saw a limb she didn't want to cut off."

"Well, that is what happens when people are in territory disputes.

Civility is the first to go." She sighs and looks around at the empty table next to ours, then reaches over and grabs a tankard and downs whatever's in it. I say whatever's in it; the cellars here are hardly overflowing with choice so I'm going to guess it's more moon ale.

"We have become complacent," Raven says. "We put our future in the hands of the vampires. We let them dictate this century, waiting on them to take on the Grays for us, and we have failed to address the effects of Grayfall on the wolfpacks. We should have had more of these councils before now. We should have had . . . fuck. Maybe that clawbrain Silver has a point."

"Silver Stubbe? The ones you had a little rant about earlier?"

Raven glares at me, a little of her old fire coming back. "A very small point. Among a lot of very stupid ones." She drains her mug and looks around for another. Seeing alphas start a brawl obviously got to her. All the time I have known Raven, she has always been about control. Even her fighting, which I've seen much more up close than my bladder was comfortable with, is a lesson in controlled aggression. You might think it looks primal, unleashed, unhinged, but you're not looking properly. There was something truly disquieting in watching her think, *Ah, by the bloodmoon, I'll have a drink anyway.*

New tankard in hand, she sits back down and stares at me, unblinking. "You know what, mage? I'll give you what you want."

*That's a comment that can go in a lot of unexpected directions* is what I want to say, but even I know when to hold my tongue sometimes.

"Extinction Valley. You want the story?"

"Yes," I say, meaning it. "I do."

Raven nods, and then leans back into her chair. For a while she doesn't say anything, and, with her hair obscuring her eyes, I half wonder if she's taken a nap. But then her voice comes, distant and low, and she tells a story I'll soon wish I hadn't heard.

"The Battle of Extinction Valley, mage, took place halfway through the Twin War. At that point it was just us and the bloods. Three years of skirmishes, battles, swinging one way or the other. Nothing concrete. Nothing gained. Much lost. The sorcerers had stayed out of it, or so we had thought. Eventually, both sides decided the time was right to end this stalemate. It was not called Extinction Valley then, of course. It was just the valley, a valley that sat in the Borderlands, between First Light and our forests.

"The vampire forces were all camped out on one side of the valley, and the wolfkind forces on the other. It was too hard for an army to pass around the northern mountain ridge, as it went almost to the edge of the forest line. South of the valley would mean for the vampires having to move back north at some point into the thicker part of the forest; for us it would have meant fighting in the clearer Centerlands south of First Light, where the winged vampire battalions would have a clearer sight and better time of it. So if one side wanted to make progress, they would have to cross it.

"So the wolves came down from the forest on the east side of the valley in their pack regiments, all the way down to the valley floor. And I mean all the wolves. We were not fucking about. The vampires stayed on the western mountain ridge, ready to march down to the valley floor to fight us. Or fly, I suppose. You could not have had a more traditional battle. But the battle never happened."

There's a long silence then, aside from the sound of scratching, and I see Raven is dragging one long nail down the side of the table, adding her own marks to the ones gone before. I almost think the story is over, but then she resumes.

"We wait there, on the valley floor, waiting for the army of blood to come down to us and commence battle. Except the vampires do not do anything. Nothing at all. So we make camp. Two days pass, and nothing happens. The vampires stay on the ridges overlooking the valley. Some of us start to get angry, wanting to take the mountain pass and engage the enemy. But we stay disciplined. We stay in our packs. Which, of course, is exactly what the bloodfucks wanted. After three days, some of us complain of odd symptoms. Rumors fly around that sorcerers are helping the vampires and bewitching them. Then, on the fourth day, it happens. The blood Lords ready their army to march down. But first, they throw small charges of firepowder into the valley. Even if they had been able to hit any wolves, they would not have hurt us, so we were not concerned. But that is not why they are throwing them. For where the explosions are set off, great clouds of dust rise into the air all over the valley floor. Then it begins. One by one, we start to writhe in agony. Some near to the explosions collapse instantly; others who are farther away begin to weaken as the wind carries the dust toward them. Soon, our entire army is struggling to even stand, weakened and poisoned and unable to defend ourselves. That is when the vampires finally descend to the valley floor, all five thousand of them.

"You see, as it turned out, Jacob, the sorcerers had been helping the vampires. But not in the way we might have expected. No Atmos come to make hail the size of boulders or lightning strikes to our hearts. No mountain-moving Kinets. No Cloaks come to craft illusory vampire battalions. Instead, the vampires had taken all the wolfsbane they could find from the farthest southern shore where it grows—almost all of it in existence."

"Wolfsbane?" I say, confused enough to interrupt. "I thought that didn't exist anymore."

"And you are about to hear why. We got rid of it after the Twin War, I can tell you that. Even back then there was never enough to poison an entire army. Not with its leaves, at least. But the Kinets, the tricksy subset of them who can move small things, just like the ones who strengthen the blood for the nobles in First Light these days—they had mixed that wolfsbane into the grass and the soil in the valley secretly, weeks before the battle. They had seeded the very valley floor with it.

"As we made camp, some of it was disturbed. But not enough to really make us notice, a few instances of mysterious illness aside. But when those explosions were set off, it released clouds of wolfsbane dust all across the valley, great billowing clouds of death. The air itself became lethal to us and we began to slowly die on the floor of the valley, our very blood poisoned by the air. Easy meat for the vampires; it was carnage. Slaughter. All the vampires had to do was march down there and pick us off, pack by pack. The grass ran red with wolfblood, great streams of it. The vampires ripped our throats out. By the time morning came, you could not see the valley grass for the corpses. They were executing us methodically, killing us off wolf by wolf. It was cowardly. It was brutal. It was genius."

"But you're still here," I say, lost in this crazed tale.

"Well, that is the only light in this story. The small glimmer of light on the dark side of the moon. You see, the wolves on the northern side of the valley had a few more minutes before the vampires reached them than the others. The ground there had not been seeded as much as farther south, so some of us were still able to stand. One pack that could were the Ansbachs. Ashen Ansbach himself—not the alpha of the pack back then, just an underwolf—was the one who had the idea, the masterstroke, which would give us enough time to run. Because that's the only thing we could do now. Run. So we all began to use our strength to knock down boulders from the ridge on the vampire side of the valley.

"A wolf in full strength, sorcerer, is a real sight, but a whole pack of us—even ones beginning to weaken from clouds of wolfsbane—well, we can really do some damage. We caused a rockfall on the northern half of the valley that completely cut the valley in two and delayed the vampires getting to us. It allowed many of us to escape. Led by Ashen, we dragged each other free, desperately, with what little strength we could before the vampire Lords smashed through the barrier.

"It made us as a pack. After that, we were considered the leaders in all but name, and Ashen led the council. Not that there was much choice after the losses were sustained. In one night, two-thirds of our kind were killed. If it had not been for Ashen's quick thinking, they might have been wiped out altogether. The vampires were aiming for nothing less than our extinction. Hence," she says, "the name."

I give it a few moments. Outside the antechamber, the noises of conversation and growling and singing can be heard. In here, there's only the weight of history, choking me. I think on horrors so shading bad the mind can't even begin to process them. I think about being able to live forever but bleeding out on the ground instead. I think about losses that never fade as the years pass, of realities that defy the generations. For once, I don't have something funny to say.

"That must have been horrible for you," I say eventually.

"I have seen worse," she says quickly, almost reflexively, sniffing like all good liars.

"No, you haven't."

"No," she replies, dragging her claw through the scratches she has made. "I have not."

# 20

# Everything Is Golden

Wolves, of all the races of the Everlands, have a better success rate in long-term matings, or as the other races would call it, marriages, than the others. Various explanations have been proffered for this over the centuries but to my mind the explanation has always been simple. If you are to survive a relationship over literal hundreds of years, then the model that vampires have, or occasionally vampire and sorcerer or wolf and sorcerer (or even rarer still, vampire and wolf)—the model of living with each other in enclosed spaces and constantly seeing each other every day, or at least frequently—is doomed to fail. No goodwill or passion can survive that, surely? Look, then, to the model of the wolves, who frequently separate from each other for months, sometimes years at a time, to roam the forests or the world, before always coming back, the zest for each other renewed. It may not suit all, but you only need look at the comparative failures of other models to see that there is something in it.

Amber Morbach, *The Uniqueness of the Wolfekind*

## Raven

The morning after the revels in the Great Hall, I decide to see my alpha. Ashen's rooms are at the top of the central tower of Ansbach castle, which sits in the middle of an expansive courtyard, around which is the rest of the castle main. The tower stretches up dizzyingly high; a winding circular staircase takes you all the way past other Ansbach rooms to Ashen's chambers.

When I reach his rooms, I see no sign of him, but Golden, his pack mate, is reclining on a loungeseat in the receiving room, naked. I am still wearing my furs, but the informal clothing rule inside the castle does not stretch to actual living quarters. She is wearing a silver necklace around her neck, the moon-plus-stick-of-wolfsbane design of our pack its pearl centerpiece. The necklace hangs loosely; it has to survive the constant switches between wolf and person form. I do not bother with such things, but that does not mean I do not think it looks nice. She jumps up to greet me as soon as I cast eyes on her.

"Raven!"

"Golden." I grin and embrace her, nuzzling her neck as she sniffs my hair.

"It has been too long, Midnight, girl," she says, and stands back, properly appraising me. Her sun-bright hair, which gives her that memorable-sounding moniker, falls down her shoulders, much longer than mine, to halfway down her back. Normally she braids it, a style leftover from when many of the Ansbachs lived in Lightfall and all the new wolf fashions there. But it is natural now; that said, it is still more well-kept than mine. Golden is much more concerned about her appearance. But I judge her not for it; that is another way we differ from the bloods.

"How has it been?" she asks, a sly grin on her face. I see she is wearing a dash of lip daub, another Lightfall fashion. Not all the Ansbachs—or the other moon pack, the Gevaudans—adjusted well on our forced return to the Wolflands. We are not as culturally vampire as the Morbachs, but we did love the mores of city civilization, though they have fallen away in the last century. But some, like Golden, hold on to them, and I do not begrudge them that. Myself, I was as made for a city as a half-gutted fish is made for a tower's worth of stairs, which is ironic given the role I've been handed.

I shrug in reply. "You know the bloods, Golden. Arrogant. Careless. Everything we are not."

Golden nods. "And now mass murderers." Her lip curls and her fangs show, and I am reminded that although fashions abound, she is still a wolf, and a fearsome one, at that. I fought near her at Extinction Valley; her hair was not perfect then. I remember her wild eyes when she knew that both her sons were lost.

"Ah, yes. Of course," I reply. "You know I keep forgetting. It is so fucking insane that I have to remind myself of it, like a strange dream."

Golden laughs, but shorn of all joy. "It felt like that when Ashen told me, Raven. To think the vampires have been using us. It is almost as bad as Extinction Valley. Not quite as many killed, but a whole century wasted, and all of our blood given over to them. To think we thought them allies."

I nod. "We were fooled. I suppose we have short memories."

Golden's eyes close briefly, and I see her head turn slightly to the portrait above the loungeseat, of her and Ashen lying next to the fire in wolf form, sun-gold and crypt-ash beasts together, with two wolves in front of them, both golden, albeit slightly darker than her. The portrait is slightly faded with time, almost two centuries of time, to be precise. The two wolves were her and Ashen's sons, and they did not come out of Extinction Valley.

"No, Raven," she says, hanging halfway between fury and sorrow. "We have very long memories, indeed." Then she shakes her hair back around her shoulders and nods to the rooms beyond. "Do you think it'll be war?"

I shrug. "Maybe before Grayfall I could tell you the minds of the alphas. Things were much more settled in the period after the end of the war. Not now. There is a lot of anger out there for different reasons. The Stubbes would go to war with the vampires, certainly. They are always angry. But the northern packs have their own territorial dispute they are concerned with. We still have the Gevaudans on our side in all things, and Soissons are not warmongers. I would not like to call it, but I feel keeping the peace is more likely."

"What do you think Ashen wishes?" she says, her large round eyes fixed on me.

I am slightly taken aback by this, and she sees it.

"Oh, Raven, you know him better than I do in that department. You're all politics and that, even though you say you detest it. You know his mind in those ways better than I ever did."

I smile, agreeing. If you were a blood you would think that comment barbed, for one pack mate to say to another wolf that she knows the other's mate better in one way. But wolves do not have that kind of jealousy. It would be absurd, too; jealously and envy and secret attractions and affairs are all the prerogative of vampires—and sorcerers, in their way, at least when they seek to get involved with the other immortals. But for wolves such things are almost impossible when your nose tells you in the most detailed way imaginable what the other person is feeling. Golden will know that I'm attracted to Ashen, that I care for him deeply. It would be strange if I didn't, as we were once almost mates ourselves, four centuries gone, so long it almost seems a separate life ago. She will scent it on me. But she will not smell decay—the scent of lust for wolves—because I am not in love with him now, not in the packmate way, at least, and that will suffice. And even if she did, she would not attack me with words but challenge me as wolves. As it is, she will resent me not, for what is the point? It is hard to understand if you are not of the wolfkind, and it is best that it is not attempted, as it would be so far from your nature that you would be pondering on it till the moon has a fucking face.

"I think he still wants peace. He is an Ansbach, after all, is he not? We remember Extinction Valley. We are all here because of what we did. You, I, he. We still do not want war."

Golden smiles and nods but holds my gaze. "Even after all your time in First Light, the way it is now? Even after what you uncovered?"

I pause. I consider telling her how I reacted when I heard the ruse of Grayfall. How I wished a great purge of the city, of wolves tearing through it, ridding it of this infection. How I felt the ancient primal urge of the hunt, but a greater hunt this time, one of teeth that never ended and carnage that never stopped, until the bloods were gone forever and the forest run never ended, even beyond the forest. The final hunt, a hunt through centuries.

These thoughts are beyond her nose, though, and I decide to keep my counsel. Even other wolves are best not privy to the true midnight within me.

"War now, with the amount of wolfblood they have from us and our reduced numbers . . . We are lucky to still have all our forest, after everything. I would have us still run through it."

Golden breaks the stare finally. "Yes. I agree. You know, whenever I get angry, whenever I feel the fury, I remember that our Midnight Assassin, the most dangerous wolf who ever lived, would call for peace. It calms me."

I have never heard Golden speak of her anger so. I am a little surprised. But I am also gladdened. Anger is the only sensible currency at the moment; it deserves to be in the air.

"Right," she says, back to her usual self. "I won't keep you from Ashen. Make sure he puts on all his formal furs, won't you? He always tries to get out of the boots."

I grin. "I'll make him wear the whole clawdamn lot."

"And let's talk sometime, me and you. Down by the waterfall, maybe. We can hunt a little, and you can tell me what the bloods are up to when they are not plotting."

"I would like that, Golden. Well, the hunting bit, at least."

"Ha!" she says, flicking her sunlit locks back. "I know you hate talking for long, Raven, but that's the price of being friends." And then she is gone, picking up her furs from an antler hook on the wall as she goes, leaving me alone in the entire quarters with Ashen.

"How many times do I have to say this, Raven? There's nothing to worry about."

"Ashen, please, there is everything to worry about."

My alpha, my oldest friend, stands in front of a long mirror, adjusting his fur robe. It is a grander version of the one Jacob met him in, with various extra furs stitched on top of different shades of the same ash as his hair. The effect is as if someone was lying down and a variety of different animals were dumped on top of them and tied there when they got up. It is not pretty like the bloods, but it is representative of the creatures we share the forest with. And all of these were hunted for food; none were killed for the dressing. An important distinction, which bloods also often fail to appreciate. The moon-and-wolfsbane sigil on this fur is stitched in gold.

"Fuck this for a wolf run," he announces, giving up. "I feel ridiculous wearing this, whichever way I adjust it." He turns to me and grins. "For once I wish you had your way, Raven, and we could go to the council stark-bollock naked."

"Ashen," I begin, "you are my alpha and it is my duty to protect you, and I am telling you, as an assassin and a hunter, that you are in danger." I balk at my own seriousness. What I really want to do is ask my old friend about the forests: how they have been for the nine years I have been skulking the Borderlands of First Light hunting our own kind and doing other work besides. I want to tell him of the more absurd realities of the vampires and their city ways. But when I scent something not right, when I half scent steel and something worse on my nose, when all my instincts are on fire . . . well, then I am a very singular wolf.

Ashen sighs and steps away from the mirror. "Raven, in one hourglass I will tell the assembled alphas that, whether we choose war or other means, our life has, once again, changed forever. My life will always be danger, even in these days of stability and peace and all the moondamn rest of it. I've survived sixteen decades as alpha of the council. I'm sure I can last another bloody day."

I say nothing but walk to the window, which looks down onto the courtyard far below that surrounds the central tower. Below me, various Ansbach underwolves are rushing around making the organizations for the official dinner to follow the Outside Council, and the ceremonial games that will hopefully wash the stink of disagreements and bargaining from the council by showing the leaders of all packs working together. Above me, the sun rises higher in the sky and its beams glance across my face. Half in shade, half in sun, I clear my throat and speak.

"Do you remember the battle of Shadowfall?" I ask, carefully.

"You mean do you remember *after* the battle? Of course I bloody do, Raven. All that carnage, all our dead, but it's still one of my happiest memories."

"Me too," I reply. "When we raced to that waterfall, halfway up the Antumbra peak. We knew we had just escaped with our lives in the fiercest battle yet. I still had the faces of all the bloods and mages I had killed in my mind, and a lot of parts of them still on me."

"We washed the blood off, and we carried on racing," he says, eyes not on me but on the memory.

"You thought you were going to win, but you tripped on the rocks."

"Uh, excuse me, I did not fucking trip on the rocks, you knocked me over. Very selective memory of that you have for someone who never forgets."

I grin. "As if I could knock your massive arse over."

"Are we recalling memories, or are you insulting me now?"

I push my dark locks from my face and I turn to him. "We carried on so far up, even though there was no forest left, just rock. It was almost impassable, but we carried on."

Ashen nods. "We did."

"I felt so alive. I was mourning friends, but I felt happy. The two coexisted. It was a pure feeling, shorn of what was happening below, something I could embrace. I could understand the war below, and the death, but I could also understand that none of it mattered, not in that way, up there in the clouds, just as deep in the forest."

"Or in the light of the moon," says Ashen, voice low.

"Exactly. But I don't feel that now. I'm not mourning any dead. I'm not fighting battles. I'm seeing wolves behave not like wolves, like . . ."

"Bloods?"

"Yes. Exactly. We have become lost. We are in a state of suspension. And I do not know how to get out of it. I can't see through the clouds."

"You're not halfway up a mountain now."

"Exactly. But I wish I was. I cannot see what is all around us. I feel blind."

Ashen sighs. "You were built for war or built for peace. You do not like the middle." He waves his massive paw at me as I go to protest. "I mean it as a compliment, Raven. You're the most wolflike wolf I've ever known."

"Golden tells me that I am good at politics."

"I love my mate with all my heart and half the moon, but she's not a wolf in the way you are, and she'd be the first to admit that. She cannot understand you. You are not in times made for you. I am. I wish I wasn't. But I'll help guide us through this, Raven, because we have seen much, much worse than this, have we not?"

I think on poison, airborne and fierce, and more death without honor than I have ever witnessed; I think of sadness blood and true. The Extinction Valley song, never dimming, never dying, loud across the ages.

"We have, old friend." My claws lengthen, short and long, by my side. "We have."

"Raven, I'm going to say this once. Stop worrying and enjoy the ceremony. Or at least what comes after. Not often we get to muck about with ones like us, who know the burden of leadership. Yes, everything is changing. Yes, we may go to war. But I'm ordering you, as your alpha, to have a bloody good time!"

I shrug. "I cannot kill anything or fight anything here, and this afternoon I have to wear more clothes than I have worn for ten years. I do not think I can make that promise." I allow a half grin to sneak up on my face.

"There you go," says Ashen, heartily clapping me on my back and roaring his laughter. "There's that midnight smile."

## Jacob

When I wake, I reach for the jug of ale next to my bed and take a little sip. Not a great habit to get back to, reminding me of those days before Sage found me when I wandered the innhouses of Quantile, winning at cards and starting fights with other Quantas (safe in the knowledge that none of us have any powers, so said fights would not end up with me in several pieces on a wall).

But I didn't get much sleep—hard to rest when wolves periodically howl awkwardly close to your window—and I need a lot of the desert courage today. Mainly because Ashen, in his infinite shading wisdom—or maybe it's just Raven playing with me, who the Light knows—has requested I be present in the council meeting.

This makes sense if you see me as the diplomatic representative of the Archmage and thus all the sorcerers, to record crucial events that may lead to the first interimmortal battle since the Twin War. It makes less sense if you know that not only have we sent shade-all messages to the Archmage since Sage and I lied to him about the true events of First Light, but that I'm also the worst possible representative, by which I mean I can barely represent myself at the best of times.

But refusing Raven is not advisable if you're attached to all your fingers, so to the meeting I will go. I stretch, feel my joints pop, and quickly stop stretching. Sorcerers live forever, or at least so we're told, and it's quite hard to kill us, so why in all the five shitting magicks do I still ache after the liquor nights? Shorn of any answer to this, I attend to my wash, make sure my robe is as clean as it is ever going to be, and then make my way down from my chambers to the ground level, where everything is abuzz with far too much hubbub at this time of morning for my liking.

Ansbach wolves rush past me, cleaning the antechamber off the hall of all the detritus from last night. I smell the heady aroma of meat coming from the kitchens: forest boar, by the scent of it, but maybe venison, too, or hoptail, perhaps. I stare at the wolves, thinking how strange it is that none seem like they're the servants but simply the same as the others. From what I've gathered in my fairly rapid education on the wolfkind this last month, wolves do not have servants. They just pitch in when they fancy. I suppose when half your life consists of running through the forest naked, then a rigid class structure is not first and foremost on your mind.

I begin to follow one of these definitely not-servants, hoping to grab some of the late breakfast meat off a platter, when an arm reaches out of the shadows and grabs me. I stifle a scream—my scream is not as masculine as I would like, so I thank the Light for small mercies—and I turn to see the shadowed form of Raven stride out of the darkness. Her hair looks almost neat for her, as straightened as I'll ever see it, and she is wearing an alarming amount of fur-based clothing.

Composing myself, I muster, "Why is it that you seem to be wearing more clothes in the Wolflands, where no one cares, than I ever saw you in First Light, where nudity is not at all a thing?"

Raven narrows her eyes. "These are ceremonial furs. For when the Outside Council meet."

"They don't look that ceremonial, more like you've just doubled the amount of furs."

She ignores this, as is her wont, and pushes me roughly in the opposite direction. "Eat later, mage. Council is now. You have overslept, unsurprisingly."

I gawp at her. "You mean I'm going to the meeting by your side? I'm honored."

"No," she says. "I will not be at the meeting. The meeting is only for alphas of the packs."

"Then that means I'm . . ." I begin, feeling a numb sensation on my arms.

"Yes, it will just be you and the alphas." Raven's mouth twitches at this point, and I'll be Lightdamned if she isn't trying to suppress a laugh. "You will be the first sorcerer to have ever been in the chamber with them."

"Yes, I feel very lucky. Just me and five of the most powerful wolves, who could eat me in a moment, discussing war. That feeling of luck has gone right to my bladder."

Raven rolls her eyes. "You will be fine, mage. Just stay in the back and don't interrupt."

"Oh, good, thanks for that. I was actually planning on heckling them, so that really puts a crimp in my plans. . . ."

Raven grabs my arm again—I am not enamored with this new trend of being physically manhandled by the continent's most feared hunter—and pushes me into lockstep with her as we walk through the Great Hall to the chamber. I spy the wreckage of the night before: beer stains, chunks of meat, furs discarded, a pool in the corner of the room that I hope is not the wolfkind adhering to what you'd expect of a big dog at a party.

"I see why you don't have much nice furniture in Ansbach castle now," I add.

Raven doesn't reply. At the eastern end of the Great Hall is a set of large redoak doors, and Raven opens them to reveal a small antechamber, at the end of which is another set of doors. These are larger, thicker, and have a shiny, dark-brown sheen to them.

I gasp. "Is that . . ."

"Castaray wood, yes."

I gawp at the doors. "I've never seen so much used. How in shade's name did you get a bloody great pair of doors made from a material only found in Last Light?"

Raven shrugs. "When Last Light fell, a small amount of base-material castaray wood was brought over with the survivors. Much of Ansbach castle was still in ruins after the war, despite it being two decades on, so Ashen paid one of the survivors to make them. It cost a significant amount."

"Why?"

Raven's voice is hushed when she replies. "A statement. Castaray wood never weathers and does not scratch. It will remain long after much of the wood of this castle is gone. The wolves will never again be fractured by the vampires. The Twin War cost us three entire packs. What were seven became four, before the Stubbes made us five. We will not be amputated like that again. We will not be worn down. We will remain."

"That sounds like a very expensive lesson. I'm beginning to think you wolves have more money than sense. Or you just don't care about money."

"Well," says Raven, knocking loudly on the doors. "You have accidentally found yourself some wisdom there for once, mage." As the doors open, she turns to me, her dark eyes unreadable, some of her newly straightened hair already falling round her face. "Good luck." And then she leans in to me and whispers, "Use some of that intelligence you are always masking, Jacob. You are my eyes in there. Do not let me down."

And then she's gone, and as I enter the chamber as the first sorcerer ever to do so, my mind is set on only one thing: how much I seem to be threatened by her, and how much I liked her breathing into my ear.

Anyway, she's right. What is there to fear? It's not like anyone is getting murdered.

# 21

# Ashfall

Not all meetings of the Outside Council have been particularly interesting affairs; most have broadly focused on smaller matters that arise between the wolves and sorcerers and the bloods over the years. Perhaps the most memorable was the one held the year before the Twin War broke out, when the alpha of a wolf-secessionist pack raised the idea of wolves being able to choose to adhere to vampire law in cities where they lived side by side with the bloods. This resulted in the unfortunate alpha being killed on the spot, and the bloods thereafter used this as one of the (many) excuses for the aggression that followed and triggered the beginnings of the Twin War.

Argent Morbach, *A Brief Historie of the Wolf Politick*

## Jacob

After the impressive castaray-wood doors to the council chamber, the chamber itself is . . . a disappointment, to say the least. Aside from a nice-looking vaulted ceiling, the room is mostly empty—literally of people currently but also of most furnishings, aside from a circle of five fur-backed chairs arranged in a circle. If this was a castle of bloods or mages, the walls would be adorned with murals or friezes, maybe some hanging tapestries, depicting great events or at least the great ceremonies that take place in here. But wolves, I am coming to realize, really don't care. Well, some may care more than others, if the rapid-fire lessons I've been getting recently are anything to go by—some acting more like vampires; other of the bastards are more feral—but Ashen Ansbach is clearly not one to preside over any fancy ceremony.

I think I might be warming to the beast.

As I'm currently alone, my nerves immediately recede, and part of me hopes that perhaps it's all just a bit of a jest by Raven. Stick the hungover mage in a room, tell him he's about to witness one of the most important wolf meets for years, make the lad piss himself. Then I remember that japes and prankeries are not really the Midnight Assassin's style; she's more a glower-and-sarcasm type of woman, and my frayed nerves slowly return.

Unhelpfully, I am then met by the booming voice of the most important wolf in the land. "Jacob! Good of you to join us." Ashen half lumbers, half lopes toward me, grinning wide, a mug of ale in his hand. He slams the mug onto the nearest chair, some of its contents sloshing over the side—yes, real important ceremony, this—then clasps me by both shoulders, forgetting his strength and almost imprinting his giant wolf mitts into my very bones.

"I hope Raven impressed on you that you don't have to be here. But given that it's you who came to us and warned us, and that this involves the whole damn Everlands now, I thought it's only right and proper you get a chance to watch what happens here today. Some of the others won't like it, but sod 'em, frankly." He grins at me, and I see he has a little bit of gristle stuck between one of his teeth from some poor forest creature.

I take a beat to reply as I process the news that this was optional (try telling that to Raven; thank you for that, Midnight Assassin) and then before, frankly, that piece of information is fully digested his other statement that some of the other huge, hungry wolves might not want me here hits. By the five magicks, what a fine day this is turning out to be.

"It's my pleasure, Ashen," I reply. "And my honor," I add pathetically, trying to cover all bases.

"Ha!" he booms, a little bit of spittle flying from his mouth and landing in his giant dark-gray beard. "There's no honor round here, mage. You'll find that out soon enough." Then he unclasps what remains of my shoulders and bounds over to the chair he left his mug at, and sits there. "They won't be long now, probably. The rest of the alphas. Just sit yourself down"—I turn and notice a decidedly unpadded chair hiding in the shadows in the corner of the chamber—"and try not to be bored off your arse."

I take the first part of his advice and place myself gingerly on my tiny chair—so small that it surely can't have ever seated a wolf; they must keep pathetic specimens like these in a store cupboard for visiting idiot mages—and decide that the second part I definitely won't be in danger of breaching, as nothing about this, I fear, will be boring.

There follows an interminably long and mildly awkward interval wherein Ashen ignores my presence and proceeds to down half his mug of ale—wiping his mouth of beer with his fur sleeve as he does so; good hygienic use of ceremonial furs, that. Thankfully, the strange moment is soon broken, but not-so-thankfully this is because, one by one in remarkably quick succession given that they do not seem to have arrived together, the other four alphas enter the chamber.

Each one greets Ashen first, bounding in their various different styles over him. Some greetings are effusive, a couple almost like big puppies greeting each other. Others are more restrained. In the case of Silver Stubbe—who I recognize immediately, as wolves really give you a large clue to strangers' identity with that naming system—it feels obviously hostile, neither of them doing much more than barking the most cordial greetings at each other.

Then they are all sitting down in the circle, and as they shift about and prepare to start the meeting properly, I take the chance to take them in and test what I've learned so far. Raven seems to think I have some uses in this Lightdamned Wolflands, so I may as well put some basic effort into remembering things.

On the chair at the base of the circle nearest to me, back facing me, is Silver Stubbe, which is fine by me, as I didn't much like my first look of his face, which was that of a man who gives you a backhand compliment before giving you a stab in the back. Makes sense, if the Stubbes are the young agitators who want to go to war with the vampires. Raven doesn't like a lot of people, but I suspect she might have cause to particularly hate him.

Next chair to the left is the huge hulk of Verdant Soissons, forest-green fur vibrant in the torchlight. Just like when we played cards last night, he gives off the reassuring friendliness of Ashen. The Soissons, as Raven informed me, hail from the northeast of the Wolflands, in the deep forest just before the northern shoreline. I can't imagine them wading too deeply into wolf politics. They are of the tree, Verdant said last night, and I feel that that probably makes them less inclined to be aggressive than the moon or the claw packs, but I'm still learning, so who the Light knows. Plus, they have that territory dispute with the Morbachs that, as the terrifying fur fight in front of me last night signified, does not seem to be going well.

Next around the circle, completing it back to Ashen, are two wolves I didn't meet last night but—and shame Sage isn't here to witness the absolute feat of memory and attention I'm displaying here—by process of elimination I know are from the two remaining packs, specifically Bronzed Morbach and Berry Gevaudan. Berry is female and, unsurprisingly, blue-haired, like the summer fruit she's named after. She has a wide, jolly face and big expressive eyes.

Bronzed is male and dark, orange-golden haired. He has a face I suppose you'd call haughty, and is sitting like he's the guest of honor at a lavish dinner, not like he's in a ring of wolves sitting on padded wooden chairs. I mentally put him in the Silver Stubbe category of "wolves that are probably a bit of a shit."

Ashen's boom drags me from my half-arsed appraisal.

"Right!" Everyone looks to him immediately as he speaks, showing that though they don't necessarily all look like they're in the presence of someone they consider their leader, they want to show him some respect at least. That sounds like something Sage would say, but I stand by it.

"Let's bring this bloody meeting to order, shall we? I appreciate you coming. And I know some of you have a bit of a head from last night—"

"That's one way to shitting describe it," guffaws Verdant.

"—so I won't drag this out too much. Well, the news anyway. I suspect the discussion of it might take a fucking while."

As I take in this opening salvo I can't help but compare it to meetings of my own kind. I've never been in a meeting of the Archmage and the heads of other sorcerer sects, obviously, but I've seen other formal gatherings from afar, or public occasions on my few visits to the capital, Luce. Sorcerers like their ceremony. And vampires never need an excuse to throw a bit of pointless ritual in there. But this? It makes Sage's meetings with the rest of the Cult of Humanis seem formal.

Wolves are strange beasts.

"Uh, before we proceed, Ashen, I have a question," says Bronzed, expression still like he's been forced to smell shit.

"Yes, Bronzed?" says Ashen.

"Why is there a sorcerer in our meeting?"

All their heads snap round at this, most with surprise, which means—and oh, how good is this for my sense of self-worth—that they actually hadn't noticed me sitting in the shadows of the chamber. Which begs the question: If they hadn't seen me, surely they smelled me? Wolves have the best noses in the land and literally smell emotions, so surely . . . unless, of course, they were so preoccupied with the meeting they didn't even think to sniff.

I have led a life of being fairly and in some cases remarkably inconsequential, but this is a new low, even for me.

"Oh! Him," barks Ashen. "Yes, that's Jacob, second deputy or something or other, of the Cult of Humanis. I think that's right?" He gives me an apologetic smile. "Not that I'm much of an expert." He grins at everyone, as if this explains it.

"Yes, but why is he here? In our meeting?" asks Morbach, who I have decided I really very much do not like.

"He's an observer," replies Ashen, surprisingly patient. "He represents the Archmage himself, for all intents and purposes—"

*All intents and purposes* is doing a great deal of work there, I reflect.

"—and it's important he's present to see what we decide. You'll see why. Just pretend he isn't here, if that helps."

"Oh, wonderful, so it's sorcerer business," Hawk mutters.

Ashen puts his big paws up in a placatory fashion. "It's a little more than that, Bronzed, as you'll see."

Silver Stubbe clears his throat, which is clearly unnecessary and equally clearly in character. "Ashen, are you telling me that we are meant to trust this mage with our most intimate secrets?"

"Intimate!" guffaws Verdant, his long green locks shaking. "We're not trying to mate with each other, Silver."

Silver ignores him and pushes his long, straight hair from his face in annoyance. "How do we know he isn't working for the bloods? I don't want those Lords to know our business. This is . . . this is unprecedented, Ashen."

"Silver, you ain't impressing nobody with those long words, darlin'," says Berry.

"He has a point, Berry," says Bronzed.

"Why do you care?" Berry retorts, pointing at Bronzed. "You Morbachs love the fuckin' bloods, you're always dressing like them!"

"Oh, I did wonder how long it would be before someone made that gibe. . . . But Silver's right, we should ask him to leave." Morbach glares at me.

"Oh, don't you start, Morbach," cuts in Verdant. "The lad's all right, we had some drinks last night, played some cards. . . ."

"Well, we're not all as trusting as you Soissons, Verdant," Morbach replies, glaring at him, the scent of their mutual dislike lingering in the air.

"Some of us are fighting battles back in our pack lands, not just howling among the trees. We need to be on our guard."

"Ha!" Verdant slaps his knee. "You mean on your guard against the trouble you started, you mean."

"*All right!*" says Ashen, not shouting but loud enough that everyone stops their squabbling. "Jacob has been in the company of Raven for the last few weeks. Raven vouches for him without hesitation. That is enough for me, and I hope it is enough for you . . . unless any of you wish to question Raven's loyalty?"

A silence descends. I smile. I suddenly realize I have a very powerful ally here, and then remember that she is not, technically, here. My smile leaves.

"Very well. But I'm not discussing the finer details of my pack in front of him," says Bronzed. Meanwhile Silver, wordless, turns round on his chair and studies me. His eyes narrow, and I see a small curl of his mouth, and I can't tell if he's smiling or twitching, but I don't like it one shading bit, that much I know.

Berry winks at me though and sticks her tongue out, and I immediately decide I'm going to like her.

"Now that we've got past that," Ashen continues, "it's time I told you why you're all here, unless we want to still be yapping away when we could be feasting later." He pauses to take a long swig of his mug, so long he practically drains it, then throws it down on the stone floor next to him, where it falls to the side and rolls a little. Very statesmanlike. Then he wipes the flecks of beer from his beard and mouth with the sleeve of his ceremonial furs, slowly and thoroughly (whether they're still ceremonial if they're so stained is something I'll ponder another time) and clears his throat.

"This is the situation." He pauses. He clears his throat loudly.

"This is the situation," he tries again, but interrupts himself with a deep cough. Then another. Then he tries to clear his throat, louder this time.

"Bloody moons, Ashen, how much did you neck last night?" asks Verdant, chuckling.

Berry frowns. "Ashen?"

Ashen coughs again and suddenly begins to choke, his large shoulders bent over as his huge frame shakes forward and backward. The coughs begin to turn into convulsions and he collapses onto the floor, knocking his mug and sending it skittering across the chamber toward me, where it rattles a little and stays still, while Ashen himself writhes around.

For a moment, no one moves. The entire room is frozen in place, frozen for almost too long, it feels like, as if they are having trouble accepting the sight of their eyes.

Then the tableau breaks and it's Berry who reaches him first, lying beside him, calling out, "Ashen!" She tries to pull his body over, which is now on its side, still convulsing. "Fuckin' help me then!" she cries to the others. Verdant gets there first, and together the two of them turn Ashen onto his back and push down on his limbs, trying to stop his movements or at least prevent him from hurting himself. Then, slowly, the convulsions suddenly stop and Ashen lies there, wheezing. Everyone is out of their chair now, except me, still struggling to process this. Little dribbles of ale from the dregs of Ashen's mug slowly roll toward me, the ground on a slight incline. I watch them for a moment to take my eyes off the horror show ahead of me.

Then the doors burst open and Raven enters. She turns first to me, takes me in, then the mug. Then she switches to Ashen. Wordless, she races over, her hair covering most of her face so I can't tell her expression. She crouches down on my side of his body, next to Verdant, who looks at her helplessly. Silver has backed off into the other corner at this point, a shocked look on his face. Morbach is still in his seat, hand over his mouth.

I turn back to Ashen, and I wish that I hadn't. Ashen's skin has darkened to a purplish-black pallor and his veins now stand out against his face and neck, pressing against his skin. Still choking, he tries to speak, but he can't form the words. Blood trickles out of his nostrils, first a few drops and then, as I watch, it runs into a steady stream, soaking into his furs beneath him. His skin looks like it must be burning to the touch, and as if to confirm this, Berry puts her hand on his forehead and pulls away quickly, shocked.

Then Raven lifts her head up, staring at the ceiling, as if to howl, but instead she half shouts, half spits a word out, a word that reverberates around the chamber and through the skulls of everyone there.

"WOLFSBANE!"

The word has a pretty striking effect on those in the chamber. Verdant backs slowly away from Ashen's body, his gaze alternating between

Berry and Silver and his mouth open in a wide O. Berry puts a hand over her face.

Silver scrunches his face up. "Impossible," he says, but the word comes out like a soft breeze, with less conviction.

Something, some mad, fevered thought in my brain, tells me that I should speak. Maybe if I speak I'll wake up. "Should . . . should I get someone?" I ask.

Raven turns to me, and I see her snout is elongated, her fangs lengthened, her eyes burning yellow, and her body is so angry that she's struggling not to turn to wolf form completely. For a moment I think she's going to charge me, and then she growls out, "There is nothing you can do. There is no one you can get. He is dead." And then she turns back to Ashen, and her voice goes soft, and I have to strain to hear her whisper. "Oh, you fool, what have they done to you? Ashen. Oh, Ashen."

At this point his skin is so dark that it's hard to distinguish from the pulsating veins that have also turned black. His face has seemingly shrunk and almost disappeared among his unruly locks and only his eyes remain clear, pupils turned yellow and green and purple and orange, like a rainbow version of a wolf's eyes when they change. At some point, someone has ripped his furs open to reveal his chest, and I wish they hadn't, because his body is also a sickly violet black.

Someone else rushes through the doors then, a woman with long blond hair, golden even, dressed in tightly wrapped, elegant-looking furs that cling to her body.

"Golden!" cries out Berry.

*I'm really excelling with these guesses*, I think, and immediately hate myself for my thoughts. *Can you not be serious for one shading moment, Jacob?* The woman who I assume from her choice name and her expression of utter panic and terror must be Golden Ansbach, Ashen's mate, crouches down next to Ashen and puts her hand on his face.

"No," she gasps to herself, and then turns to Raven. "There must be something, Raven, please."

"It is wolfsbane, Golden. I . . . I am so sorry." Raven turns to the others for a moment, as if begging someone to challenge her, but most have averted their eyes at Golden's agony. Only Silver still stares on, his expression at this point unreadable. I can hear commotion outside the doors, countless wolves rushing around, but no one daring to join the tableau outside. Somewhere in a room far away, someone howls.

As Golden puts her face next to Ashen's, his roving, desperate eyes suddenly recognize her, and he tries to speak, but guttural chokes are all he can manage, and as his eyes meet his pack mate's, she shrieks his name over and over, her snout elongating, her claws lengthening, her voice alternating between person and the soft yelps of a wolf.

Then, suddenly, Ashen's guttural sounds stop, as do the convulsions, and the Ansbach alpha's eyes flash silver for a brief second before his head falls back and his face grows still, his body almost immediately losing its blackish hue and the veins receding, until a mere moment later his body lies, serene and peaceful, on the chamber floor.

There is silence then. Absolute silence. Then Golden, who is still somewhere between a human and wolf, raises her head to the ceiling, tears pouring down her face, and howls, once, then collapses onto Ashen.

I can't watch that, so I look at Raven, and I see her staring at the others, and I know Raven by now, I do, I know that look, and I see there is bloody murder in those eyes.

# 22

# The Idiot

Given that wolfsbane is certain death for wolves and there is no cure, as you can imagine many of the vampires have devoted their lives to finding ways to administer it without us wolves detecting it first.

One of the most ingenious was the assassination attempt of vampire Lord Giacomo Cottone, who managed to drink enough wolfblood to fly all the way over to Gevaudan castle in 250 AL while the alpha of the Gevaudans at that time was bathing outdoors in a steam pool. They dropped wolfsbane from a great height into the pool, believing that the steam would make the alpha inhale the noxious vapors from the plant.

It did not work; the wolfsbane simply floated harmlessly in the pool until it was discovered by a shocked underwolf the next day. But less ridiculous schemes over the years have certainly worked.

Of course, now that wolfsbane has been completely removed from the Everlands, such clever, complex tactics can be confined—thankfully, from the wolf perspective—to the past-scribing books.

Ruby Morbach, *The Great Feud: Vampire and Wolf Battles Through the Ages, 100 AL–475 AL*

## Jacob

Raven finds me on the bench again, back in Golden's garden, staring at the herbs before me. All is silent in this part of the castle, except for the gentle trickle of the fountain and the occasional buzz of a bee inspecting the multicolored roses.

For some reason, trying to name all the herbs calms me. And by the five magicks, do I need a bit of calming now. As before, I quickly identify the takelily, chalkweed, and wolf parsley. Then there's that incongruous mageweed, which only takes root where sorcerers have been. A remnant of some previous diplomatic visit, perhaps. Next to it are some small, vivid, green and yellow sticks of some herb I've never seen, and I've seen a lot. Beyond that, I spy small circular leaves of lightguard, the tear-shaped indents in them being pretty memorable. I smile. I have that back in my herb garden in the cult. It has strong hallucinatory properties. Golden likes some fun, I see.

I suddenly remember I'm thinking about a very recent widow, and I feel that quick tinge of self-hatred again.

"Bold of you to sit in Golden's garden at a time like this," says Raven, an unexpected voice from the shadows, as is ever her way. I couldn't even hazard what entrance she came in from, but I'm fairly sure she's behind me.

"I doubt she'll come here. She's busy doing widow things." Even as I say it, I want to punch myself. "I'm sorry, I didn't—"

"You make jokes around grief and death and stress as a coping mechanism. It is fine. I have the measure of you now." She pauses. "Actually, I had the measure of you very shortly after meeting you."

"Who's making jests now?"

I feel the breath on the back of my neck. "Point taken, mage."

To my genuine surprise, she stalks into view to my right and joins me on the bench.

"I'm sorry, Raven. I really am." I turn to her and stare at the profile of her face. As usual, her long hair shields most of it, but I can see the parting of her lips and the hint of short sharp canines under there. Always waiting to be lengthened. I can't really see her eyes. A shame. I'm starting to like them, idiot that I am.

She doesn't reply to that.

I try a different tack. "How is Golden?"

"I have not spoken to her yet. She needs space. There are no words for what she must be experiencing right now. They have been mates for the best part of three centuries."

I nod. I can't imagine that. I managed five years once, back in the thoroughly unpleasant days of Quantile, before Sage. When I was just a depressed drinking Quantas in a whole city of them. They were the only good times of that part of my life, but I know I could never have managed a relationship like that for centuries.

"What happens next? Who is going to be—sorry, that's too soon."

Raven turns to me then, and I get to see those eyes. To my surprise, there's a hint of a tear in the left one. The wolf emotes. "Why? It is important, is it not? We can grieve and talk, can we not?"

I'm not sure if she is haranguing me or convincing herself, so I just nod. She turns away from me again. I miss her face already. Lightdammit.

"What happens next," she continues, "is that there will be an *ehcielnehesredeiwfau*."

There is a long pause. "A party?" I ask hopefully.

"No. Not a party," replies Raven, her tone neutral. "The literal common-tongue translation is *goodbye corpse*."

"Ah, I see. I can probably guess it from that."

"Then a new leader will be chosen for my pack. A new Ansbach alpha. Then the other alphas will have to choose a new leader for the Outside Council."

I nod, trying and mostly failing to keep up. "An alpha of the alphas."

Raven sighs and crosses her legs. "If you must."

There is a pause. It goes on for a while. This is normally when Raven vanishes, but she is still there, still naked, still in my company. This might be the longest we've ever spent just the two of us. Shame the circumstances are so shading depressing.

"Raven," I say eventually, deciding she must be waiting for me to speak. "This is all well and good, this talk of process, but . . . that is to say . . . oh, Lightdammit, Raven, *what the fuck happened in there*?"

Raven's reply sounds dry as the desert I hail from. "What do you think happened, mage?"

"How in the five magicks should I know? I'm not Sage."

She ignores that. I sigh and give it a go. "Well, given the fact that you shouted 'wolfsbane' quite loudly at the time and that wolfsbane is a deadly plant that kills the wolfkind, I'm going to hazard a guess that Ashen was killed by it."

"And?"

For Light's sake. This feels like one of Sage's tests. Why are people always testing me? "And I imagine someone put it in his drink."

"But?"

"You know, this would go a lot quicker if you took over yourself."

Silence.

I sigh again. "But wolfsbane is not meant to exist anywhere. You lot got rid of it after the war. After Extinction Valley. It shouldn't be a thing anymore."

"And?"

"Raven, come on. . . ."

*"And?"*

"I don't know what more you want. . . ."

She sighs. "Why were we able to get rid of it so thoroughly?"

I think on this. I give it a while. After all, Raven herself likes her long silences, so I'm allowed some on occasion.

"Oh," I say eventually, with the satisfied glee of a man proving to himself he is less slow than he thought. "You smell it. Like you do every other shitting thing. You can smell wolfsbane, from ages away, isn't that right? That's how you scoured it off the land."

"And so we can conclude?"

I smile. I have the lay of it now. A little slower than Sage, but fuck it, he's not here. "So we have two questions. One, how is wolfsbane still around? And two, how did it get in his beer, given that every single wolf in the castle should have been able to smell it, never mind the wolves in that chamber?"

"Good show, mage." I can see a hint of a smile on her usually unreadable lips from here.

"There you go, Sage, you're not needed now." I grin, wishing my best friend and prime agitator was here to see me now.

"Let's not go that far."

"Yes, that's fair."

There's another pause. Somewhere far off, a couple of wolves begin to howl. I want to ask Raven if these are expressions of grief or just normal wolf things, but I decide to restrain the thought.

"It is actually more complicated than that," says Raven.

"More complex than an impossible murder?"

"No, just another reason to make it more impossible."

"Oh, good." I half laugh to myself. "Excellent, please go on."

Raven clears her throat. "The wolfsbane wasn't in the mug."

"I'm sorry?"

"You heard me, mage. It wasn't there."

"And you know this how, Inquirer Raven?"

She turns to me again, her dark eyes narrowed.

"That was a jest, you see," I say hurriedly. "Inquirers investigate murders in Luce. Sage used to be one . . ."

"I know what inquirers are." She turns away from me again. "I know it was not in the cup because I drank from it. I took a sip when he first poured it, before he went in. I have been doing that the whole time the Outside Council have been here. Well, I caught most of his drinks anyway, he sometimes has one behind my back, the cheeky bastard." She catches herself using the present tense and stops. I notice one solitary nail on her right hand lengthening and shortening into talon and back.

"So what . . . you're his taster here? You're risking your own life for him?"

"Only while the other alphas are here, like I said. I do not trust them. Some of them, at least. And I have been proven right in that respect." A pause. "And, if I am honest, I never expected to have to deal with wolfsbane. There are lesser substances that cannot kill a wolf but can leave them ill for a time, ones that are harder to scent than wolfsbane and can be disguised. I was worried that any incapacitation of Ashen, no matter how brief, could be used by others as . . . political advantage. Or worse."

"Silver Stubbe again?"

"Yes, or others. The Wolflands are not as stable as they have been, you may have noticed."

I reflect on this. "Could it be that while you only took a sip, Ashen downed the whole lot, and so you were not affected by it?"

Raven shakes her head. "That is not how wolfsbane works. If it was in there, I would have been killed, too, even after consuming only a little bit. That is why it is so fatal. Only the tiniest amount can kill, and there is no cure, nothing that can be done. If it had been in there, then he would not have died because he would have drained the whole mug; no, he would have been dead from the first sip. It just would have taken a little longer to hit him, in diluted form. But as I sipped it first, and here I sit, it could not have been in there."

"Hold on," I say. "If such a small amount kills, why didn't vampires win every single past war with you easily, when it still existed?"

"Because we smell it, mage, remember." She makes no attempt to disguise her impatience.

"Yes . . . but in that case, I have the opposite question. This locked-room murder mystery aside, how did any wolf ever die from it if you can smell it so well?"

Raven shrugs. "Our enemies the bloods—and on occasion, your kind—have always been nothing if not inventive. Wolfsbane on an arrow shot from far enough away . . . Or overpowering the wolf when they already know of its presence and then administering it . . . Or, as I told you from the tale of Extinction Valley, seeding it deep in the ground then blowing the moondamn ground up."

I give that a few moments to sink in, thinking of all the centuries of cunning and death. The Everlands is full of pieces of shit, when you really come down to it.

"Well," I say eventually, "in summary, the questions you need to answer are how Ashen ingested wolfsbane, how no one smelled it beforehand, and how it existed in the first place." I breathe out. "Good luck, Raven. Seriously."

"Thank you, mage," she replies, uncrossing her legs and stretching them out, and relaxing into the bench. "But I do not need it. You do."

A cold chill flutters down my spine. Sometimes my instinct for bad news gets there ahead of the news itself. Benefit of being an eternal pessimist.

"Sorry, you're definitely going to have to explain that," I say with a smile that has no right being on my horrified face.

But before she can, we're interrupted by a wolf with long blond hair and a practical arrangement of furs for work more than show, which indicates that she's one of the wolves seconded to castle duties for the council's stay.

"I'm sorry to interrupt, Raven," she says, standing in the archway to the garden, a panicked expression on her face. "But you need to come and see this."

Raven narrows her eyes, then stalks off after blondie. At the archway she pauses and turns to me. "You too, mage."

I sigh, annoyed at our conversation being cut short and alarmed at what further drama there could be in this mad castle I'm regretting ever coming to. But I quickly follow her, because it's best not to keep the Midnight Assassin waiting, I've learned.

We hurry across the central tower courtyard to the southern wing and then east to the Great Hall, where the doors are wide open and a crowd of wolves—all the remaining alphas and at least a dozen of the castle Ansbachs—are gathered around Silver Stubbe, who has a triumphant shit-eating grin on his face.

But I'm not concerned with Stubbe. I'm concerned with the two people he has forced to kneel in front of him, facing the crowd. Two faces I recognize.

Silver sees Raven then, and grins. "Ah, Raven. There you are. I have wonderful news. Ashen's killers have been found in the nearby forest, fleeing. Your pack mate can be avenged already."

I stare at these alleged killers.

Samantha Ingle, the maid who got us into this whole mess and almost brought her city down.

And my oldest and best friend.

Who else but Sage Bailey?

I'm still in shock when Silver speaks again. "Now do you see what I have been trying to tell to deaf ears?" He turns to each of his fellow alphas in turn: to Verdant, to Bronzed, to Berry. "The vampires haven't finished with us. And they still like the old ways, the wolfsbane ways. They sent a mage and a Worn to see it through.

"Well, thanks to one of my unders scouting the woods"—he nods at one of the two other Stubbes who are part of his retinue, a beefy brute lurking behind him—"we found the assassins. So now, once we've shown them the mercy of the claw"—he strokes a lengthened talon down Sage's shoulder beneath him, making it clear what *mercy* really means—"and we have avenged Ashen, we must finally start looking toward the old enemy, who are as far from done with us as we must now be with them."

At that point my shock dissipates like the initial cold after you've plunged yourself into an ice bath and I start to move forward, a shout of "Sage" on my lips. But two things stop me. One is the firm grip of Raven, holding me before I can take a single step. The other is Sage's eyes. He's staring at me. He looks tired; his new short beard is somehow more unkempt than mine, and his hair is longer. But the stare. That's a stare I'm used to. It is the *shut the fuck up* stare. But more than that, it is the *you do not know me, wait for my words* stare. Once you've been on enough hair-raising adventures with someone, which we did before Grayfall when we scouted the entire Everlands for mortal relics, you become an expert in the in-danger stares of your coadventurer. Sage's stare is not just saying words, it's saying whole sentences. And having read them, I reluctantly step back, relieved to find Raven's painfully tight grip loosening as a result.

Then Sage's voice, low and calm, sounds out across the hall. "We are not who you say we are. We claim the right to sanctuary, as laid down in Clause 58 of the Wolf Pact, post-Grayfall. I was persecuted in an outpost of Luce as a Quantas, and forced to flee with my wife here from the Desertlands to First Light. But we encountered Grays, and took the southern route, round the remains of Dawn Death to the Wolflands. We were arriving, not fleeing when you found us. We claim sanctuary, we claim—"

At this point Silver shouts, "Enough!" and pushes Sage so hard he falls forward and almost smacks his head off the stone floor. I see Sam, who has so far remained admirably stoic, gasp and instinctively move to his aid, but Silver clamps a hairy palm down hard on her shoulder.

"A risible excuse," roars Silver. "The vampire Lords aren't even trying with their cover stories these days I see. Evading the Grays! No one evades the Grays."

I wince inwardly, as he has a point. I don't know why Sage has suddenly returned, with Sam, to boot, but I would hazard a guess that he didn't expect a welcome like this, or that his timing would be so poor, and he has not had long to concoct an excuse. It does have some fair points. The claim of sanctuary makes sense. When the wolves and the bloods did the deal after Grayfall to allow the vampires to take the wolf criminals and drain them of their wolfblood, they did throw in a fairly random clause about any immortal, including mages, being able to claim sanctuary with another if waylaid in their journey across the Centerlands by Grays. At that point it was still thought possible to cross the Centerlands without being killed by Grays, even if you didn't end up at your final destination. You've got to respect the optimism.

And the point about him being a Quantas and having to flee? Again, plausible. The other sorcerer types are not always welcoming of our kind in certain areas. *Not always welcoming* being a poetic way of saying magic-class cleansing was frequently attempted. And yes, sorcerers often take vampire wives.

But them actually reaching here alive? That's where it falls through. But more than that, why not just tell them who he is? Tell them he's representing the Archmage in First Light? Not that we've done much reporting back to him, frankly, but still true in the literal sense. Why come up with this, for Sage, frankly shit cover story?

This is all too much. I'm at a shading loss, as usual.

"Silver," Raven says, stepping forward, her voice low and composed.

"Before you go executing strangers on no authority, I have a couple of questions."

Silver's expression doesn't change, but I see his eye twitch a little. "Of course you do, Raven."

"First question," Raven continues, as a couple of watching Ansbach wolves part to let her through, so she directly faces Silver, Sam, and Sage. "Have you any evidence these two were involved in Ashen's murder, other than their appearance in our forest?"

Silver smirks and turns to the other alphas. "We all respect you, Raven, certainly enough to hope you didn't fall for that terrible story."

Raven puts another step forward, gently, carefully, and it is just as threatening as if she had lengthened all her claws at once. Suddenly the room feels hushed, as if it's just Silver and Raven alone, facing off.

"I'm not talking about the story, Silver," Raven continues. "I'm talking about the need for evidence before we kill people. I cannot speak for the practices of the bloods or mages, but I know that here in Ansbach territory we take that very seriously indeed."

Silver huffs. "Ashen was killed by wolfsbane; mages know how to secret it anywhere. And they appear just after the murder. What more do you need?"

At this point Berry Gevaudan pipes up, her large eyes narrowed. "A little bit more than that, Silver, darling." I remember Raven saying that the Gevaudans, like the Ansbachs, were of the moon, and a bit more studious than the Stubbes, who were of the claw. Luckily it sounds like that includes having a bit of respect for the investigative process.

Silver shrugs. "I'm sure we can get them to confess, which is all the evidence we will need."

I suppress a shudder at what that means. I see one of Raven's talons lengthen a little. I know by now that means anger.

"I'm not going to dignify that with a reply, unless you want to sully Ashen's name right here in his own home, his own hall. Wolves don't torture. That's for bloods."

"A lot of reply, that, for someone who doesn't want to dignify themselves with one," says Silver, a smug smile creeping onto his face. He can't help himself. He really is a dislikable bastard. I see Bronzed Morbach badly suppress a smirk to his left. That means at least one of the alphas has fallen for Silver's schtick, worse luck.

Raven breathes out slow and takes another step forward. "And then there is my second question. Who . . . is in charge?"

Silver furrows his brow. "I'm sorry?"

"You heard me, Silver Stubbe. Under shared wolf law, who is in charge?"

Silver lifts his hands up as if offended by the question. "No one, Raven, obviously. Ashen is dead, so we await the next alpha of the Outside Council to be voted in."

Raven shakes her head. "I am not talking about the Outside Council, I am talking about the Ansbach pack. Since you are on our pack territory, the dealing of outsiders within it is very much our prerogative, unless I have read every pack's individual wolf laws wrong."

"You Ansbachs haven't chosen a new alpha yet! By the claw, Raven, where is this goin—"

Raven's voice comes out louder now, lower, half a growl. "*By the moon*, Silver, you do not know your own laws. When a pack alpha dies there is not a vacuum before a new one is chosen. Instead, the residues of the alpha remain temporarily in the pack mate until the new alpha is made. Which means Golden Ansbach is, for all intentions, as Ashen was for the time being. Now, if you want to go to explain to the grieving mate who is dealing with her whole world falling apart that you want to shit on every principle that Ashen believed in, and that you can be very fucking sure she still believes in, too, then please go ahead. Or, if not, you can follow my word in her stead and work with *me*, a representative of the Ansbach on Ansbach territory instead of this . . . whatever this is, this *dnatsfualedur*!"

I don't know what that last word means, but I know it gets a sizeable reaction among the gathered crowd, including the other alphas. Morbach's eyes widen and he looks like he is about to shit himself in those overly fancy furs of his.

Whatever it means, it wipes some of Silver's confidence off him, and his smug countenance wavers a little. "Very well, Raven. Let us play it your way. I am only trying to seek honor for Ashen, nothing more. What is your counter, then?"

"We put them"—Raven nods toward Sage and Sam, the bloody married couple, as I suppose I have to think of them now—"in some guest quarters." She holds her hand up as Silver goes to protest. "We do not have jails in Ansbach castle, we've never needed them, and if these are seeking sanctuary I would not have us prove to be the most foul of hosts. Believe me, if they are guilty of Ashen's murder they will receive justice swift and most bloody. Until then we will put them there under guard, of course, until the investigation is concluded."

"Your investigation," says Stubbe foully.

"Your sharpness has returned, at last," Raven replies.

Silver narrows his eyes. "As usual, it seems you have your way. But my two unders will take turns as one of the guards, round the clock. That is not negotiable."

"We are not negotiating, Silver, but I have no problem with you wasting the time of your own unders. One Ansbach guard, one Stubbe guard. Now if you do not mind, I would quite like to return to investigating the murder of my pack mate, just in case this grand theory of yours is wrong and the murderer is among us laughing at your distractions." Before Silver can think of a riposte, Raven nods at one of the Ansbach wolves lingering nearest to Silver, who goes forward to grab Sam and Sage up. Silver doesn't stop them but just stands there, glowering.

The wolf takes them past me, and I stare at Sage, who makes no effort to stare at me back, and as the hushed confrontational silence that had descended dissipates into the hubbub of a roomful of wolves trying to digest what just happened, it sinks in with me just how utterly shading ruined the situation really is.

I'm back in Golden's garden, watching the last of the sun give way to the chill of night. Back staring at herbs and plants and flowers and a fountain. I've been sitting here in, I suppose, shock, for a couple of hourglasses, waiting for Raven to come and tell me what happens now. She might not come. But if she is as good as they say she is, she will smell my desperation, for answers and, maybe, some kind of hope that she will tell me what to do or, even better, do it herself.

By the Light, Sage. You've really gone and done it this time. And for once, he can't even blame me. Probably.

At length a shadow enters my periphery and lingers behind the bench to my right.

"You know, mage," says Raven. "Sitting here all day hoping to be somewhere else is not a plan."

"Says you. You've no idea how many times it's worked in the past."

Raven sighs. "I do not suppose you know why they came here."

I shrug. "I've had no contact with Sage. The idiot went underground after leaving us, doing his secret stuff with Sinassion. And I had nothing from any of the rebels. Maybe they've made some progress? They wanted to update Ashen?"

Raven ponders this, moving from behind me to the fountain in front and looking up at the marble cast of the moon centered on it, over which the water trickles, as if she wants to be back where the river races and the moonlight lands on forest, not stone. "Then why not send a honegull? Why come themselves?"

"Maybe they don't trust all the wolves. Seems sensible, from what I've seen of that bastard Silver Stubbe. He's the classic 'rabble-rouser actually in league with the enemy' type. I wouldn't put it past him to be the vampire Lord's wolf in the Wolflands. You don't have to have watched too many musicscenes to gather that tired old plotline."

Raven grunts. "Hmm. Maybe. But it was, mage, the worst fucking timing they could have chosen."

"Agreed. And why choose that cover story? Why not just say who they are?"

Raven turns from the fountain to him and narrows her eyes. I see she has changed from her earlier set of furs, ceremonial-looking ones, to more practical evening wear that covers less of her body. I feel like I'm becoming an expert in these endless furs. As for her body, probably best not think about that too much. "I cannot answer that. But I can tell you a positive effect it has had."

"If you're trying to spin some good news here, Raven, you'd better have eight legs, because I'm not buying it."

Raven ignores this. "It means that no one knows you are acquainted with Sage. Which retains your authority as my guest here. And it means that we have an easy solution to the whole thing."

"I'm not going to like this, am I?"

Raven stares at me. "I need you to find the murderer for me. I need you to do it in three days. It solves everything. Sage and Sam can be cleared. The wind can be taken out of whatever Silver's plans are. A new alpha can be chosen for the Ansbachs and then to lead the Outside Council. The Stubbes can be put to heel and the Wolflands can continue to be stable. Find the murderer and how they did it, and everything else falls into place."

"No, sorry," I say, my expression fixed, half imagining being somewhere else, somewhere with alcohol and bedsheets in the near proximity of said alcohol. "Still need quite a significant amount of explaining there, Raven."

Raven walks from the garden toward my bench and stands in front of me, arms crossed, long fingernails tapping her ribs impatiently, threatening to extend to claws. She sighs heavily, and I catch a scent of her breath, half pine, half forest air. It's not unpleasant. I tell myself to look at her face, not down, the weary reminder of the predictable mage I am. This has always been hard as her face often has the expression I'd imagine her having moments before eating me. But as I stare into her deep-shadowed, half-feral eyes, and take in her lips, perennially half curled with the hint of sharp teeth, and watch her long locks settle as she fixes on me, I find myself finding it easy to stare at her face. Far too easy.

"Look, mage, I cannot do it myself. I hunt, and I kill, and I stalk, and I smell. Some of these skills are helpful to the task ahead. But the finer details, the motives, the hows and the whys and the seeming impossibility of it, I am not patient enough for such things. I am . . ." She pauses, obviously struggling with the next part. "I do not have the sufficient intelligence for it, either."

"But I do?" I ask, genuinely bemused.

Raven studies me then, studies me for a while, and even in the increasing comfort I have with her features, I quickly grow discomforted and feel a blush creeping up round my neck, damn traitorous neck that it is.

"Jacob," she says, doling out that rare use, for her, of my actual name, "I am only going to say this once. Do not expect it again. You are not the stupid fool you think you are. Sage Bailey, the most intelligent mage I have ever associated with, did not purposely choose an idiot to be by his side. You are clever, and you are observant, and while you may not match Sage in these attributes yet, you still have them in greater quantities than most people in this world, and you also possess something that Sage does not. You can get people to talk to you, and like you. You are perfect for this role. Or at least," she says, clearly tired of complimenting me, "of those I have in this castle, you are best suited for it."

I try to take all this in. The intelligence bit is clearly a canard, a lie for my benefit. The people bit, perhaps, but still a stretch. "I can have a drink with people on occasion, Raven, I'll give you that, but I don't see—"

"You got the secrets from Tenfold. You walked right into that house of the vampire elite, the Rushes, and you got them all from him when really you should have got a beating."

I remember how shit-scared I was when I finally confronted Tenfold. "I almost did."

"But you didn't. You have skills." She pauses. "You magickless mages . . . you Quantas . . . this, negative feelings about yourself, is a thing with some of you, is it not?"

"What does that mean?"

She doesn't reply.

"Look, maybe I have a few things I have picked up along the way, maybe even a couple of skills from Sage or whatever. But I'm a sorcerer in a castle full of wolves. I'm the last person who should be doing this."

"No," Raven says, half growling, and she turns away from me, stalking back toward the herb garden with alarming speed, and remains with her back turned as the crescent moon waxes above us. "You are the only one who should be doing this. I am full of murder, Jacob, I am full of rage. I can feel it now, clawing its way out of me. I can feel it howling in the base of my skull. I can feel it screaming in every edge of my soul. Do you know how I managed to not attack every wolf in that room, pin them down, rip a finger off to show that I mean it, demand they tell me who it was else I sink my teeth into their throat?"

"No," I say quietly, not entirely enamored with the idea of being so close to such an angry wolf assassin.

"Because of Ashen. Because I do not want it to fall apart. The peace he built, his legacy. I have to stay in control. But to speak to them all, to dig into this, to investigate . . . my control would break, and my wolf would take over. And we do not want to see that happen, do we, mage?" Her voice grows husky as she says that, and I swear the evening shadows start to shift around her.

"No, we don't." My voice comes out croaky and malformed. But then something happens. Something I haven't done for at least a century. I shovel my fear down, my inherent terror, and I replace it with something approaching boldness.

"But it can't be me, Raven. I'm sorry." I stand up. "I can talk to some people, see if we can get allies to free Sage and Sam. Or you can send me back to First Light." I pause, thinking of what Sage would do. But such thoughts are pointless, as I can't be an inquirer. I can't mimic Sage. I'm not that person, I never was.

I start to walk out, fearing as I do the rage she spoke of loosed on me: claws on my back, her fresh breath in my ear, not like I want—Oh shit, I want, don't I? But in the worst way imaginable: the last feeling before her primal fury rips me to pieces. Maybe it was always meant to end this way, this odd coupling of ours.

But no rage or death or terrifying attack comes, thank the Light, and as I reach the stone archway leading back to the castle, her voice cuts through the air to me, clear and emotionless. "He was my best friend."

I turn round. She still has her back to me. She hasn't moved from her position at the garden's edge. She is even more bathed in shadow now.

"What?" I ask, pointlessly.

"Ashen was my best friend. Maybe my only real friend, at least in these last two centuries. He understood me, knew my depths, and he still loved me, in his way. We have known each other for four centuries. He is the only person still alive that I know of who remembers my mate."

She has never mentioned a mate. We've never talked this long, I suppose.

"The grief in me is so large, Jacob, that I can only barely see the edges of it. I do not even want to look at it now. I cannot engage with it, not yet. But it is in me, and I know it will kill me for all the centuries I have left. I . . ."

A pause. A very, very long pause. The air stills. Whoever was responsible for the sporadic howling earlier has chosen to stop. The faint noises of the main castle behind us seem fainter by the moment. In the evening gloom, we may as well be the only people alive. There are goose bumps on my arm.

"I cannot do this alone, Jacob. I need you." She turns round, and a single tear has tracked its way down her face, her still-unreadable, shadowed face, and it's fallen onto her chest. She looks like the most beautiful fucking thing I've ever seen in my life in her grief, and for once I decide not to loathe myself for a thought like that, not to truly despise myself. For a moment, just a moment, I give myself a break from that.

Then she says, softly, "Will you help me, or will you leave me?"

Is this her? Does she mean this? She's the most honest person I've ever met, but she has her whole kingdom at stake. She might have found her will to lie and deceive me. Might have sensed how I might be starting to feel.

But I've never wanted to believe anything more, and sometimes it's not bad to be a fool.

"I'll help you," I reply, embracing my idiocy.

# 23

# Flight Plan

> Of the nine great wonders of the worlde, our limited conception of the worlde being the Everlands alone, my personal favorite (with apologies to the astounding Atmos weather tower of Luce) is the waterfall that comes off Ansbach Castle. There are various reasons why it should not be there, or at least the castle should not be there if the waterfall is. But to perceive its majesty as you approach the castle from the south is a true sight, a true wonder. If you can journey safely through the Wolflands, I most highly recommend it!
>
> Kinet Lamarstion, *A Journey of Wonders*

## Sam

I do my best to get to sleep but it's not easy. After a lifetime of sleeping in the day, getting to sleep at night is even harder than I thought it would be, and I didn't think it would be a walk in the garden. I tried to train myself for my stay in the Wolflands by missing out on my last day's sleep during the trek down from First Light, but of course the brain and body aren't that easily fooled. At least in one sense being taken as a prisoner and being given some windowless guest quarters as a prison is actually quite useful, as I don't have to worry about dodging rays during the day. Most of Ansbach castle is free of the day's light; there's a lot of gloom. But it is still facing up to be a bit of a risky stay, wolf castles not exactly built with vampire comforts in mind, especially since they went to war with each other.

But now? Lovely, simple, safe. Relaxing, if you don't count the imminent threat of execution for a murder I didn't commit.

I turn over restlessly in my basic bed, a hemp mattress over a worn wooden frame, obviously built for mages and sorcerers as wolves wouldn't be seen anywhere near an actual bed. It's a little better than the bed I had for a decade at the First Lord's palace, much worse than the bed I slept on at the new Leeches' abode in Westfall.

Back to the old-school comforts for me, it seems.

As I fail to drift off I consider my predicament, at least the bad luck of it. When Sage and I announced our grand plan of traveling to the Wolflands to seek the support of the wolf armies to protect First Light from a future Lords' attempted take-back of the city, I was full of the classic Sam sense of fate: we would be the ones to swing the numbers in our favor, gift the rebels-cum-rulers the support of a whole new army. It would take some persuading, but after all, with the intelligence of Sage and my ability for, I don't know, making things change very quickly, who would bet against us?

But instead, after a hurried journey from the Wolflands, a week of walking all night and little talking, we walked into a murder of their leader and set ourselves up, it seems, as the perfect fall folk for some other angry werewolf who seems very keen to pin the blame on us.

Now I'm just trying to work out if I'm in worse or less trouble than the time I was a palace prisoner, set to be executed (twice, come to think of it). This feels worse, as I just don't know what's happening.

But I'm not afraid. Yet. Crying with First Lord Azzuri, sharing our pain, our trauma, cured me of that. My guilt is gone, too, for now. I didn't come this far to falter.

Fuck these wolves.

*Knock knock.*

The knock makes me jump, slightly putting the dampeners on my confident thoughts, and I sit up in bed and light the candle on my rickety gelmwood bedstead. I don't need to put my day gown on as I'm wearing it—wolf castles are draughty, especially since I'm not on any good blood at the moment, just the carafe of rabbitblood they supplied me with—so I hurry to the door, and say, carefully, "Yes? Who is it?" as if I could stop anyone from coming in anyway.

"Open up," comes the bark in reply, and I recognize the gruff tones of one of the wolf guards who was stationed outside my quarters. Left with little choice, I open the door and see him before me. He's tall, I'd guess almost seven foot, tall even for a wolf, and broad, as well. His long red hair is tied back in a ponytail, a rare affectation from what I could tell of the wolves I've seen here so far. He has a mean face and bulbous nose and small eyes and I can see he is perfect *guard the suspects* material. His guard furs—already I can tell the difference between some of the fur outfits they wear—include large black shaggy shoulder pads and a much trimmer yellow two-piece. It seems pointless to me, especially after knowing Raven in her nakedness back in First Light, but there's obviously some rule about clothing in the castle they're all dutifully sticking to.

"We're movin' you," he says, his accent a strange mix between a Southwestfall broad twang and the more clipped foreign-sounding accent of a wolf like Raven.

"Why?" I ask, suddenly afraid that Raven's demand for investigation will have been overruled somehow and that sinister Silver Stubbe will have gotten his way for an execution.

He shrugs, and indicates the corridor to his right. "This way."

I do as he says, not having much else to do, after all, and not in the habit of overpowering wolves built like a brick pisshouse, and walk ahead of him, following his directions as we turn right. The corridor is cold, dark stone lined with torches, fairly standard castle décor, I'm beginning to realize, for this castle that is not built with the vampire's idea of finery in mind. I smell wet dog, and I can't work out if it's the wolf behind me or just the aroma seeped into the stone.

We take another right and come to a door similar to my own "guest" quarters, and my wolf guard knocks on it and is answered by Sage. A swell of relief fills me. His eyes look even more tired than before and his hair is slightly rumpled, so he's been attempting sleep, too; maybe he succeeded. His eyes dart to me, and he looks relieved. Then concern flashes across them as he, too, must have realized that our execution reprieve could have come to a hasty end.

But he leaves, as I did, with no protest, and we walk together ahead of the wolf. We take two more rights, then descend a stone staircase, small and tight. I couldn't tell you where we are. We walk down this staircase awhile, and the air grows colder and the torches grow less frequent, and the expression on Sage's face grows more concerned.

"Where are you moving us to?" he asks eventually, as the staircase opens out to a dark, stone corridor, the smell of damp heavy in the air. On my basic-blood eyes I can hardly see a few feet ahead of me. If this isn't the castle basements then the castle basements must be really depressing.

The guard wolf doesn't reply.

That's when I realize that while we *are* being moved, it's not to new prisoner quarters. It's to our place of death, secret and cold and dark.

One of these nights someone will stop trying to kill me, but tonight is not that night. We march down this new . . . *tunnel* is a better word than *corridor*, the roof sloping right, almost cave-like in its formation. Definitely some catacomb under the castle. There are no torches ahead so the wolf guard grabs one of the lingering ones on the wall. He won't need it, and I can maybe manage at a slow, careful crawl in pure dark, but I assume it's for Sage so he doesn't have to carry him to his murder.

After a few more moments of torturous walking, we arrive at the end of the tunnel into a wide, expansive room with no seeming exit that I can see in the torchlight. I see Sage study it intently, starting at the walls. Even for his clever mind, I don't see much hope here. If I'm right, it will be us and a massive wolf in here, and I'm not on any proper blood and Sage has no magick. I wonder how quickly Sage can pull out that invisibility cube of his. I asked him about his other one, the one that turned him into a large metal suit of armor and shot twelve winged bloods out of the sky, and he said that it was a "one use" thing and the thing to "charge" it was very large and located back in the Desertlands, deep in the vaults of the Cult of Humanis.

So my heart instead is set on a quick dose of invisibility.

"It wouldn't work, Sam," Sage says, doing that annoying thing where he knows where my train of thought is going. Who needs a Neuras when you have a Sage? "Werewolves smell just as much as they use their eyes, even more so." He's not looking at me, though, just staring at part of the stone wall behind me.

The wolf ignores Sage's conversation with me and just grins at us. "You're not stupid. Not if you pulled off that murder, anyway. So you know you're not leaving here. So let's just get this over with." His fangs lengthen within his grin, and he unties his ponytail, his red hair falling around his face.

"What are you called then, Redbush or something stupid?" I say, summoning the same false, adrenaline-fueled bravery that I've done for Rufous. They're all the same, these overconfident killers, these slavering men. They're not worth my pure terror. They're barely worth my rage anymore.

"Redsky Stubbe, you Wornblood," he replies. "Pleasure to meet you." He looks down at his hands, which are shimmering and shifting, a brief kaleidoscope of colors, within which the shapes of hands are growing larger and hairier and clawier, and he grins. "Do you know what's funny?

I don't need to change to kill you. You're both so pathetic, I'll just shift my hands alone." He looks down at this paws, now fully changed to wolf.

Sage, who's backed himself up against the far wall, narrows his eyes at him. "Another Stubbe. Like the one who accused us of Ashen's murder. I know three things about Stubbes. One, you're all pretty Lightdamn stupid. *Really* stupid, to be clear. Angry morons easily led by Silver. More beast than man, and stupid beast at that."

Redsky laughs, but he can't conceal the anger in his eyes.

"Two, you're particularly stupid, if you're here. Silver brought two underwolves with him, like all the other alphas, I assume. One for diplomacy and intelligence. And one as a bodyguard, as the brute. I wonder which one you are."

No laughing now, just anger on his face.

"Three, I'm sorry."

Redsky narrows his small eyes further and steps toward Sage menacingly. "Sorry about what, mage?"

"I'm sorry your father didn't get killed at Extinction Valley so the world didn't have to deal with you. Would have been a lot better if he'd choked to death on the wolfsbane clouds so the Wolflands didn't have to put up with your stupid bloodline making your pack even thicker."

At that Redsky loses all composure, raises his paws, and points to Sage with the paw not holding the torch.

*"YOU FIRST."*

Then he blows out the torch.

I instinctively jump back, expecting claws in me despite his claim to be going for Sage, but in the new ominous blackness I can just about make out the looming shadow figure of Redsky lunging forward toward the sorcerer, still backed up against the wall. I hear the wolf half growl, half roar, and sense rather than see his two huge paws balled into fists, ready to punch Sage in actual half.

The mighty blow comes, but Sage isn't there, as he's ducked just in time.

Instead, the huge wolf fists hit the stone, and Redsky roars in pain, and retracts what I can't tell in the gloom but imagine are bruised and bloody paws. But I also hear the sound of something breaking, and crashing, and falling, and more roaring, and it looks from my poor weak-blooded night vision like the whole room is coming down. The wolf's roars grow louder this time, obvious pain, and then for a brief moment there is silence.

Then a hand grabs me out of the shadows.

I don't scream, I'm glad to say, but my heart does do a couple of dives off a steep cliff. But it's Sage, lightly covered in dust, I think, grabbing me by my arm.

"This way," he says hurriedly, and pulls me toward where there seems now to be a hole in the wall that the wolf tried to plow Sage into.

"How?" I ask as we approach it. "It's a thick stone wall, I don't—"

"I'll explain in a moment," Sage says, and I see his head nod toward a large pile of rubble to the side. "He's under that, but he won't be for long, we need to go."

"Okay," I say, turning back to the entrance to the tunnel we came in through.

"No," says Sage, pulling me back to the hole. "Through there."

"Uh," I reply, struggling to process something that has no right to be processed at all. "You mean into the hole in the wall."

"Not a hole," adds Sage, his voice next to my ear now, almost as close as when we kissed one month ago. He smells, not unpleasantly, a little of cedar. Why does he always smell of cedar? "A tunnel."

"A . . . ?" I ask, finally processing, but Sage has already dived in, and so I follow, finding as I do that the hole indeed has revealed a tunnel, half my height and twice my width. There is a slight breeze, and I immediately get some gist of what this might be. I crawl on my knees beside Sage, expecting any moment to feel a giant paw reach out from the rubble behind me and grab my ankle. But no paw, and no grab.

I crawl on, wishing I'd drunk some better blood to sort out the ache in my knees and the scratches of the sharp rocks lining this tunnel. I'm still virtually in the dark, just focused on Sage crawling in front of me. Water starts to drip around me, and my knees begin to get wet. At some point he turns right, and so do I, dutifully following him. I don't like being in the dark on where we're going, but the downside of knowing a mysterious so-and-so like Sage is that sometimes I, who like to know everything, have to accept that I have to wait to be told it. I'm sure he could have told me quickly before we went in the tunnel. Now he must extend the surprise. But as a flaw, it's not that bad.

And I'm warming quickly to his strengths.

My thoughts are rudely interrupted by my face walking right into his arse, and I stop, muttering an apology, and then suddenly realize I can see clearly thanks to the light of the opening ahead.

Moonlight. And the sound of rushing water, almost deafening. A river?

I shuffle next to him. He sticks a hand in his robe, deep into the concealed pocket the wolves didn't bother to check for, and comes out with several bloodvials, wrapped in fur.

"Here," he says, giving me one. "Sorry I didn't get a chance to give it to you earlier. But you'll want good eyesight for this." I take it from him, quickly unstop it, and down it in one. It's fox. Of course; a Hocquard special. A Midway blood but enough to give me terrific eyes. Eyes to show me clearly that the tunnel ends here, and beyond is a thin lip of rock one person can just about stand on. The waxing crescent moon is high in the cloudless winter sky, and with that and my new blood in me, I can see far and perfectly.

In the distance are snow-covered fir trees, continuing on for miles, ringing this backside of the castle we've come out on. To my left and right the great castle walls loom high on all sides. But it's the scene directly below me I'm more concerned about.

The huge bloody waterfall, specifically.

"It's a waterfall," I say numbly, staring at the cascading water glimmering in the moonlight, the soft spray of it lightly dusting my face as I peer out onto the lip of the rocks above.

"I'm afraid it is."

"You knew about this?"

Sage sighs. "As soon as we were led into that dead end, I wondered if there would be a secret exit. There always are in all the wolfpack castles, a residue of the wars past where they might need to make a quick exit. We'd gone down a long tunnel with no other exits. And then to this room. A room the wolf guard was clearly just told was a nice place to kill some people quietly. I spied the stone to be a slightly different color in the gloom, and I felt a tiny breeze when I stood against it. I took a calculated risk, and angered our newly rubble-covered friend enough for him to smash the thankfully quite flimsy stone covering the exit. I wasn't sure if it would knock him out; that was very lucky, to be honest."

"And the waterfall?"

Sage turns to me with an awkward expression, rubbing his beard. "That I was not expecting. I knew there was a waterfall on the southern end of this castle. I just didn't expect the secret exit to come out above it. There's a lot of reasons why there shouldn't be a waterfall coming off a castle. I'm going to have to ask about this."

"Impossible geography aside, may I just say that it is an extremely stupid place to put a secret exit."

Sage thinks on this. "It makes sense if you're a wolf being pursued by a squadron of vampires or sorcerers. Unless the vampire's on wolfblood, or the sorcerer is a proficient Atmos, they can't follow you over the waterfall without incurring damage. A wolf has a better chance."

"A better chance."

"Yes."

"So even a wolf will be injured."

"Um . . . yes."

"So we're going to turn back?"

"Not exactly."

"We're going to jump, aren't we?"

Sage looks awkward. "Well, if you want to."

I peer over the lip of the outcrop again. The thunderous waters must fall, say, two thousand feet. The scent of mineral rock and petrichor assaults my fox-improved nose, and I see the white lines of spray that outline the water and watch as it flicks into the air and out into nothing. Far below I can just about make out the water depths, surrounded at fairly random intervals by unappetizing-looking rocks.

"I can't emphasize enough how much I don't want to." I sigh. "Can I have my magicked stag?"

Sage nods. "Good idea." He takes another vial out of his secret pocket and hands it to me. Daphnée and I had conversed at length about what blood to take on my journey to the Wolflands. The obvious choice would have been wolfblood, an instant get-out-of-danger salve and easier to get now the rebels had the city stores. But if the wolves had found it on me? Not exactly fitting for a diplomatic begging mission to have the blood of the people we're coming to for aid. So we took a risk and took stag instead, alongside some lesser Midway bloodvials like fox.

Which now I'm regretting. Because yes, magicked stag is the king of noblebloods that aren't wolfblood. I'll be ten times as strong and fast and feel hardly any pain. And moodwise I'll feel amazing. But it isn't wolfblood and it can't stop me breaking into pieces if I come down bad on the rocks at the bottom.

"I read once that hitting water at this height is like hitting rock," I say.

Sage smiles then, not a grim smile, either.

"What?"

Sage shrugs. "It's just nice to be around someone who reads."

Despite myself, I smile, too. "Well, let's do this then before we're caught and I've scraped my knees for nothing."

"You might be the bravest person I've ever met," says Sage.

I turn to him, the stag filling my veins, hardening my skin a little, giving me the thrill of the blood, the spark of life, the zest of the outdoors, but also removing all my anxiety, all the extremes of emotions. I'm so used now to the semihallucinatory madness of wolfblood that I forgot how beautiful and balanced stag can be.

"If that's a prelude to kissing me, Sage, you missed your chance," I say, bold as you like, and then I wink at him.

And then I jump off the blooddamn waterfall.

# 24

# To Catch a Wolf

If you wish to spot a liar, you must be alive to certain things. The first is their body talk, the way they give themselves away with their facial expressions and their stance and, in the unlikely event you have a trusted wolf nearby to assist you, in the scent they give off.

The second is the small details they give. Lies will tend to the nondescriptive or the bizarrely overdescriptive. Think on how people remember things. Learn to spot a learned repetition from a true memory.

Yet another is the confidence of the liar who thinks they have got away with it. Let those who you suspect not know the extent of your suspicions, and they will respond with relief at their continued success by getting lazy over the finer details on which it was built.

Above all, be patient. And be intelligent. You cannot learn the latter. But anyone can become an expert in the former.

Sage Bailey, *An Instructive Pamphlet on the Art of the Inquirer,* written circa 403 AL

## Raven

My goodbye to Ashen is exactly what I expected. Soulless, numb, lacking in any sense I will remember the moment. I stand on the edge of the forest outside the castle grounds, next to Golden. The two wolves who were closest to him. We are naked, the light morning snow gently covering us in a thin film that slowly melts with our body heat. Eventually this will feel a little cold, but we will not be in person form for long.

In front of us, a small, shallow pit has been clawed out of the hard winter ground, just deep enough to place a body. It sits under the shade of a great beech tree, branches bare, trembling in the frosty winter wind and shaking snow onto the grave below.

Behind us, a respectable distance behind, are the rest of the Ansbachs. They came from all over the Wolflands, answering the chain of howls as quickly as you would expect. Most of the six-hundred-strong pack were either in the castle or its grounds or in the nearby forest, of course, having marshaled their strength for the Outside Council. Just in case. But some would have been roaming in other forests, in the routes between the pack lands where wolves can run completely free. A few, those on the coast or the south where the Swamplands start, would have been a little too far to reach in just two days, even at full wolf running. But wolves never wait for more than two days for this ceremony. The forest is waiting.

Behind the Ansbachs are the rest of the alphas, standing in a respectful line. Normally for the death of someone like Ashen, all those from other packs who wanted to pay their respects would be there, too. But the atmosphere is a barrel of firepowder waiting to be lit and so I did not allow anyone else to come into our territory. The howls I ordered made that very clear. The murderer cannot leave, and any of their reinforcements cannot come in.

As for how I feel? I do not feel sad, I do not feel angry. Those emotions were present yesterday when I spoke to Jacob. They will be present soon again. But today, in the early morning air, when I am meant to be feeling things, they are absent. I would like to think this is the sense of the forest taking over, the thought of what we wolves believe happens to us upon death replacing grief with a sense of wonder at the land.

But I know myself too well. It is not the forest. It is my refusal to bow down to the forced occasion. It is my stubbornness. Part of me is furious I let Jacob see a sliver of the extent of my feelings two days ago. It got him to stay. And I did, deeply, want him to stay. After the proceedings today, he will begin his work. But I felt a little sick afterward, like a layer of skin had been stripped from me.

And so now, I respond with numbness.

As Golden softly yelps next to me, her fangs and nails gently lengthening, Ashen's body is carried toward his shallow grave on a dense raft of tied spruce twigs. The wolves carrying him deposit him next to the grave.

As they wait to put him in, everyone turns to Golden, to see if she wants to say anything. Sometimes the bereaved wolf wishes to speak, sometimes they do not and will let their time in wolf form do the talking instead. Golden stands frozen for a moment, as if considering it. I study her. Her long, shining hair is braided into a pull-through ponytail, as is the Ansbach way for mourning. At least for the last two centuries—when I was young, wolves gave less of a shit about that sort of thing. Her face, shorn of lip daub or any of her usual additions, is stark and desolate. She smells of deep grief, rose-lily and rose itself and some jasmine underneath that. A little bit of pine as well, mild excitement, which is to be expected, the adrenaline of such an event. Jacob can rule this suspect out, at least; even if I did not know her and her love for Ashen so well, her grief is obvious on the air and she is not cunning enough to fool my nose.

After a few moments more, she shakes her head, and Ashen's corpse is placed into his shallow grave, completely naked. In the cold, he looks strangely lifelike, his face warm, like he is about to leap up and challenge me to a race across the forest, a race he knows he will lose but won't give a fuck about it, because he knows I'm the competitive one.

Or like he wants to make fun of the way I howl, even as I have the blood of five vampires slathered around me, and everyone else is staring at me in alarm, or in some cases terror, the scent of metal and steel so strong it almost bowls me over. They saw what I did to that vampire company in the skirmish, me alone. But Ashen doesn't care. He finds my death howl funny.

Or like he wants to hold me as I howl as a person, too distraught to even shift to wolf, as the corpse of my mate lies before me and the world collapses in on me, so long ago it hardly seems real.

I turn my face away, numbness giving over to something, now.

Then, as I look away, I hear the soil being thrown back over Ashen. There is not much of it, because of the shallowness of the grave. It's that shallow because his body does not need to be there for long. The closer it is to the ground, the quicker it will rot or be eaten by the forest, and the sooner his forest spirit will rise and permeate the trees. I will join him someday, as will Golden.

Will we speak? Will we be aware, in the sense we know it now? Perhaps. Perhaps not. But we will all gather, eventually, all of us in the forest. The inevitability of it is the only balm for the gut-wrenching grief to come in the centuries that will follow.

Once he is covered as good as he needs to be, we all stand there, waiting. After a while, Golden's hair and nails lengthen, and she growls, the growl getting lower and longer as she turns. Her eyes go yellow and feral. Her body starts to shimmer, and break, and fall apart and meld itself back together, a shape-shifting kaleidoscope of skin and bones and flesh all on the periphery of the vision, impossible to pin down, coalescing. Her transformation is fucking beautiful, but I suppose it would be, it being her. It's over in a few moments, and she stands there, a great golden wolf sitting on her haunches, howling to the moon, a long, drawn-out howl, over and over again. Then I transform, too, and join her, the chorus gaining in strength, my own notes undulating and cresting over Golden's, in tune with them but adding to them, a vibrant dirge.

Next, the Ansbachs behind me join in, and now the forest edge is alive with the song of the wolfpack, the chorus of the Ansbachs.

Then, finally, a respectful amount of time later, the other alphas change and sing. And as all howl, I hear the wolves of the forest around join in, too. In the crisp winter air I can just about hear the Gevaudans, miles away over the gorge. And I know, even as I howl my feelings into the forest, that slowly but surely all across the Wolflands, the chain of howls will form, every wolf in every pack who wants to acknowledge the man who saved us all in a valley far, far away and long, long ago.

Extinction Valley in my dreams, Extinction Valley blood-filled streams.

A memory that never leaves.

A wolf I will never forget.

We skip the funeral feast. No one wants to feast with a potential murderer. There will be time for that when this is over. We will celebrate Ashen properly, not under this fucking cloud. The alphas stick to their own chamber suites or, in Verdant's case, the forest grounds, as that great big green bastard is a wolf who never sleeps indoors, which I can respect. After we have all eaten in our respective ways—I chose to race through the snow-covered forest floor and catch a hare or two, almost invisible in the white panorama—I cautiously head up to Ashen and Golden's chambers. Now just the lair of a widow mate. The wind is fierce today and I can hear it whipping through the window of one of the other rooms. She must have removed the animal skin covering the window. She wants it cold.

Golden is lying in the same place I saw her last time, on the lounge-seat, naked again, but her necklace is gone and her hair is out of her ritual braids and flows all around her, halfway down the loungeseat itself, but not straight, not shining. Dull and with the beginnings of matting. Her scent is like earlier at her mate's grave: deep pungent petals of grief. The pine of adrenaline has been replaced by something more like the potent vegetation of seaweed, just like you'd find on the northern coast. That, for wolves, is the scent of nothing, the scent of listlessness and struggling to emote itself. That is concerning. I had hoped for the fine scent of lemons: fury.

She looks up at me, her eyes bordering on the vacant, and a little life comes into them, but not much.

"I can't wear it at the moment," she says, reading my thoughts. "Memories." She shrugs, content to leave it at that.

I move up to her. I want to nuzzle her, but her entire aroma is telling me to back off.

"We will find them and we will kill them," I say.

She sighs. "I heard that Silver has already caught them."

I huff. "A sorcerer and a vampire? Who were not anywhere near the scene? As if they could be running round secreting wolfsbane without being scented. Some ruse by Silver, to what end I will discover. No, the real killer is still here."

She nods, tiredly. "You can only keep everyone at the castle a couple more days under wolf law, Raven. Then they'll be gone, and even if you find them you'll never bring them to justice."

"Then we will race to their fucking pack territory and rip their throats out and any of their unders who helped them," I say. "Terror and blood, I will bring to them. You know I speak true." I'd hoped for a reaction to this commitment, but her expression barely changes.

"How will you find them?" she asks.

"I—" I stop. I am not sure how she will take this bit. If anything will provoke a reaction, it will be this. "The sorcerer. Jacob. I have tasked him with finding out how it happened and who did it."

"The sorcerer?" she asks, eyebrow half raised. "I assume you mean the one who came here first, not the one under guard." If her comment sounds cutting, I probably deserve it.

"Yes. Jacob. He . . . he comes from a cult that has a history of inquiring. . . ." I stop, annoyed with myself for using Jacob's term. I have spent too long around that fucking mage. "Investigating murders, discovering secrets." I inwardly wince at the slight lie. The second part is certainly true, discovering secrets. But it was Sage Bailey who investigated murders, back when he worked for the Archmage in the sorcerer capital, before the war, at least if Jacob's words are correct. Jacob himself has no such history. I am, in fact, putting a huge amount of faith in the mage. I tell myself I see something in him that is justified but, as I explained to him a little too honestly, it is also because I cannot do the things I need to both literally and also without losing my temper and ripping the throats out of the people I am meant to be talking to.

I do not say any of this to Golden.

"So this sorcerer will spend the next couple of days talking to the alphas, and he will tell us who killed my Ashen?" she asks, raising her head off her cushion.

I sniff. I cannot detect any wave of anger. No lemons.

"Yes. I—it is not what I am built for. I want this bastard found, for Ashen. For you. He is a resource at our disposal, and I have chosen to use him."

I brace myself for her fury. We have never fallen out, not since Extinction Valley, at least, but I have seen her lose her temper with others. Never Ashen. Never at all. But she has a fury about her, like all wolves with such heritage.

"Good," she says. To my relief—both at her lack of anger and the fact she seems to be feeling something finally—she actually smiles. "You're right, Raven. I know you. You would snap Silver's arm off or something and suddenly we'd be at pack war. I trust your instincts. You're doing what Ashen—" Her smile goes and something hitches in her throat. Another wave of flowers comes my way.

I look away and give her a moment. When I look back, I notice that the portrait of her and Ashen and her sons above the loungeseat is gone. She sees me looking.

"I can't bear to look at it. I'm the only one left."

"You have the rest of the pack, Golden, you're not alone." Even as I say it, I know it is the wrong thing to say.

"That's easy for you to say, Raven," she says, suddenly finding that citrus rage. "You never had children, you've been alone for centuries, you don't have the concept of family." The words come quick out of her mouth, and even as they leave she looks at me in shock. "Oh gods, Raven, that's the worst thing I've ever said, forgive me."

I move to her then, and I reach out a hand and I stroke her face.

"There is nothing to forgive, Golden." And I mean it. Words are nothing. Actions are everything. Her scent tells me that was not her, anyway.

She buries her face in the loungeseat then, and a low keening comes from her, a mewling. I kneel before her and nuzzle my face into her legs as she wolfs out some of her grief. After a while, her face still buried, her voice comes back to me.

"My sons should not have been on the wrong side of the rockfall. Did I ever tell you that?"

I raise my head and look up at her, brief surprise etched on my face. I do not know why, it is natural to be thinking of them as well as Ashen. The grief for her will never go, nor should it. Her two sons were killed during Extinction Valley. When the deadly clouds of wolfsbane were released into the air after the vampires set off the firepowder explosions that released it from its seeding below the valley floor, the two young Ansbachs raced across the valley to try to save another wolf from the Chalon pack. One of the sons was in love with them, a rare interpack love. The fact that the Chalon pack does not exist anymore and that almost all of its members were killed that day should tell you all you need to know about what side of the valley they were on. They were one of the first to be covered in the clouds of wolfsbane. Neither son ever made it back in time for the rockfall that Ashen coordinated, that cut us off from the clouds of wolfsbane. Their bodies were found two days later when the wolfsbane had dissipated, just yards from the rocks. On the wrong side. Of course, I already know all this.

"They are with their father now," I say. "Their spirits are in the forest."

She doesn't reply to that. Some wolves are more comforted by that than others. I tell vampires who ask that we think of our afterlife differently. We do not need the idea of *being* with our loved ones after we die, not in the usual sense. We just need the knowledge that we are all one in the forest, whether we are aware of ourselves or not. But what I omit is that this idea is better for some than others.

I do not think it comforts Golden much. She has had too much grief to find comfort in anything, I suspect.

"Do you remember when we went to the Gevaudan waterfall?" I ask instead. "You, me, Ashen, the cubs. They were only a couple of decades then."

She smiles at that, and doesn't say anything.

"I caught a deer, and Ashen did, and the cubs were desperate to hunt themselves, but then we came across that grizzled bear. And you were going to step in but they leapt in front to protect you, as if you needed it, but they faced off the bear and it scarpered away. I remember how proud you were. And," I say grinning, "how pissed Ashen was that the bear got away, because he fancied some bear meat."

"Brave of you to make me think of a happy memory like that, Raven," comes her voice, neutral, scent finely balanced between grief and curiosity.

I cease my nuzzling and stand up before her. "I did it on purpose. You were right. I have never had a full family, whether on purpose or by life. But you had one. And those memories that hurt can never be taken away from you. Do not flee from them. Do not lie on this loungeseat and think only of their death. Think of their life. Run through the forest and howl of their memories."

She lifts her head up then, and I get a half smile, which will have to do for now. "Maybe I will, Raven. Maybe I will."

## Jacob

I begin my investigations the day after Ashen Ansbach was buried in that frankly insane shallow grave. I don't know how the wolves can be okay with the idea of his corpse being so open to the elements, but I think if I want to keep my wits in the couple of days I've been given to solve this murder—all of those words are incredible, by the way, both the short amount of time I've been given and the fact I am apparently *solving a Lightdamn murder*—then I have to accept I don't really understand the first thing about wolves.

Which is a problem, obviously, for someone trying to root out a killer among their kind. So I must revert to the basics. All the basics that Sage has told me in many incredibly dull lectures about his time as an inquirer.

First, the interviews. I try to recall Sage's words about trying to get the most out of a suspect. All that nonsense about inspecting their features, listening to the details they give, whether they're overelaborate or not sketched out enough, what feels *real*, and not giving myself away too much, allowing them to walk overconfidently into their own trap. It all sounds so good coming out of his mouth, but he has the advantage of his brain to go with it.

My only advantage is that I didn't drink last night, so I have a clear head for once in my life.

The interviews take place in the morning, and in an antechamber off the Great Hall. I am entirely unsurprised to find that it's bare of anything except a chair for them and a chair for me. I've taken to wearing furs under my desert robe. It takes a lot for sorcerers to feel cold too badly, something about the magick inside us, they say, although whether Quantas actually have magick inside us given we can't use the bastard thing is a source of great religious and general controversy.

My first interviewee is Berry Gevaudan, bright-blue hair in waves around her, wearing nothing but a thin white fur robe with the sigil of the Gevaudans—an hourglass over a crescent moon—stitched onto it. The robe is short and doesn't cover her legs, and is open suggestively at her cleavage. Her body is fuller than Raven's but just as attractive. *Oh, by the five magicks, Jacob, can you not be you for* just *one hourglass?*

"Hello again," she says, winking, standing next to the chair. This might be my first murder interview, but I'm fairly sure a suspect winking at me is not a great start. I like her a lot from the small amount of time I spent watching her in the council chamber, and I find myself trying to desperately scrub that feeling from my mind. One of these is a killer, I tell myself over and over again. The voice that comes back tells me that means I could be in a room with a killer.

I decide not to speak to myself again.

"Take a seat, Madam Gevaudan." Even as I say it, I realize how ludicrous it is calling a wolf a vampire title, and I grimace.

She smirks. "Berry, please. And I'll stand, if you don't mind, darling. Chairs are boring for wolves."

"Berry it is," I say, trying to give her my best friendly-but-not-friendly smile, which I suspect comes across as mild constipation. This is not going to be easy. This isn't me drinking by the fire, trying to get Commander Tenfold to loosen up and give me all his secrets. There's no drink, for a start.

I clear my throat and dive straight in. "Berry, have you any idea what happened in that chamber?"

She smiles at this. "This is something, isn't it? A mage asking me how Ashen Ansbach died. This whole thing is . . . fucking bizarre. How are you feeling? Can't have been nice for you, watching all that."

"I don't . . . it wasn't. It wasn't that pleasant," I reply, not expecting a question back at me. Already I feel the silent disappointment of Sage, like a particularly judgmental ghost hovering above me.

"By the way," she continues, still smiling, moving from her position by the chair to within a few feet of me, like we've just met each other in passing. "I appreciate you not ogling me. My body. Not my usual reaction from sorcerers, I have to say. You lot really don't benefit from there being no women among you, I have to say. You should intermingle more."

"Some of us do," I reply.

"Not enough, I reckon," she says, grinning.

I get that meaning immediately. "Don't you have a pack mate?" I ask.

"Oh, darlin', you don't know the first thing about wolves, do you?" she says, cocking her head at me.

I decide to give that remark a good deal of distance. A few miles, if I can help it.

"Berry, I have to ask again—"

"I know, I know. I'm sorry. I'm not trying to evade you or anything. This is just my way, I'm afraid. I'm a bit . . . friendlier than Raven." She pauses to give me a look, and I'm not an idiot so I get it straightaway. "It's just my way, I'm sorry."

Then she moves back to behind the chair. "But since you're obviously besotted with Raven . . ."

"I'm not . . ." I reply, wishing I could start this whole interview again and maybe down a few Atmos fireshots beforehand first.

"I'm jesting, mage. Look, I don't know what happened in there. Like everyone else, I thought wolfsbane was gone. And I didn't smell it. The whole thing is clawdamn nonsensical."

"Forget the wolfsbane, then. Who do you think did it?"

"That's a strange question to ask," she says. "Given that I might have done it."

"Did you?"

"Ha! It would be an easy morning for you if I said yes, wouldn't I? But I didn't, I'm afraid. The Gevaudans, as you must know if you've done even the most basic amount of preparations, are the closest pack to the Ansbachs. We have always supported them. Whatever Ashen was about to tell us—and some of my fellow alphas are going to start getting quite impatient, by the way, if you don't tell us what that was soon, fair warning, Jacob, darling—I would most likely have supported his instinct on.

We are both of the moon, our packs. We are careful, we are wise. We are mere miles from each other. We have no bad wolfblood. I am desperately sad that he is dead."

"You don't seem desperately sad."

"Can I not flirt and be sad? Or must you try and understand wolves again?"

I smile at that, whether wisely or not. "Fair point."

"As for who killed him, I haven't a bloody clue, I'm sorry to say. Silver Stubbe hates the Ansbachs, because the Stubbes want war with vampires, revenge for all the past they had no part in, so you might want to start there. But would he kill him? Even if he could, that is a bold move. And I have always seen the Stubbes as cowards. But then I've been alive awhile, and all I know is that ultimately I know nothing. Bit of wisdom for you there, darling." Then she winks and starts to walk out of the room. She stops. "Oh, sorry, did you have any more questions for me?"

I sigh. This is going well. "No, Berry. Thank you."

"Good!" she says brightly. Then at the door she turns around. "Oh, and if you ever stop mooning over Raven—don't worry, I won't tell—then feel free to come and fuck before you go." She sees my mouth form an O of shock and continues, "Oh, don't deny it, we smell lust, remember? Wolves can lie to each other if they try hard, but mages can't. That's a good thing to remember, Jacob." Then she winks again and she's gone.

I decide to pretend that last quart of an hourglass did not just happen.

Next into my, for want of a term I deserve, interview room, is Bronzed Morbach. He's wearing a much larger fur robe than Berry, in a light-blue color, with fur pantaloons in the same color. Small rubies are stitched into the robe's lapels. I understand now the things that are said about his pack, how they're envious of the vampires' finery. This kind of dress looks absurd in these bare, careless surroundings and compared to the other wolves.

He gives me no greeting, or any kind of acknowledgment, and just like Berry he ignores the chair, opting to stand in front of the far wall. He doesn't lean on it. Just stands there. He strikes me as the least impressive of all the alphas, and the shortest. He can't be more than six feet tall. But his whole demeanor makes him seem smaller. His burnt-orange-gold hair is the shortest cut I've seen, barely halfway down his face, and his expression is the same as in the chamber: haughty, disinterested. It's like he almost doesn't want to be a wolf.

With the strong feeling that I did not perform to the best of my abilities, I decide to immediately go on the offensive.

"You are the pack closest to the vampires, both in location and disposition. Did you do their bidding and murder Ashen Ansbach?"

From the look of his outraged, puce-red face, the offensive has certainly had a reaction. "Who are you to talk to me like that, mage?! I could have you killed on the spot for that, you worm thing!"

"You definitely couldn't," I reply, very much hoping that this claim of his is as full of shit as I assume. "Unless you want to kill Raven first." I make a wager that whatever he's made up won't survive contact with my assurance of my protection from the Midnight Assassin, and from the frustrated look on his face I feel I can cash in my monies.

"I may have to tolerate this, but I don't have to answer your questions."

"That is fine, as I don't have any." I didn't know I was going to say that until I said it, and now it's too late to take it back.

He gives me another shocked look, his stupid thin lips wide apart, and then he stalks out. At the door, however, he stops and spins round—I'm beginning to suspect wolves like this tactic a little too much; it's not as clever as they think it is—and says, "If you want someone to take a look at, look at Verdant. Those tree-loving Soissons are not as innocent as they make out." Then he stalks out, and I breathe out, partly annoyed I let my temper prevent me from getting much out of him but also wondering if I didn't accidentally get something after all.

When Verdant Soissons comes in, I make a promise to myself to get something good out of them this time. Verdant, just as tall and green as ever, and, unsurprisingly, naked, ambles over to the chair, moves it aside, and sits down on the floor, cross-legged, grinning at me. "Has anyone used that bloody thing yet?" he asks by way of greeting.

"No," I admit.

"Of course they haven't! The five of us you saw sitting on chairs in the chamber—that's as many as you'll ever see sitting like that at one time."

"You sat on a chair to play cards with me," I point out, deciding to use the fact we've drunk and played together to my advantage in my increasingly desperate ploy to have a strategy for one of these chats.

"Well, that's cards." He grins. "That's different. We should play again, before we leave. Not often I get to play with a mage. If you're not too busy doing Raven's bidding, that is." He sees me frown and adds, "Oh, don't be so glum! I'm just fucking with you, Jacob. We're all doing Raven's bidding, anyway."

"What do you mean?" I ask.

"Oh, mage," he says, and gives a deep belly laugh that sounds like two bells coming together deep underground. "You think we're all staying here, after Ashen's been killed, in another pack's territory, just because it's the right thing to do? We're doing it because Raven asked."

"You fear her that much?" I ask, used to Raven getting that reaction but not expecting it from Verdant.

"Fear?" He shakes his green-bearded head. "No. I mean, don't misunderstand me, I'm not going to be quick to get on the wrong side of her, she has a reputation for a reason, but it's not fear that's keeping us here. Most of us, anyway. It's respect."

"Respect." I nod. "Anything in particular, or just the general kind?" I'm in unfamiliar waters here. Respect is not something I know much about. It's certainly never been thrown my way.

"You don't know the story?"

I shake my head. "I have a feeling you're about to tell me it, though."

He lets out a bellowing laugh again. "You cheeky bastard. But you're right. And it's a good one. It goes back to Extinction Valley, which I assume you *must* know about?"

I nod.

"Well, that's something. You see, after the battle, it was brutal. Bloodmoon brutal. All the packs were mourning their losses. I mean, a couple of packs pretty much no longer bloody existed at all, but those that did, the four you know today minus those annoying pricks the Stubbes, who weren't around then, well, we were hurting. Angry. Too weak to do anything about it. Facing a war against the vampires we were no longer able to fight. In those terrible months after, we were liable to give up completely. And then Raven did the most crazy thing I've ever seen."

He pauses then, in love with his own story, and I can't blame him, as it's setting out to be a good one.

"She went behind vampire lines. For six months. And one by one, the crazy, beautiful bitch *hunted* them. Specifically, the majors of the battalions who had been overlooking that ridge, over the valley. The ones whose eyes we looked into before they gave the orders to blow up the clawdamn ground. She hunted six of them, across the whole goddamn Everlands: out of sight, undetectable, unkillable. She hunted six of them, one for each pack during the battle. Every time she killed one, she brought their head—their *head*—back to the Wolflands, to a different pack. *Six times* she did that, with the entire fucking vampire army out to stop her, up in arms. But they couldn't lay a finger on her. And those of us who were mourning, we stuck that head on a pike and we paraded it round, and it didn't stop the grief, but by the bloodmoon, did it take the edge off. It kept us going, at least till Sinassion intervened and suddenly our enemy wasn't our enemy no more."

He pauses, and there's silence, and I imagine a midnight-black wolf stalking across the land, the whole vampire army on her tail, a vampire head in her jaws.

It's an image.

"Even for her, it was incredible. And we never forgot. Us alphas, most of who weren't that at the time, we never forgot." He beats his massive chest emphatically, and the expression on his face is fire and blood. "We never will forget."

"Right," I say, nodding. "So you like her then."

"Ha! You could say that. I can't speak for everyone, such as Silver or that poncy fuck Bronzed, but the respect is there, at least."

I nod. "Speaking of Bronzed Morbach, he cast the finger at you." Even as I say that, I realize it's a bold move, trying to set one wolf against the other. Especially given Bronzed literally threatened me. But his reaction is, to my surprised, relaxed.

"Of course he did, the little shit. The Morbachs hate us."

"And why is that?"

"Well, they, as you know, communicate the most with the bloods, and clearly want to be them given the way they dress. They do deals with them, offer them things, in exchange for access to all the finery and bear shit that vampires are good at—jewelry, precious stones, and so on."

"Deals? Like?"

"Like access through their forest to catch the animals they want to bleed. Those they need for their Blood Farm, when their breeding levels go low. And that's the problem. They want us to agree to give them access to the bloods. An agreed route all the way from First Light through the Morbach territory through to ours. All the way to the northeastern coast."

"And you didn't agree."

"No, of course we didn't agree! We're not having bloods trampling through our beloved forest. We're a pack of the tree, after all. We're not offending the trees by having fucking bloods wandering around getting lost trying to snag a bloody bear. A terrible idea. And Ashen thought so, too. So now they're pissed at us. Clearly. And instead of just accepting it, they've started to challenge some of our territory. We keep ourselves to ourselves, but we won't let them take away a single tree of our land."

"I see. Well, I appreciate your honesty," I say, thinking it wise to throw in a compliment now, though I have no reason to mean it.

Verdant grins. "You're welcome."

"As to the wolfsbane . . ." I start.

"Oh, I can help you there, too."

I stop. Again, I do a terrible job of disguising my look of, I suppose, hope. In the corner of my eyes, Sage's ghost grimaces again.

"Ha! You thought I'd be clueless like the rest so far, yes? But there is an explanation for what happened to Ashen. Whether that's what happened here, I'm afraid I can't tell you. But it's the only thing I can think of that makes sense. And it involves you." He sticks his finger out at me, so suddenly I have to brace myself not to physically pull back on my chair. It occurs to me how ridiculous this scene is, me on a chair and him on the floor in front of me, like a child. A massive green child.

"Me?" I ask, not completely enjoying this turn.

"Well, not you precisely," he says, grinning again. I'm beginning to get a little tired of his jesting. It must be a wonderful joy to be his pack mate.

"Your kind . . . mages," he continues. "Specifically, the Kinets. Well, even more specifically the bloodmages. You know, the ones who fuck about with small things, like changing the blood itself. Let's just put it this way. They don't just do blood."

He pauses, clearly wanting me to keep up. I hazard the only logical guess. "Plants as well?"

"Exactly," he says, clapping his hands together, enjoying this story far too much. "They can change the way plants are with their magick. The characteristics of the plants. What they look like, even. They used to do it a lot more when their kind, the Kinets who focus on moving small things, were growing in attention, in the years between the end of the war and Grayfall. Now they're obsessed with the blood. But first, they were obsessed with plants."

"You seem to know a lot about this," I say.

He shrugs. "Well, we Soissons are a pack of the tree, so nature itself, plants and shit, is very much our domain."

"Yes, I can tell by the way you said 'plants and shit.'"

"Ha! Good one. But it is not just us who will know this. Because one of these mages came round to the Wolflands. Visited all the packs, in fact. As well as the vampires. Bringing gifts."

"Gifts?"

"Yes, to show their power. Show they could be hired. And paid. And this is where it gets interesting. Because rumor has it, they took round a wolfsbane plant that did not smell of wolfsbane. And did not look like it, either. Not to all the packs. But just to one. Someone who'd paid them a lot of coin to make it."

"Oh. Oh."

"Exactly. Fucking 'oh.'"

"Wasn't this the time when wolves were making sure that no wolfsbane existed round the entire land?"

"It was."

"Right, so this would be . . . very bad for wolves. So why not give it to the vampires?"

Verdant nods. "That's the question we wondered. It sounded stupid, so we dismissed it. But then when another of the mages came round our way, the Soissons patch, we . . . asked him."

"By the pause in front of 'asked him' there, I'm guessing that there wasn't that much choice in the asking. Very little, I would wager."

Verdant smiled. "I am friendly, like my pack. Until we are not. Wolfsbane is no laughing matter. I lost . . . many at Extinction Valley. So we . . . forced some answers out of him, after we forced all his teeth out, too. And he admitted that one of his fellow Kinets had been hired by someone very important in a wolfpack to make this special wolfsbane, and then had sold it to them. That they had not done it for anyone else. But they didn't know who."

"Someone very important? Like an alpha?"

Verdant shrugged. "You would assume so."

"And why is the whole of vampire territory not awash with this new innocent-smelling, innocent-looking wolfsbane?"

"Well," the forest-green wolf replies, standing up, evidently done with the session, "probably because they didn't want Raven fucking Ansbach coming after them and taking their head, so I'm guessing they kept it to this one sale. So find who they sold it to, and I reckon you'll work out which of my fellow alphas did the deed."

And then, with a final chuckle to himself, he walks out, and I know exactly what I have to do.

Before I can do exactly what I have to do, however, there is the small and highly annoying matter of the remaining alpha wolf to speak to. I am impatient to follow up on what Verdant told me—the world of mages being very much more to my liking in this inquirer business—but I have no choice. I'm also not keen to speak to Silver Stubbe, though the fact he's currently my number-one suspect, given how keen he was to pin the finger on Sage and the fact he's a massive cock, means I can't exactly avoid him.

When Silver walks in, I realize something. I thought the Stubbe pack were of the claw. Wild, aggressive. But nothing I've seen of him so far has given that impression. He has more of the air of a secretive vampire Lord about him. I half want to just completely ignore the little prick.

Which is ironic, because he completely ignores me. He walks over to the wall on the far end of the chamber, as if to study it. He looks down at this nails, as if there's some dust on there. He runs his hands through his flowing, annoyingly perfect argent hair, as if looking for burrs. Then he starts patting his furs absent-mindedly, looking for something.

I patiently wait, controlling my emotions by imagining him being electrocuted by an Atmos, perfect hair frizzing up as the bastard fries. It's a violent image, I grant you, but it's been a long morning and I'm still completely sober.

Eventually he deigns to notice me. "Oh, hello. Sorry, I didn't see you there. You didn't want to talk to me, did you?" His voice is oil, slick and greasy. His face is judgment, thin and cruel. "No, surely not, because a wolf would not have to answer questions from a mage, would they? That would be absurd. Especially after what the mages did at Extinction Valley. How they helped the bloods kill us with wolfsbane. No, you must have heard Raven wrong. . . ."

I feel like correcting him and pointing out that that was some of the mages for hire, paid by vampires. Not all sorcerers. But I don't think he'd listen. He is the fanatical type, perhaps, but definitely not the listening one.

Suddenly he edges toward me a little, smiling gently, patronizingly. "I think what she must have said is that you should leave here now, before your guts end up steaming in the cold winter air, feet from your body." He smiles wider. "Or something like that, anyway!"

Then he turns and heads toward the door. But—of course he does, my kingdom for some originality—he stops just as he's about to leave and turns back to me. "Funny thing about Raven. She's all about honesty and hates deception—and politics. And she's all about peace, these days, too, or so she tells me. And yet I wager she hasn't told you about her little disagreement with Ashen, has she? Well, it was more than a little disagreement. She's not been quite the patient peacemaker these last few years that she makes out."

I mustn't disguise my reaction because, Lightdammit, he grins wider. Forget the drink; I would go sober for a decade right now to be able to beat that shading grin off him.

"No, I didn't think so. Oh well. I will see you later, anyway. In some form."

And then he's gone.

I leave soon after. I have two places I desperately need to be. One of them is wherever the shit ale is. And the other might determine the entire murder inquiry, and, it seems from these threats, my chances of surviving these fucking Wolflands.

# 25

# Silver-Tongued

One of the weaknesses of our kind is that we tend to assume that all of us accord to some of the more traditional wolf values, those of openness and honesty and hashing things out under the light of the moon instead of in secret corridors.

But this is, of course, not true; some wolves can be as secretive and cunning and manipulative and odious as the best vampire Lords, and it is often they that surprise the more traditional, powerful, lethal wolves who are expecting attacks by the claw, not of the backstabbing.

Greysky Gevaudan, *The Ten Different Types of Wolf*

## Jacob

As soon as I leave the antechamber in which my various failures and, maybe, one success of an interview took place, I honor my desires in pretty quick fashion. First, I race through the Great Hall and the drinking rooms that spin off it, which I notice have all been completely cleaned up from the chaos of the night before Ashen's death and have remained that way, clear evidence that no one is having any kind of a piss-up out of respect for their fallen alpha.

I head quickly to the kitchen down the corridor to the right, and intercept someone coming out with some unnamable game meat spread out over a wide platter, presumably to be delivered to some alpha and their two underwolves. "Ale. Any kind," I say to the harassed-looking wolf, a thin man with a moustache and thick sideburn whiskers and a deep-black mop of hair. He's probably called Inkstain Ansbach or something.

He goes to say something, most likely "Can you wait till I've delivered this sodding meat first?" (which is what I would say, I suppose; I am being a complete prickard to him, I'm aware, but desperate times), then checks himself, presumably remembering my status as Raven's special one or something. Then he carefully puts down the meat, which, to be fair, is not going anywhere, and retreats to where he came from and soon after returns with a large flagon of ale. He hands it to me and, admirably deadpan, says, "Ale. There's only one kind here."

I down it in one as he watches, mildly stunned, maybe thinking sorcerers didn't have it in them. After wiping my mouth with my robe sleeve, I see his expression and shrug. "If you'd been in there, you'd understand. Now, please, if you could tell me where the library is."

Definitely-not-called-Inkstain's face screws up in confusion.

"The library," I repeat. "Place where books are kept. Place where—actually, I can't describe it any better than that."

"I—I know what one is," he says, and then remembers who I am. "We don't have one, mage, I'm sorry. Not many libraries in the Wolflands."

"You . . . you don't have a library," I say, feeling a chill in the air.

"No. Pack Morbach have one, I think. But not us."

"But how do you . . . record knowledge?"

He starts to look a little impatient, but he knows he can't seem too impatient to me, and the result is a slight twitch in one eye. "Through passed-down pack lore. I mean, there are wolf books by wolf authors in great libraries in all the Centerland cities. And First Light. We just don't keep them here."

I struggle to get past this. "Very well. Where would a book be kept, then? Or parchments of importance. Any writing. A collection of writings."

He raises his eyebrow. "You mean a library?"

"No! For fuck's . . . I mean anything."

He shrugs. "I'm sorry. Now, if you don't mind, mage, I need to . . ." He points pointedly at the platter of meat. I nod and walk off, not bothering to disguise the slope of my shoulders and the desire for another drink.

The immediate collapse of one of the best ideas I've ever had has hit me hard, and the last thing I want to see is Raven, but then I suppose it's my fault for sitting in Golden's garden again. I can't help it. It's the one place in this fucking castle I don't immediately feel out of place in. It's the herbs, I think. Mageweed, the wolf parsley, the takelily, the lightguard, the green-and-yellow one I don't recognize. It takes me back to my own slice of nature in the Desertlands. Right now, the way I feel, I would sacrifice a finger or two just to be back there, getting harangued by Sage, trying to find a place to nap, complaining about the lack of drinks. Anything just to be rid of this cold, constantly dangerous prison I seem to have been thrown into.

Raven sidles up to me, from the left this time, and stands just outside my periphery. No sitting next to me this time. "How did it go?" she asks, her voice neutral.

"I'm surprised you weren't listening in. Wolves have great hearing, don't they?"

No reply.

"Sorry, that was somewhat flippant. It was . . . hard."

"I'm sure you were up to the task." Still cold, neutral. I'm not sure where the help-pleading Raven has gone, but I'd quite like her back.

"Well, let's see. To summarize. Berry wants to fuck me; Bronzed implicated Verdant, but I think Bronzed is a moron; and Silver threatened me. So very successfully, thanks for asking."

There is silence to this. Eventually her voice comes out from the shadows she seems to have returned to. "You are frustrated. You are annoyed with me for giving you this task. You are angry at yourself. I understand."

"You smelled all that on me?"

"I did."

"Good to know my scents are so easy to read."

"You are not a wolf. Of course your scent is easy to read."

"Well, at least you understand."

Her next line comes as half growl. "I said understand, not tolerate. Time is not in our favor."

I want to say a lot of things then, but I still have a good feeling about our last conversation, and I'm not immediately about to throw that away. Not yet. "It wasn't completely useless. Not at first."

The silence goes on. Then: "For the love of the bloodmoon, Jacob, obviously I want you to go on."

I grin to myself despite my despondency. "Verdant told me that one of the Kinet mages had come round all the wolfpacks, offering their services. The ones who move small things. In the time before Grayfall, shortly before they were all hired by the vampires to be bloodmages. Apparently they claimed they could make a wolfsbane plant that didn't look like wolfsbane and didn't smell like wolfsbane. And someone took them up on their offer and paid them. They found this out by torturing another mage, by the way, so I fucking hope that protection of yours means something."

"But he didn't know who had paid this mage," says Raven, ignoring my comment about my own safety, I note.

"No."

"Do you think Verdant is telling the truth?"

"I didn't get the feeling he is using me. But, as Sage would say, that feeling knows nothing, and I don't have Sage's way with the body signs or whatever the shade he calls them. But you know him better. Can we trust him?"

"The Soissons do not have any history of being deceitful. Or too aggressive." She must hear my quiet snort, as she adds, "Torturing mages does not count as aggressive for a wolf, I am afraid. No, out of all of them, aside from maybe Berry, Verdant is the one I would trust the most."

"Well, that's a good start."

"So we need to find out who this mage sold this so-called new wolfsbane to, do we not?"

I laugh, though it has absolutely no mirth in it. "That's the thing. I had a plan. For a moment, I thought it genius. But of course, it's me, so . . ."

"Slow down, Jacob," she says. A rare use of my name, this time, I feel, in anger. "Tell me."

"Well, you see, Raven, the Kinet mages are strange creatures. The ones who move small matter, anyway. And by strange I mean fucking bizarre. They are methodical, almost obsessively so. They like to write things down. Record everything. And they like to leave these records wherever they go. We once had one visit my cult. They insisted on leaving some parchments with us about their visit. It's like they're leaving a walking trail of information."

"Already very strange, you are right."

"But it gets stranger and, at least I thought, more useful. Because this habit of leaving records, it has another use. They were always wandering places, you see. Selling their skills, at least last century. In the span of about fifty years since the war, when a lot of the talented bastards who could move mountains and shit had been killed, the ones remaining—the ones who learned to move smaller, invisible matter—got very clever about it, and went round the Desertlands, hawking their skills and their wares.

"Except the Desertlands can be a very dangerous place for wandering Kinets, especially those more skilled in making crops grow or improving blood than hitting you in the face with a tree. So they took to leaving records of their sales and their presence where they went, not always with the permission of the people there. But secreting them. Placing them in libraries, hidden. So if something happened to them, their kin would know where to look. For evidence they were there. Or else they could use it as a form of blackmail. So . . ."

"Yes, yes, I see your big revelation coming a mile off, mage," says Raven, interrupting my excellent flow. "If the mage who came round all the wolfpacks had come here, they would have left some record of themselves."

"Well, yes," I say. "Even if they didn't sell the wolfsbane to an Ansbach, they'd still leave a record here, in case they needed it later. Protection for them, in every castle." My excitement leaves my voice as quickly as it had entered. "Except you don't have a fucking library, you book-hating freaks, so the first great idea I've ever had was quashed before it ever got started. Only the Morbachs have a library, apparently. So whichever Kinet would've come traipsing round the packs looking for a sale wouldn't have left anything. There's no place for anyone who came looking for them to look."

Part of me wants Raven to contradict me at this point. Tell me about a small trove of books kept somewhere that the mage would have known about and could have secretly added to. But she doesn't. She lets the silence do the talking.

"It was a good plan," she says, quietly.

"No, no, no," I say, feeling frustration bubble up from me, all the doubts I've had all morning, and in some cases the outright humiliation, pushing their way out of me like a constipated geyser. "You don't see, do you? Surely you at least *smell* it. That wasn't just a good plan, it was my *only* plan. I'm all out of ideas. I was barely holding my ground in there. I'm not capable of this. It's like I told you before, I can't do this. I've never been able to do this kind of thing. I'm just an animal that Sage uses to do his tricks occasionally. Drink with this person. Flirt with that one. The rest of the time I just follow his instructions and try not to get killed. I can't do this. I'm not good enough. I'm going to get my best friend killed because *I'm not good enough*."

I realize I'm shouting now. I turn slightly to where Raven lurks next to me, anger and shame sparking equally in me. "I'm not good enough," I repeat, almost a whisper this time.

A hand on my shoulder. Nails slightly digging in. "I disagree."

"You don't mean that. You're not stupid. You know I'm out of my depth. You just don't want to get involved with the other alphas. You're just protecting yourself. Using the annoying idiot, hoping some clue will fall out of his fumbling hands."

"You think I am lying to you? Have you not noticed that I cannot abide that shit? That I like to be fucking honest? Have you not noticed that about me yet?"

"Oh, really," I say, a part of me wanting to reach and hold that hand on my shoulder, but too far gone in my self-hatred now to recognize that part or even do anything with it. "If you're so honest, then why didn't you tell me about your little *disagreement* with Ashen?"

The hand withdraws from my shoulder. I hear a slight hiss through sharp teeth. I want to take that back and rephrase it. But the fucking words are out there now.

"It does not take a . . . what do you sorcerers call it, a *quickmind* to work out that it was Silver who told you that."

"And yet your reaction tells me there's some truth to it."

A pause. The scratching of nails on the bench behind me.

"Oh, fuck this," I say, standing up, twisting round to face her. "This terrifying act. I'm not scared of you, Raven Ansbach. If you were going to eat me you would have done it already."

She cocks her head and pushes some of that midnight hair out of her face. "Maybe I was not hungry then."

"Why did you lie to me?"

Her eyes narrow and a claw on her little finger lengthens. I realize I am lying. I am still a little scared of her. But fear and other things can still go together.

"If you're not scared of me, why is there metal in my nose, mage?"

"My name is Jacob, Raven."

She sighs and relents. "I never lied to you. This is not important information."

I move closer to her. She smells of freshly cut woodland grass today, which makes no sense as it's all snow out there, but I'm not in charge of the way people smell.

"I'll decide that. I'm vulnerable here."

She laughs. "You are as safe as me."

"Really?" I stare straight into those half-feral eyes, dark-rimmed, green-irised. "Then why did Silver threaten to separate me from my guts if I didn't leave here?"

Silence. Then: "He did that?"

"He did that. So thank you for that protection."

She thinks on this. "Shall we sit down, or are you just going to keep moving closer to me?"

I say nothing and move to the bench, furious but also confused.

She follows me and we sit there a few moments, staring at the herbs.

"When the bloods and us were due to make the Pact after Grayfall . . . the Pact where we send out wolf criminals to First Light to be bled for fifty years at a time so the vampires can get stores of wolfblood to fight the Grays . . . I . . . challenged it."

"Challenged it?" I ask.

"Yes . . . I went to Ashen and I said it could not happen. I was not going to let the vampires have control over our kind. Not after Extinction Valley, which was not even a century old by that point."

"And Ashen refused you."

"Yes. He said it was the only way. Said the Grays were all that mattered now. Said we could not just be trapped in the Wolflands. That there were other forests that we had the right to run through, and this was the only way to get them."

"So what did you do?"

She doesn't reply to this immediately but looks up at the afternoon winter sky. It's a clear day and the sheer cobalt blue of the Wolflands sky is dazzling. I can hardly look at it, but she stares at it, unflinching.

"I was so full of anger. Decades of peace with the vampires, decades of having to pretend that Extinction Valley had not happened, all because of Sinassion and his devastation of the continent. I felt like the bloods had not been punished. And now they were getting what they wanted."

A long pause. She scratches her nails softly on the bench, leaving thin marks. I see there's a smudge of dirt on her thigh. I turn away quickly.

"So I went to Silver."

"What?" I did not expect that.

"I knew he felt the same. That the vampires must be punished, not helped. I was . . . so angry. I felt so powerless. I . . . was not used to this feeling."

She must have been angry if she went to that prick.

"I did not know him as well then. Or know his nature, at least," she adds, as if reading my mind like a coinshop Sinassion. "It turns out he wanted more than the Pact to fail. He wanted war. To press the advantage on the bloods after Grayfall. It was insanity. Even in my rage could see that. So I backed away. But . . ."

"Let me guess. Ashen found out."

"He did." She hangs her head, and her hair covers her face completely. It is a look I am used to. "And the terrible thing is that he was not even angry. He was just disappointed. He sat next to me and he said, 'All that rage, Raven. It can't be good if it takes you to wolves like Silver.' And he was right, of course. He was right, as ever, the bastard." I still can't see her face. I hope she's smiling, not sad.

"So Ashen made you work with the bloods all these decades, liaising with Saxe, chasing down the wolves who escape?"

"No. He would never have done that to me. I volunteered myself."

I gasp. "But you hated that!" I sigh. "That was the point, wasn't it?"

A few moments of silence. Then Raven almost spits out the next words. "What good is my rage if it turns me away from my best friend? What good is my rage if it leads to things that would cause the deaths I stew over? What good is any of my fucking rage?" Nails scratch fiercer now. "I am just as much a liability as any who would start war. I must learn to live with peace, no matter how much I wish death on others."

I'm not feeling quick-witted enough to take that last comment on straightaway. So I stare at the herbs instead. "So it was a lie out of shame," I say.

"It wasn't a . . ." She stops. "Yes. I feel shame."

"Well, look at that. We aren't so different after all."

She turns to me then. "What do you mean?" Her hand is near mine. Her nail almost touches.

I laugh. "You said it yourself earlier. 'You Quantas . . .'" I go to explain more, to tell her my truth, my shame, my past, but I'm so tired and defeated from the morning I just can't be arsed. As usual, I retreat to what I know.

"I'm done, Raven. I can't help you. I've proven that this morning. I'm tired of all these lies and games and wolves and this world I'm in where I don't belong. I'll do what I can to help, and I'm not going to let them kill Sage. But you have to do this, not me."

Raven's hand retreats. She gets off the bench.

"So you are giving up," she says, ice-cold. "You are right, you do not belong here, in this land where we always fight, even when we should not. I should never have expected anything from you. I should not be so surprised as I am to be disappointed in you."

And then before I can reply to that, she's gone. I don't see her leave, but this time not because she's so fast but because my head is hanging in shame.

## Raven

I feel immediately regretful after my conversation with Jacob. Especially my reaction at the end. I am not in the habit of regret, but its keen sting flows through me, and I do not like it. I had been uncomfortable at the memory of asking him for help the previous day, and even more uncomfortable at telling him the stories of one of my deepest shame. And I let that discomfort say things I regret, and it . . . it bothers me.

But first, something important must be done.

I search all through the castle for the one that I want, trying to track his overly washed, faintly astringent scent through the thousands of other scents assaulting my nose at any given moment. Eventually I find him communing with one of his two underwolves in a chamber on the west side of the castle in the warren of rooms that sit below the western guest chambers.

"Leave us," I say to his underwolf, a diminutive silver-haired woman who takes fright just at the sight of me. No doubt picked by Silver as his closest underwolf for her skills in stroking his ego.

To my immense pleasure, she immediately vacates the room, and I sense a quick brass tang of fear from her.

Silver turns to me, frowning. "Raven, what the moons—"

He never gets the rest out, because I give him a strong right hook and he stumbles back, almost crashing to the ground.

"What the fuck . . ." he starts, his lugubrious greasy voice replaced by a harsh bark.

Before he can fully right himself, I swipe an arm out at his legs and he buckles to the floor. "You crazy bitc—" he begins, before I haul him up and throw him against the wall. Stubbes wolves and their love of the derogatory meaning of *bitch*. When will they learn how ridiculous it is?

His shock has given way to the steel hint of fear now, much stronger and sharper than his underwolf's moments ago. I stride over to where he lies and I haul him up by the scruff of his neck.

"I always wondered if you would be as cowardly in a fight as I suspected. I suppose now we have the answer," I say, staring into his terrified eyes.

"You've finally lost it. I'll have you—"

His words are interrupted by my fist against his teeth, knocking out his front two. It is not as easy as it looks to knock out another wolf's teeth, so I put my all into it. They clatter to the floor, and blood jets out of the holes they leave behind.

"Oh . . . oh fuck."

I grab his tongue. "This next?"

"Hmmmmmmm."

I go to yank it out, but then I let it go and carve a nail down his forehead and then his cheek instead, a deep gash. Nice and slow.

"Ughhhhhh."

Then I reach under the stupid fur he's still wearing and I grab his cock and squeeze. A little blood flows under my finger where one of my nails scratches his balls.

"What about this?"

"You can't . . . you . . ." He struggles to talk over the blood in his mouth, his eyes blinking from the blood in them, too.

I let him go and he slumps to the floor. I watch him a few moments, this pathetic lump on the ground, and then I reach down and I pull his little finger off him.

*"Aggghhh what the—fucking moonfuck oh shit ahhhhhhh . . ."*

I eat it.

"Tastes of nothing," I say, then I turn around and march to the door. At this point, his underwolf has come running and she stops there, staring at me in horror. "Fuck off," I say, "unless you want to lose some eyes for a bit."

She gives Silver a guilty look, then flees. Those Stubbes, they really are cowards.

I turn back to Silver, who has managed to get himself into a sitting position against the wall, head lolled back, cradling his finger stump, blood pooling from his mouth and face.

"If you ever threaten someone under my protection again," I tell him,

"I will kill you, and I do not give a fuck about the consequences." Then I start to walk out.

I stop when I hear him laughing. There's some gurgling in there, too, but there is definitely a laugh. I walk back into the room.

"Kill me if you want. You can't stop what's coming," he says. "Ah, bloody claws, that hurts. Shit."

I advance toward him. "What does that mean, you coward?"

Silver laughs again, the gap between his teeth turning it into a whistle. "I may not be able to fight you, but I can outsmart you. I was going to surprise you with this, but it doesn't matter now."

I wait, wanting desperately to rip his head off to end this, but breathing in and out to control myself.

"You see, Raven, *aghhh—*" He spits out a gobbet of blood. "I'm going to be the next Outside Council alpha. I'm going to be the next Ashen. The wolf of all wolves. I've got the support of Bronzed, who hates you Ansbachs. And soon I'll have Verdant's vote, too, if he doesn't want his life to be made clawdamn miserable by the Morbachs to his west and us Stubbes to his south. That'll be four votes against three. And who knows, maybe I'll get Berry, too. And then you smug Ansbachs are done."

Everything in me wants to rip his eyes out and then, when he has had enough pain, slowly bite his head off. He can tell, as he adds, "Go on, then. Kill me. Prove how terrifying you are. My death will damn you. Make it all happen quicker. The Stubbes below me will ascend. We'll be even more powerful. My death will unite all the packs and we'll take the fight to the bloods like we should have been doing all this time."

I calm myself and my hatred, and I try to breathe out.

"Good luck," I reply, and then I walk out of there.

# 26

# Never Going Back

> Please don't look for me, my love. I know you would do it out of duty, and guilt, and still love, I think, but I know, and you know, there is a part of you that is relieved . . . a part of you that welcomes your freedom. You want to know the secrets of the world, and I can no longer stand getting in your way. I'm sorry.
>
> Sofie Clarke, in a letter to her husband,
> Quantas Quantantion, dated 380 AL

## Sam

I wake up with a throbbing head, tired and hungry and feeling on the verge of fainting. I'm alive, though, which is a start. I didn't impale myself on a jagged rock. A brief memory comes to me of hitting a rock, though, of plummeting down toward it and desperately trying to corkscrew myself out of the way, as if I had wolfblood wings. But all I had was magicked stag, great normally but not enough to save me from a hard landing. I remember nothing after that.

I open my eyes to see what new peril awaits me. But instead of peril, I see Sage, a very concerned expression on his pale, weary face, standing over me. I turn around and see I'm resting against a cave wall, the nearby opening showing me it's night. Not recaptured. And not dead. Things are looking up.

"We're alive," I say, as good a beginning as any.

He grins, and then to my surprise he hugs me.

"Ow," I say.

"Ah, sorry," he says, releasing me, and for a moment we both feel awkward at the sudden personal contact, but then I grin.

"We jumped off a blooddamn waterfall, Sage Bailey. We actually did that." And then I burst out laughing, and it goes on a little longer than it should, and I wonder if I want to cry or go mad. Just another night in my new action-packed life.

Sage laughs back, but I can tell it's forced. The more I study him, the more exhausted I see he is. And, maybe, something else. Sad?

I study my surroundings more. Outside of the cave entrance I see a forest of redoaks, thick, dark, scarlet trunks racing up to a dense canopy that towers above the rock outcrop we're in, so dense that almost no moonlight filters through, and I only have the fire Sage has made and my basic bloodless vampire night eyes to go on. Fresh snow blankets the forest floor. I smell the forest night air, a little bit earthy, and I hear some type of owl screech three times not too far away. But all these senses are not particularly sharp, so I know my magicked stag has worn off.

I look back at Sage, who is still studying me, concerned, eyeing me up and down.

"Do I have fleas or something?" I ask, trying to keep it light.

He laughs politely and shakes his head. "No, it's just . . . you were . . . quite badly injured." I raise my eyebrow questioningly. "But it's okay. You look . . . completely healed now. You'll just be feeling a little, uh, hungry for blood, a little sore."

"Yes to both points."

"Here," he says, proffering me a recently caught rabbit, a small wound in its side. "It's not much but it will allow you to walk for a bit."

I study it. "You caught a rabbit for me? I'm impressed. Wait, how?"

Sage shrugs. "I made a bow and arrow and I shot it."

I squint at him and notice the bow on his back, made from what looks like a branch and some kind of animal gut and not looking like it would do much good at hitting anything. "Do you have much knowledge of shooting arrows?"

"It took me a couple of hours to learn and get my aim. It's not a particularly difficult skill."

I laugh, and then wince at the pain in my ribs as I do so. "I think the archers of First Light would be offended by that." I grab the rabbit then, and I bite into it and quickly suck its blood, draining it dry in ten seconds, suddenly consumed by bloodlust.

It's only when I finished that I realize the sight I must have been, canines ripping open fur, mouth greedily exsanguinating it in mere moments. Most sorcerers will only have ever seen vampires drink from vials or carafes or glasses rather than straight from the source. I've not drained an animal since my days of being street orphans with my sister.

I look nervously at him, but he seems happy, if anything. "I'm glad you're hungry. Just a shame vampires can't drink from sorcerers, as I'd offer you mine. But I know you've read enough to be aware of the results of that."

I stop, bloodlust temporarily sated, and try to stand, wiping blood from my mouth as I do. I'm a bit woozy, a little tender on my feet, but I feel I can walk. My travel furs and pants are a little worse for wear, ripped almost as much as they're stitched, and my boots are in a bad state. But it'll do. Then I turn to Sage and sigh. "I know you well enough now to see something in your eyes. Tell me everything. How long have I been out, and what happened?" I pause and turn to where the cave deepens, and seems to widen, and try to peer into its gloom on my rabbitblood eyes, which don't prove particularly helpful. "Are we safe?"

Sage nods. "For now, maybe. But we need to keep moving. I'm fairly sure that Redsky Stubbe, after extracting himself from the rubble, will have begun hunting us. If it was Silver's plan to have us killed, claiming an escape attempt gone wrong, presumably, then having us actually escape will not be something he can abide. We're far enough away from Ansbach castle that we have a head start, but that head start will be gone soon."

"Don't you think others will come help us, too? After they hear what happened? Like Raven? We were being guarded by an Ansbach, too, weren't we?"

Sage shakes his head. "I honestly don't think they'll even know we've gone. I didn't see any sign of our Ansbach guard on the way out, did you? Maybe he was killed by the Stubbes or convinced to betray Raven . . . either way, Silver won't want anyone knowing we're gone until we're dead and he can use whatever escape excuse he wants for our deaths."

"So he's definitely the murderer of Ashen Ansbach, then?"

"Maybe, maybe not. Maybe he just wants us to be blamed so he can show how dangerous the vampire Lords are and use that to take power. Look, Sam, all this theorizing is all very well and very *us*, but we need to get going."

I nod, but then I fix him with a stare. "Then we'll get going. But after you tell me everything. Everything that happened after I jumped off that waterfall."

Sage stares at me, deep exhaustion circles under his eyes, and I start to think he's just not going to reply and walk off. But then he rubs his increasingly large beard, sighs, and begins.

"After your fall in the waterfall you were . . . quite badly injured. Your body was swept along the river in the extremely fast current. I swam after you. Well, I tried, anyway. I was lost to the current myself and ended up several miles downstream. I carried on following the river, looking for your body, which was washed up another mile east. I suspected, or I hoped, at least, that the small amount of magicked stag would do its work, so I carried you deep into this part of the forest, into this cave, where the sun does not go. I built us a small fire and I hoped that would be enough to keep us warm. And I watched you heal."

He stops then, breathing in and out quickly, and turns away from me, and you don't have to have spent a lot of time in his company to know the signs of him trying to control his emotions.

I walk over to him, still turned away from me, and I reach out and hold his hand.

"How injured were *you* when you were doing all this for me?"

His voice comes out quiet. "I was . . . a bit bruised. But fine now. Sorcerers don't heal as fast as vampires, but we have our ways."

I squeeze his hand. "You're lying. But I appreciate the intent . . . and how badly injured was I?"

A long pause now. "You had some wounds, let us just say that."

"Some wounds."

"Yes."

I let go of his hand and I step in front of him. He has the start of tears in his eyes. "How badly was I injured, Sage?"

"Sam, it doesn't matter, I—"

"Then why do you want to cry?" I say kindly, gently, knowing the gentler thing would be to leave it, but I have to know. I always have to know. We're so alike in that way.

"It's just exhaustion, I'm normally more in control, I'm sorry."

I pause, wait for him to continue. I give him time.

"Half your head was gone. Completely gone. You smashed it on the rocks." He breathes out and takes a moment. "Any less than magicked stag, I think it might have been too late. But I thought you had a chance on that blood, even on just a vial. So I watched you, praying to the Light that I don't really believe in that it would be enough. I watched you, broken, healing, for two nights and two days. It was . . . I don't wish to repeat it." His voice breaks slightly at the last bit.

I let that hang for a while. I genuinely don't know what to say.

"You're a good man, Sage" is my final effort. "You're the best I've known, I think." And I kiss him lightly on the forehead before he can react. He's so tired he doesn't even flinch in surprise. We lock eyes, and I study his tears, not large enough to fall, and then I lean in again, but this time for his lips.

But at the last moment he does flinch, and pulls away, and turns from me. "We . . . Sam, we really need to get going. There's a wolf on our tail, and time is of the essence."

He tries to say it firmly, but it comes out weak and tired. I stare at him, confused and a bit hurt, and I try to think of something to say to assuage the awkwardness, but as I do something hits me.

A smell. A smell I know, but stronger. I'd been smelling it since I woke up, I think, but the rabbitblood helped it grow in strength. I walk deeper into the cave, where the scent is coming from, and for a moment I'm confronted by an abyss of black, too faint too discern on my blood, but it seems to be a cavern with things stacked in it, and that smell is fiercer, a clean smell of polished metal and something else even cleaner beneath it.

Like the cubes Sage carries. The relics of the mortals.

All I hear is the drip of moisture from somewhere beyond me. And then something else. A hum, like something not of this world. Something that has sensed me.

And then light comes into the cavern, comes out of the walls, small globes like I've never seen before sparking up. Their light is fierce but not blinding, soft but powerful, and that's when I see what the shapes are on the cavern floor. Large cubes, must be ten by ten feet. Gray, smooth, astonishingly unweathered, from the looks of it made out of the same material I've held in my hand. One wall of each cube is open, and they are all empty, the interior the same material as the outside.

Sage walks up behind me. "Ah, yes, I was going to get to that."

I turn to him, slightly annoyed, the confusion of before still irking me even as the joy of discovery tries to edge it out. "Going to get to it eventually, were you?"

I turn back to the cavern and breathe in, as if by breathing I can inhale the secrets before me, transform my lungs into the repositories of all the truths I, like Sage, would love to know.

"This is one of the mortals' sites, isn't it?"

"It is," says Sage. "I've been here before, with Jacob. That's how I knew we could shelter here."

"Is this it?" I ask. "Just these big cubes, and whatever was in them?" I think on this. "You took the contents back, didn't you? Back to your vaults in the Cult of Humanis."

Sage nodded. "Many years ago, now, yes. This was one of the first finds we made. There are . . . bigger sites than this. But this was just a storage center, I think. Storage for their relics."

I breathe out, awestruck. "It's one thing to be told of these things by you. Or even to see the evidence you carry, the work of the small cubes. But to be in a place where they were, it . . . I never doubted you. But this makes it real."

"Yes, I suppose it does. You should see the one in Shadowfall, though. There is . . . a lot more to see."

"Maybe you'll take me there one day," I say, part of me trying to unwisely pick the scab from the awkward moment before. But then I think better of it and cut in with "Wait, if this is just here, open to anyone, then how have you kept these relics secret all these years?"

Sage squints at me. "It's . . . hard to explain. Essentially, only Jacob and I can get in the cave."

I stare at him. "Yes," I say, carefully, looking meaningfully at the very wide open entrance back the other way. "I can see how that is hard to explain."

"Well," Sage adds quickly, "I think the mortals designed it so that only someone already familiar with their artifice, maybe already carrying it, or someone who has interacted with the relics enough, could enter. I don't know, it's frankly impossible to gather much data on this. But Jacob and I have tested it out extensively. Here and in other places. It's not that other people are physically barred from entering, it's just . . . they don't know there's a cave here. They can walk right up to it and think it's a wall. We've even left a trail to lead people to such sites on purpose, so wolves and bloods could find the entrances. Then watched them from afar. Jacob's idea, as you can tell from the sheer recklessness of it. But no one other than us has ever gone inside."

I reflect on this. "Sometimes I think there's so much I don't know that immortality isn't long enough to find out."

"Sam, I—"

I hold up a hand. "You're about to tell me that we need to be going, and the knowledge must wait."

Sage nods apologetically. I turn to go, to leave this cave of comparative wonders behind, when I notice something. Something painted on the far cavern wall. There are cave paintings across the land, a relic of the span of time, no more than a century, pastscribers think, when vampires, werewolves, and sorcerers went from mindless beasts to civilized races. It was a strange sped-up event, known as the Great Intelligence, that happened somewhere before, at least a few centuries, dating began properly with 0 AL, After Light, which is when First Light was built.

But this is not those paintings. This is bolder, better designed, vivid, like the paints were there before the wall. And it seems to glow, not just in the arcane mortal lights but with its own light.

The illustration itself is of a round blue ball, with green shapes across it breaking up the blue, shaped like wedges, with some tapering at the top and widening out, and others doing the opposite. Next to the ball, perfectly symmetrical, impossibly well-designed painted letters depict the word, in the common tongue I speak, EARTH FIVE.

"What is it?"

"Sam . . ."

"Just this last question, Sage. If you didn't want my curiosity, you should have left me in the river." I mean it as a jest, but it comes out severe, a reprimand, even.

Sage sighs. "I think it's our world. Not just the Everlands but the entire world and its continents."

I think on this. Then I nod. "Kinet Levestion has always said it was round. I read his treatise on it, not that I understood all of it."

Sage smiles then, his first proper smile for a while. "It's amazing that you even read it. Not many people know of it or would bother to try and understand it. It's pretty impenetrable starcraft."

Sam shrugs. "I understood the basic point. Round ball. Us." I pause. "So the mortals called this world *Earth*. Imaginative, that." Then I narrow my eyes, as two more points occur to me. "But that picture seems quite specific. All the edges of the continents, almost like they fit together. How would they know what all the lands look like? You'd have to be up in the stars, looking down."

Sage studies me silently, and his face seems to glow in the impossible cave lights.

"And what does the number five mean? Unless it means . . ."

Sage just stares, letting me come to the conclusion.

I breathe out, trying to stay pathetically afloat in the current of revelations. "Actually, I think maybe we should get going now, or my brain is going to explode out of my skull, and then you'll have to wait for me to heal again."

We walk for what feels like at least two hourglasses through the same thick forest, neither of us saying anything. I feel a little bit of an idiot for thinking that Sage recalling what seems to have been the considerable trauma of saving me and then waiting for me to heal was a great time to lock lips. I also feel stupid for even thinking of any of this when I've just seen more evidence of the mortals, we have a wolf on our tail, our mission to the Wolflands has turned into a battle for survival, and we are further than ever from getting the wolves as an ally. At this rate we'll be fighting them, too.

Then again, apparently I only recently had half a head, so maybe I should be a little gentler on myself.

Eventually the forest gives way to a valley spread out before us, dotted with copses of redoaks and pines but mainly bushes, with a fast stream rushing past to join up with the river that somewhere contains half my old skull. The valley climbs to our west to a high point, and above that are cliffs leading to more forest. The waxing moon is almost full now, and gives me enough light to see across the vista before me. Still, I would do anything for even just a Midway blood now. Especially if we're being hunted.

"Up there," says Sage, finally breaking his silence, pointing to the cliffside above the valley. "That's where Ansbach territory begins, I think. We're in Gevaudan land now. But if we get up there, we can proceed back to Ansbach castle."

"We're going back?"

Sage turns to me, and I feel a little sheepish, realizing I'd not even asked where we were going. *Again, Sam, you have a new head and who knows what else, how about we be kind to ourselves?*

"Sorry, I should have said." He hangs his head low and I realize just how tired he is. "I just don't see any other way. The Gevaudans would have no reason to trust us, and their alpha is at Ansbach castle anyway. I don't see how we can survive all the way back to First Light if we're being hunted. But if we can get back to the castle ourselves, and get to Raven before someone else gets to us, well, I trust Raven."

I nod. It does make sense. I can't think of anyone I'd rather have protecting me in the entire continent, with no offense to the mercurial genius in front of me.

I sigh. "Let me know if you see any animals, then. Not sure my rabbit-blood is going to sustain me much longer, at this walking pace, anyway." Sage just nods. I wish this awkwardness would end.

A wolf howls, worryingly close. Long, almost mournful. It echoes through the valley, and the hairs on my neck shoot up. We wait. There's no follow-up.

"That is bad, isn't it?" I ask.

"No one is replying." Sage looks around at the valley. "And this territory border, between the Gevaudans and the Ansbachs, is not likely to be full of wolves. And most of the Ansbachs will be nearer the castle. So I imagine it's a message. A message for us."

"Why would a wolf send a message to its prey?"

"It's part of their code. If they're hunting someone, they must know they're being hunted. They're very strict on this, I believe."

"Redsky Stubbe or any of the Stubbes didn't strike me as wolves who follow any kind of honorable code."

"Wolves are complicated."

*Not as complicated as sorcerers*, I think.

"Well, then," I say, stretching my legs. "Forget blood, let's get walking."

We manage to get all the way across the valley and up into the cliffs above it, almost into Ansbach territory, before we hear the next wolf howl. There's a path up the cliffside, more rocks than my tired legs would like, but ahead of me it winds round to where the next part of the forest begins, and I launch myself after Sage, who has already crested the ridge above me.

Ahead are dense trees, wolfland-pine ones this time, not redoaks, and I turn behind me to peer over the cliff edge to the valley we've just come from. We took the winding side path up, but below me is a steep fall straight down, and I imagine leaping off, hitting the ground below, just like I hit the rocks. Maybe the deep snow would break my fall. For a moment my exhaustion whispers at me to jump, to get a rest, wake up with Sage over me again, having healed me. It's convincing, this voice, and that's when I realize I really need more blood. I'm about to start getting desperate, look for insects or slugs to suck on, when the wolf howl echoes across the valley.

I turn to Sage, who looks deathly pale, his sleepless nights and archery crafting catching up to him. "How near?"

He thinks. "Half a glass away? Hard to be certain."

"We're not going to make Ansbach castle, are we?"

Sage doesn't bother to challenge me. "No." He reaches for his bow. "If I can shoot the right arrow at the right point, I can maybe hold him off for a while as you run."

"Right, Sage Bailey," I say, forcefully enough to stop him in his tracks. "No more of that. A wolf is not a rabbit, as I hope I don't have to remind you." I breathe out and sit down. "You've saved me enough times recently. It's getting concerning, frankly. Time for me to save us both."

Sage rubs the bags under his eyes and stares at me skeptically. "Do . . . do you have a plan?"

I stare at the cliffs behind me, and some absurd attempts at planning rattle through my brain. Most of my ideas have been made on much better blood. Now I have nothing. But I am more than the animal in me. I am Sam, blood-hungry or not. I brought down an entire city, and I'm not going to die in a forest far from home.

I turn back to Sage. "Do you still have the invisibility cube?"

He nods. "Yes, but as I've already said, wolves can smell you so it's no help."

I grin, slowly, that old feeling creeping back into me. "That's what I'm counting on." Then I look at the beginnings of the forest around me, and back to the cliffs. "We're going to need to collect some things if we're going to do this in time." I try to stand up, but faintness overcomes me. "And by we, I mean, for the time being, you."

The forest is silent as Redsky Stubbe comes trotting up the cliffside path to the top where we are. The chirps and owl hoots and night-starling song is shut off. The land respects the wolves enough to give them their peace on a hunt, evidently.

I stand with the cliff edge to my left, facing the forest ahead where my escape route lies. Behind me to my right are several trees where the cliff curves into the forest. Directly behind me is what appears to be a thick bush.

I am invisible to the naked eye, with the cube in my right hand. It feels warm, and softer than the material it's made of should suggest. I hold it tight and breathe the pine-fresh forest air in deep. Sage found a vole in his collecting of the materials for my very hasty plan, and I have a little strength back. I've never had voleblood before. It's a little better than rabbit, I'm surprised to find. Makes me feel surprisingly calm for a Wornblood. Or maybe I'm in the eye of the storm, my nerves having jangled themselves to death and my mind now still.

*Come on, Sam. You had half an army of Grays pointing their guns at you not so long ago. One stupid wolf is nothing.*

Speaking of the stupid wolf, he rounds the cliffside-path corner and comes onto the crest of the hill and faces me. His jaws are massive, saliva dripping from them, rows of fangs as long as my index finger and almost twice as thick. His deep-red fur is scored with orange mottling—I see the sunset implication of his name well enough—and his bulk is huge. Bigger than Raven in her wolf form by far. I see why he is Silver Stubbe's muscle. His legs are thick and end in huge paws, with the claws lengthened unnervingly. He sniffs the air and immediately sets his small, wild yellow eyes on me. He can't see me, but as Sage said, he most certainly smells me.

I breathe in. I breathe out. Redsky trots a little closer, grinning if a wolf in wolf form could be said to grin. It does feel like his slavering, fang-filled maw is wider, anyway. He howls then, this one I can tell in victory. Then he sniffs again, and I worry he is trying to find Sage. Sage who has taken his clothes off and rubbed himself vigorously in snow, not a pleasant experience for sorcerers, who deal better in heat than cold, but hopefully, maybe, enough for the wolf to focus on invisible old me.

Then, suddenly, I drop the cube, which winks off immediately as I let it go and lands dully in the snow. And I start to shriek. "Oh, Blood Gods, you smell me, don't you! I knew it!"

Redsky shimmers then, and there's that shifting collection of hues and shades and time and space and something metallic in the air and now he's a naked man, chest covered in rust-gold hair, more muscles than sense, laughing in the cold snow. It's a cruel laugh.

"Sorcerer tricks! I see your friend has abandoned you. Shame he didn't tell you that a wolf nose cannot be fooled. I'll make it quick, girl, as I have to catch up to your cowardly friend." He raises a hand and lengthens his nails into talons. "This will hardly hurt a bit." Then he runs at me, full pelt, and I scream again, and scream some more. I give it all my might.

And then at the last second as he is upon me, I summon all the temporary buzz of my vole meal to quickly dive to the right, into the trees.

Redsky's momentum carries him into the thick-looking bushes next to the trees, between them and the cliffside.

Except they're not that thick, and they're not really bushes, more the hastily assembled—but in the snow and the night, surprisingly convincing—grouping of foliage and branches that Sage collected, which serve to cover the rest of the cliff edge as it meets the trees.

Redsky, expecting some proper greenery to slow his charge, careens almost off the edge, but for a moment it looks like he's stopped himself in time, his feet sliding just inches from the edge, his arms flailing.

And then I recover from my dive and run up behind him, and with all the waning strength of one small mammal inside me, I shove him as hard as I can. He turns as he falls, his red-haired face the picture of confusion, turning into alarm and a little fear as he goes, his mouth a comical O. For a second I feel bad for him, then I summon the dead faces of those who bullies like him have consigned to death—my mother, my father, my sister, Beth, Redgrave—and I make sure the last thing he sees is my tired, worn-out grin.

Sage is shivering against a tree a hundred yards in, naked, covered in snow. I bring him his cloak, discarded a hundred yards farther beyond him.

His exhausted eyes barely register me as he tries to extricate himself from the snow and wrap himself in the cloak while preserving his modesty, though he summons relief at my survival with a genuine smile. "You did it."

"I did. I'm too tired to work out if my debt is wiped out with you." I shiver myself, and sit against a tree opposite him, keeping an eye out for any winter rodents. "Which I think shows how, at some point, we need to slow down and stop putting ourselves in these positions."

Sage grins tiredly, now fully cloaked, and slumps back down against the tree. I look at him with concern. "Can you last?"

He nods. "Sorcerers are very hardy, even in extremes. It takes a lot to end us just by exhaustion or the elements. They say the Light is in us all, even a magickless Quantas like me."

"Is it?"

He laughs. "One mystery at a time."

"So now what?" I ask. "Back to Ansbach castle, as before?"

He nods. "I might just take a moment, if that is all right."

I narrow my eyes. "I thought sorcerers were very hardy."

"Yes, but—"

"I'm jesting, Sage, take as long as you need."

"Glad you've found your humor after pushing a wolf off a cliff edge."

I shrug. "Murder makes me mischievous." I feel a little nauseous at the jest, and it occurs to me that though I hated Redsky, for what he represented, if anything, I don't know if I actually want him to die. "Do you think he'll be dead?"

Sage studies me before he answers. "From that fall? Probably not, for a wolf. But he'll be far too injured to catch up with us now." I decide to accept this as truth, not Sage's kindness, so I don't have to examine the pure rage inside me that gloried over his death, if even for a moment.

There's a silence then, but it's not awkward, like before. Sage breaks it first.

"That was an incredible plan, Sam."

"Thank you." I mean it. "It came to me easily. It's like I made one big plan to save First Light, and now my brain wants to see what else I can do."

Sage nods. "I found that myself, once upon a time."

"Oh, good," I reply, rolling my eyes. "So I'm on track to be you."

Sage laughs. "You're already better than me, Sam, in a lot of ways."

I eye him. "You had to add 'a lot of ways,' didn't you. You couldn't mitigate it." Sage starts to sputter but I hold up a hand. "Jesting, again."

He laughs at that, free and loud, and then it cuts off, almost like he's remembered something, and he sighs. "Oh, Sam. Sam, I'm sorry."

I raise an eyebrow. "About what?"

He doesn't reply immediately but stares back where we came, at the cliff edge and the cloudless moonlit sky beyond it. One night to full moon. When his voice comes, it's soft, and I can smell the regret in it almost like I'm the wolfkind.

"I had a wife, Sam. A vampire wife. Many years ago. Several centuries and more, now. Decades before the Twin War, before I first founded the cult, before I was an inquirer, before I had properly traveled to start seeking out the mortals, even. When my name was not Sage Bailey, the name I chose for the cult, but my given birth name, Quantas Quantantion. We lived in Quantile, my wife and I, with the other magickless mages. We were happy, for a while, though I can't ever say that was a life she deserved."

He pauses then, lost a little bit in the remembrance, and I try and fail to imagine Sage Bailey in boring domesticated bliss.

"But my lust for traveling and finding out about the world, and the legends of the mortals I'd started to get obsessed by, was growing and growing. I wanted to know everything, and go where I needed to find it. She wanted a home and a stable life. She wasn't stupid, Light knows, in many ways she was more intelligent than me." He smiles then, recalling my earlier comment. "She was simply more intelligent than me. But our dreams for the future became so different I . . . it never occurred to me till too late that our paths were splitting. I was so caught up in my own world. But she was more than self-aware for the both of us. So she wrote me the most honest, beautiful letter, and she left me, and I—"

He stops then, and bows his head. When he raises it again, his eyes look haunted. "I thought it would be fine to think of it two hundred and twenty years later, but I forgot I had to speak it aloud." He rubs his eyes. "I'm so tired I can't cry."

I go to hold his hand. He doesn't try to stop me. "I'm very sorry, Sage. Have—have you been in contact since?"

"No. I—held out hope that one day my thirst for the truth would leave, and we could just return to how things were. The centuries are many and long if you can survive them, after all. Nothing ends, I told myself. But she died in Grayfall. I've had it confirmed to me many times over."

"Oh, Sage . . ."

"It is fine. I have grieved long, and the sting of it has gone. But not the regret."

I give him a few moments, our hands still held.

"I'm sorry," he says eventually. "I wasn't trying to be maudlin. My point, Sam, is that I'm not a man to be . . . thinking of things with . . . and if I gave that impression with my impulsive kiss on that field those weeks ago, then I'm sorry. I like you very much. But I'm not a real person. I'm just an obsession, who has to go where he may, who has to . . . who has to *know*. I can't make anyone happy. I doubt I ever will be myself, even if I find out all I need to. But I can't stop myself. And I don't want to."

For a moment I go to tell him, *That's me too*. That's my ambition, not for knowledge really (though I crave that, too) but for achievement, for never going back to how I was, for never again cleaning the piss off a noble's floor and dreaming of things I thought I'd never see. For never again feeling that there is a world beyond me, electric and true, all happening far from me, where I should be. For *never going back*.

For a moment, I want to tell him we're the same.

But I don't. I tell him what I think he wants to hear.

"Friends?"

Sage smiles, exhausted, shivering in his cloak of a magickless man.

"I very much hope so."

"Right," I say, glad to have things clear and stuffing any other thoughts deep where I kept my guilt not so long ago. "Let's get back to that pissing castle then."

## 27

# Planted

Sorcerers love to hide things. They love it. If you find an abandoned sorcerer temple, you'll spend the next century finding things they've hidden. I don't think wolves have ever hidden anything that wasn't meat and liable to rot soon. Vampires don't hide things; they put them in great vaults and dare you to steal them. But sorcerers are the squirrels of the immortal world, secreting their acorns in the most ridiculous places.

Kinet Lankastrillion,
*Some Prudent Observations of My Fellowe Sorcerers*

### Jacob

Morning comes and finds me sitting on my bench in Golden's garden. What a surprise. I might ask to be buried here. It's certainly taken the place of my favorite corner in the temple or the corner of my favorite inn back in my pre–Sage Quantile heavy-drinking days in terms of places to be when I'm feeling shit.

Winter sun slants down, winking off the fountain. I don't expect Raven to join me this time. Even if she wanted to. I'm sure she'd scent the self-loathing and depression on me, smelling something like chalk or stale farts or however it works for wolves' noses. I allowed myself to think I was something I wasn't and, as ever, I wasn't up to the job. But there's a strange peace in the shroud of depression that follows remembering something like that. Like putting on an old familiar cloak. The mind clears, and all you have on your schedule is sadness. It's relaxing, in its way. Just me and this fountain and these roses and this herb garden and this soft layer of snow and me sulking.

Something stirs in the back of my mind, but all I want to do is find a proper drink here, just like the old times, and stare unthinkingly, unsoberly, at this fountain and this herb garden and this soft layer of snow and . . .

And . . .

I look at the herb garden. At the mageweed, specifically.

I shake my head. *No, it's a stupid idea. Even by your low standards, that's a stupid idea.* I shrug it off, settling back into my comfortable fog of nothing, my black dog, my . . .

I could check, though, couldn't I?

Could I?

I stand up and walk over to the edge of the herb garden. I stare at the mageweed, at its small red leaves and blue stalks, nestled between the takelily and that thin-sticked herb I don't recognize. Mageweed. Grown by mages, unsurprisingly. Kinets, specifically.

I stare at the soil underneath it.

Could I?

For once I seek Raven out—and now I'm in her chambers.

I realized I had no idea how to find her, because she always finds me, so I asked one of the hundreds of wolves ambling round the castle where her chambers were, and they gave me a look that suggested that my sanity had left me and that this would be followed soon by my life. But they told me.

Her chambers are in the central tower, where all the Ansbach chambers are, of course, and so I crossed the courtyard from the main castle to the tower with the pace of a mage on a mission and the mild fear of someone who has had their life threatened. The courtyard was busy, wolves running round with bits of wood seemingly building things. I'm not much on construction so I couldn't hazard a guess on what these things are. Crossing the courtyard the other way was Verdant. As the only wolf here who hasn't completely fucked me one way or the other, I went to give him a friendly glance, but the scowl I saw on his face—a scowl ill-suited to his normally jovial features—stayed on there even when I swore he saw me. If anything, his face darkened. Wonderful.

When I got to the tower, I took the right staircase as instructed and climbed as it wound all the way up to about two-thirds the height of the tower and then, hoping my not incredible memory for directions wouldn't abandon me here, I took the right off the staircase and walked down the torch-lined corridor, passing several other doors, to a door at the end, which I knocked on, receiving a short sharp growl in response that I very much hoped meant *enter*.

And that's how I found myself standing in Raven's bedchamber, notable for not actually containing a bed.

"Oh," I say, watching Raven sprawled out on a thick gray fur rug, her head staring at the ceiling, the left side of her face covered in her dark locks. Her naked form became almost second nature to me back in First Light, if second nature means suppressing my thoughts like water back into a blowhole, but I've only seen her in furs while in the castle so I have to reorient myself back to a normal I've never really been very oriented to in the first place.

The look she gives me, though, quickly quashes such thoughts. Her eyes are dead, almost catatonic. If she hadn't grunted for me to enter, I'd almost wonder if she was sleeping awake.

"I . . . I thought this might have been your receiving room. Not your bedchamber. Chamber. Rug chamber. Something chamber."

Nothing.

"Raven, I have something you need to see."

Nothing.

"I found something. . . ."

That brings a little bit of life to her, and she lifts her head up to stare at me, a reanimated corpse.

I hold up some sheafs of parchment, faded, worn, ripped in the corner, covered still in a little dirt. "I should have realized. Just because a Kinet mage couldn't hide anything in a library, or any place of books, doesn't meant they'd give up. No, they'd put them somewhere they could tell someone about if they ever needed to. But somewhere no one would think to look. Open to anyone in the castle. And marked clearly. But still completely secret."

"Please get to the point, mage."

"It was *under the mageweed*. The herb, grown by sorcerers only. In Golden's garden. Buried deep. In a little box. I, uh, tried to not make a mess but . . ." I clear my throat, deciding to skip over my soil desecration. "It makes complete sense. The Kinet seller comes here. Kinets love plants, everyone knows that. Move the soil around and all that stuff. He offers to add to the garden, as a gesture. He takes the opportunity to leave his stash." I whistle. "And what a stash."

I point at one parchment in particular and drop the others. It has a series of small pictures on it, drawn meticulously in quill ink, and next to each picture is a series of words and letters. "These are records of what that Kinet who came round to all the wolfpacks sold. And who they sold it to. The date on the back is 470, which accords with the time when they would have been touring the Wolflands, according to Verdant."

Raven sits up completely now. Still vacant but life returning.

"Look at these pictures. Three plants." I point to each in turn. "Next to each plant is a pack name." Again, I point. "And next to the pack name is the wolf they sold it to. I think it's their initials. So the top one"—I point accordingly to a drawing of a herb plant with tube-shaped petals coming off it, and thick stalks—"this was sold to the Soissons. The initials 'M.S.' must refer to someone in the Soissons pack they sold it to."

Raven's eyes have a bit of fire in them now, though not as much as I'd like.

"And the next one," I continue, finger moving down, pointing to a picture of a plant with a small spiky ball of stalks, almost like a painhog. "This was sold to your friends the Gevaudans. The initials of the buyer are 'T.G.' And then we have this one." Now I point to the final drawing; this time the plant is just a few long thin sticks with no flowers. "This one was sold to an Ansbach." Raven's eyes narrow now. I finally have her. "The initials next to this one are 'W.A.'"

"So this means . . ." says Raven, processing a lot of information at once. I know the feeling; I've been friends with Sage for fifteen decades.

"It means that the person who has the new wolfsbane plant—the one that doesn't look like wolfsbane or smell like wolfsbane and that most likely killed Ashen—is probably from one of these three packs, and is one of these three people, whose initials we now have."

Raven keeps on staring.

"Don't you see?" I ask, impatient. "This is the breakthrough!" I shake the parchment in front of her, as if I can force its meaning off the page and into her skull. "This is it! One of these plants is the murder weapon, and one of these packs houses the killer . . . I mean, probably."

Raven gets off the bed then, and moves to her small window, her back to me. The protective animal skin of the window is pinned aside, letting the cold winter air in. She doesn't seem to mind. No one here does. I never thought I'd say this, but I can't wait for the reassuring all-year-round sweat of the Desertlands.

"'M.S.' and 'T.G.' obviously do not refer to Verdant or Berry," she says.

"None of the unders they have with them here have those first initials. So it would be someone in their pack. Someone not here."

"But they might have given it to them to bring here."

A shrug. "Maybe."

"And what about the Ansbachs?" I ask.

"What about them?"

"Well, who's W. Ansbach?"

"I do not know. There are a few Ws in our pack, not many. No one I can think of who would have enough coin to buy such a thing."

"Might Golden know?" I ask. I don't particularly want to talk to a recent widow, but I'm not letting this go.

"If she knew about such a sale, she would have said something already."

"Unless she was involved."

Raven spins her head round. "Careful, Jacob. Besides, she was not in that room."

I feel a little anger surge. "What's your ailment, Raven?"

She sniffs. "What do you mean?"

"I mean that you asked me to solve this shitting murder and now I come to you with the best clue yet and you don't seem to care."

"Maybe because I am not sure I care."

I take a few moments for that to settle in.

"What do you mean?"

Raven's voice, when she replies, is lower and softer than usual. I can't tell if it's fury or resignation. Maybe both.

"I mean Silver more or less has his ascendancy to Ashen's position sewn up. He has the support of Bronzed. He just needs Verdant, which I have a feeling he will get through threats. That is enough for a majority."

That might explain Verdant's expression on the way here, I realize, but keep this to myself.

"So you work by majorities. I thought there might be a fight or something. Naked in the forest, that kind of thing."

Normally that would get something from her. This time, nothing.

"Once Silver chairs the Outside Council, and uses his standing from that to influence all the other packs, he will continue to whip up resentment against the bloods. I know him and I know his kind. He will most likely blame Ashen's death on the vampires—"

"But that makes no sense," I reply, unwisely interrupting.

"It does not need to. Rumor and fear will do the work for him. He is a clever bastard, I will give him that. Then the wolves will be roused to be more aggressive toward the bloods. They will break the Pact and insist on their wolf criminals back and supply no more wolfblood. When this is received as badly as they know it will be, it will be war again."

"But . . . but that would be a terrible idea. The vampire Lords could use the Grays, if it came down to it. If they had to. You'd be massacred."

"And if I tell them that now, you think I will be believed? It will be seen as talk against Silver, to stop him. This is a bad time to tell them the truth, sadly."

"But you're Raven Ansbach. You saved them all. You Ansbachs. They respect you. 'I will never forget.' That's what Verdant said. That's what he said about you and what you did after Extinction Valley."

Raven runs a hand through her hair. "Fear triumphs over respect and honor every time, Jacob. Even among wolves. Verdant has the responsibility of protecting his pack from those packs around them. Bronzed is nearest the vampires. Always vulnerable. Even the Stubbes have a point; the vampires did almost wipe us out. We are not united like we used to be. We are just scared cubs, when you come down to it. And I? What have I done to help? I have been fury these last two centuries, and no good came of it. And what of my peace? No good has come of that, either. I am an old wolf in a new time and there is no fucking place for me anymore."

I sit on her bed. It is so hard it may as well be the ground. I can't imagine she actually sleeps in here.

"So that's it. You've given up finding Ashen's killer. You've just given up. Raven Ansbach. The Midnight Assassin. Defeated. Is that it?"

She laughs then, sad and dark. "I am not the fucking Midnight Assassin. I never was. That name was given to my mate. Long ago. His name was Midnight Ansbach. Black-haired like me. But he died so many centuries ago that people have forgotten, and now I have the name."

She turns to me, and her eyes are the saddest I've ever seen. "That is what happens if you live long enough. Everyone forgets. Everything falls apart. Maybe this is when the Wolflands do, too."

I move toward her then, and I clasp her hands. My heart leaps at my own action, fear and adrenaline strong in me. For a moment our eyes meet. I try to think of the right words.

Then she releases her hands from mine.

"I am never going to fuck you, Jacob."

I stare at her. Then I back away. "That wasn't . . . I wasn't . . ." I feel it all then. The humiliation of a life without magick. The cold shame of my birth. The loneliness of my hometown, hard and fierce. My shame turns to anger, lithe and quick, that old proud fury at a world that never wanted me.

"You fucking wolves," I say, spitting out the words. "You're as bad as everyone else."

Then I start to walk out and, at the doorway, like everyone else in this dog-breath shithole, I stop and turn for my last comment.

"You can't give anyone a chance, can you?"

She gives no reaction, and I walk away.

On my way back to my own chambers, to drink, then sleep, in that order, hopefully, I come across Berry Gevaudan bounding down a corridor. She almost bumps into me. She's wearing furs, and her shining blue locks are braided behind her.

"Well, hello, mage," she says, grinning at me.

I'm not in the mood for much enthusiastic conversation.

"Hello, Berry. I didn't think I'd see you before the new council leader is chosen tomorrow."

"You know? Of course you know. You and Raven." She winks at me but must see my expression, because her smile drops a little. "Things not progressing well for you, I see," she says, cocking her head a little.

"Not unless you're here to help." I try to muster some of my usual spirit when all I want to do is leave this place behind me. Stop-and-talks are dreadful.

"Sorry to disappoint you," she says, her grin returning. "But I am off to meet with Silver."

I nod, unsurprised. "You're off to swear fealty to him, I see."

"Hmm, you really do know everything. Actually, I'm going to tell him that I'm keeping my opinions to myself until tomorrow."

"And what happens tomorrow?"

"Well, what happens is we all go to a glade in the forest at first light. And we do some ritual nonsense, and then we choose the next alpha of the council."

"Which will be Silver."

"Maybe." She frowns. "What do you care?"

I sigh. "You know what? I don't. I'm done with the investigation."

"I'm sorry to hear that. You've been quite the entertainment."

"Have I?"

"That's what I just said, darling."

I want that to be it, but something, that annoying ghost of Sage again, makes me ask the next question. "Someone in your pack bought this plant off a Kinet mage one hundred and thirty years ago," I begin, brandishing the parchment that went down like a cold barrel of sick in Raven's room. "Do you know who? Their initials are here. T.G."

Her mouth drops open a little, revealing slightly longer canines than Raven's. Maybe she's lengthened them for my benefit. I can't tell with this one.

"I told you you were entertainment, mage. That's the most random shit anyone's ever asked me with absolutely no context."

"I could do with the help."

"Yes, you sound like you need it." She squints at me. Then she sighs. "Very well, to the moon with it. Let's take a look." She takes the parchment off me and studies it for mere moments, then hands it back.

"You can't help?" I ask resignedly.

"No, on the contrary, my curious little mage," she replies. "I know exactly what that plant is. I remember the Kinet who sold it, and who he sold it to."

"Really?" I was not expecting that at all.

"Yes, really. They called it falsedawn. The plant itself produces a strong glowing light, more so than even some of the night mosses in the forest. Grow enough and you can light a castle in the dark, say, with little need for torches or lamps or suchlike. Pretty useful. It was bought by one of the trader unders in my pack. Cornflower Gevaudan."

"But . . . the initials say 'T.G.'"

"Yes, well, that's the funny thing. Whoever wrote this didn't use their own initials. They used the nickname. Traitor Gevaudan. Bit of a mean nickname really, as they left for the Morbach pack three centuries ago but then slunk back to ours. Not really the done thing, that, as you can imagine. They had good reasons, I think, but that gets lost, you know?"

"Great," I mutter to myself, looking at the increasingly less helpful parchment clues. "So these aren't even accurate names."

"What's that?"

"Nothing. Thank you, Berry. Thank you for being one of the few wolves who spoke to me like an actual person."

She mock-bows. She is so tall that her head still doesn't reach mine even in the bowing. "You're very welcome, Jacob. I'd ask if you're still wanting that fuck before you go, but you're in deeper than you were before."

"I'm sorry?" I said, trying to process both the sex offering and the immediate retraction of it.

"You stink of decay."

"I'm sorry?" I repeat, increasingly lost.

"Lust, Jacob. Smells like decay for wolves when it's lust for someone else? What's Raven been teaching you . . . ? Anyway it's more than lust for you, by the smell of it. You're in deep, lad, you have my sympathies."

"I don't—"

"Not that you have a chance, no offense, but it would be nice for her to get around for once. A sad one, she is."

I desperately want to leave this conversation. "I don't like Raven like that."

"Oh, really? Well, she likes you."

"Wh—what?"

"Oh, you haven't heard? She beat Silver to a pulp because he threatened you. I mean, really hurt him. Classic Raven beating. I mean, he'll have healed completely by tomorrow, even regrown his two front teeth, but I bet it bloody hurt." She smiles. "He's not told anyone, of course, you wouldn't, would you, but some Ansbach wolves were nearby and they told me what happened."

I don't know what to say to that.

"Ha!" Berry laughs. "Young love, eh. Well, in this case, pretty old love. She's ancient, you know, you have no idea . . . anyway, best of luck to you, Jacob. I hope you don't give up, but if you do, take care. Things might not be safe round here much longer."

And then, with a wink and an unexpected but expectedly strong squeeze on the shoulder, she's gone, and I leave for my chamber in a daze.

# 28

# Not the Fall That Kills You

Twas sad to see the hero die,
Twas sad to see them fall
Their bones lay broken in the gorge
I don't like it all
I wonder if they'll live again
We never give up hope,
But blood is blood
And death is death
They should have used a rope

Stone Soissons, *The Ballad of the Wolfman*

## Jacob

Morning comes after a fitful and interrupted sleep—interrupted by various wolf howls, as usual—and I wake in the worst mood. I also wake later than I wanted, which is not, I must admit, unusual for me. It must be around nine bells, not that anyone actually rings any shading bells here. They don't have hourglasses, either, so I assume they just sniff the air to tell the time or something.

I heave myself out of bed, but not before swigging some of the Wolfsbane whiskey I found last night. It's a bad habit, first thing. The kind of habit I used to show back in Quantile. Before Sage. Before the cult. It doesn't bode well.

Outside my chamber door is a large metal bathtub, still impressively warm. Obviously one of the wolves in charge of attending to me thought I needed a good bath. More to wake up than anything else, I accept it and bathe. I do it in the corridor. Why not? Everyone has left. They woke me up at morning five bells with all their howling. Gone to that forest clearing, wherever the Light that is, to choose the next Outside Council leader. Not just the alphas. But all their attendant underwolves, and more importantly all the Ansbachs in the castle, hundreds of them. I'm pretty sure it's just me left, and the sound of quiet all through the place seems to confirm that.

Once bathed, I head down to the kitchens where I confirm that I really do have the castle to myself. Well, look at that. I can do anything, if by *anything* that means I can walk into any bare room I want and steal a chair that no one wants to sit on. I slump down on a bench in the small hall off the kitchens that smells of wolf hair and dirt.

Depressed with all those thoughts, I decide to liberate the wolves of some of their terrible ale for a prejourney drink. It goes down quickly and it goes down tastelessly. I sigh, then I belch. I slowly wipe the sleeve of my desert robe against my mouth, liberating it of some beer droplets, and immediately regret it, as I have to wear these robes without washing for a while and so it might be best if they don't stink of beer the whole time.

And then, like a skybolt from an Atmos, a thought hits me. And a memory.

I rush through the kitchens and to the rooms at the back. Searching. They can't all have left. Someone needs to prepare things for later. Come on. They can't all be gone. And then I hear the golden sounds of movement, and I suddenly see a medium-height wolf (so, six foot something) with blond hair tied up in a net, wearing light furs, in front of a giant steaming vat, vigorously washing various other furs.

"Oh, thank the damn Light," I say, making them spin round. They probably won't know the information I need. It will probably be a dead end.

I ask anyway.

It wasn't a dead end. Not by a long way. And what they said makes my head spin. I attempt to act nonchalantly, and once out of sight I grab another tankard of ale from the kitchens and hurry back to the herb garden, not keen to be seen doing any kind of investigating anymore.

It might be nothing. It is probably nothing. And it still doesn't answer the other questions. I still can't do this. And I still need to go.

I will sit here a few moments, imagine myself back in more peaceful times, and then I will forget I found it. It's not enough to solve the murder, and it will probably make things worse. And anyway, Raven won't let Sam and Sage die. I'll just suppress this information, like I suppressed memories of my Quantile years. It's easy to forget the first few decades of your life. You just leave the memories alone, and eventually *they* leave *you* alone, except in fleeting moments, and if you have a bottle or a bed to distract you, those moments can be over pretty quickly.

So I sit there on the bench, staring at the herbs, willing myself to walk away.

I sit and stare at the roses beyond the herbs: cobalt blue, verdant green, deep crimson red. Thriving even in this season, through botany I couldn't even begin to guess at. I smell the frosty winter air, let its chill cool the end of my nose. I listen to the calming quiet flow of the fountain. I look back at the herbs. At the takelily, at the lightguard. At the mageweed. By the five magicks, I made a bit of a mess of digging up that mageweed! I disturbed some of the plants next to it, too. Not the biggest problem at the moment, granted. Hope that thin-sticked yellow-and-green fellow next to the mageweed isn't a sought-after hallucinogen or something, because I've really done a number on that. Whatever it is. Whatever—

Oh, fuck.

I pull out the parchment. The parchment I almost threw away in my resignation and sulking. I look at the pictures. The pictures of the herbs.

Then at the initials. The initials that don't all represent proper names.

And in one, terrifying instant of pant-wetting, crystal-clear clarity, I solve the murder.

Having done my final act, my new evidence in my pocket, I have nothing to do now but to wait. A part of me desperately wants to just ride away from here, let my revelations die with my absence. If what Raven says is true about what is happening now somewhere in the surrounding forest, it won't matter anyway. Or it will matter so much that what I have to say will mean I never leave this land alive.

Do I want to risk my life for this? Do I even value my life?

I remember a time, surrounded by bottles, surrounded by lightguard herbs, drowning in self-pity, when I wanted to die. My latest venture in Quantile had failed. My last friend had left me. And I saw all the centuries to come, stretching out. And I knew then that my life had no value.

I knew it in my bones, a scripture written in my being before I was even born. I knew it at my core.

It's in this memory, shriveled up on the bench like a man burned by his own actions, that I feel a nail on my shoulder. Sharp, not enough to draw blood but with the promise of blood, to come, perhaps.

"You are still here," says Raven.

"Oh, thank the Light. Thank the Light. It's you." I turn to her in utter relief, forgetting how we left things. Then I remember, and I allow the moment to hang there awkwardly. From the look of her, she feels that, too.

"Why . . . why are you here?" I glance around, as if expecting an explanation from the air. "I thought it was just me and that bloody washerwoman."

Raven frowns at me.

"The *washerwoman* sounded a little offensive, didn't it?"

"I forgot how annoying you were," she says.

"You forgot in half a day?"

She sighs. "I am still here because there is no reason for me to be at Silver's ascendancy. There is a whole pack to represent the Ansbachs. I will not give Silver the satisfaction of watching all his plans come to fruition."

I think on this. "So right now it's just me, you, and the washerwoman in the entire castle?"

Silence.

"Right, if you don't want me to call her the washerwoman please, for the love of Light, give me her name."

"Ivy Ansbach."

"She had blond hair."

"We have blond ivy."

"Right. I—never mind. It's just us, though?"

"And Golden. She is still holed up in her quarters. She also does not need to be at the council vote."

I stare at her, mouth fully open, fully embracing my moronic shock.

"We need to go and see her. Right now."

Raven's eyebrow cocks. "Why?"

"I'm going to say this simply, and I need you to trust me, because I'm thinking fairly quickly on my feet here, and this is something Sage normally does, and if I stop then I'm afraid it will all come crashing down."

"You need me to trust you."

"Yes."

If I see a hint of a smile on that face, is it my imagination?

"I trust you, Jacob."

"Really?"

"Really. I should . . . maybe discuss what I said to you last night. I was . . . in a black mood, and I—"

"Raven," I say, almost grabbing her shoulders, which I still think even at this more advanced stage of our relationship could have been fatal for me, "while I appreciate the imminent apology and then my apology and then all the good things that come with that, I cannot emphasize enough how important it is that we go see Golden now. If I'm right, she's in great danger, and we need to warn her. I'm balancing a lot of things right now in my head and very soon I won't have the balls to do what I need to do."

"She is in danger? From the murderer?" asks Raven, claws lengthening at the thought of protecting her friend.

"In a manner of speaking, yes. I'll explain everything when we speak to her."

We move to leave the garden, but as we start to break into a run, I stop and turn to Raven. "But definitely don't forget about the whole apology thing, will you?"

Raven bares her teeth at me, and I take that for a yes.

Golden's—formerly her and her mate's—rooms are at the very top of the castle tower. As I climb the endless corkscrew stairs, the wind whistling with increasing pitch through the slats in the stone as we climb, I try not to dwell on what I'm about to say, because if I do I might wish to jump off the tower when we get to the top of it.

After what seems a torturously long ascent, we finally reach Golden's chambers; Raven goes first and opens the unlocked door to the receiving room. I raise an eyebrow at her presumption to just enter, but I don't say anything. It must be a wolf thing. Or a friend wolf thing. Or yet another rule I don't understand.

Belly full of rampant nausea, I follow her in and take in the lounge-seat, the elegant furs draped everywhere, the fine quacian-wood dresser in the corner. It might be the most finely furnished room I've seen in this castle, albeit orders less refined than your average Midway vampire townhouse.

Golden isn't here, so Raven turns to the left of two doors opposite, and this time she knocks lightly. I wonder for a second why she doesn't announce herself, then I remember how smell functions and realize Golden will have known she was here since she ascended the staircase.

"Raven," a soft, honeyed voice from within calls out. Raven gingerly opens the door to reveal a study, with a fine varnished desk and, I think with a little bitterness, some bookshelves behind it. Also behind the desk is Golden Ansbach, sitting on a tall, fur-backed chair, wearing light-blond furs herself.

To our left, a thin wooden door of slats leads out to a balcony, which I imagine must give some fairly fear-inducing views if you aren't used to that kind of thing. The wind screams through the slats. I'm not sure I could work up here.

"Raven." She smiles and then looks at me. "I'm glad you're still here. I thought it might just be me." Then she turns to me. "Jacob I have not met. Well, apart from . . ." She stops, presumably reluctant to relive the horrific scene where I first saw her wailing and howling over her mate's dead body.

I study her for a moment before I reply. Her hair is flowing free, and is so sun-blond it almost seems to glow. She has round, warm eyes, much different than Raven's, and she has a smudge of lip daub on. She doesn't look happy, but she's not exactly bawling.

"Glad to see you are up and about a bit," says Raven. "I was . . . a bit worried before. You looked . . ."

"Catatonic?" She smiles. Even her sharp canines look more refined than Raven's. "I was. I still am, honestly. But I find that carrying on with my work, or at least trying to continue—" She pauses a moment. "—Ashen's work, all his dull things he had to do . . . well, it's keeping me going."

Raven smiles. "I am glad. And I am sorry to intrude, but Jacob has something important he needs to tell you." She pauses and side-glares at me, which is something I was not aware was possible until she just did it. "At least I hope he has."

Golden smiles at me and pushes some of her beautiful locks out of her face. "Of course. Can I get you a drink first?"

"No—" Raven starts, but I cut in.

"Actually, yes, please," I say. "I'll have what you're having."

"Well, I wasn't going to . . . you know what, I'll have some Wolfsbane whiskey, if you want to join me." She must see my look of surprise. "Oh, you think because I straighten my hair I can't drink with the best of them?" She flashes me some teeth then, and rises to get the drinks. *Stop flirting with the widow*, I think, and then from Raven's fairly terrifying expression I suppose she must be thinking the same.

She returns with the goblets of whiskey and places them on the desk in front of me and her. "Thank you," I reply. "I'll need this for what I'm about to say."

Golden raises an eyebrow. "Do you always need alcohol to talk?"

I ignore this. "I think I know how your . . . late mate was killed, and I might know who did it."

Golden's jaw drops. "You do?"

Raven's face is unreadable.

"I do, and . . ." I stop myself and squint at her bookshelf behind her. "You do have that book! I can't believe it!" I point at the top left of the bookshelf, and Golden turns round in surprise, and Raven turns her head left to stare where I'm pointing.

"What book?" asks Golden, turning back in confusion.

"*A Storied Overview of the Many Cults, Volume I*, by Neuras Sondallion," I reply. "I've just . . . never seen it in the flesh before. It's so rare."

"What does this have to do with Ashen's murder?" asks Raven, who is giving me a very suspicious look.

I sigh and put up my hands in apology. "It doesn't, I'm sorry. I got distracted. It's been . . . it's been a very long and stressful few days." I look at Golden, who is as confused as Raven is suspicious.

"Obviously not as stressful for me as it is for you . . ." I start, sweating a little.

"Jacob . . ." says Raven, voice descending into a growl.

"Yes, yes, sorry." I down some more whiskey, readying myself for what comes next, and the sheer audacity of it. "I can tell you right now who killed your mate, Golden."

I pause and then mutter a silent prayer to the Light of Luce. Then I lift my finger and point to the blond wolf opposite me.

"It was you."

Raven spins round to face me then, instantly growling. "What the fuck, mage?"

Golden looks shocked and tries to mouth words. "Is this a jest?" She turns to Raven. "Is this a jest, Raven? What is this? Is this meant to be funny?"

"Jacob," says Raven carefully, placing one suddenly very long nail claw meaningfully on my left arm. "Think very carefully about your next words before you accuse the one person in this world who cared more about Ashen than me, and my one friend left in it."

I gulp and try to imagine what Sage would do.

He would, of course, persevere. "I can prove it," I say, slowly. Then I take a sprig of a herb from one of my robe pockets. I place it on the desk in front of me, next to my whiskey cup. It is green and yellow, and is shaped like small sticklike stalks. "This is a herb that grows in your herb garden, Golden. It's been right in front of me this whole time. I didn't know what it was called, I've never seen it before." I twirl it in my fingers. "Oh, and one more thing, when you were both distracted with that book I was pointing at, I put some of it in your whiskey."

Before I've even finished my sentence, Golden bolts up from her chair and backs away and puts a hand to her throat, eyes wide with shock, nails lengthening and facial fur sprouting in what I guess to be sheer horror. "You. . . . You . . . little . . ." And then she moves toward me with fire in her eyes and lip curled and fangs lengthening, and I realize what's about to happen, and I quickly shout, "Fuck, I didn't really!"

She pauses in the first arc of her swipe at me and glances at Raven, who has raised herself off the chair in an automatic fighting stance, confusion etched on her face. Then she slowly sits back down and glances at the spilled whiskey.

"Raven," she says, clearing her throat and smoothing her wild hair back down. "I'm starting to want to hurt this mage very badly."

Raven says quietly, face unreadable, "Jacob, speak, and speak quickly."

"That was a wild reaction from someone who'd just been told a normal herb from their garden had been put in their drink, Golden," I say, my eyes trained carefully on her in case she decides to go feral again. "Wouldn't you say, Raven?"

Raven does not reply.

"But it was a very logical reaction if you knew that the plant on the table in front of me, the one that was just casually in your garden all this time, next to the mageweed—which only grows around mages, of course—was in fact wolfsbane, and that you had a very short window of time to live."

I hold the stick up and look at it. Raven moves away slightly. Golden's eyes are fixed on it, and her jaw is tight.

"It's not the wolfsbane that you two have feared for centuries, of course. The kind that was eradicated from the very face of the continent around the time one particular Kinet mage was trying to adapt it. It doesn't smell like wolfsbane, which is how no one detected it in the room. And it obviously doesn't look like it, which is why you just left it in the middle of your herb garden, which, by the way, is *incredible* overconfidence, although I suppose the fact that no one else knows what it looks like helped. No one, that is, aside from the mage who helpfully recorded it on this parchment."

I take out the document that had so frustrated me the night before and had been received with such disinterest by a depressed Raven. "This was under the mageweed, by the way. I find it a bit funny that you didn't know the clue was next to the evidence of your crime. I think there's a word for that, Sage would know it, anyway."

Then I point at the bottom picture of the plant. "You see? It's a good likeness, isn't it?" I move my finger across. "And of course, here the mage has written that it was sold in the Ansbach territory." I move my finger across a little more. "And here. The initials. W.A."

I see Raven's look of confusion, and I quickly add, "Yes. Not Golden's initials. But, as Berry Gevaudan helpfully informed me last night, these initials are not necessarily the actual names. More code names or nicknames. Or in your case," I say, pointing again at Golden, "it's a literal description, isn't it? Not 'Ansbach.' But *A* for 'Ashen.' *W.A.* 'Wife of Ashen.' Of course, very like a mage to think of you in vampire or sorcerer language, using *wife* instead of *pack mate*, but what can I say? Not all us mages are enlightened."

For a second, Golden's face has such a shocked grimace plastered across it that I expect her to confess there and then. But then she shakes her head and replaces it with a disgusted look. "How dare you. How dare you come here with such a ridiculous tale."

I frown. "Please explain to me what is ridiculous about it. I'd love to hear it."

She laughs, dry and harsh. "Well, how about the fact that your evidence consists of some tattered parchment that could have come from bloody anywhere, your doing, even, and a bit of a plant from my garden, which is open to anyone, by the way, and whose word for it being wolfsbane, or new wolfsbane or whatever nonsense, we have to take from you."

I shrug. "Eat it then."

She ignores me. "And while we're at it, please, oh wise mage, please tell me how I killed my mate when I *wasn't in the bloody room*."

She growls at me, revealing her entire set of canines.

"Well, I can't prove that completely," I say, and she smiles. "But I can give it a pretty convincing go. You see, it came to me when I was downing a quick ale earlier . . . which I may have stolen from your kitchens." I look at them both. "Not relevant, sorry. Anyway, I wiped my robe sleeve on my mouth when I was done. And I was suddenly transported to a memory of the last person I saw doing that in such an exaggerated way." I pause. Just like Sage, I am learning to be a drama mage. "Ashen Ansbach. He did it once at the start of the council meeting. And then he did it again when he'd downed his mug completely. And I suppose it was that second time, when he properly wiped across his lips the bits of this wolfsbane plant that, I propose, were ground up into his sleeve. Rubbed onto the fabric of his ceremonial fur. By someone who knew he had that habit. Someone with easy access to his furs that morning."

Golden is quick to snarl. "That is the most ridiculous thing I've ever heard."

I shrug. "It's a bit of a stretch. And like I say, I can't prove it. But here's the funny thing." And at this point I turn to Raven and her unreadable face. She's the one I need to convince, anyway. "The reason I can't prove it is because the furs Ashen was wearing, those valuable ceremonial furs, were destroyed. Burned. By the washerwoman." I look at Raven. "Person whose job may include washing for this weekend, but who does other things, and just happens to be a woman."

Raven narrows her eyes slightly. I continue. "She burned them at your request, apparently, Golden. You came to her immediately after his death. Demanded they be burned. She was surprised. She asked if you didn't want them kept. You said no, they must be destroyed immediately."

I stop and lean back. "That's all. The murder weapon, method of murder, and a trail of evidence leading back to you, Golden."

Golden stands up then. "Someone put a herb in my garden. I got rid of the furs my pack mate died in because I couldn't bear them being around. And I unsurprisingly reacted badly to someone claiming to have spiked my drink. It's hardly the case of the clawdamn century, mage. Now piss off, before I throw you out the window." She bares her teeth at me, but a single tear rolls down her cheek as well.

"The idea I would kill my Ashen." Her voice goes to a whisper. "My Ashen." Then she turns to Raven. "Why have you let this . . . fool talk to me like this, Raven? How can you sit there and let him say such things?"

I turn to Raven, who, during Golden's performance, has been rooted to the spot. She is staring past Golden, her eyes looking far away.

"Raven?" Golden asks again. "You can't trust this mage, surely? It's me. It's Golden. The wolf you've run with. Hunted with. Spent centuries bitching about Ashen with." She laughs, a little too loudly, and comes round the table suddenly and kneels at Raven's feet. She grabs both of Raven's hands and stares straight into her eyes. Raven's eyes, hazy, refocused, gradually take her in. "It's *me*, Raven. I don't know what's going on here, but I need you right now. You're all I have."

She turns to me and sneers. "You can't trust *him*, Raven. Please tell me you don't trust one of the same kind who spelled our doom at Extinction Valley. Please tell me you don't trust a sorcerer over me."

Raven stands up then, quickly, so quickly Golden almost loses balance. She backs away from Golden a little bit, till she's almost at the window. Golden stands, too, and for a moment neither of them moves.

Then Raven's voice, slow and sure, comes in. "I do trust him, Golden. Moons help me, I do trust him." Then she takes a hand and drags it down over her face and shakes her head. "But more importantly, I trust my nose. The nose that told me how you felt when you thought the herb was in your drink. The nose that gave me the sharpest tang of citrus I've felt for a while. Pure lemons, so pure I could hardly breathe for a second. Fear, deadly and certain. The knowledge of your certain death. You can fool me, Golden. You can fool me for centuries." Then she smiles, a sad smile, of knowing what must come and the things that must be broken. "But you cannot fool my nose for a moment."

Golden stares at her. Then she takes a step back. "Oh, Raven. Raven. I cannot tell you how much I didn't want this to happen." Then she hangs her head low, as if about to buckle. And then, quietly, "Fuck it."

She moves so quickly that I leap back in my seat, but she moves not at me but straight at Raven, head down, charging like a bull, and Raven, who wasn't expecting the charge at all, has a moment to look surprised before Golden barrels into her, at a rapid force for such a small run-up. She charges her into the slats covering the window and straight through it onto the small oval balcony beyond, ringed by a low stone wall.

Raven starts to grab ahold of Golden to stop her charge, but she's flailing back at the same time, struggling to stay on her feet, and Golden keeps on charging right to the edge of the balcony, and the momentum carries Raven off her feet and right over the edge.

For one almost comical moment, Raven is suspended in air, feet over head, and I see her look of genuine bemusement. And then, as I sit helpless in my chair, I watch in indescribable horror as she falls. She's instantly out of sight. I stop caring about Golden, and I leap out of my chair and run to the edge of the balcony. I hope beyond hope that there's another balcony below, or that Raven's hanging off the edge or sticking to the tower walls or some other superimmortal stunt that I have no doubt she's capable of. But instead I get there in time to see her land with a sickening distant crunch on the ground below, splayed out, blood instantly pooling underneath her, neck at a sickening angle. One of her legs has changed fully into wolf, not that it did her any good.

"Oh no," I say, willing myself to look away. But I can't. I stand there, feeling more empty than I have for fifteen decades, and I stare at Raven's broken corpse. I put my hand to my face and I find it wet with tears, though I didn't feel them fall.

Then I hear the growl behind me.

"Do it," I say. "I don't care anymore. If I got her killed, I don't want to live. Fucking do it."

Nothing.

I turn round, feeling the tears now, breath hitching.

*"DO IT!"*

Golden walks up to me and runs a long nail gently down my cheek, caressing me. "I had to kill her like that. You left me no choice. There was no other way. But I don't have to kill you like this. I can do it properly."

"I don't . . . I don't know what you mean."

She snorts. "That's because you don't know the first thing about wolves. And you don't know the first thing about me. Just because I had to kill my pack mate, and now my friend, doesn't mean I stop being a wolf. I haven't gone insane. There is a way we do things. I will not dishonor my pack."

A part of me feels like saying *Why not? You dishonored your husband pretty thoroughly*. But I'm too empty to even bother. All too aware that behind me, a few hundred feet down, is the smashed cadaver of someone who I wanted—

"So I'm going to hunt you."

"What?" I stare at her like she's a new type of animal I've just found in a puddle.

"You heard me. We don't kill on the spot, unless it's self-defense. Which is what that was. Raven would've killed me. She always liked Ashen more than me. Well, that was easy, since I despised him."

"What?" I say, feeling my mind slowly shutting down.

"Oh, this isn't my confession, don't worry. This is your chance. The way it works is I give you an hourglass head start. Then I hunt you through the woods. If you can get to safety, or lose me, or kill me, then you survive." Her head tilts. Her long blond hair, down to her navel, shines brighter than ever. "Any questions?"

"No. You don't understand. I don't care. Kill me now. I'm not going to play your stupid game."

She snarls at me then, and drags her nail down my chest, not caressing anymore but drawing a thin line of blood. "It's not a clawdamn game, mage. It's what we do. It's who we are. And I won't kill you. I won't do any more damage to my pack. So if you don't want to live, then jump off and join the friend that you made me kill."

"'That you made me'?" I laugh. "You're a special one, aren't you?" I feel a little something stir. Not much, but enough. "Fine. Hunt me. But don't be surprised if I make a few friends along the way."

She grins. "Good luck. They're quite far away, mage."

And then she turns and retreats back into her study. "Your time starts now. So I'd get running if I were you."

I take a last look behind me, almost hoping to see Raven gone, knowing that any moment she'll appear back up here ready to rip Golden's head off. But she's still there, and there's a lot more blood now. I close my eyes. "I'm sorry, Raven," I say. And then, because one way or another, I doubt I'll be back in Ansbach castle, I whisper, "Goodbye."

Tears flowing like a river now, I follow Golden back into her chambers and start running.

# 29

# The Last Time You Ever Call Yourself Pathetic

Why do wolves revert to person form as they are dying? It is one of the great mysteries and the source of much debate. Those who have always asserted the truth of the wolf form—that it is the greatest of the two, that the beast has supremacy—must ask why we go to the great forest in the land in our weak people forms instead.

But perhaps we are looking at this the wrong way. Maybe we should instead be asking why on earth a wolf would want to die. People wish to die all the time. But never a wolf. I am glad that, in a manner of speaking, wolves are invincible. It is the people, as ever, who are the truly fallible ones.

Grassy Soissons,
*The Greate Questions Answered: Musings of an Underwolf*

## Jacob

I'm not enjoying being hunted by a wolf. It's not meant to be an enjoyable experience, I realize, but even so it's worth emphasizing just how shading annoying this is.

It wasn't meant to come to this. I was meant to be the hero for once. Not Sage. Me. The mage who drinks too much who solved a murder and stopped a war. But now I'm going to be disemboweled and probably eaten in the middle of a snowy forest, deep in the Wolflands, hundreds of miles from home, and I'm suddenly discovering that the price for trying to be the hero is one that I seriously can't afford.

The trees rush past me as I push myself to the edge of my speed, the edge of my abilities. Which, for a sorcerer, is not that fast. Maybe if I was an Atmos I could summon some currents to fly on. Those smug shits get around pretty speedily. But any other sorcerer, especially a magickless kind like me, can run for, what, twenty miles an hourglass for . . . a while? We don't get tired too easily but we can't keep on forever. A full wolf can run at the peak of their fitness at forty-five miles an hourglass for a full glass. I didn't use to know that. But I had a lot of time to spend reading about these bloody wolves in the past two months in the Wolflands, even before Raven put on me the frankly unfair need to solve a murder.

I realize as I think it that Raven is dead, and for a moment the thought lances through me like a venom-tipped spear, almost freezing me in my tracks.

The point is, even though I know I can't outrun the wolf on my tail, I know I can't rest, unless I want my rest to go in a little more permanent direction than I'd like. I've already wasted precious time at Ansbach castle, searching for winter furs to cover my robe. Sorcerers can tolerate the cold fine but not as much as the heat, and though I'd not die for a good while out there in just a robe, I wouldn't be much good at running fast. So I wasted time, and now I am keenly aware of the imminent arrival of Golden; I feel her breath on the back of my neck.

And then I hear the howl. It's not close, but it's not far, either. How much time have I wasted? I can't measure time through the fucking sun or the sky or any of that shit. I can't count time in my head like that smug prickard Sage.

Sage. Another person I'll never see again. Another person I failed. There's no Raven to save him now. And I never told him how grateful I am that he saved me from my old life.

More regrets, from a dead mage running.

I come to the crest of a hill. Beyond, the valley stretches out before me, a flat expanse of white. Mages are not built for running in the snow. I'm running in snow boots, and despite these I'm starting to lose sensation in my toes, and honestly things are not looking good.

At the end of the valley, hidden by a copse of eastern pines but there all the same, is the territory of Pack Gevaudan. More knowledge from my recent studies. That's where the wolves closest in allegiance to the Ansbachs are. The ones most likely to help me. More to the point, they're the only other wolfpack for a hundred miles, so most likely or not they'll have to do. But then the person on my tail knows that, too, and they won't let me get there. I have a funny feeling that they could have caught me by now, and that they might be playing with me.

I look down at the canopy of trees below the crest, a hundred feet down. I could jump, I suppose. I can't practice magick, but whatever made me strong like all the sorcerers put the Light in me, and I'd break a couple of bones and have one of the worst days of my life but I'd heal eventually. But what good would that do? It would only delay the inevitable. But if I don't jump, if I don't at least try, then a lot of people are going to die. Beginning with me, primarily.

Jump it is, then.

"Let me save you the bother."

I smile at the voice, and acceptance comes immediately with the smile. I turn and face Golden, who at some point between catching up to me and watching me contemplate the jump has shifted to person form, naked and smug amid the snow, teeth and claws still long and sharp, eyeing me with a predatory gaze.

For a moment, I pause and I imagine Raven darting out of the trees beside me, to save me. I imagine the last conversation we had, the look in her eyes. I would have liked to continue that. I would have liked to apologize properly and hear her apology. And then maybe tell her certain things, even if they're not reciprocated. Put my self-hatred aside just for a moment and reach for the moon. But it's too late for that. That is not an option anymore.

"That wasn't a particularly impressive hunt, was it?" I say.

She shrugs. "It was a hunt. I followed the rules. That's all that matters."

"Could I have done any better?"

She smiles, showing rows of sharp teeth that have stayed sharp even after the shift back to a person. "Well, simply running was a little moronic, if you don't mind me saying so. You were never going to outrun me. You would have needed half a day for that at minimum, not an hourglass."

"So what was I meant to do?"

"Set a trap. Something with trees. Start a fire. Lure me into firepowder explosives. Trick me into jumping off a ravine. There's not been that many magickless mages or vampires who've survived a wolfhunt, back when we hunted them, of course, but I believe they used those tactics."

"I honestly wouldn't have known where to start."

"Well, then, don't feel too bad." She advances toward me.

"You're not even going to tell me why you did it?" I ask. "Why you killed your mate? Why you killed Ashen?"

She shrugs as her nails lengthen back into claws. "Not to you. Why would I? How could you possibly understand the depths of my pain?"

I leave that be, and I back away some more. Her snout lengthens then, and her body follows it, great and golden, eyes blazing, jaws slavering.

"It isn't fair," I try. "I don't deserve this. This isn't how it should have ended."

But even as I speak the words, they sound ridiculous to me. I allowed myself to think I was someone else, that the drunkard who Sage found all those years ago in an inn, bitter at his destiny, at being a Quantas, the worst of the five kinds, the magickless fucks, could be someone better. The person who Sage always wanted me to be, who Raven had helped me become. But I realize now that the more you dream, the more you can't see the ground shifting below you.

Out here in the Wolflands, there's no hiding from the reality of life. No one is thinking about what you deserve. Certainly not the forest, anyway. I take comfort from the fact that, despite being a mage in a land of wolves, I'm thinking like a wolf in my final moments.

Maybe, then, people can change. But my transformation has come to an abrupt end.

"I wish," I say, facing my death, as she looms before me and opens her jaws, jaws ever so wide, "that there had been pockets in these furs for a drink."

And then those jaws close, and that's the end of me.

Or at least, that's what I wait for, eyes closed, mind at some sort of peace.

But I hear a roar instead, and feel fur brush past me, and hear a great clump and a cut-off growl.

I open my eyes, hoping they're not about to be clawed out, and I see the strangest sight.

A large wolf, larger than Golden, anyway, is on top of her. A wolf that's bleeding from dozens of places, with open holes in some. A wolf whose two hind legs don't seem to be at the right angle. A wolf who looks like it has a broken jaw. A wolf that is midnight black.

A wolf that is Raven black.

"By the five shitting magicks," I say, laughing and, I think, crying at the same time. "You have to be jesting."

And then the golden wolf below the black wolf pushes her off and Raven yelps in pain, and it doesn't seem so funny anymore.

You don't have to be a quickmind to know that on her worst day, the wolf they all fear to fight—Raven, the Black Death—could make short work of Golden.

But this isn't her worst day. It's much worse than that. She's broken and I don't know how she is still here.

And so I do not know how it is going to go.

But it starts like this. Golden, having pushed Raven onto her haunches, immediately leaps at her. Raven tries to bound to the side, but she is slow, so slow, and so Golden's bulk lands on her, and Golden's long, thin wolf jaw, smaller and weaker-looking than Raven's but still capable of ripping your head off, by the looks of it, snaps at Raven's face and almost clamps over it. Raven pulls away just in time, but Golden is on her now, and her claws dig into Raven's haunches and I see Raven's eyes wince in pain.

Then, just as Golden goes to bite into her underbelly, Raven somehow summons the energy and momentum to push Golden off her, blood streaming from the new claw marks in her side. Golden readies herself to jump onto Raven's back, but Raven has rolled to the side and then leapt up, facing Golden again, broken jaw drooling, eyes wild with pain and ferocity. She almost stumbles on what must be a broken leg, or a leg having an extremely bad day, at least, but she stays upright, and when Golden leaps forward, she flops down onto her belly at the last second, leaving Golden to fly over her and land hard just beyond her.

Then she whips round, yelping in pain at the movement required, and bites Golden deep on the hind leg. Now it's Golden's turn to roar, and she shakes herself out of Raven's jaws—jaws that never let anything go except for today, when the agony of using them must be immense—and scurries away, then turns back to face her and almost simultaneously leaps, but Raven has leapt as well, and the pair collide in midair.

The sound made at that collision makes me wince, a sickening, bone-crunching thump that I fear must only come from Raven. Raven falls out of the air like a sack of rocks and lands painfully and at all unnatural angles in a snowdrift under a tree.

I don't know how much longer I can watch, but I can't leave her. But I also can't help. Any other sorcerer could have helped her. No, scratch that: any other sorcerer wouldn't have got themselves into this position. But I am a magickless mage and my impotency hurts. In my home in the Desertlands is an underground cavern full of devices strange and powerful. I don't have any with me here. Sage would have had something with him.

But I realize, finally and inevitably, I'm not my mentor. I'm not my friend. I do not best the circumstances of my shitty birth with the arc of my skills.

I am a Quantas born, and a Quantas ever shall I be. And I've done absolutely piss all to account for that in my two centuries.

So I watch the fight, my hands stuck in my useless robe pockets, like a child watching—

My pockets. I feel something.

Golden whisked the wolfsbane away from her study. But there is a stick of it left in my pocket that must have broken off when I originally revealed it.

But it's a tiny amount.

*Any amount of wolfsbane can kill.*

Look at that, I do listen to people. But what's the point? What am I going to do, ask Golden to take a quick food rest? Remind her that it's almost mealtime?

And then, as I watch, Golden barrels into Raven so hard underneath the tree Raven has sought temporary refuge under that the entire tree shakes and a branch snaps off and falls on Raven's head, dazing her. Golden takes advantage by biting into her side, and Raven half growls, half yelps, and I see one of her wolf legs shimmer and coalesce into a human arm. Then she picks up the branch that almost concussed her and hits Golden over the head with it.

Golden immediately lets Raven go with a yelp and staggers back, then Raven's other leg transforms into an arm and she leaps onto Golden's back, now with two wolf legs and two human arms like some grotesque Kinet experiment gone wrong, like a drawing etched out by a madman too long in the desert. She starts using her longer human arms with extended wolf claws to rip into Golden's neck.

Golden howls in rage and pain and tries to shake Raven off her back; Raven almost falls but clings grimly on. Then Raven's face twists and flickers and eddies in the air, and suddenly she is a wolf with a human face, broken-jawed, bruised, blood streaming from deep wounds, one eye swollen. She looks very concerned at this development, and that's when I realize she's losing control.

In her pain and brokenness, she is reverting to human to die.

That's one thing I do remember from my wolf reading when I arrived, and the slow terror of what's about to happen freezes me in my place.

And tells me what I have to do.

Oh, by the five fucking magicks, even by my standards this is a bad idea.

Without thinking, I rush forward from my spot above the glen toward Golden, who is still growling and yelping, trying to dislodge Raven as the Midnight Assassin rips chunks from her neck. Raven is barely hanging on, her own eyes glazed, her arm movements becoming increasingly weak. Blood oozes from her person ear, and her wolf torso is slowly shifting to human, her whole body like some kind of warped taxidermy unstitching itself before my eyes.

Golden barely registers me, so concerned is she with Raven. I think about throwing the tiny piece of wolfsbane into her open jaw. Then I think, *What if I miss?* Or if she just spits it out—would it still have worked, then?

And then I remember the actions of someone I called the bravest person I've ever met in a clearing not two months ago. A maidservant with balls of fucking brass. And I laugh, part despair, part inevitability.

"Oh, you crazy bastard, Jacob. This is going to hurt."

I run up to the slavering, howling Golden with the tiny stick of new wolfsbane in my fist and I ram that fist straight down her open jaw, and then I let go.

Three things happen then.

The first is that she knows exactly what I've done; she smells her own herb, her own death, and the moment it hits the back of her throat her eyes go wild with fear and fury.

The second is that she tries to spit it out, but she can't as I reach with my other arm to hold the back of her head and I jam my first arm farther down that warm, terrifying gullet.

The third thing that happens is that she bites down on my arm with all the force of a thousand pounds of pressure and her teeth slice through my flesh and hit bone, and I scream, and oh by the Light, that fucking hurts, and I feel her fangs graze my bone and scrape it as my blood flows out of her mouth in a great stream.

"*Aggghhhhhhhhhhh*," goes my voice in a guttural shriek of unending agony.

She tries to bite my arm off completely but she can't as I'm too far down her throat for her to clamp on enough. So she chews desperately, and snot and tears flow down my face as I feel my arm being shredded to pieces.

And then Raven jumps off her back and punches Golden in the side of the head with all her remaining strength, even as the Midnight Assassin has almost fully reverted to person form, and in her shock Golden releases her grip on my arm and I stagger back, and then in reflex she swallows. Her eyes blaze and she howls in fury and then she goes to choke up what she has swallowed but she can't heave it out, too concussed from Raven's blow, and Raven hits her again, even as she falls to her knees herself, her strength almost gone.

Then the Golden wolf shimmers and strobes, and snout becomes mouth and fur becomes skin and she shrinks in size as kaleidoscopic colors strobe before my eyes and flesh expands and shrinks and snippets of blood and bone wink in and out of existence like a deformed galaxy of anatomy imploding in on itself, and then there is just a naked blond woman collapsed against a tree, heaving, black veins already pulsing on her face.

Raven collapses next to her, eyes rolling in pain.

I stare and I think about the worst most inappropriate gallows-humor joke I've ever said, and then, for once without feeling guilty for it, I shove the poor threesome jest into the recesses of my brain and I suddenly become aware of the blinding, phenomenal agony of my arm, which is little but exposed bone and strips of flesh. I vomit into the snow, then collapse next to Raven, cradling my ruined joints.

As Golden's breathing gets more labored and her face starts to throb and darken, Raven turns to her, wincing at the movement, and whispers, blood pooling out of her mouth with every word. "*Why?* Tell me why, Golden. While there's still time."

Golden's eyes, dark and purple and wild with pain, briefly focus on her, and she tries to mouth the words, but her mouth is too swollen and she can hardly get her breath.

Raven holds Golden's hand and squeezes it. "*Please, Golden. Please tell me why. You have to tell me. TELL ME.*"

But she can see Golden is too far gone now, and as her purple-and-black body and face slowly fade back to normal skin color, and her eyes lose their vitality, and her breaths start to go shallow, Raven gives up and simply squeezes her hand harder.

Then the life is gone from Golden Ansbach, and her head flops to the side, and Raven lets go of her hand and collapses her head onto the tree.

Her eyes register my presence, then swivel toward me. "That . . . was brave, mage." She tries to smile but coughs up a lump of something gristly and red instead.

"It . . ." I try to get the words out as my body screams in lightning agony. "It wasn't brave. It was insane."

"No." She finally manages to grin. "I have seen insane. I know insane. That was just brave."

I grin back, even as tears stream down my face. "Well, don't go expecting it again. I'm running out of arms here."

"You will heal."

"I hope so. I need both my arms to—oh, by the fucking Light, that hurts—hold multiple drinks in my hands."

"Do you remember the way back?" she asks, voice fainter.

"What?" I turn to her, even as the action makes me shriek as I twist my arm. "What do you mean, where are *you* going?"

"Do not be stupid, Jacob. I am done. I fell off a tower."

"Yes, I was meaning to ask you about that. . . ." I stop, deciding that this is definitely not the right time, and then her words properly hit me. "No, don't talk stupid, Raven. You're not done. You're Raven Ansbach, the Midnight Assassin, and we're going to get back and heal up and then . . ."

She grabs my hand then, and I can see how much the action hurts her. She slowly turns her face my way, her onyx hair covering half her face, eyes half hidden in shadow as ever, mouth open with that curl exposing her canines, that Raven look, that face I can never get enough of.

"I am old and I am done, Jacob. The world is moving on without me. I do not even know why Ashen died. I am tired and I am broken. I am tired of being angry all the time, every day, every year. I cannot do this forever. I'm sorry. This is not fair on you. But you have to let me die now." Her head collapses back with the effort of the words, and more blood pools from her mouth. Her eyes start to close.

I want to lie back and give in to the pain of my arm, too. Lie back in the snow and rest while Raven dies.

But instead, something in me snaps and I grab her shoulder and shake her, hard. Then, Light help me, I slap her.

Her eyes snap open. Her voice is like leaves in a gust. "Did you just fucking slap me?"

"I . . . did."

"I am trying to die here."

"Well," I say, finding my way slowly. "You can't."

"I . . . can't?"

"Yes," I continue, every step a cautious one. "Because I won't let you."

A long pause, and for one moment of sheer terror, I worry she's died with her eyes open. "Why?"

"Because . . ." I go to say one reason, go to say how I feel, but I know in that instance that it's founded on selfishness. On what I want. And if she doesn't want it back, where does that leave me? And even if she does, what power can that have over someone who's lived for so long who finally wants to die? I'm not that enchanting. So I think more. And then I know exactly what to say.

"Back before I met Sage, I lived in the city of Quantile, where most of the Quantas live. Not a great place. Very depressing. Sorcerers who can't practice magick feeling very bitter about it and all that. After a lot of sulking in my initial years, I finally decided to do something. I convinced a group of fellow Quantas to band together in a sect, just like the other sorcerer types, too, and start to petition, and build a proper community on the outskirts, where we could work out our place in sorcerer society. What we wanted to do in this pitiless, unforgiving world."

I pause and sigh. Other than Sage, long ago, I've never told anyone this. A deep well of shame and fear threatens to overwhelm me. I feel the crest of its wave, but, maybe because of the greater agony of my arm, it doesn't have a hold on me like it normally does. I gird myself to carry on.

"I got too bold, I suppose. Didn't think it through. Left us too exposed, I . . ." I breathe in, then out, using the agony of my arm to steady myself. "The Atmos sect, who hate us the most, sent some . . . assassins, I suppose you'd call them in vampirespeak. Not sanctioned by the Archmage. They wiped us out in an hour. I fled, covered in the blood of my friends. The only survivor."

I grip my arm as the memories try to equal the pain.

"A true coward. So you see, I've been where you are. I've wanted to give up. I've seen the future, and not seen it get any easier. I looked at myself and I hated who I was. And I sat in the desert in a city of people, who hated themselves, too, and I decided to just let myself go. And if the pathetic Quantas, the pointless Lightdamn Jacob, can have fought that feeling and struggle on, then you, Raven, you who does what no one else can or no one else will, you can do it, too."

Raven stares at me for a while, her breath a wheeze and her body stinking of iron, even in the cold where my nose has given up. Then she whispers, low. "Lean into me."

I lean in. Her breath is metal and pine.

"That is the last time you ever call yourself pathetic, Jacob. As long as I am alive."

That's when I know. That's when I know how I feel, and that's how I know she'll live.

She coughs. More blood.

"So what's going to happen now," I say, more alive than I've felt in years, "is I'm going to take this bottle of Wolfsbane whiskey that I have under my furs, and which I really should have used to numb this fucking agony of my arm already, and you're going to down half of it. And then you're going to get up. And then I'm going to drag you back."

"How are you going to do that? In the snow with your arm and my size and—"

"Well," I say, procuring the bottle and removing the stopper. "Because I'm going to drink the other half."

30

# One Wolf to Lead Them All

For better or worse, remember this:
For wolves, actions speak louder than words.

Dandelion Gevaudan, *The Forest Life*

## Raven

We stagger along, my mage savior and I. The shame of having needed help in the battle is only mildly lessened by the knowledge that I saved his life in the first place and also had just fallen from a very high tower.

As I explain to Jacob in long, drawn-out whispers on our torturously slow journey back, I slightly shifted my entire body into wolf form as I landed. Not enough to prevent some continually agonizing injuries, although pain is a thing to me I have long made peace with—it is the weakness injuries lead to I cannot abide—but enough to not kill me. It is a trick I learned long ago from a wolf with more skills than any alive today whom most have forgotten about. It is often the way. We think of advancement in knowledge as a line, rising over the centuries. But there are often dips, where lost knowledge stains otherwise more enlightened eras.

Listen to me. How wise I am when I am half delirious with pain and drink.

And now I lean on a sorcerer, a sorcerer a good foot smaller than me, as we stagger along in the snow. In truth I do not know how much it is him that is helping or the half pint of Wolfsbane whiskey I downed. But I am here, and we are staggering.

And as we stagger, I reflect on how he saved me not once but twice. Once with an arm down Golden's throat, an arm that now hangs uselessly by his side, bone shining through the wraps of ripped flesh. From what little I know of sorcerers' bodies, it will heal completely or mostly in time, but it will take longer than a wolf and be considerably more painful.

The second time he saved me was when I had given up. For a moment, all the centuries and all the loss became too much to bear. My anger, never ceasing, but for so long impotent, became too much to bear. My failure to see Golden for what she was, became too much to bear.

I must contend with that shame, too.

But for now, at least, the edge of that shame is taken off by being in the company of Jacob.

Maybe I will even tell him.

Or, if we do not make it back, eat him.

Option, options.

An hour into our pathetic journey through the forest it becomes clear we are not going to make it back. We are both flagging, the whiskey wearing off, my horrific injuries and the strain on Jacob of dragging me along and the shock from his arm beginning to tell.

And then we hear the howling. To our west, away from the route back to the castle.

But nearer than the castle.

I do not want to say it. It is not a good option.

But Jacob, whom I underestimated for so long and I will never do so again, says it for me, his own voice almost as quiet as mine now.

"Are the council nearer?"

"Yes," I whisper.

"Let's go then," he says.

"It . . . it will not go well for you. To interrupt that."

Jacob considers this. "Do I have more of a chance than if I collapse in the forest before we ever get back to the castle?"

"Mildly."

"Well, then."

"Jacob?"

"Yes?"

"Nothing."

"Thanks, Raven."

I do not want to say my words of true thanks to him now. I do not want it to be a product of my pain and my weakness.

If we survive this, he shall know. A little, anyway.

We trek for another hourglass through the forest west toward the howling, which is occasional and comes mainly from all the assembled Ansbachs. Mainly howls of support when whichever Ansbach is replacing me is speaking, or general background noise.

It must be frustrating for the other alphas to be having a meeting in the middle of such a show of force from my own pack, but it is the only reason I can be reasonably confident that Jacob and I will not be immediately killed by Silver or his unders or whichever alphas he has under his thumb now as soon as we arrive.

Suddenly, we come out of the forest onto a semisteep incline down into a great open clearing. Here trees have given way to shrubland and a vast expanse of field, fenced north and south by tributaries of the same river that almost fully encircles Ansbach territory. The vast midafternoon winter sky covers the snow-covered field in soft sunlight, and its blue expanse for a moment makes me feel completely insignificant.

It is not a feeling I am used to, and I can only blame my weak state for it.

Perhaps this is how you are meant to feel, when you are not as proud and as foolish as me.

My Ansbachs, my precious Ansbachs, are lined up in wolf form on the western side of the clearing in one great huddle. There must be two hundred of them, almost half the pack. All those who were in the castle, and more who have joined them from the forests around.

To their east, and a hundred feet in front of us, Silver holds court in person form, naked, his two underwolves a few yards behind him. Watching him, in a fairly uneven line, stand the rest of the pack alphas, also in person form, also naked.

It looks and sounds like he is getting into his stride. This meeting to choose a new council alpha has been going on for hours, so this could well be his closing argument. Not that it will matter, I imagine. He had the numbers before this meeting started.

I have been chasing murderers and communing with sorcerers, and he has been sewing up his ascendancy.

Stupid, stupid Raven.

I stare at his smug face and self-satisfied smile as one by one Jacob's and my presence begins to be noticed.

I smell the soft scent of pine on the air, growing excitement from some. Also a strong aroma, I am pleased to report, of chalk, concern from my Ansbachs at the Stubbe takeover they are witnessing. If the roles were reversed, if the Stubbes had been witnesses to an Ansbach ascendancy, I wonder if they would have sat there so calmly.

But my pack know better than to think everything can be fixed with the claw. We look at the moon and we know better. I am proud of them.

I am worried for Jacob.

I am also finding it hard to stand anymore.

## Jacob

Any benefit the Wolfsbane whiskey—and one of these days I need to ask someone why the most popular spirit in the Wolflands is named after certain death for the wolfkind—gave to me has long gone and now pain is my close friend, so close it's making my vision go hazy and my limbs, the ones that aren't completely shredded, go cold.

Raven making my shoulder go numb by leaning it on it for two hourglasses hasn't helped magnificently, either.

But to be fair I am in better shape than Raven, who's now close to collapse.

So I have no choice but to wander down the verge from the forest into the clearing, with every single eye of the watching Ansbachs on me, a sea of colored furs, every shade, every hue. A small army of wolf eyes absolutely stunned.

Not as stunned as Silver, though, who was not expecting his wonderful oratory to be interrupted by two broken idiots moving at a snail's pace toward his circle.

The other alphas watch me with a mixture of concern and confusion. Verdant's big friendly mouth drops open in shock. Berry's wide eyes narrow, as if she can outsquint the strange sight before her. Morbach's haughty expression turns a puce shade of outrage. The remaining wolf, a chestnut-furred one who I assume is representing the Ansbachs on the council, stares, too, expression unreadable.

I wonder if it's not just the injuries and the interruption that have so perplexed everyone, but the fact that Raven is so injured at all.

Is this the first time they have seen her so broken?

Is that why no one rushes to her aid?

Are they waiting for her great plan to reveal itself, or even more tantalizingly, her great fury?

They might be waiting awhile.

Finally I arrive in the middle of them. Silver in front of me, his face enraged, fists closed by his sides. The alphas behind me. Ansbach crowd to my left.

"Right, Raven," I whisper. "This is where you speak, please."

Raven turns to me, heaves herself off my shoulder, and clears her throat.

And then she collapses to the floor and lies there, semiconscious.

Fuck.

For a second there's complete silence.

I can feel there are mere moments left before this all breaks. Before someone rushes in to help her, to take her back to the castle. To maybe help me or gut me. But either way, there is an opportunity here. Maybe I'm delirious. I think I'm definitely delirious. Half your arm hanging off will do that to you. But there is something here. Something on the edge. I can sense it.

All my life I've hated myself and thought myself useless. I know I can't do this, or at least shouldn't be able to.

But I don't have to like myself, at least right now.

I just have to like Raven.

"WOLVES," I shout, as several of the alphas start toward me. I face the council, but to my delight, my voice carries far across the clearing. Light bless whatever last gasp of energy has given me this.

Everyone stops again. It's funny how far curiosity will get you.

*Come on, Jacob. What would Sage say?*

*No. No. What will* you *say.*

"I have no right to speak," I begin. "I have no right to be here."

"Exactly," says a voice from behind me, as Silver advances, but to my amazement, Berry Gevaudan points to him and shakes her head, and Silver, the endless coward, stops.

"I am not wolf," I continue. "But she is." I point to the semicomatose Midnight Assassin at my feet. "And she cannot speak. So I am speaking for her. If anyone disputes that, then kill me now."

I wait. You can hear a pin drop in the clearing, and you could probably also hear the rabbit-tail beat of my Lightdamn terrified heart.

I continue to remain unkilled.

"Raven Ansbach has avenged Ashen Ansbach. The injuries you see before you are a result of that."

I tell them then a brief version of what happened. I have to hawk out a large gob of blood and gristle at some point, which doesn't bode well, but I get it out.

Shocked faces replace curiosity. Some of the Ansbach faces in the watching crowd go pale. It occurs to me they were probably friends with Golden, too. They don't challenge my account, though.

"I never doubted Raven," says Silver, having found the lugubrious prick tones in his voice, and having regained the confidence shorn from him when Raven emerged from the forest line. He must have thought she was coming for him. Now he sees the truth of it, and even without a wolf's nose I can almost smell the relief on him.

"And we will thank her, and deal with this shocking news later. But now we must get you both to the castle, and what is happening here must continue. This is wolf business, mage." He spreads his arms out magnanimously, like a vampire prayhall preacher. "Can someone—"

"No," I say. Then I shout again. "*NO.* I will speak for Raven."

Silver signals to his two underwolves, but Berry steps forward. "Leave him, Silver. You heard him. He speaks for Raven. She deserves to have a voice here."

"What in the bloodmoon are you talking about? This isn't how it goes. Those aren't the rules." Silver's voice has lost a little of his oil and now sounds plaintive and pathetic in the winter air.

"The rules? What rules are those, the ones where you threaten me and my pack?" says Verdant, his booming tones cutting across Silver's. "Don't play the referee with me, boy."

"This isn't a rules-based system, you know that," says the clipped, boring voice of the chestnut-furred Ansbach representative. "We do this our own way on the day, and only the final vote is essential."

"But you can try and stop him if you want," says Berry, winking at me and extending her claws to show that her words have force.

I see Bronzed has a glower on his face, but he stays quiet.

Silver's unders turn to Silver for guidance, and the alpha Stubbe stares at the wolves across from him, then at the hordes of Ansbachs to his right.

"You fucking Ansbachs . . ." he growls, tongue licking his lips nervously. But he nods at his unders, and they back away from me back to his side.

*Right*, I say to myself. *Now to get this right.*

"Look at how Raven has suffered for you," I begin, pointing at her slumped form. "She has avenged your alpha. And paid for it. While you were all here, playing politics, she was hunting and avenging and falling off a fucking tower to do the right thing. Just like she always has. Just as she helped save you all during Extinction Valley. Just as she brought you the heads of the ones who killed your friends and family, when no one thought she could."

I see Verdant smile at me for that one.

"Just as she worked with the vampires this last century, because she had to, even though she hated it. Always alone. Always for the good of the wolfkind."

This started off a speech, but now, by the Light, now I *feel* it.

"*LOOK HOW SHE SUFFERS*," I say again, pointing. "And I know you respect her, but maybe you're complacent. Maybe you assume she'll always be here, always help you when you need it. Well, she almost wasn't today. But she survived when no one else would. So maybe it's time to stop being complacent. Maybe it's time you took her out of the shadows. Maybe it's time a wolf I know most of you would follow and most of you would die for actually led you."

Silver laughs, high and crazed. "As if she would ever want that."

I smile. I couldn't have planned it better myself.

"*EXACTLY*," I shout, using the very last reserves of my energy to put all the power into my voice. "She doesn't want it. And that's why she's *perfect* for it."

I can't speak anymore. I'm done. I glance to the other alphas. Berry gets it. Verdant, too, I think, I hope. The Ansbach representative smiles. Will it be enough? Will they put my crazed speech into wolf terms and stitch the plan into something before Silver can axe this new train of thought?

I don't know, but I know I'm done.

I collapse, and as darkness clouds my vision and I slip into unconsciousness, I smile.

It won't work.

It can't work.

But fuck, did it feel good.

# 31

# It's Just Sad

A Quantas born and a Quantas ever shall I be.

Anonymous sorcerer ditty

## Jacob

A day and a half on from my far-too-close brush with death by wolf jaws, I lie in bed in my room in Ansbach castle, my ruined arm a good sight less ruined, as sorcerers heal quickly. Not as quickly as vampires and wolves, but close enough. It's still in a bandage, though, and will be for several more days before the entire arm grows back. After a week there will be no sign at all that it was ever mauled to the bone. Currently it is numb, with the help of a herb from, fittingly, Golden's garden. Wastewhile, I think. I wasn't really listening properly at the time.

Raven, who never knocks, I've realized, enters my bedchamber. This is the first time we've been alone since it all happened. The first day I mostly spent asleep, and today Raven has been constantly surrounded by other wolves, I was told by my wolf nurse, a fact that she has not looked particularly happy about, but then she has always had resting rage face, so it's hard to tell.

She's wearing her ceremonial furs, which makes sense because she's about to go to a ceremony. This time I won't be invited, which I'm quite glad about. Not sure I'm much of a lucky amulet when it comes to wolf meetings.

Incredibly, almost all of Raven's injuries are completely healed. Well, perhaps not incredible for a wolf. The only sign that the Midnight Assassin fell hundreds of feet from a tower and then fought a fight to the death are a few lingering bruises and scratches on her arms and neck, and a slight swelling still to her previously extremely broken jaw.

Raven lets the silence linger.

I break first.

"I can't believe it worked," I begin.

"Neither can I," she replies. She appraises me properly then. I do the same back to her. Her long wild hair looks a little straighter, though not much. I thought she might braid it for the ceremony, but then I suppose I wasn't thinking. She has put some kohl on her eyes, though, not that they ever needed it, already dark and brooding, but it's the first time I've seen her with any kind of face paint.

She must sense—or more accurately smell—my surprise as she says, "It highlights the eyes, which represent the discs of the moon. Moon packs daub their eyes on very formal occasions, claw packs daub their nails, and tree packs paint their arms."

I nod, thinking this through. "That last tree part made no sense, though, you realize that, don't you? The tree packs just couldn't think of a body part like a tree, the lazy bastards."

Raven ignores this, but I see her trying to suppress a smile.

I jump on it. "You're starting to find my jests amusing, aren't you? Admit it. Smiling is better than scowling."

She raises an eyebrow at me. "Let us not go too fast there, mage," she says. "I will tell you what is amusing, though. That a sorcerer stood before the alphas of the council and told them who to choose as their next leader, and they listened." She pauses. "As I lost consciousness, I had fully expected to come round to see you being eaten." Another pause. "At that point, I would have been so hungry I probably would have joined in."

"Oh, now you're allowed to make jests, too? Very well, I retract it." I lean back on the bench, cradling my arm. "Why did it work?"

"Well, as much as it would amuse you to know that you alone were responsible for a complete reversal at the heart of wolf politics, in reality you triggered a much longer discussion that followed. I suppose you could say you broke the spell that Silver had woven over some of them with threats and promises. Silver's majority—himself, Verdant, Morbach—fell apart when faced with what had happened, and the reminder to them all that for wolves, actions should always matter more than oiled words.

"Essentially, Verdant found some courage against the threats Silver had thrown his way about his territory being nibbled at. That just left Bronzed. Bronzed, like all Morbachs, is a coward, just like the bloods they so often ape with their behavior. As soon as he saw the tide turning, he buckled, too. Silver was on his own in the end."

"So what happens now? Now you're the big dog, in every sense."

"Well," says Raven, "now I tell them we are going to war if the new First Light needs us. Not everyone will agree, but once this ceremony is over I will be both alpha of the Ansbachs and Outside Council leader, and a leader with new authority is normally listened to. So we will talk, and discuss, and come to the right decision."

"Wow, just like that. You know, it's funny, it's just when I used the word *leader* a few days ago at the start of this all to try and understand your wolf system, you gave me a considerable amount of grieving over it."

Raven glares at me. "And I will continue to give you some grieving if you go down that line of reasoning."

I go to smile, but then something occurs to me. "Wait, you said 'new First Light'? If *new* First Light needs you?"

Raven grins. I'm not used to this new smiling Raven, and I'm not sure I'll get used to it. "Yes, there has been . . . some news. It is why Sam and Sage came. There was a rebellion. Sam's idea, in fact. It worked. The Lords were kicked out of First Light. They have retreated to the Centerlands, moved into Lightfall. But it is likely they will try and retake First Light soon enough once they have marshaled their strength. And so I am going to pledge our aid, the aid of the Wolflands, to the new rebel alliance, should they need it."

I absorb this. It's a lot to take in, and I feel like a lot of it dribbles down me, so to speak. "Fuck."

"Exactly, mage."

"Oh, shades! I almost forgot. Sam and Sage, they've been released unharmed?"

Raven thinks on this. "Let us just say there is more news."

"Raven . . ."

"One of Silver's thugs tried to kill them. They escaped. Jumped off a waterfall in the process. They were hunted. They killed the wolf. They returned here of their own volition, arrived shortly after your big speech and my ascension. Too late to help, but they were not in a fit state anyway. They are recovered now."

I try to absorb this, too. "I'm not really a great advocate of being told insane things in big reveals like that, I think, without drink." I narrow my eyes. "Any drink for me?"

Raven stares at me, deadpan. "You are in recovery."

"You're a lot of fun."

"I can be," she says, tilting her head at me, hint of another smile on her face, and I lose all ability to reply to that, so we just sit in silence for a while. Funny how my confidence with women wilts with this one. Somewhere above, a honegull flies over the gardens from the aviary, a small parchment tied to its leg. I recognize it as the kind addressed to the vampires. Red-and-white feathers. A message going to First Light. Raven sees me looking.

"It is to tell them that the wolves have pledged their aid, and that Sam will be with them overnight. We are giving her a lot of wolfblood—she has earned it—and she is going to fly to First Light on it, a five-hour journey. They need her now, and they need her quickly."

I nod, and imagine a weeklong journey walking taking five hours in flight. A marvel.

"Raven," I say eventually. "Did you want this? I was so caught up in the moment and, honestly, the pain, that I didn't stop to think. Do you want this?"

Raven stretches out her legs on the chair. She inspects her nails for a while, lengthening and shortening them at will, but not from anger this time.

"Ashen said something to me," Raven says eventually, "in our last conversation before he died. He said I was not in times made for me."

"Do you believe him?"

Another long pause. "No. I do not. For a long time I thought my problem was I was too angry. Too willing to kill and get revenge and be of the wolf. And my guilt at that forced me to be someone I was not, in order to keep the peace. But, thanks to you, or possibly thanks to the revelation I had due to the horrific life-threatening injuries—"

"Let us say both," I add helpfully.

"—I realize now that my problem has never really been anger. No, it has been fear. Fear that I am only one thing. Rage. Claw. Midnight, black and red all over. Death. However you want to put it. Fear that I will lean into my true nature too much or not enough, but can never get a balance. But I forgot one thing."

"What's that?" I ask.

"The Ansbachs are of the moon. I am not only my fury. I can be more things than that. Perhaps. Maybe even a good . . . leader." She looks sideways at me, daring me to challenge her.

"Honestly, Raven?" I say. "I don't think you'll be a good leader." I let that linger as long as I dare. "I think you'll be a fucking fantastic one."

"Hmm," snorts Raven. "And now I remember why you are an idiot."

"Back to the insults, I see."

Raven turns to me then, and pushes her hair out of her face so I can see all of her features. She holds my stare, and not nervous for once, I hold hers back.

"But if I am to be this wondrous leader you speak of," she says, slowly, "I will need you by my side."

"Ha!" I laugh. "Well, no worries there, I'm not going anywhere until I'm fully certain my arm is healed and that I've drunk all the free ale that I feel my heroics have warranted." I start to laugh, but the intensity of Raven's stare holds me.

"You misunderstand me," she says. "I want you by my side . . . permanently." Something occurs to her then, and she quickly adds, her expression holding firm, "As my advisor, I suppose you would term it in your kind." But I see the tiniest blush there, just a little, and my heart does cartwheels, the stupid bastard.

I try to laugh again but my throat goes dry. "I'm waiting for the complicated jest to be revealed here."

"I am serious." Her eyes hold me.

"What . . ." I try.

"Not forever. But until we have finished what we started, together, in First Light. Until the Grays are gone and the Centerlands are free, and the Lords have felt my teeth in their heart chambers."

"That sounds a lot like forever." I feel the heat of the desert, and of a faraway home.

"Jacob, I am asking—"

"I'm not a wolf, Raven, I don't understand. I'm . . . me . . . the one you just called an idiot." My hands have gone sweaty now and I feel my pulse throbbing in my neck.

"I do not care that you are not a wolf, you can still be at my side. As an advisor," she adds again quickly. "Equal to my others. I am Raven Ansbach, and I will not care about things I do not want to care about. And as for you being an idiot . . ." She drops her head for a moment and laughs. A rare and, oh gods, a beautiful, laugh. "For moon's sake, Jacob, that is just a jest, and you know it is. If you cannot get rid of this thing of yours now, then when . . ."

She stops, and sighs, and tries again. "You solved a murder that no one else could. You saved my life. You stopped Silver. You helped put me here. You are not the sorcerer who almost gave up all those years ago in Quantile, Jacob. You are not the man playing second fiddle to Sage all these years. You are the man who chose to be a leader, once. But more than that, you are a wolf, Jacob. *And* a sorcerer. The best of both. Bravery and wisdom."

I bow my head, struggling to take in the words, struggling to accept them, a lifetime of struggle. "But I'm a Quantas," I say, watching as a tear drips from my face to my lap. "'A Quantas born and a Quantas ever shall I be.'"

Raven holds out a hand and lifts my chin up and puts her other hand round my face. "And right now is that not a fucking brilliant thing to be?"

I don't reply. I'm afraid of how happy I'll be if I do.

"So what do you say?" she asks, holding my gaze, both hands still on my face.

I briefly close my eyes, and then when I open them she's still holding me, and staring at me.

"I say, When do I start?"

She smiles then, a great wide smile, sharp canines and all, and she cocks her head at me. She still holds my head—one hand under my chin, one on the side of my face—and for a moment, I think—

But then she lets me go, and the moment passes, and I realize I've accepted something very different from what I really want.

But it won't stop me feeling happy.

Sage comes in after Raven. He looks more tired than the last time I saw him, kneeling in front of Silver Stubbe, which makes sense after the brief tale Raven just told me, but his eyes have life in them, and I see he's shaved off his beard and done something a little better with his hair. His robe is clean now, too, and his grin is wide when he claps eyes on me.

"It's been a while, old friend," he says, grasping my outstretched hand. I wince a little at my arm as he sits down on a plain pine chair next to my bed.

"It's only been a few weeks," I reply.

"Yes, but that's the longest we've been apart for, what, a century?"

I grimace. "Well, that unending proximity to you explains a lot of things in my life."

"Oh, because you're doing a lot better now," he says, indicating my arm.

"Point made."

There's a slightly awkward silence then, and Sage, rare for him, misinterprets it. "I know you must be angry at me."

"Going to have to be more specific there, Sage. We've known each other too long, this could concern a thousand things."

Sage doesn't take the bait, and I see genuine sadness on his face. I sit up, girding myself for a serious conversation I'd hoped to avoid.

"For leaving you in the Wolflands, to go off and meet Sinassion. I know it wasn't fair. And I'm sorry."

"Are you?" I ask, inspecting his countenance.

"Yes."

"Then tell me everything, and for once, no more secrets."

And, to his credit, he does; at least it feels like it. He tells me about how he founded the cult with Sinassion, and what happened with him back in First Light. He tells me all the details of the First Light revolution. And then he finishes off with his recent travails being hunted in the forest with Sam, which is clever, really, because it's hard to be angry about him keeping all the secrets about this former life with Sinassion when I've just heard his frankly traumatic tale about watching the subject of his obvious infatuation grow her face back.

"That is a lot," I conclude, uselessly.

"It is, yes."

More silence.

I sigh. "Go on, Sage, out with it. I know you too well. Stop brooding and say it."

He exhales then, half laugh, half sigh, and he stares away from me at the window as he talks.

"I never told you about Sinassion partly because I felt ashamed, I suppose. That the man who'd killed so many had once been my friend. But more than that, I felt like I wanted a fresh start. I wanted the cult to have a proper origin. A narrative to sustain it through the centuries. But it was an unwise . . . an irrational . . . no, no, a *shitty* thing to do to not trust you with that information, to not trust my friend. And it was stupid to just abandon you for my thirst for knowledge. I didn't know how to explain it to you, and I couldn't wait, for fear I'd never learn Sinassion's secrets. I panicked, and I abandoned you. And I'm sorry."

I squint at him. "You are?"

"I am."

I shrug. "Well, that's that then."

He turns to me and narrows his eyes. "That's it?"

"Yes, that's it. I had most of my arm bitten off by a murderer a day or so ago and I'm inclined to enjoy myself a little now, and I'm not going to sulk over something that happened centuries ago. I missed you. I'm really glad you're here."

Sage grins. "I always knew you were soft at heart."

And then, in a smooth motion, he whips out a tall, thin, glass-corked bottle from his cloak, which has the imprint of a lightning bolt melded into the glass.

"Lucemead!" I cry, so loud he actually flinches.

"Yes. From the Atmos distillery, it looks like. That cheery fellow Verdant Soissons brought it with him to the castle for some reason, and he felt like you might need it more."

"To be clear," I add, nodding at the bottle, "*that* is why I am glad you're here."

He hands me the bottle to take the first swig. "Some drinks with an old friend?"

"Why not?" I say, then stop as something occurs to me. "Look, Sage, there's something I need to—"

"Raven has asked you to stay here as her advisor, and you've accepted."

My jaw drops. "She told you already?"

"No," says Sage, "but . . ."

I hold my hand up to stop him. "Please, no. I've had decades of you showing off, and I've been dying for a drink. Let's just assume you're very clever." He shrugs as I plan what to say. "You see, the thing is . . ."

This time it's Sage who holds up his hand to stop me. "Do you know why I asked you to be my second brother in the cult, Jacob?"

I frown. "Because you needed someone to remind you to sleep every now and again?" But I see his serious face has returned.

"It's not just because we got on well, when I found you, or that I needed someone who . . . had some qualities I didn't, with people and other things. It's not just because you were there at the right time, and you felt like a good fit. It's not just because I saw a drive in you, beyond your jesting and drinking. Although it *was* all those things. It's because soon after we met—and just before I formally asked you to join me—I investigated the deaths of your Quantile friends, your attempt at forming a new sorcerer sect. I spent a couple of days looking at it properly, like an inquirer. And do you know what I concluded?"

"No," I say, my throat suddenly feeling parched and my voice coming out croaky.

"I concluded that you had had some very bad luck to be targeted by a rogue Atmos squadron, and that you'd actually been very careful. And very good. That the Quantas sect you were making could have been a real force for good, could have given our kind a real purpose if it had grown, could have gotten some recognition in Luce, even. Maybe given our kind a chance at a formal sect in the capital. I concluded that you had done something special in a very sad place, and that one day, you would do something even greater. And I wanted to be there when you did."

Sage pauses and fixes me with a stare. No awkwardness. None at all. "I am very proud of you, Jacob. Prouder than you know. And whatever you do with Raven, I will be cheering you on, and glad to see my best friend shine."

I let that lie awhile. If I cry, I cry. It's fine. But I don't. I just feel, in all honesty, wonderful. "And now who's soft at heart?" I say, and we both laugh at that, and I take a swig of the Lucemead, and by the Light, it tastes good, like honey and lightning down my throat at the same time.

"Besides," says Sage, "if the Lords attack First Light, then I'll be seeing you sooner than you think."

"Oh, so you're staying with the vampires?"

Sage shrugs. "Maybe, for a little while."

I grin. "You old dog."

He frowns. "Sam and I are just *friends* now, Jacob. I mean to see what happens to Sinassion, and get more answers from him."

"Yes, of course." I nod and roll my eyes. "Obviously." Then I glance at the bottle meaningfully. "But you're not going back to First Light for a couple of days, though? Pretty sure this can't be the only bottle lying around, and I've got a spare pair of hands to search now."

Sage nods. "I think I could do with a brief rest, yes."

And then I raise my bottle to my old friend, and hand it to him. "Good. Well, get drinking, you lightweight."

Raven returns later, after Sage and I have finished the bottle and I've napped off at least some, though definitely not all, of the Lucemead. I'm surprised to see her again so soon, but as soon as I catch her expression I begin to understand why.

"I know why Golden did it." Her eyes avoid me and study the end of my bed. "I only found out thanks to you, I should say to begin with."

"Oh, really?"

"Yes. All that nonsense you were talking about sorcerers always leaving their records in books and suchlike. That I did not really listen to at the time as it sounded like the dullest thing I had ever heard."

"Rude, but carry on."

"Well, it occurred to me that she might have left . . . some kind of explanation. A . . . diary, I suppose, vampires or your kind might call it." She pauses. Her little nail starts to lengthen. What comes next will not be easy, I realize.

"And I was right. She had. Hidden behind the books on that bookshelf you so memorably used as a distraction to expose her. Only a few bits of parchment, but they told her story well enough."

I give that a while, as I'm not sure if Raven wants to tell it.

"I will not read you her words. They were meant for no one really, but especially not someone who did not know her. But you deserve to know, so I will give you the outline."

"You don't have to—"

"Yes," says Raven firmly, her voice suddenly full of the depths of winter. "I do."

She clears her throat, and then: "Golden and Ashen's two sons were killed in Extinction Valley. They were on the wrong side of the rockfall that Ashen instigated and the rest of us Ansbachs carried out. The rockfall that cut off the clouds of wolfsbane from us, and saved so many of the wolves, but condemned the others to be trapped, although they were surely dead anyway. They had gone to rescue a potential mate of one of theirs who belonged to another pack. They almost made it back in time. Their bodies were found the next day just the wrong side of the rockfall."

"But . . . I don't see how that's Ashen's fault," I say, trying to put out of my mind the image of a mother finding her sons' corpses feet away from safety.

"She begged him to wait, but he said he could not. That they would all die if they did not do it soon. He was right, of course. We would all have been killed by wolfsbane had we waited. But . . . in her grief, she still blamed him. And that blame became pure hatred as the centuries went past. Ashen always grieved, of course, but he . . . forgot, I suppose. He forgot them a little, he forgot how to be sad about it after so much time."

Raven pauses here. Her hair covers her face. For once I don't think it's an accident.

"But she *never* forgot. And the centuries never dimmed her grief, they just focused it and strengthened it. And seeing the lessening of the grief in him, and how the centuries had forgotten her boys . . . I think it drove her mad. I smelled her strong grief, when we said goodbye to Ashen. It ruled her out as a suspect in my head, thinking the grief was for her husband." Another pause. "But I see now it was for her boys. Her never-ending grief, strengthened even more as she said goodbye to the mate she had killed. And do you know the worst thing about it, Jacob?"

"No," I say, holding her hand. She doesn't try to stop me. I feel her nails shorten and lengthen against my fingers.

"I think she knew. I think she knew it was not Ashen's fault. But she could not stop it. The grief was too much. She wrote this one line. It . . ."

A very long pause, this time.

"She wrote: 'I just want time to stop, and acknowledge what it has done to me. I just want time itself to take some responsibility for my pain. But it never stops. And neither does my pain.'"

I don't reply to that. We are silent for a while.

"This was written a while ago," says Raven eventually. "I suspect after that her awareness left her, and by the time you met her, I think her mind had gone a bit."

She squeezes my hand then, once, fierce, and then she gets up quickly, her hair still covering her face. Before she leaves, she turns back to me.

"Sorry, Jacob. I had hoped answers would make it better. But when everything is said and done, it is just sad . . . and that is all there is to it."

# PART III

# The Shape of Fangs to Come

## 32

# A Seat at the Table

The early rulers of First Light, whenever they wanted to scare the Lords underneath them into submission, used a simple prop: a circular wooden table, left in the corner of the palace hall. They would point to it and tell the Lords that it was only the firm grip they held that stopped the entire city's fate being decided by a bunch of Worns, sat round the table, dividing up the city's wealth into everyone's hands. It was much more effective than threats; terrifying possible futures always are.

Garnetia Manganesi, *Rulers Throughout the Ages*

### Sam

The wolfblood runs out around ten miles from First Light, five hours after I left Ansbach castle, so as I feel my wings start to lose their strength, I glide down to the forest floor and walk the rest of the way across the mainly forested region known as the Borderlands, which lies between the Wolflands and First Light. I'm exhausted; even the normal lingering effects of wolfblood have left due to the exertion of the nonstop flying. I'm a little bit in shock, too; the scenes of the forest rushing by below me as I soared through the clouds were incredible. I've flown on wolfblood briefly before, but this was something else.

Ahead and around me the forests of the Wolflands stretched out, and as I headed north I could spy the great Endless Ocean up ahead, a twinkle of blue, promising further mysteries. Despite the night and the cloudy sky, hiding the full moon from me most of the way, my eyesight would have made a hawk jealous, and the entire range of evergreens and hues of snow on bare trees were crystal clear to me. I heard all the chirpings and stirrings and rustlings of the night forest below, like a menu of sounds I could choose from and focus in on, pinpoint each one. I realized I wanted to live like this all the time, and for now I didn't let it worry me.

My wolfblood brain, normally so vocal, like having a hallucinogenic voice commenting on things that no one should know about (would be a very shit way of describing it), was quiet during my flight, again because of all the energy required, I expect. But it did start whispering to me of how from up here you can imagine a different world, one before civilization began. Before the Great Intelligence. I recall my conversation with Sage, about the need to know. One day, I'll know this, and all other things.

But for now, the city I'm heading to needs me.

When I walk out of the woodland that marks where First Light begins proper, I spy a large four-horsed carriage waiting for me, on the path that stops before the line of trees. It has the same red-blue noble crest pattern on it of a palace carriage, but daubed over it is a purple coat of paint. I nod to the driver, who puts his hand on his chest and bows to me, which I did not expect at all.

Then the carriage door opens and none other than Daphnée Hocquard is waving at me, beckoning me in. "Well, come on, Sam, darling, there's a whole city waiting for you!" she cries. "I hope you don't mind the welcome, it's just that you were sighted over the forest heading this way by the winged guard, and I was on tenterhooks anyway after the honegull that Raven sent explaining everything the day before, so I was all ready to greet you, and well, frankly, I missed you, my dear."

For a moment I'm speechless, not expecting anyone to greet me, never mind her, and then I jump in the spacious carriage and I hug her, hug her tight, and she says, "Oh, Sam, it is good to see you."

When I pull away I realize what, in my shock, hadn't been obvious to me: that she is dressed just as she was as a Lady. The same as she was when I first met her, in fact. Her hair has its luster back, the dark brown shining and intricate braids turning into cascading curls once again, with many white flowers pinned in them now, not just one. She has lip daub on, and face paint, and her eyes have a ring of kohl. Her fox pendant around her neck is there, although I don't think that ever left her, but now she has pearl fox-shaped earrings as well. I remember her thin blue scarf with roses stitched on it, and her white gloves, and the figure-hugging scarlet dress that now completes her look.

She sees me looking, and laughs. "I know, Sam, I know. It is bad. I should have remained in my Worn clothes, yes? Not exactly the look of the revolution. But I liked looking like this. It was never about power or status. I just liked it. It was who I was. But still, I wasn't going to. But then Alanna said something wise, as ever. She said that it's not the style of dress that makes you the villain, it's being the villain."

I narrow my eyes. "That wasn't what she said, was it?"

"No, not really. She used the word *cunt* more." We both laugh then, and suddenly it devolves into something else . . . I don't know who starts it, but the tears of laughter become tears of another thing entirely, and we quietly cry as the carriage rolls along, and I lay my head in her lap as she strokes my hair, much like my mother used to. "So much has happened in such a short space of time," I say between tears.

"I know," says Daphnée. "Things will calm down, eventually."

*I'm not sure I want them to, that's the problem*, I think. Instead, I say, "I'm not sure they ever will."

Daphnée sighs as she runs her hand through my tresses. "Me neither, darling, me neither. Astounding work with the wolves, by the way. You might have saved the city, once again. I want the full story, soon."

"I don't think it was me, this time, but you'll get it, don't worry."

I only raise my head up from her lap when our carriage rolls past a scene of destruction. We'd taken the road from the eastern border of First Light through Northeastfall, where the Lords' mansions are. Or at least were. What I saw now was scattered piles of rubble, and the burned remains of furniture, and a large hole in the ground like something had exploded within it.

Daphnée nods, seeing my shock. "Some of the mansions were destroyed in the initial riots, by some of the Midways who had lost everything in the crash. Some more were destroyed in the last week and a half since you've been gone, by Worns on various supplies of magicked noble that is commonplace now. Tenfold got it all under control, though. He let them blow off some steam, but we did not allow it to get out of hand. And the few Lords who pledged to the Worn cause have been allowed to stay in their homes. For now."

I nod. It all makes sense. It's not exactly the peaceful scenes I hoped for in my nonviolent revolution. But it's not blood in the streets either. Just rubble on the grass. I can live with that. For now.

Then, after the carriage has rolled on past the smaller paths threading through the land of mansions and joined the larger Lord's Way that will take us into Centerfall, I see an even bigger scene of destruction a quarter of a mile ahead. The palace, the centuries-old home of the First Lord, until Lightfall, then back again after Grayfall, the ancestral seat of the ruler of the vampires, is . . . gone. Completely gone. Not just rubble or debris. But nothing. Just a few acres of scorched earth.

"What?" I ask, turning to Daphnée, who goes a little pale.

"I'm sorry, Sam. It happened a day after you went. I wish you'd have been consulted, all those memories . . . but it was the condition Hands Parker made, for her to agree to all the other buildings of the Lords to be left standing. We needed a symbol. A symbol of renewal. And what better than for the palace—that place of torture, of oppression, of obscene wealth—to simply disappear?

"It took two nights, and four hundred Worns. Tenfold wouldn't let them use the stores of wolfblood, hence why the numbers and the time. But piece by piece it was torn apart, and the debris was taken to the quarries of Northwestfall, to be used for good when building construction starts again properly."

"It's fine," I say, trying to process the idea that a decade of my life was simply gone. "I won't miss it." I think I won't. They were mostly bad memories, but they were still memories. And they weren't all bad. Beth, the library—

"Oh, Blood Gods, the library!"

"Do not worry, Sam. Entirely relocated to the Invisibles building, which, you won't be surprised to hear, is no longer used for Invisibles-market trading. It was overseen carefully by the palace librarian, a Midway, who was on our side, it turns out."

I think of the frescoed dome, of the library stacks that had been my savior. Of the scented and musty smell of the parchments and the vellum and the paper. Of a place of peace in a time of mostly misery.

It is sad, in a way. But not in a way that overtakes the pain of those who have suffered at the hands of the people in that building. Their rage has validity. It takes primacy.

We are silent for a while then. I want to ask Daphnée about her and Alanna, both how they were together and whether she has asked Alanna about their miraculous escape from harm in the second destruction of the First Guard. But all that can wait. I need to see my city again, the one that had hurt me that is being made afresh in an image still to be determined.

Soon the Lord's Way turns into the Center Road, which takes us past Centerfall, the scene of the market crash I orchestrated just short of two weeks previous but feels like a lifetime ago now. Then we move onto the Blood Road, which takes us south, and we head toward Southwestfall.

"Not going to Westfall?" I ask, thinking of the new headquarters of the rebels that had been quickly made in a townhouse there, where I had a comfortable bed I was looking forward to falling into.

"Not yet, Sammy. If you can bear it, in the last few hours of the night, there's a meeting I think you should attend."

I raise my eyebrow. "A meeting?"

Daphnée nods. "The first of its kind, actually. The first meeting of the new First Council of Lightfall. No First Lord, just an entire council of equals. Molly's idea. She thought you would approve."

I nod. "I do." The city didn't need a new overlord. It needed a group of wise heads. How you go about choosing that, however . . .

"Who's on the council?"

Daphnée smiles, and raises one gloved hand, and counts off her fingers. "Well, let's see. I'm on it, I'm afraid. Can't get rid of your old mentor that easily."

I grin. "As if I'd want to."

"Tenfold is on it, commander of the Guard, obviously. Molly and Hands Parker. Sorry about that last one."

I shrug. "I'm actually sort of warming to her."

"She tried to kill you."

"It's a slow warming process."

Daphnée cackles. Then she resumes her counting. "Representing the Midways, the third of them who stayed in First Light, anyway, and didn't go with the Lords, is Redflute Silverside. Used to be on the Blood Bank Council. Appears to be an idiot, but actually very clever. Reminds me a bit of Jacob, in that way. Hands wasn't very happy with that. She wanted only Worns on the new First Council. Well, and me, whom she makes an exception for. But Molly said that a lot of the Midways were not that different from the Worns, and deserved representation, and not being lorded over."

"Wise Molly, as usual." I nod.

She switches hand. "Next is Vermillion."

My mouth forms an O of shock. "As in Vermillion Azzuri?"

"The very same. Our old ruler, on our new council. Funny how things turn out, isn't it?"

I nod. "I'm glad." I think of our moment together in the smoke a few days ago, crying, healing, mourning our respective losses. I never thought I would have grown so close to the man I once saw as an enemy—not evil like Rufous or Spymaster Saxe, someone misguided but not the active problem. But grief and clarity have changed him, genuinely. He is not the same man, and I'm dearly looking forward to seeing him.

"Even Molly was not an advocate of that one, sadly. But he needs to be on there. The handful of Lords who were always with our cause were instrumental in the rebellion, and convinced and marshaled by him. We owe him a lot, and me and Tenfold and Alanna agreed. Molly and Hands do not like it, but they will get over it. I hope."

"Oh, wait, Alanna . . . she's on it, too? This will be fun."

"Oh no," Daphnée says, a twinkle in her eye. "She refused. Said she likes the shadows."

"But she'll be at the meeting nonetheless, standing behind us in the shadows."

Daphnée winks at me. "Sharp as ever, darling."

Just as she's done listing the council members, I see us enter Southwestfall. The tight collection of rickety homes, low and basic, all squashed together in the nosiest night streets you'll ever ride through. Worns rush along, shouting, greeting, looking up at the full moon and basking in its glow for a moment, then rushing along to shout some more. The scent of all kinds of bloods, Worn and Midway, assaults my nose, still potent with the lingering residue of wolfblood, and even a thin thread of noble blood comes from somewhere . . . hawk, or maybe bear?

"The bloods . . ."

Daphnée smiles. "Yes, it's not just Wornblood in Worntown anymore. The blood redistribution has begun. It is a long process, and we've got to work out how to do it properly, especially as we don't have any Kinets to magick it anymore, they've all fled with the Lords. But we have the Blood Farms, and nonmagicked Midway and noble animals were good centuries before the Kinets began their tricks, so we will be fine."

"And we've got the wolfblood stores, and the wolf prisoners for more."

"Yes, though we're saving that for if the Lords come back with an army, so Worntowners won't be flying at all for a while."

"When."

"Sorry, dear?"

"*When* they come. They won't allow this to lie. We will have to kill Rufous and his army at some point. Every single one."

Daphnée stares at me then, and for a moment I think she's alarmed or disappointed. But then she reaches out and strokes my hair. "Taught you well, my girl, didn't I?"

I nod and remember her words. "Taught me how to burn it down."

Then the carriage stops at a familiar site. The Five Cuts, the inn where the revolution began in earnest. I laugh. "Of course. I should have guessed. Fitting."

We get out of the carriage, and we're about to enter when I realize something. Everyone on the street around me has stopped what they're doing and is looking my way. And all doing the same thing.

Right hand on the heart, where the blood flows.

Left hand on the neck, where the carotid artery is, where the blood also flows.

The old salute for a warrior who has saved you.

And they're singing. Four notes. Three ascending, final one low. Over and over again. The song of the Worns. The song of hope, where there is misery.

Daphnée speaks behind me, a gentle hand on my arm. "They're singing for you, Sam. The maid who saved us all."

For a moment, as the notes wash over me, so clear on my blood, I see every line on their faces, the faces of those who already look stronger and younger and more fervent than they ever did, with better blood rushing through them, and the hope of its bitterness filling them with ideas, filling them with the future, a future they won't age into but remain forever young. Not trapped by the blood they drink but freed by the blood they share.

And then the final remnants of the wolfblood inside me chime in to the dark recesses of my mind, like my voice but distorted. And they say, *I've seen the future. And it doesn't last. This is too much. You will never live up to it, and you will let them down. And all that is temporary will prove to be so, and everything will crumble, as it should.*

Maybe, I tell myself. Or maybe not.

I unfreeze, nod at Daphnée, and enter the Five Cuts.

And then I take my seat at the table.

## Epilogue

# Where Else Did You Think They'd Be?

Sometimes I wonder if this cursed city will be the death of us all.

Princess Alanna, personal diary, 270 AL

### Sage

The wolf jail is a much less formidable building than I'd imagined. A simple tall iron gate with a stone wall running all round the perimeter and no signage or decoration indicating what lies beyond. Past it is a nondescript low stone building with no windows that may as well house tools as opposed to wolves. I can only assume the wolf prisoners—the ones whose blood is drained to keep the Lords in stores of wolfblood, or *was*; I'm completely unsure of the situation now—are kept in more secure locations underground, beneath this unassuming frontage.

In all surrounding directions are scrub-covered fields, lightly covered in snow, which give way to currently woodland and beyond that the largely evergreen forests of the Wolflands, whose lands I've no wish to return to in a hurry.

To the west is Southeastfall, and the rest of First Light beyond, full of important people I must see once I've done this.

Once I've spoken to Neuras Sinassion.

The leaders of this new First Light were as good as their word: they kept him alive and let me talk to him and find my answers. That gives me a little hope for this strange new citywide arrangement, though this is early days and there's still plenty of time for my hope in progress to be dashed.

A guard dressed in the standard blue-and-red uniform opens the gates. He's tall and burly, the kind I'd expect to be stationed on what I assume is the most dangerous posting in the city: the kind where if something goes wrong you're confronted not with an angry Worn but an angry wolf, the kind of wolf so angry and deranged that their own kind were happy to part with them.

The guard doesn't say anything, just inspects me with an amused expression and points to an archway in the east side of the building. I walk across an expanse of nothing but dirt and then go through the archway. Beyond it is another guard, waiting for me before some stone steps that descend to what seems like a tunnel, curving round to the left and preventing me from seeing around them.

This guard has three blood drops on his scarlet epaulets, indicating a senior captain. I can't see his hair under his bright-blue hat, but his moustache and neat small beard are blond.

He studies me, and I wait for an introduction, but none comes. Just instructions.

"The jail below is empty but for Sinassion. It's just him down there. He can't get out. But we play it safe. After that Gray thing, at least, we assume mind control. So there'll be three guards watching you, looking for signs of his control. And three more watching them. If you try and release him, they'll kill you." He clears his throat, expression giving nothing away. "So, you know, don't do that."

"Noted," I reply. "Anything else?"

"You've got a quarter of an hourglass. Use it well. And don't come back here. It's bad enough stopping these psychopath wolves from escaping without having to account for sorcerers coming for a chin-wag with that bastard."

I nod. "Lost a friend to him in the war, did you?"

"Friends, plural, mage."

"Noted."

And then, wishing to be anywhere this conversation isn't, I turn from him and descend the stairs, which corkscrew round for what must be several hundred steps.

I don't know what I expected at the end. Some elaborate prison cells. Some strange security contraptions.

All I get is a long, torchlit tunnel that culminates in a jail cell eight feet long by six feet wide: stone floor, stone walls, a rough woolen mattress in one corner and a hole in the stone floor opposite in lieu of a pisspot. I wonder if Sinassion even needs it yet; sorcerers can go several weeks without drinking and, if need be, months on end without eating, and Sinassion was always one to test those limits to the extreme.

Speaking of Sinassion, the man himself, dimly lit by the torches on my side of the ten-inch-thick iron bars, is standing against the back wall of his prison, black hood up, eyes ablaze with those unyielding furnaces. Watching me or in his own world, who can tell?

I turn to the three guards who are watching me a dozen meters back, and see the other three beyond them.

I wonder if they understand that if Sinassion wanted to leave, he could leave.

That he's here for me.

*Hello, old friend.*

His voice enters my head unbidden, lounging in the corners, creeping throughout my inner recesses. It never gets less strange.

I want to defy him again, speak back to him, not think back to him, but I don't want the guards eavesdropping, so I reluctantly acquiesce to his choice of communication.

*Hello, Sinassion. I see they've not killed you, yet.*

*I see you're still full of resentment, Sage. I would have thought a trip to the Wolflands would have cured that. New land, new faces.*

*How do you know?* I start to ask, naively hoping that his claims to not root in my mind without permission are true, or that my old mind guards against him still work in these new days of his growing power.

*I'm not sneaking around in there. It's just obvious. I know you well, remember. Plus many other details of your appearance. You are not the only one who trained his observation skills for years, I'm afraid.*

*Fair enough,* I reply. *But I don't have time for carefree talk. I did what you said. I helped you train your new powers, though you couldn't free the Grays in the end. And now I come for my answers. The full story, this time.*

*So impatient.*

*I've been through a lot in the past week, so yes. My patience is in recovery.*

He shrugs then, an actual physical action, and I'm so used to him being creepily still that I almost jump back. But then he speaks again.

*I first started hearing the voices in my head many centuries ago. Before the founding of First Light. Yes*—he pauses, sensing my surprise or seeing my expression, or maybe both—*I am that old. As my powers slowly grew over the passage of time, the voices got louder. At first they were a whisper. They followed me around. Too quiet to be heard, but not so quiet as to ever give me peace. It almost drove me mad. In some ways, perhaps it did.*

*But as I grew my mind powers over the years, so did I exert my control. Enough to tolerate them. And enough to pick out words. Most of it was indecipherable, strange words in a strange language, almost like our common tongue but not quite. Over the years, I learned some words and phrases, put some sense into the jumble. Some of it was locations. Places that fit descriptions of areas in Shadowfall, Dawn Death, Luce, First Light, Lightfall.*

*I went to these places. Found relics, like the ones we collected together in the early days of the cult. The voices grew stronger, clearer, near to the relics. That's how I knew that the voices in my head had made them and the place I found them in. I grew convinced that these voices were the mortals that are so ensconced in all our myths and bedtime tales, and that they were a race of far greater power than us, and that if they returned we would be nothing against them.*

Sinassion pauses, seemingly lost in his retelling. I feel a tang of something in the air; most likely in my mind. But it feels like this is a time when these truths can finally be heard. I almost feel it in the air: thin, frayed. A time for belief, and a time for stories. A time for other worlds. This is what I live for, after all.

*I tried to tell people*, Sinassion continues eventually. *But no one believed me, and I knew if I used the relics that they would seek them for themselves and chaos would reign.*

*Wait*, I interrupt. *That's not the Sinassion I know. You very much wanted to use them. That's why we parted. That's why the cult fell apart the first time.*

A long silence. For a moment I wonder if I've caught him in his own lie he's told himself, but I should know better with Sinassion.

*No. It is what I really thought at first. Why I wanted to work with you. And then, it is true that I grew frustrated over time. That I wanted more . . . direct action. To use the relics. But then, when you resisted me, I did not try and claim them for myself, did I? I simply left. You always thought we disagreed, but that is not true. I listened to you, and left the relics to you, and sought faster methods through my own way, through war and my Shade army. But I knew if I stayed working with you at the Cult of Humanis, then my desires would one day overcome my respect for you.*

*Your respect for me?*

Sinassion's eyes seem to dim. *I know you still feel bitter about it. But I always respected you, Sage. You are better than me in ways you cannot know and could never understand.*

I sigh, outwardly. *Do you get paid per cryptic riddle?*

Sinassion huffs inside my head, and I assume that's his version of laughing. *I get that a lot. Anyway. You know of what came next, my attempt to intervene in the Twin War, with my army of Shades. It almost worked. I underestimated certain things, though. How much enemies would work together to stop me. I was impatient, careless. But I had reasons to be impatient. The threat in my head did not go away. In fact, it grew. Just like my powers. And the voices started getting stronger and harder to drown out. And then two momentous things happened. Which take us to where we are now.*

*The first is that the voices became one repeating message. Over and over again. Never ceasing, never stopping. A word similar enough to ours that there was only thing it could mean.*

Inside and outside my mind, I hold my breath.

*"Return."*

*The second is that I was able to work out where the voices were coming from. Where they have always been. The most obvious place, when you think about it.*

Sinassion's eyes burn fierce.

*The mortals are from Last Light.*

*Wha . . . what?*

*It's where they've always been, Sage. And be honest, if you were going to guess, you could do worse than there, yes? The city of secrets.*

*But . . . but Last Light was only founded three hundred and fifty years ago. And now it is a dead city.*

*I'm not talking about what vampires built on top of it. I am talking of what is beneath it. What may have ventured up above it.*

For a moment I think of Alanna, the only person I know from Last Light. I think of her miraculous fall from First Gods when we were trapped on its roof, with her dying lover in her arms. I think of how she somehow saved Lady Hocquard's life. I think of what Sam told me about how she saved them both recently during the explosion that killed most of the new First Guard.

Is Alanna a mortal?

Then I switch to the bigger picture, and think of what this could mean, if Sinassion's claims are true. That I have a location. That the mortals might not be dead. I think of worlds beyond mine, and things I have only dreamt to touch. I think of answers, and the need for them, burning in me ever since I came into this world, desolate and disappointed. I think about what I said to Sam: that I'm not a real person. I'm just an obsession, who has to go where he may, who has to . . . who has to *know*.

*So*, I think to Sinassion, hesitant, the future in flux and everything to play for. *We're going to Last Light, aren't we?*

*Of course. I wouldn't have it any other way. But we'll need others. We can't go alone.*

*Others?*

*Yes*, thinks Sinassion, laying out my path. *I have a funny feeling you know exactly who to bring.*

**End of Book 2**

# ACKNOWLEDGMENTS

In book one I thanked more people than could fit into Wembley Stadium, so this time I'm opting for the short and sweet version, in the hope that the legendary people around me will understand that their original thanks was in perpetuity. One day I'll get the balance right, but like a serial killer's playground, I'm prone to violent swings.

So a hearty thanks to those directly involved in the existence of this book: my agent, Harry "Yorkshire Hitman" Illingworth, whose legend increases yearly; my excellent international rights agent, Helen Edwards; my iconic editor, Pete Wolverton, whose notes that led to this book being substantially rewritten played a key part in it being (hopefully) not a complete mess; and the rest of my St. Martin's Press team: Claire Cheek, Sarah La Cotti, Stephen Erickson, Layla Yuro, and, finally, Ervin Serrano for the excellent cover—and anyone else at my publisher I have missed out, forgive me! Thanks also to MaryAnn Johanson for her astute copyediting. Oh, and my resplendently magnificent audiobook narrator, Shakira Shute.

A new thanks entry to my devastatingly cool horror crew: Anna "Super Dupes" Dupre, George "Sub-Genre" Dunn, and Charlie "Rizz" Battison.

And finally, to all the kind readers and reviewers and Bookstagrammers and what have you who *got Lightfall*, really *got* it: I may be broken, but you give me the best fix.

# ABOUT THE AUTHOR

Julia Boggio

**Ed Crocker** was born in Manchester, United Kingdom, and has managed to stay there ever since. By day he writes books and edits other people's—his clients include *Sunday Times* bestselling authors and award-winning indie authors—and by night he reviews books and interviews authors for various publications, watches horror films, and plays video games, so evidently he has not matured since his last author bio. His first book, *Lightfall*, book one in the Everlands trilogy, has been translated into seven languages.

You can find him on some socials as @edcrockerbooks and sign up for his newsletter at ed-crocker.com.